Rita Bradshaw

Forever Yours

headline

First published in 2010 by
HEADLINE PUBLISHING GROUP

First published in paperback in 2011 by
HEADLINE PUBLISHING GROUP

1

Cataloguing in Publication Data is available from the British Library

ISBN 978 0 7553 5937 0

Typeset in Bembo by Palimpsest Book Production Limited,
Falkirk, Stirlingshire

Printed and bound in the UK by
CPI Mackays, Chatham ME5 8TD

Headline's policy is to use papers that are natural, renewable
and recyclable products and made from wood grown in sustainable forests.
The logging and manufacturing processes are expected
to conform to the environmental regulations of
the country of origin.

HEADLINE PUBLISHING GROUP
An Hachette UK company
338 Euston Road
London NW1 3BH

www.headline.co.uk
www.hachette.co.uk

For our beautiful granddaughter, Emily Rita Anderson, born 17 June 2009 – perfect in every way and infinitely precious. Baby sister for Georgia and cousin for Sam and Connor. So much prayer went up for you, little one, when we thought we were going to lose you – you really are our beloved miracle baby and cherished more than you will ever know.

All praise and thanks to the Lord for His grace and mercy, and thanks to our darling Faye and Roy too, for doing their bit in producing the most adorable and exquisite pair of little girls the world has ever seen. Those genes are pure dynamite!

Love that is constant knows no boundaries,
It is the dew in the morning and the night's
  breeze.
Its melody can be heard in a child's laughter,
Its warmth in a mother's smile.
It gives and gives without measure
And when it is spent, it gives again.
It sees the worst and the best in the beloved
And it is not shaken.
It believes all, endures all, trusts all.
It is constant; it is love.

ANON

Contents

Prologue

Sacriston, Durham, 1880

'Where are you off to, this time of night?'

'Out.'

'Aye, I can see that – I'm not stupid. I didn't think you were going to park your backside in front of the fire wearing your coat and muffler, now did I?'

Vincent McKenzie cast a cold glance at his mother but didn't reply. He reached for his cap, pulling it over his thick brown hair. He then waited for her voice to come at him again, and as he opened the front door her nasal tones followed him as he had known they would.

'Well? I'm waiting for an answer, m'lad. Are you off sniffing after a lass? Is that it? 'Cos I won't have some little baggage back here, so think on. This is my house and I say who comes in and out.'

Knowing his silence would rile her more than any retort, he stepped outside, shutting the cottage door behind him and walking down the garden path to the gate. He'd just opened this when his mother wrenched open the front door and let loose a tirade worthy of any dockside fishwife.

The night was as black as pitch and bitterly cold but to the tall, well-built man striding away from the cottage it wasn't overly dark. It was the same with any miner. They'd say to anyone who'd listen that you didn't know what darkness was until you'd been down the pit. That blackness was consuming, a living entity so thick and heavy you felt you could touch it.

But Vincent wasn't thinking of the pit, nor of his mother. His thoughts were concentrated on the news he'd heard that morning. Hannah had had a baby. His Hannah. His beautiful, pure Hannah had had Stephen Shelton's bairn. She'd lain with Shelton, let him kiss and fondle her and impregnate her with his seed.

He made a sound deep in his throat that could have come from an animal in pain, the muscles in his face working. Why had she done it? Why had she married Shelton?

It was beginning to rain, icy droplets that carried sleet in the midst of them, but Vincent didn't feel anything besides the white-hot rage which had burned him up all day as he'd laboured down the pit. It had been bad enough this time last year when she'd married Shelton. Having to stand by and watch her on her wedding day, dressed in white and walking down the aisle to that nowt. That had been betrayal enough. But to bring forth living proof of what they got up to . . . His thin lips curled back from his teeth as though he was smelling something foul.

Hannah had been the one perfect, spotless thing in his life, a being apart. From a bairn he'd adored her, worshipped the ground she walked on, and she'd returned his love. He knew she had, although they'd never spoken of it. He'd made up his mind he was going to ask her to walk out when she turned sixteen, but Shelton had got in first. However, he'd waited for her, knowing she'd come to her senses. What could Shelton offer her, after all? A two-up, two-down terrace in the village, whereas his mam's cottage—

No, his mind corrected him in the next moment. *Not* his mam's cottage. He'd been the man of the house since his da was killed down the mine the very week he himself had gone down as a lad of thirteen. The cottage was his – he paid the bills and put food on the table. And situated as it was just outside the village and with gardens front and back, it was a cut above the colliery housing typical of that provided by the mine-owners all along the Durham coalfield. His grandfather had built the cottage, brick by brick, and it was comfortable and roomy; three bedrooms upstairs and a separate scullery and kitchen and sitting room downstairs, with a wash-house and privy across the paved yard outside. Aye, most lasses'd give their eye-teeth to live there, even with his mam.

As always when he thought of his mother Vincent channelled his thoughts in a different direction. It was an art he'd perfected long ago as a young boy of seven years old, the first time she had come into his bedroom at night and told him that the things she'd done to him and made him do to her were what every mother and son did.

The cottage was on the edge of Fulforth Wood, and as Vincent came out of the narrow lane into the wider road which led to the colliery village a quarter of a mile away, his eyes scanned the darkness. It was gone eleven and he didn't expect to run into anyone, but you never could tell. One thing was for sure, he couldn't afford to be seen for what he'd got in mind. If he met someone he'd have to abandon his plan and try again another night, but he was loath to do that. He didn't think he could endure another hour of knowing they were playing Happy Families while he was in hell. And it was hell, a hell more real than anything Father Duffy scared everyone with in his fire and brimstone sermons.

When he came to the crossroads where Witton, Durham and Front Streets met Plawsworth Road, he stood looking down Front Street. The lines of housing called Cross Streets in the area to the north was in total darkness, but the inn to the left of the grid of streets showed a light in one of the bedrooms. Moving into deeper shadows, he stood and waited.

The village was growing fast. There was talk of the colliery owners partly funding a new Catholic school as they had with the Roman Catholic church presently being built at the far end of the village. He and Hannah and the other colliery children had had their lessons in two cottages on Front Street, used as a school on weekdays and a mission chapel on Sundays, but it looked as though that would soon be a thing of the past.

He hadn't enjoyed his schooldays. His brown eyes narrowed. Living as he did some distance from the village, he'd been the outsider – and the other lads had never let him forget it. It hadn't helped that his father was known as the village drunk; when his da wasn't down the pit he could normally be found propping up the bar in the Colliery Inn, and his mother had had to meet his da at the pit gates come pay day and wrestle enough money off him to buy food for the week. Many a night his father had slept in the sawdust and dirt on the inn's floor; sometimes three or four days had gone by before they saw him.

But his da had never missed a shift. He could say that about him.

Vincent flexed his big shoulders, his eyes unseeing as he looked back down the years. When his mother's night-time visits had become a regular occurrence he'd thought about running away, because even as a little lad he'd known that she was lying and other women didn't do that to their bairns. But there had been Hannah. Beautiful, golden-haired Hannah, his angel, his undefiled, perfect angel. For such a slender wisp of a thing she'd been like a small virago when she'd defended him from the other bairns' bullying, even though he'd been inches taller than her — an awkward, lanky lump of a boy who'd known he was dirty, filthy, inside. But she had liked him. She had been his friend.

Or so he'd thought. But it had all been lies. The sound came again from his throat. She was no better than the rest — worse, in fact, because she had made him believe she cared about him and let him dare to dream about a future where he would be like everyone else. That's all he'd ever wanted, to be like everyone else. But it couldn't happen now and he was done with pretending.

She had to pay. He breathed deeply, struggling for control. He had to be thinking calmly when he did this. There could be no mistakes. *Clear your mind. Focus, man.*

His fingers felt for the can of oil in his deep coat pocket and he straightened as the light in the inn was extinguished. He'd wait another minute or two before making his way to the Cross Streets, just to be sure.

'Leave her, Stephen. You'll wake her up and she'll want feeding again.'

Hannah's voice wasn't cross, on the contrary it conveyed

tenderness as she looked at her husband bent over the cradle at the foot of the bed. She knew that some miners, like Stephen's brother, Howard, would have been miffed if their first bairn wasn't a boy, but not her Stephen. All along he'd insisted he wanted a miniature version of herself and it was clear, once Constance was born, that he'd meant it. He was besotted by their daughter. Her mam had said she'd never seen a man so unashamedly thrilled with his child and it was true.

'She looks like you.' Stephen Shelton's voice reflected the wonder he felt as he stared down at his tiny daughter. 'Our Howard's little lad looked like a wrinkled prune for weeks, but she's as bonny as a summer's day.'

'You'd better not let your brother hear you call Daniel a wrinkled prune.' Hannah's voice carried a gurgle of laughter in its depths. She agreed with her husband; even now, at six months old, his brother's child couldn't be called handsome by even his nearest and dearest. And when Stephen still hovered by their daughter's cradle, she added, 'Come on, love. Come to bed.'

As he joined her in the iron bed that could hardly be called a double but which had been a good price in one of the second-hand shops in Sunderland, some fourteen or fifteen miles south-east of Sacriston, the bedsprings zinged their protest. Hannah immediately snuggled up to her husband, for in spite of the coal fire burning in the small grate, the room was cold and what warmth the fire gave out was soaked up by the baby's cradle directly in front of it. As Stephen put his arms round her, she murmured, 'Do you think she's warm enough?'

'She's as snug as a bug in a rug.' Stephen kissed her brow. 'How are you feeling?'

'Tired.' It had been a long labour, thirty-six hours from start to finish, and the last few had verged on the unbearable. She hadn't expected it to be so awful but the midwife had assured her the first was always the worst and the next one would be better. She hadn't wanted to think about the next one; she still didn't. Lifting her head to look into Stephen's face, she smiled. 'All the pair of us have done today is eat and sleep – your mam and mine have seen to that.'

'Good.' He stroked a strand of hair from her forehead, marvelling – as he always did – that this beautiful woman was his. 'I told them when they arrived this morning that I didn't want you putting so much as a foot out of this room.'

'Well, they obeyed your instructions to the letter.' She had tried to persuade her mother and mother-in-law that she was perfectly capable of going to the privy in the backyard rather than having to use the chamber pot, but they wouldn't have it. Mind you, when she'd got out of bed to use the pot she'd felt so sick and giddy she'd thought she was going to pass out, so perhaps they were right. 'I've never been so cosseted in me life and Constance only has to squeak and they're whisking her up.'

'All the lads wanted to be remembered to you, by the way, and send their best to you and the bab.' Stephen pulled her closer into him. Constance had been born late on Saturday night and the next day being the Sabbath, Stephen hadn't gone into work until this morning. 'All except Vincent McKenzie, that is. Surly devil. I swear he gets more moronic with each passing day. Just stared at me, he did, when the lads were asking about the bab and didn't say a word.'

'Vincent's not moronic, Stephen. You know he isn't. He was considered bright at school.'

'Bright or not, he's got a side to him that's stranger than a nine-bob note. You'd know what I mean if you worked a shift or two with him. Never says a word to no one unless it's the deputy, and he's all over him. Got his eye on the main chance, sure enough.'

Hannah shifted slightly in his arms but said nothing now. She knew Stephen had a bee in his bonnet about Vincent. It dated back to when they'd been bairns and she'd used to stick up for Vincent when the other lads had a go at him, which was most of the time. But she'd felt sorry for him. She still did. It couldn't be much of a life for him; his mother like a millstone round his neck and her with a tongue on her like a knife. She'd said as much once to Stephen in the days when they were courting and asked him if he couldn't be nice to Vincent, make a pal of him, but it had caused such a row between them she hadn't mentioned it again. Stephen had got it into his head that Vincent liked her in *that* way and nothing would dissuade him otherwise, even though she knew Vincent thought of her as simply a friend. Probably his only friend, poor thing. Not that she'd seen hide nor hair of him since she'd got married apart from once or twice in the distance, and then he'd made no effort to pass the time of day even though she'd smiled and waved at him.

'Bob Hutton reckons Vincent's after being second in line to the deputy when old Walter goes, and that'll be the day I'll get meself set on elsewhere. I wouldn't work for that nowt if I got paid in gold nuggets.'

She wanted to ask him to stop talking about Vincent, but knowing that would provoke an argument, reached up and kissed his stubbly jaw instead. 'I missed you today,' she said softly. 'It was lovely having a day to ourselves with Constance yesterday, wasn't it?'

Her reward for her tactfulness was his voice coming deep and warm when he murmured, 'Aye, my idea of heaven, lass. You hear some of the lads talk, ones who've been married less time than we have, and it makes me thank me lucky stars for what we have.'

Hannah nodded. Beryl and Molly, her two older sisters, seemed to *expect* their husbands would disappear on a Saturday afternoon to watch the footy and spend Sunday lunchtime – and more than one evening a week too – at the Colliery Inn with their pals. But Stephen had never been like that. From the first week they'd been married he'd been content to spend all of his time with her.

'I see more than enough of my mates down the pit, lass,' he'd stated, when she'd shyly brought the matter up one day. 'I might have the odd half with them afore I come home now and again, just to be sociable, but I'd rather look at your pretty face than their ugly mugs and I've told 'em so.'

Shocked, she'd asked him if they'd been offended and he'd roared with laughter. 'Any one of 'em would swap places with me like a shot, given half a chance,' he'd told her. 'They know it and I know it. I'm a lucky man.'

She knew she was lucky too, she counted her blessings every day. Cosy and snug now Stephen's body warmth was enveloping her, Hannah knew a moment of pure joy. She had the best husband in the world and God had given them Constance: she couldn't ask for more. And they'd never had to live with in-laws as so many young couples did. The occupants of Sacriston had doubled in her lifetime, and although the mine owners were constructing more housing, it was a slow business; however, just two weeks before they'd wed last year, old Mr and Mrs Atkinson had gone to live with their married daughter in Sunderland. Mr Atkinson being a close pal of Stephen's da, he'd tipped him the wink and Stephen had been first in the colliery office. She'd never forget the look on Stephen's face when he'd come to tell her.

'Good night, lass.' Stephen's voice was slurred with sleep as they lay close, breathing almost the same breath. 'And I'll bring the little 'un to you when she wakes up; don't you go getting out of bed.'

''Night, love.' Oh aye, she was lucky all right. In this tiny world that was hers, she had everything she wanted. With careful managing they paid the rent each week, and if towards pay day the stew held more dumplings and less scrag ends, Stephen never complained. Not that it'd been like that over the weekend though; her mam had brought a ham-and-egg pie and a basin of sheep's-head broth, and Stephen's mam had been determined they didn't starve too, bless them.

The baby was fast asleep, just the odd little snort or snuffle disturbing the silence, and the glow from the banked-down fire took the edge off the blackness. Hannah's eyelids closed and she drifted off too, her last conscious thought of her daughter and how long it would be before she woke them for a feed.

Vincent knew exactly which house he was making for in the ten rows of terraced streets which made up the Cross Streets and stretched in regimented lines from Front Street. For months on end after Hannah had married Shelton he'd left the cottage in the middle of the night and come to stand across the road from where she lived, hidden in the darkness as he'd stared for hours without moving. Nothing was violent enough or deep enough to describe the hatred he'd felt towards Stephen Shelton, a hatred and rage which had stretched to include Hannah when he'd first heard she was expecting Shelton's child. He'd prayed with a passion that Shelton would be killed in one of the numerous accidents that occurred weekly down the pit, and that the shock would cause Hannah to miscarry. Only then would he be able to sleep at night. He had pictured it in his mind so often he had been stunned when he'd heard the baby had been born alive and healthy.

The terrace of eight houses was in darkness as he had expected, since there were no street lamps in the Cross Streets. He stood, his hands deep in his pockets and the fingers of his right hand stroking the can of oil as the sleet fell, melting on contact with the ground. He would be best going round the back — it was more feasible a fire would start in the kitchen. His mind was giving him instructions almost independently and he obeyed it, making his way to the back of the terrace and walking along the dirt lane which bordered the tiny backyards and shared privies, one to each two houses. When he reached Hannah's backyard he again became still, waiting.

What exactly are you waiting *for*? his mind asked him derisively. You've been waiting long enough, haven't you? Get on with it. You've either got the guts to go through with this or you haven't.

He'd got the guts. His body jerked as though a puppeteer was pulling the strings. From the day he'd walked away unscathed from the rockfall which had taken his father and six other miners, and told his mother he'd kill her if she ever touched him again, he'd known he could do anything. Twenty-four hours trapped in the bowels of the earth before the rescue team had got them out had taught him a lot. The terror he'd felt in that pitch blackness as he'd waited to die hadn't been as bad as the numbing fear and shame he'd lived with for six long years. He had vowed then that if he got out alive, she wouldn't lay another finger on him. It had been a baptism of fire, that first day down the pit, but it had saved him. That was the way he looked at it. The pit – and his mother – had never held the same fear for him again.

He made no sound as he entered the backyard which was shared with the house on the left to Hannah's, passing the lavatory and the communal tap which was the sole means of water for the residents. His heart thudding fit to burst, he tried the latch on the back door and it opened immediately. No one ever locked their doors in the tight-knit mining community.

He stepped first into a tiny scullery just big enough to hold the tin bath which was hung on the wall by a long wooden peg. On another wall there were more pegs and Stephen's working clothes hung there with his boots beneath on the stone flags.

There was a step up into the kitchen, and he could see dimly by the glow coming from the banked-down fire in the open black range. In front of the range was a steel fender, three feet long, and positioned by this was a clothes horse on which various articles were drying. A scrubbed kitchen table with four chairs tucked beneath it, a high-backed wooden chair with faded flock cushions, another much smaller table holding a tin dish for washing dishes and pans, and an enormous clippy mat in front of the range made up the sum total of the furniture, and all the items looked well-worn. There were no cupboards on the bare whitewashed walls, merely four shelves on the wall opposite the range, and these held a conglomeration of crockery and cutlery, along with items of food and other bits and pieces.

Vincent's lip curled as his gaze swept round the room. And she'd settled for this rather than what he could have given her? In the last few years he'd taken any extra shifts that were going and seen to it that the cottage looked real bonny, but what was the use of that now? All his striving had been for one thing and one thing only – and that was finished with. He wouldn't have her now if someone paid him to. He couldn't begin to explain, even to himself, why the birth of the child had affected him the way it had, but something in him – something elemental and primitive – was repelled and enraged by it to the point of madness.

He shook his head as though the action could clear his mind. The night was quiet and still, the only sound was the ticking of the wooden clock on the mantelpiece over the range.

No more hesitating. He fetched the can out of his jacket pocket along with a box of matches. He doused the clippy mat, the flock cushions on the chair and the clothes horse with the oil, before tipping an oil lamp standing in the middle of the kitchen table on its side and letting the oil spread out in a thick flow. Then he lit the first match.

Matthew Heath had the stomach-ache. He had been holding his belly and wriggling in pain for over an hour in the bed he shared with his two older brothers. As the cramps intensified, he knew he'd have to pay a visit to the privy in the backyard. He also knew what the problem was. He had filched a couple of the big cooking apples his mam had left from the sack he and his brothers had brought back home in the summer. The apples were stored on brown paper under the eaves in the roof and were forbidden fruit: his mam had issued dire warnings as to what would befall anyone who had the temerity to pilfer one.

He had worked hard for them apples though, he thought to himself in justification of the crime. Not like his brothers who'd messed about something rotten. Farmer Todd had said he'd done the work of a man that weekend, and he wasn't one for buttering you up, not Farmer Todd. And yet whenever his mam baked one of her apple pies or crumbles, his brothers got the same portion as him. It wasn't fair. And so he'd decided to level things up, that was all.

Another cramping pain made him squirm. Stifling a groan, he slid out of bed and fumbled in the darkness for his jumper and trousers laid ready for morning on the back of a chair, pulling them over his undershirt and drawers. It'd be freezing outside. The day had been biting cold and their mam had said she could smell snow in the air and she was never wrong.

Picking up his heavy hobnail boots, Matthew crept silently on to the small square landing separating the brothers' room from that of their parents. He didn't want to wake his mam. She had a nose on her like one of his da's ferrets for smelling things out, did his mam, and even though he'd moved the other apples along to disguise the fact that two were missing, she'd know somehow.

He stopped in the hall to feel for his coat on the row of hooks attached to the wall, but didn't pause to put it on, such was the urgency in his bowels. It was only when he was sitting on the wooden seat with the hole in the middle that he pulled it on, his teeth chattering.

The power of the fermenting apples in his system ensured it was over half an hour before he left the privy, and his only thought was to get back to the warmth of his bed. He was frozen, inside and out. But halfway across the yard he paused. There was a light brighter than he'd seen before shining from the house next door where the Sheltons lived. He liked the Sheltons. Mrs Shelton was bonny and Mr Shelton hadn't told on him when he'd accidentally kicked a can full of pebbles he and some of the other bairns had been having a game of footy with, straight through their kitchen window. Mr Shelton had been mad, but he'd said the fact that he hadn't run away with the others but had stayed to face the music made them square. Aye, the Sheltons were all right.

It was only when a curl of black smoke dimmed the light for a second that he realised he was seeing leaping flames. He stared transfixed as the kitchen curtains blazed, the material eaten up so quickly he barely had time to blink before they were gone. And then he was galvanised into action. Wrenching open his own back door, he yelled for his parents at the top of his voice before again running into the yard, and as he did so the sash window in the bedroom above the kitchen next door was pushed up. He could hear the sound of coughing and choking, but when Mr Shelton leaned out, he was holding what looked like a tightly wrapped bundle of clothing in his arms.

'You down there. Can you catch her?'

15

For a moment he didn't realise Mr Shelton was intending to throw his bairn out of the window, but when he did he braced himself. 'Aye, Mr Shelton. It's me, Matt. I'll catch her.'

He didn't have time to think about it. One moment he was under the window and the next he'd fallen to his knees with the impact of seizing the bundle before it hit the ground.

He heard Mr Shelton say, 'Thank God. Good lad,' before he turned back into the room moments before smoke billowed from the open window. He sat on the cold flagstones cradling the baby and he thought he heard Mr Shelton coughing and shouting, 'Wake up, lass. Wake up!' as his parents and brothers ran out into the yard, along with the neighbours on the Sheltons' other side, Mr and Mrs Preston.

When his father and Mr Preston tried to enter the house the flames and smoke beat them back, and although his mam was shouting and screaming up to Mr Shelton, he didn't come to the window again. Nor could Matt hear him coughing any more.

The fire was out and he was sitting in his da's armchair in front of their range when Mrs Shelton's mam and da arrived. He knew his da had gone to fetch them — they only lived in the next street — and when they came into the kitchen he heard his mam softly say, 'We can't get him to let go of the bab, Mabel. He keeps saying he had to catch her.'

When Mrs Shelton's mam crouched down in front of him he raised his eyes from the baby's tiny face to look at her, but his arms tightened round the bundle on his lap. He saw that the lady he'd always known as Mrs Gray was crying, although her features were blurred with his own tears. Her voice sounded broken, funny, when she said, 'You're a brave lad, Matt. Do you know that? A brave lad. But for you, Constance wouldn't be here right now.'

Her voice quivered and her husband's hand pressed her shoulder as he murmured, 'Hold on, lass, hold on. There's the bab to think of. She needs you now.'

Matthew saw Mrs Gray swallow hard before she spoke again: 'I'm Constance's grandma, hinny. I know you've got two nice grandmas, haven't you, and you like to visit them, no doubt. Well, Constance is coming to stay with me so I can feed her and look after her. You can come and see her whenever you want, would you like that?'

He gulped over the lump blocking his throat. Mr and Mrs Shelton gone, just like that. 'You look like her.'

'What's that, pet?'

'Mrs Shelton – you look like her.'

'Aye, well, that's to be expected. She's my daughter.'

Mabel Gray's voice cracked and she made a little sound which caused Ruth Heath to wrinkle up her face in sympathy. She stood looking down at her neighbour kneeling by Matthew, unable to take in the enormity of what had happened. That lovely young couple, and them only just having had the bairn. And Mabel was right. But for the lad, the bairn would be lying alongside of her mam and da. After all the neighbours had formed a human chain from the tap in the yard and put the fire out with every bucket they had between them, they'd discovered the two rooms upstairs hadn't been consumed by the fire. Nevertheless, the young lass and her husband had been lifeless when they'd reached them. It'd been the smoke, of course. The lass had still been lying in bed, it didn't look as if she'd ever woken up, but after Stephen had got the bab out he must have been overcome. Tragedy, it was. Terrible.

When Ruth saw her son pass the baby to Mabel a moment later she expelled a silent sigh of relief. Thank goodness. For a while there, she'd thought the whole thing had turned Matt's brain, the way he wouldn't let go of the bairn an' all.

Mrs Preston had made a pot of tea and now as she silently handed everyone a cup, Ruth took hers with a nod of thanks. The smell of smoke was strong; it'd take days, weeks even, for it to disperse, and the damage next door would take some putting right, but that was nothing compared to the lasting heartache this night had caused. There was no telling what had started the fire. The clothes horse might have been too close to the range maybe, that was easy done, she herself had scorched the odd thing or two over the years, but whatever had caused it the result had been devastating. A babbie robbed of her mam and da and two sets of families grieving.

As though her thoughts had conjured them up, a knock at the back door preceded Stephen's parents and three younger, unmarried sisters entering the kitchen. The girls were crying and Stephen's father looked stricken, but such was the expression on Stephen's mother's face it brought a rush of tears to Ruth's eyes.

No one said anything, but as Hannah's mother made room on the settle where she was sitting rocking the child in her arms, Stephen's mother sank down beside her, reaching out and stroking the downy forehead of the sleeping baby with the tip of her finger. The two looked at each other, as one in their pain, and as Ruth wiped the tears from her eyes with the sleeve of her dressing-gown, she thought, At least the bairn will be loved. There's no doubt about that. But it won't be the same as having her mam and da, will it, God bless the poor little mite.

They had the funeral on the following Sunday so everyone could pay their respects and not lose a shift. The whole village turned out despite the deep snow and ice which had hit the north-east the day after the fire. It being the Sabbath, all the shops were closed and the quietness which pervaded the village on a normal Sunday was more intense, seeming to pulse like a live thing as the men and boys from both families walked the funeral route, surrounded by male friends and neighbours.

Every pair of curtains in the village was closed and the women and children who lined the street were silent as they watched the cart carrying the two coffins make its way to the graveyard north of the Cross Streets. Afterwards, family and close friends gathered at the Grays' house where Mabel and her two remaining married daughters and Stephen's mother and sisters had prepared a spread.

Vincent McKenzie had followed the coffins along with his workmates, knowing it would raise eyebrows if he didn't, but that wasn't the only reason. He wanted to be near Hannah one last time. The short service was held over the open graves and when the first clods of earth hit the wood and Hannah's father stood shielding his face with his hands as the tears dripped through his fingers, the man's grief didn't move Vincent.

'This is your fault,' he wanted to say. 'You let her walk out with Shelton, you let her marry him. This is your fault – and now see what's happened.' But of course he remained silent, standing slightly apart from the other mourners, his stomach churning with the sickness that had been with him for days.

He watched as Matthew Heath was called forward by Hannah's father to lay a wreath at the foot of each grave which would eventually be laid on top of the mounds of earth when the grave-diggers had finished their work. His eyes became pinpoints of black light as he stared at the young boy. But for this lad's interference Stephen Shelton's brat would be where it should be – six foot under. Instead it was alive, a reminder of Hannah's duplicity and her union with Shelton.

He was almost the last person to leave the cemetery. The sky had been heavy and low all day and now the snow began to fall in great white flakes.

'We're in for another packet.' One of the grave-diggers passed him as he stood just outside the gates. 'All this afore Christmas don't bode well for the New Year. It'll be a long, hard winter sure enough, you mark my words.'

Vincent didn't bother to reply. Turning away from the direction of the village, he pulled his muffler more closely round his neck and set out towards the town of Chester Le Street, a few miles north-east of Sacriston. Chester Le Street was situated on the Great North Road and was a thriving and busy town, its vibrant industrial centre bustling with activity on a normal working day. On a Sunday the trains – both passenger expresses and the less glamorous coal trains – were considerably fewer, and the engine- and rope-works and myriad other factories silent.

Not that Vincent was making for the heart of the town. His destination was a particular house set discreetly by itself in a narrow lane on the outskirts of Chester Le

Street. Although the market town was only a short distance from Sacriston as the crow flies, most folk in the village only knew it as a place name, never having ventured further than the fields surrounding Sacriston. In the five years since Vincent had been visiting Ma Walton's whore-house he'd never once come across anyone he knew, although he was always on edge lest that might happen.

He strode swiftly through the white landscape and by the time he reached Blackbird Lane he'd consumed the contents of the hip-flask he carried in the pocket of his overcoat. He'd drunk a great deal over the last few days; it was the only way he could sleep at night. To fall into bed senseless.

Vincent paused before opening the gate leading to the front door of the house. Every time he left this place he vowed it would be the last, but then his body would begin burning again and he'd return like a dog to its vomit.

He knew the men he worked with looked on him as some kind of oddity. He took off his cap and shook it to dislodge the snow before pulling it on again. He'd never walked out with a lass and they couldn't understand that; consequently they made up their own theories about him. But he dare bet none of them came near the truth of it – that he'd known it all at the age of seven.

His features moved into what could have passed for a smile unless you were looking into his eyes.

But he didn't care what they thought. They were all thick-headed nowts, gormless as they come. He was different and he'd show them. He didn't intend to remain as he was until the day he died. His grandfather had had a bit about him by all accounts and he took after him, not his da. He was going to rise in the world and he'd see his day with this village, the whole jam pack of them. They'd soon be laughing on the other side of their face when they spoke of him.

The door to the house opened and a man stood silhouetted in the light for a moment, adjusting his muffler so it came over the bottom part of his face and his cap pulled down low over his eyes. He walked down the path, passing Vincent without a word and scuttling off in the direction of the town. Vincent watched him go until the thickly falling snow swallowed him up. Then he looked towards the house again.

The man's sheepish demeanour had bothered him, emphasising as it did the sleazy aspect of what he was about to do. He ground his teeth, his countenance darkening. This wasn't going to be the pattern for years to come, he was damned if it was. He wanted his bodily needs sated in the comfort of his own home – that wasn't too much to ask, was it? Of course there would be his mother to contend with if he brought another woman into the house, unless . . .

He blinked, his eyes opening wider for a moment in surprise at the direction his mind had taken. *Unless his mother was no longer around to object.*

Suddenly his brain was throwing possibilities at him and he realised this wasn't such a new idea, after all. It had been there for years, buried in his subconscious but festering like a deep-rooted infection.

He wiped his hand round his face, his mind racing. It would need to look like an accident of some kind, or maybe an illness? A malady that came upon her gradually and then gathered steam. But that was possible. He could do that.

22

He'd been vaguely aware of a face at one of the windows and now, when the front door opened once more and Ma Walton's voice came, saying, 'Don't stand out there, lad, you'll catch your death. No need to be shy. Come into the warm,' he moved obediently forward. His mind flung one more thought on top of the others which settled the matter: he'd never have to look at or hear his mother again if he followed through on this. He'd be free. *Free.* And it was about time.

PART ONE

The Die is Cast

1893

Chapter 1

'Now listen, me bairn, there's nowt to cry about. I should've told you before but you're still such a child . . .'

Mabel Gray's voice faded away as she surveyed her grand-daughter's tear-stained face. It was a beautiful face and so like Hannah's there were times it fair hurt her to look on it, but she had to accept the fact that Constance was a bairn no longer. She should have told her about the birds and the bees some time ago, and prepared the girl for the arrival of her monthlies, rather than it being such a shock. Constance had been convinced she was dying when she'd come running to her this morning.

'It – it happens to everyone?' Constance rubbed her wet eyes with her handkerchief. 'Every lass?'

'Aye, and it's quite natural, hinny. Now you go and sort yourself out with the pads of cloth I've given you and then we'll have a little chat over a cup of tea before your granda comes in, all right? There's a good lass.'

Constance nodded doubtfully. When the pains in her stomach had sent her to the privy and she'd seen the blood staining her drawers, she'd thought her end had come, and now here was her grandma treating it as less than nothing. She looked down at the bleached strips of linen in her hand. Her grandma had said this happened every month from now on and she mustn't wash her hair or use the tin bath when she was bleeding or she'd catch a chill. Slowly, her feet dragging, she made her way upstairs to her bedroom but after following her grandmother's instructions she didn't immediately return to the kitchen. Plonking herself down on the bed, she sat gazing out of the sash window.

The November day was bitterly cold, the thick frost of the night before still coating the frozen world outside the house in white, but although the inside of the glass showed a film of ice and the bedroom was freezing, Constance remained where she was, her small white teeth gnawing at her lower lip.

Her grandma had explained the monthly loss of blood as being necessary for her to develop into a woman, and it was true she turned thirteen soon and was leaving school at Christmas, but what good was all that when Matthew was courting strong with Tilly Johnson? And Tilly was a woman, not a bit lass.

Constance closed her eyes, her arms wrapped round her waist as she swayed back and forth. Matt had had other lasses before Tilly – he was a grown man, after all – but somehow she'd known from the first time she'd seen Tilly in the Heaths' kitchen that this one was different. Tilly had set her cap at him. That's what Matt's mam had said to her grandma when they hadn't known she was listening, and when her grandma had replied that he didn't seem to be objecting over much, Matt's mam had laughed and said it was about time he stopped sowing his wild oats and settled down, and he could do worse than Tilly Johnson.

This thought brought a soft little groan. *Tilly Johnson* with her big bust and pretty face and job in the post office. How could Matt *not* fall for her? It wasn't *fair*. Oh, why couldn't she have been born five years earlier? She would have made Matt love her then, but as it was he still treated her like a little bairn. Worse, a little sister.

Her grandmother's voice brought her from the bed, and when she entered the kitchen again it was to find a cup of tea and a plate of girdle scones dripping with butter waiting for her. By the time the scones had been eaten Constance's head was buzzing with the facts of life as related by Mabel. She knew her grandma had found the talk embarrassing, and for that reason she felt she couldn't ask any questions, even though she still wasn't sure exactly how the seed from the man was implanted in the woman to make a baby. But she mustn't let a lad do more than kiss her on the mouth and only then after a respectable courting period. 'Other' things, and here her grandma hadn't been specific, were permissible only after a couple had got wed.

By the time Art Gray came in from his early-morning shift at the pit things were as normal for a Saturday – on the surface at least. Constance helped her grandmother serve up the panackelty they had every Saturday using the chopped leftover scraps of meat from the week, but for once the potatoes rich with flavour from the meat and stock, caramelised onions and deliciously crusty rim to the dish failed to whet her appetite and she had to force the food down. The meal finished, and there being no football due to the weather, her grandfather settled himself in his shabby old armchair in front of the glowing fire with his pipe and baccy, and Constance cleared the table and helped her grandma wash the dishes. That done, the two of them took off their pinnies and tidied themselves prior to visiting the Heaths.

This Saturday routine had been part of Constance's life from when she could remember. She knew the origins of her grandma's close friendship with Ruth Heath dated back to the night Matt had rescued her from the fire which had taken her parents, and she'd grown up looking on the Heaths as part of her extended family – and Matt, in particular, as belonging to her. He'd always made a fuss of her, he still did, but now . . . Now there was Tilly.

'You all right, hinny?'

Her grandma lightly touched her cheek and Constance forced herself to smile. She loved her grandma – since her da's parents had been taken with the fever when she was five years old, her grandma and granda were her whole world – but in some corner of her mind she knew her grandmother wouldn't understand if she confided how she felt about Matt. And rather than have her love for him dismissed as something she would 'get over', she'd prefer to keep it a secret. Her grandma thought of her as a bairn, her granda too, they both did, but she knew her love for Matt was a thing apart from age and time. She had always loved him and she would always love him, it was as simple as that. And she would give up or sacrifice anything if she thought she could make him love her like she loved him.

Tilly was sitting close to Matt on the long wooden settle which took up all of one wall of the Heaths' kitchen when Constance reached the house, and this was no accident. Tilly smiled her greeting along with the others but in the jostling around to make room for the newcomers to sit down, she made sure Matt remained close to her. She knew he regarded the Shelton girl as the little sister he'd never had, and that was fine as far as it went. She was acquainted with the facts concerning the night Constance's parents had died and was aware of Matt's continuing sense of responsibility towards the girl, and if Constance had been plain with nothing to commend her, it wouldn't have mattered. But Constance wasn't plain.

Tilly looked across at her now as Constance answered something Matt's mother had said, and as had happened more than once, a dart of fear pierced her. Constance was bonny, more than bonny. She was beautiful, and tall for her age. Her skin was the colour of cream and her eyes were a cornflower blue with the thickest lashes she'd ever seen on anyone. She'd heard the lass's mam had been just as beautiful, with the same wavy golden hair, and that all the lads had liked Hannah Gray.

Tilly's hands were clasped together in her lap and she began to repeatedly move one thumb over the other in little circles. It was a sure sign she was agitated and, recognising this, she became still. How could she be jealous of a bairn? she asked herself silently. It was daft, barmy, and she'd die if anyone cottoned on.

She glanced at Matt but he was deep in conversation with his father about an incident at the pit involving the weighman, Vincent McKenzie. No one liked McKenzie. It was his job to assess the tubs of coal sent out of the pit by the miners and he had the authority to downgrade or reject the coal and inflict heavy penalties by means of cruel fines. She'd heard her own da say the weighman was more to be feared than the manager, and that McKenzie was a gaffer's toady who'd only risen to his exalted position by licking the manager's boots. Matt was convinced

McKenzie had it in for him in particular, although Tilly couldn't see why. Everyone liked Matt.

At this point in her thinking she became aware that Constance was staring unblinkingly at her; in the same manner she returned the stare and immediately the other girl's eyes fell away and her skin turned a rosy hue. *Constance no more liked her than she liked Constance.* The thought was disturbing, strengthening her unease. Instinctively she pressed closer to Matt and as he turned and smiled at her, saying softly, 'All right, lass?' she managed to nod and smile back.

She wasn't going to lose Matt. Her full, somewhat slack mouth tightened. She was eighteen years old and she wanted to be married and respectable. If nothing else it would bring an end to the other thing. She lowered her eyes to her lap, but in her mind she could see the postmaster's face and it was soft with the expression he kept just for her after their lovemaking. Their affair had been going on for over three years and she knew if anyone got wind of it she would be tarred and feathered and run out of town, him having a wife and three bairns, but where Rupert was concerned she just couldn't help herself.

Her thumbs started their rotating once more and again she stopped the motion abruptly.

Once she was wed and keeping house for Matt she would be safe. Matt was like his da and the rest of the men hereabouts, he wouldn't countenance his wife working outside the home. This thought brought another worry and it wasn't a new one. What would Matt do on their wedding night when he discovered he wasn't the first? Or would she be able to fool him? She suspected he'd had his practice before her, he'd said as much, but had always accepted that no meant no where she was concerned. Only last night when he'd tried it on and they'd nearly had a quarrel, he had been full of remorse later, cuddling and petting her and telling her he respected her for her determination to keep herself for her wedding day. He'd go mad if he thought she'd deceived him.

She felt a moment of sharp panic before relaxing and shrugging mentally. She'd cope with that if she had to, she needed to bring him up to scratch first. They'd been walking out for six months now and not a word about the future.

She darted another glance at Constance but the girl was busy slicing up a fruitcake to go with the tea which was brewing. That was another thing that riled her about Constance; she acted as though she was a member of the family rather than just a neighbour, calling Matt's mam 'Aunty Ruth' and taking other such liberties. And she was forever round here; she knew Constance often called in on her way home from school and stayed till Matt got in from the pit. It wasn't right and someone ought to tell her so, but they wouldn't. Spoiled rotten, she was.

'What's the matter? Are you all right, lass?'

She wasn't aware Matt had finished his conversation with his father and was watching her, but now as he bent and whispered in her ear, she whispered back, 'I've a bit of a headache and it's stuffy in here, that's all.'

He was immediately concerned. 'Do you want to get a breath of fresh air for a while? We could go for a walk if you like?'

She did like. It would be one in the eye for little Miss Doe-eyes. She got her coat while Matt explained to the others and as they left by the back door she had the satisfaction of seeing Constance staring after them, nipping on her lower lip.

The afternoon died for Constance once Matt had left. She continued to smile and chat with her grandma and Matt's mam and da, and when Matt's two older brothers dropped by with their wives and bairns, she took the little ones under her wing and kept them occupied by playing with them and telling them stories. The winter twilight meant Ruth Heath lit the lamps early, and the kitchen took on a cosy glow which disguised its shabbiness and added a touch of charm to the shining blackleaded range and old kitchen table covered with its white Saturday cloth.

Matt didn't return before they said their goodbyes. Constance dilly-dallied as long as she could but eventually she had to concede defeat and they stepped into the frozen world outside the warmth of the kitchen. The sky was high and ablaze with stars, the light of a pale moon turning the frosty ground to sparkling crystals.

'By, lass, watch yourself.' Mabel caught hold of her grand-daughter's arm as she spoke, nearly having gone headlong. 'It's like glass out here. It'll be a miracle if one or the other of us doesn't land up on our backside before we get home.'

Carefully they made their way into the back lane, but here the icy ridges and deep hollows were even more treacherous than the Heaths' backyard. The temperature, which hadn't risen above freezing all day, had now dropped like a stone once the weak winter sun had set, and it was so cold it took your breath away.

Slipping and sliding and holding on to each other, they advanced along the narrow back way, and they had almost reached the end of the lane when a shadow moved at the side of them, causing Mabel to scream before she checked herself.

'Sorry, Mrs Gray.' Matt's voice was self-conscious, but as he stepped forward he drew Tilly with him and even in the feeble moonlight Constance could see the girl's cheeks were flushed and her eyes bright. 'We were just talking.'

'Aye, and I'm a monkey's uncle.' Mabel's voice was indulgent rather than annoyed. 'It's too cold to be lingering out here though, Matt. Get the lass home in the warm.'

'Will do, Mrs Gray. 'Bye for now.'

Matt grinned at Constance as he turned away with his arm round Tilly's waist, but Constance's face remained straight as she watched them walk away. She hated Tilly Johnson, she thought, her throat full. And she might work in the post office and be a cut above most of the lasses hereabouts, but there was something spiteful about her and she wasn't imagining it.

'Don't take on, hinny.'

She hadn't been aware her grandma knew how she felt, but then as Mabel added, 'Just 'cos he's got a steady lass it don't mean he thinks any the less of you,' she realised her grandma didn't really understand. Not the depth of her feeling anyway.

'I don't like her.' Her voice was flat and low as she took her grandmother's arm. 'And she doesn't like me.'

'Now that's silly. Why wouldn't Tilly like you?'

Constance didn't speak for a moment. Then as they began walking again, she muttered, 'I don't know, but she doesn't.'

'Now look, me bairn, I know for a fact Ruth's for the lass and likely something'll come of her and Matt, so make up your mind to get on with Tilly, if only for Matt's sake. You can do that, can't you? He's a good lad, none better.'

Constance glanced at her grandmother. She wondered what she'd say if she told her she knew she loved Matt in the same way her mother had loved her father. It had been her grandma who'd said that although her mother could have had her pick of any of the lads hereabouts, there had only ever been one she'd had eyes for. 'Stephen was always the one,' her grandma had said. 'Your mam was like that and nothing could have changed her mind.'

And she was like her mother. Constance nodded mentally to the thought. She knew she was. Her grandma thought she was a bairn still and too young to know her mind, but she didn't think she'd ever been a bairn where her feeling for Matt was concerned.

Her mother would have understood. This train of thought stirred the deep and futile longing that had always been with her since a little girl. If she could have just talked to her mam once, hugged her, kissed her, she would be content. Her grandma was lovely and she loved her all the world, but her mam . . . Well, she was her mam. And the people who said you couldn't miss what you'd never had, talked rubbish.

'Constance?' Mabel stopped at the end of the lane, her gloved hands reaching for the sweet face that was the image of her daughter's. 'Do you understand what I'm saying, hinny?'

Constance looked into her grandma's faded blue eyes and nodded. She understood only too well. Matt could do no wrong where her grandma was concerned, and if he had chosen Tilly Johnson as his lass then she was to be welcomed with open arms. And the ironic thing was, it was because of her and the great debt her grandparents felt to Matt that this was so. When she had been saved from the fire it had also saved her grandma's reason, that's what her granda had told her once when it had been just the two of them. Her grandma had always had a special bond with Hannah, he had confided. It was like that sometimes with one particular child, and she had suffered greatly when Hannah had died. But there'd been her, Hannah's baby, to care for. And the special bond had been passed down because didn't her grandma love her more than anything or anyone? her granda had finished, patting her cheek gently. And she must always remember that. She was her grandma's sun, moon and stars.

Bending forward impulsively, she kissed her grandmother's lined cheek. 'I love you, Grandma.'

Mabel flushed with pleasure but her voice was dismissive when she said, 'Go on with you, what are you after now?' She had never been a one for expressions of physical affection. She showed her love in keeping a clean and tidy home and providing meals that were good and plentiful as befitted a dutiful wife and mother.

Knowing this, Constance now linked her arm through her grandmother's, her voice deliberately playful: 'I'll be as nice as pie to Tilly, Gran, I promise. How about that? And when she goes on about all she has to do at the post office as though the rest of us are numbskulls, I'll listen with bated breath and hang on her every word.'

'Oh you, our Constance!' But Mabel was laughing, her world having been put in order again.

Constance, on the other hand, felt hers would never be right again.

Chapter 2

It was the middle of March, and the severe winter which had seen snowfalls as high as the top of hedgerows and three months of relentless blizzards showed no signs of relinquishing its grip on the frozen north. There had been flurries of snow all week and the cold was intense, the sky lying low over the rooftops and causing folk to predict at every opportunity: 'There's more on the way, we aren't out of this yet. This winter'll be remembered for many a year.'

Matt Heath echoed this sentiment but in his case it had nothing to do with the weather. As he put it to himself, Tilly was driving him fair barmy. One minute she'd be warm and eager in his arms, giving him every signal she wanted him as much as he wanted her, and the next she'd be the outraged virago or worse, in floods of tears, making him feel like an animal.

He knew what she was holding out for, of course. Marriage. She wanted a ring on her finger before she went the whole hog. She'd never actually said so, but he knew. She was a good girl, she'd told him over and over again, and good girls didn't do 'that'.

He shuffled forward in the line of miners in the lamp cabin, waiting to draw their lamp along with the two tokens with the lamp number on. The lamp man would hang one token up in the cabin and the other would be kept by the miner; it was the only sure means of knowing if a miner had completed his shift and was safely above ground again.

'Cheer up, man, it might never happen.' His brothers were standing right behind him and now George nudged him in the ribs as he spoke, while Andrew put in, 'What's up with you these days, anyway? You're a right miserable so-an'-so most of the time.'

Matt shrugged. If he told them the truth he knew what their answer would be. Only last week George had asked him when he was going to pop the question, and when he'd replied that it was his business and his alone, his brother had asked him what he was waiting for.

It was a good question. What *was* he waiting for? Tilly was bonny and bright and she loved him; his family had made it clear they thought he'd done himself proud in catching a lass like Tilly. And he had. He had.

His lamp had already been tested and lit when he got it and he made his way to the cage which would take him into the bowels of the earth, George and Andrew on either side of him. As soon as everyone was in, the gate was slammed shut and the cage descended at breakneck speed before slowing just before it clanged to a stop at the bottom of the shaft. Matt stepped out into the coal-face along with the rest of the men. The fact that they were nearly a hundred metres under the ground he did not allow to enter his mind. It was no good dwelling on things like that.

Sacriston was near the centre of, and on the 'exposed' section of, the Durham coalfield, where the coal measures were not covered by younger rocks but only the sand, clay and gravel drift deposited by the retreating ice at the end of the last Ice Age. The area had five workable seams of coal, two of which were close to the surface but three much deeper, and it was one of these the brothers worked. The rows of coke ovens alongside the railway tracks to the left of the village was a reminder that much of the coal produced from the pit was converted into coke at the pithead and sent to the iron and steel furnaces of Teesside, and the bad winter had hit production. Now the railway was operating fairly normally again, overtime was being offered and Matt had taken extra shifts whenever he could. He hadn't liked being laid off for days on end and it had brought home to him the fact that he'd got nothing saved for the future, no nest egg. He didn't question in his mind why he was suddenly thinking this way, merely telling himself he had turned twenty-two in the New Year and it was time he stopped frittering the rest of his wage away once he'd given his board to his mam.

He was working the foreshift this week, from six o'clock in the morning until two o'clock in the afternoon, and he'd done an extra shift for the last three days which meant he didn't get home until half-nine at night. He hadn't seen Tilly since the weekend and today was Friday and they were supposed to be going to a barn dance in the church hall, so he was hoping to get a kip this afternoon once he'd had his dinner. He was dog tired. He stumbled as he followed George along the tunnel the miners called the 'roadway' which got narrower and narrower and the roof lower the further they went, and behind him Andrew said, 'You were daft doing three extra shifts in a run, man. It's too easy to make mistakes when you're knackered.'

Sharply, Matt said, 'I'm all right, you look after your own.' He'd read the censure in his brother's voice and knew it wasn't merely concern for himself that had prompted the comment. Any slight lapse or negligence by one man doing his allotted task could mean he jeopardised not only his own life but that of his companions.

The area where the cage docked was well lit; now they were in pitch blackness, the kind of black that never lifted no matter how the men's eyes got used to it. As a lad, he'd been down the pit a couple of months before he knocked his lamp over one day and put it out. As luck would have it he'd been working by himself clearing an old roof fall, which had meant he'd been plunged into immediate and total darkness, a darkness so terrifying his bowels had turned to water. Suddenly every sound was magnified, as though the roof was going to come crashing down on him, but he'd known he had to keep working; when the gaffer came at the end of the shift to inspect what he'd done, his lamp going out would be no excuse for slacking. The rats and mice and not least the ugly black-backed beetles that infested the tunnels took on a new dimension that day. He never knocked his lamp over again. Matt smiled grimly to himself.

They were walking swiftly, even though by now most of the men were doubled up as the roof was so low; no time was ever wasted getting to the work site. No one got paid for 'travelling' time, even if they had to walk or crawl for a couple of miles or more from the bottom of the shaft; the owners considered that was down to the miners. The men were paid only from the minute they reached their place of work and got started.

Behind him, Andrew wouldn't let the matter drop. 'Why are you taking extra shifts anyway? It's not like you need the money. Live in clover, you do, with Mam only having you and Da to look after and two wages coming in for a household of three. Not like me an' George with wives and bairns to feed. If anyone needs extra time, it's us.'

He knew his brother was fishing about Tilly and his intentions, but he wasn't in the mood. 'I'm not stopping you, am I?' he flung back over his shoulder. 'You've got a mouth on you to ask, same as me if you want extra.'

'I did. I asked yesterday morning but they'd got their quota.'

'You should have asked earlier then.'

'Aye, I'd worked that out for meself.'

They scrambled on, in the funny, crab-like movement all miners looked on as natural after a few months down the pit. When he'd first come down, his back had regularly looked like a piece of meat hanging in the butcher's shop by the end of a shift. He'd scraped the back of his head, his shoulders and spine constantly, but pain was a great teacher and now he rarely made contact with the harsh, unforgiving roof above him.

It was another minute or two before Andrew spoke, his tone as conversational as though they were discussing the weather when he said, 'I'd bin married a year at your age and Olive was already six months gone with our Jed.'

Steady, steady. The warning came a second after the urge to stop dead and take his brother by the throat.

But he was sick to death of being told what to do, he excused himself silently. No, not told. He could have come back with a few well-chosen words if Andrew or George or his mam and da, come to it, had voiced what they were thinking. As it was, the pressure to do what they all clearly considered right and proper and ask Tilly to marry him was worse because of its covertness.

Was it that which was stopping him? he asked himself in the next moment. He'd always been a stubborn and contrary so-and-so, he admitted it, and he didn't make any apology for it either. His da was the same. Or was it something more? He was mad about Tilly, he couldn't sleep nights for thinking about how she'd feel beneath him and what he wanted to do to her, but did he love her? And what was love anyway?

Andrew piped up again. 'It's grand holding your first-born in your arms, man. Nothing can match it, not even the best football game in the world.'

He didn't answer, but his brother wasn't to be deterred.

'It was the same when Toby was born. You look at 'em and see yourself.'

Matt snorted. 'And that's something to aspire to?' he asked with heavy sarcasm. 'Even in your case?'

'Aye, it is.' Andrew refused to accept the humour. 'It's what makes the world go round.'

He didn't want to make the world go round. He wanted—

He didn't know what he wanted. Matt walked on, his eyes instinctively checking the way in front of him by the light of his lamp. Every miner looked for some unfamiliar sign that might indicate the props were going to give, or a fault in the roof – which was the only thing between them and millions of tons of rock, coal and muck – was about to crack wide open. It was part of the deputy's duty

43

to notice such things, of course, and that was fine and dandy, but it was every miner's unspoken opinion that you couldn't have too many pairs of eyes on the job.

When they reached the area they were working on they were crawling and wriggling on their stomachs like human worms, spreading out along the coalface and beginning work immediately.

Andrew had been quiet for the last ten minutes or so, but Matt supposed it was too much to hope it would last. From a bairn his brother had never been able to leave well alone. Sure enough, it wasn't long before Andrew spoke, but this time he directed his comments over Matt's head to George. 'Hey, George man, how old were you when you got wed then?'

Matt answered before his other brother could speak. 'You should know – you were his best man, weren't you?'

Ignoring this, Andrew called, 'Twenty-one, weren't it, man?'

George's answer was a grunt. He was fully aware of his brothers' conversation and normally he would have been in there adding his two penn'orth and winding Matt up, but an abscess under one of his teeth had seen him walking the floor all night and he wasn't in the mood for the mickey-taking, joking and cursing that went on nonstop every shift.

'Aye, twenty-one,' repeated Andrew. 'Stands to reason that unless a man's a bit . . . you know, limp-wristed . . . he'll want to get himself a lass to go home to every night once he's earning.'

The insinuation was too much for Matt, but the profanity he'd been about to growl at his brother was never voiced. Instead a sound like a giant beast crunching froze his limbs and filled his head in the split second before he was enveloped in dust and rock and earth, the weight of which bearing down on his chest took the breath from his body.

The consuming darkness he remembered from the time his lamp went out engulfed him, made more terrible by the fact he was buried alive, choking and suffocating under a mountain of muck. Panic-stricken, he fought to move, and as his face and shoulders struggled against the weight holding him down, he managed to free himself sufficiently to raise his upper body on his elbows, the lumps of rock and mass of gritty slack sliding off him.

The dust-filled air was thick and heavy as he gulped at it, and he could hear one or two others choking and coughing and moving. For a moment, relief that he wasn't the only one alive in the blackness was paramount, then concern for his brothers brought him heaving and kicking the rest of his torso and legs free. One of his boots made contact with something which groaned, and Andrew's voice, rasping and dazed, muttered, 'That's right, finish the job the damn roof's done on me, why don't you?'

'Andrew.' He crawled to the sound, feeling his way. 'You all right?'

His answer was another muffled groan, followed by, 'I think me leg's broken . . . hell.' Another groan and then, 'I'm caught fast.'

He felt his way along Andrew's body and clawed at the grit and rocks covering his brother's legs, but although the right one came clear of the rubble, the left was held fast by a slab of rock. Doug Lindsay, the miner who had been working on Andrew's left, came crawling up, saying, 'By, I thought we were all done for, this time.'

'Doug.' Matt reached out and caught hold of him.

'Andrew's leg's held.' He guided the man's hands in the blackness and between them they heaved the rock clear, bringing a stifled scream from Andrew in the process.

The next moment though, Andrew gasped, 'I'm all right, see to George and the others. How bad do you reckon it is?'

'The fall was just behind me,' Doug muttered softly, 'and I reckon plenty came down.'

Matt knew what that meant. The exit was blocked and their only hope was the rescue workers clearing from the other side. There had been several men working some distance behind Doug. They would raise the alarm − if they were in a position to do so.

More moans and curses were coming from his right and then, wonder of wonders, they saw the flicker of a lamp. No sight could have been more welcome. Three miners crawled towards them pulling a fourth behind them, and at the same time there was a movement from the mound of slack to Matt's right and George coughed before heaving himself on to his hands and knees, shaking his head like a boxer coming round from the knock-out blow. 'What happened?' he asked weakly.

'Whilst you've bin taking a little nap the rest of us have bin having a picnic.' Andrew might be down but he wasn't out.

But then even he became silent when, in answer to Matt's enquiry about the men further down the tunnel, one of the three shook his head, adding, 'It's blocked both ways. It's come down either side of us and we shouldn't talk. There's not much air.'

As though in confirmation of this the lamp's light became dimmer.

'Bert?' Matt muttered, nodding his head at the man the others had been hauling and who hadn't moved.

Again he received a shake of the head and now he crawled back to Andrew, removing his own shirt and making a rough pillow for his brother's head before sitting with his shoulders resting against the wall of the tunnel. George joined him, settling himself and putting his hand to his jaw. 'Damn tooth.' He shut his eyes. 'Dora wanted me to have it out this morning but I didn't want to lose a shift.'

How was that for irony, Matt thought, his head buzzing slightly. Instead of losing a shift he could lose his life. And then he rebuked himself sharply. None of that. Once you started thinking like that you'd lost the fight. They were still alive, all except poor old Bert, and they didn't know for sure if the others either side of the fall were gone. All they could do now was wait and hope the rescue team were in time. They'd work like the dickens, he knew that. Likely most or all of them had brothers, fathers or sons or other male relatives in the accident, but even if they hadn't they'd be just as keen to get to their mates. His da had been on the late shift this week, so he'd be one of the rescue workers.

The men were quiet now, each one aware that the precious oxygen was running out and each time they breathed they replaced the little there was with carbon dioxide from their own lungs. But there was nothing they could do about it.

How long would Tilly mourn him before she got herself another fella? She was made for loving, was Tilly, with her big breasts and hips. A man could lose himself in a lass like Tilly and think he was in heaven. Would she be sorry she hadn't let him have his way when they brought his body up and she looked at his face? Would she wish she'd lain with him and let him love her?

He brought his wandering mind under control with a mental oath. *He wasn't going to die*, damn it. None of them were. How would his mam feel if her three lads were taken in one fell swoop? They had to live and that was the end of it. One thing was for sure though, if he got out of here whole in mind and body he was asking Tilly to marry him the minute he saw her again. If he'd been in his right mind he would have done it weeks ago instead of acting like a skittish lassie. Andrew was right, it was time he had a place he could call his own and a warm accommodating body to come home to at the end of a hard-working day. Tilly was ripe for marriage and she would make a grand miner's wife. She was strong and robust and hard physical work wouldn't bother her. What he'd been waiting for, he didn't know, but he was done with dallying. He'd ask her, God willing.

Having settled the matter which had plagued him for some time he became aware that he could hardly see the others; the lamp was fading fast. It was comforting to feel the bulk of George at the side of him; he wondered what his brother was thinking about. Likely both Andrew and George were thinking of their wives and bairns. As Andrew had said earlier, they saw themselves in their bairns and a part of them would live on in them. He didn't have that, he hadn't created life. There was no one living because of him. Although . . . that wasn't quite true.

The buzzing in his ears was louder and he wanted to sleep. He was tired. He couldn't remember ever being so tired. He struggled to remember what he'd been thinking about and then it came – *Constance*. Constance was alive because of him. He'd always been a bit embarrassed in the past if him saving her had come up, but now it was a good feeling, knowing the lass would grow up and have bairns of her own one day because of what he'd done that night so many years ago. She was a bonny little bairn, as bonny as a summer's day with those great blue eyes and cloud of golden hair, and her nature was as sweet as they came. He hadn't seen much of her since Christmas though. Once upon a time she'd accompanied her gran every Saturday to the house but recently Mrs Gray had taken to visiting on her own.

His brow wrinkled. He'd missed her, even though he hadn't realised it till now. Somehow their old easy camaraderie had melted away in recent months and now he felt as though he had lost something precious. Why had she stopped coming?

He continued to mull the matter over in his mind until the humming drone in his ears blotted it out. His chin fell on to his chest and so it was that his last conscious thought was not of the girl he intended to marry, but Constance.

Chapter 3

Vincent McKenzie was recovering from the biggest shock of his life. He had been at the colliery fifteen hours, not because he was part of the rescue crew – why would he risk his own life saving men who hated him, and he them? – but because of his status as master weighman. As such, along with the deputies and under-manager and manager, he had a duty to the owners to show his face at such times. That was the way he saw it. And so he'd done his bit and waited while the rescue workers did theirs, and minutes ago the last of the trapped miners had been brought to the surface.

The fall had been a bad one, but amazingly only four men had lost their lives, although several more had been injured. Most of the shift working in the affected area were 'walking wounded', however, and the management would expect them to turn up as normal the next day, even though a pocket of men had been unconscious through lack of oxygen when they were found. And of course Matthew Heath had to be among the lucky ones who'd walked away unscathed.

Vincent pulled the collar of his coat more closely round his neck, his eyes narrowing against the bitter cold.

But it was Hannah appearing from the crowd waiting at the pit gates for news and throwing herself on Heath when he'd emerged which had turned his stomach and made him feel as weak as a kitten for a moment. Of course it hadn't been Hannah; after the first paralysing impact he'd realised it was Hannah's daughter, but his guts were still churning from the incident an hour since.

How long had it been since he'd last caught sight of the girl? he asked himself now. A long time, possibly a good five or six years, thinking about it. The thought of Stephen Shelton's seed living on had been a thorn in his flesh at one time, but once Heath had begun work at the colliery and he had been able to hit him where it hurt – in his pocket – he had felt easier. He saw to it that Heath's tubs of coal were downgraded or rejected whenever he could, and the subsequent fines and reduced pay-packet carried through to the letter. Once or twice he'd cut his wages by half and there wasn't a thing Heath – or any of the other miners he penalised – could do about it. Since he'd taken the job as weighman he carried a cosh in his pocket and kept his eyes skinned once he was clear of the village and on his way to and from the cottage. Weighmen seemed to be prone to 'accidents' of the fatal kind. His predecessor had been found on a dark night with his head bashed in.

'That's the last one up now.' Collins, the under-manager, joined him, tucking his muffler into the collar of his expensive coat as he spoke. 'Damn nuisance, this. It'll affect end-of-month profit, as if we haven't got enough trouble with the unions bleating about pay and conditions. Look out for troublemakers, McKenzie, and see to it they're discouraged from becoming too vocal. You understand me?'

Vincent nodded. He understood all right. Any known agitators would find their tubs discarded over and over again until they came to heel. And if they had the temerity to complain about this treatment they'd face the sack, which meant they were thrown out of their tied cottage. During the Durham strike the year before, he'd provided the owners with a list naming the most militant miners in the colliery, and subsequently received orders to get rid of two of them as an example to the rest of the herd. The feeling of power as he'd watched the families he'd chosen to go, being evicted from their homes, had been heady.

Collins walked off without a goodbye but Vincent didn't expect one. The under-manager had recommended him for the position of weighman eight years ago but that didn't mean he liked him, nor he Collins. Vincent knew he'd got the job because he had always made it plain he knew which side his bread was buttered; furthermore he had no allegiance to any of the men under him and no family connections. He'd always been disliked by his fellow man, now he was hated, but that didn't worry him. He had made their hate work for him. He was sitting pretty in a comfortable home with good food and clothes, and he wanted for nothing. And if Collins and the owners looked down on him, he didn't mind that either, as long as he was paid the hefty commission he earned for every tub of coal he rejected for the owners. He had a tidy bit put away for a rainy day already.

Vincent followed the thin, stringy figure of the under-manager out of the pit gates. Twilight had long since come and gone and the night was raw, a bitter wind swirling the odd snowflake in its midst. Wrapped up as he was in a good thick coat which would have cost the average miner a month's wages, Vincent didn't feel the cold, neither was he really aware of his surroundings as he took the familiar route home. In his mind's eye he was seeing Constance as she'd looked when the shawl covering her head had slipped and her golden hair had gleamed in the lamplight. She was Hannah to a T, or Hannah as she had been before she'd let Shelton get his dirty hands on her, and she looked much older than her age. If he hadn't known, he'd have put her down as fifteen or sixteen.

A feeling he'd long since thought was dead stirred in him, a mix of desire and hope and fear and a hundred and one other emotions he couldn't put a name to. He stopped dead as it caused his heart to beat faster, surprise that he could feel this way etched on the features which had coarsened since his youth. *Hannah's daughter.* Excitement caused him to sweat under his greatcoat and brown tweed jacket lined with silk, both of the best quality. He always dressed as well as any fine gentleman. It denoted his position, and furthermore got up the nose of his former classmates who had taunted and rejected him as a bairn and made his life hell. One of them had muttered something about folk who 'aped their betters' when he'd been walking past a group of miners outside the colliery office once. He hadn't said anything at the time, but John Potts had been one of the men evicted from their homes last year and he hadn't been sniggering when he'd walked the road with his pregnant wife and six bairns.

Vincent strode through the village as he always did, eyes straight ahead and face set, although at this time of night

53

there was no one about and lights shone behind closed curtains. He didn't glance to the left as he passed Cross Streets although he was vitally conscious that Hannah's daughter was there living in the grid of streets as her mother had once done. But much had changed since then. The site to the east of Cross Streets had been built up in latter years and this area – Elliott and Hunter Streets, which were named after the colliery owners, and Victoria, Gregson and Blackett Streets – was referred to as 'New Town' by its inhabitants.

He paused, when after passing the Methodist Chapel and the Queen's Head Hotel he reached the crossroads, the right branch of which would take him home. He turned, looking back at the way he had come, and had the mad impulse to retrace his steps and bang on the Grays' front door then demand to see Constance.

What was she to Heath? The thought which had been there since he'd seen the girlish figure with her arms round the man's waist and her head pressed against his chest burned in his brain. What was their relationship? Knowing the story of her parents' demise and Heath's part in her own deliverance she'd be grateful, of course, and likely she'd grown up thinking of him as a kind of hero, a brother figure perhaps? Or was it more than that?

His teeth ground together, his thick black brows meeting as he turned abruptly and began to walk along Witton Street towards Fulforth Wood.

Heath hadn't responded to her as a man would to his sweetheart, he reasoned in the next moment. There had been no meeting of lips, nothing intimate. He had merely hugged her and then his mother in much the same way before other family members had hidden the two from his sight. When the group which had included the brother and his wife and bairns had walked away, the girl had been holding Heath's mother's arm, and if his memory wasn't playing tricks there had been another lass with Heath. His frown deepened. Aye, he was sure there had been, although he had been so taken up with Hannah's ghost that he hadn't paid too much attention to anyone else.

He continued to mull the matter over in his mind until he reached the cottage, and by then he had come to a decision. He'd make it his business to find out what was what over the next day or two because – excitement surged again, filling his body and causing his breathing to quicken – he intended to have Hannah's daughter as, by rights, he should have had the mother. And if Heath, or anyone else for that matter, got in his way they would be dealt with. He'd been given a second chance. He knew it.

Polly would have to go. The thought stilled his hand on the latch of the front door. But only for a moment.

There were ways and means, he told himself grimly. But first he needed to see how the land lay, and to do that he would need to proceed carefully. But he could be patient when necessary. That was one of the things the fools who had under-estimated him in the past didn't understand. He was cleverer than all of them put together. That was why they scratched a living in filth and muck under the ground like the ignorant animals they were, and he lived in comfort and prosperity.

Pushing open the heavy oak door he walked into the cottage. The appetising aroma of his dinner vied with the smell of beeswax from the many items of fine furniture he insisted were polished every day. Polly appeared in the kitchen doorway with his slippers in her hands. Her voice matched her thin frame, mousy hair and nondescript features. Dully, she said, 'The water's hot and I'll bring it straight up. Your clothes are laid out on the bed.' It was his custom to wash his face and hands on returning home and change into a clean shirt and his smoking jacket.

Kneeling in front of him she took off his boots and he stepped into his slippers. He did not thank her for her ministrations but walked to the stairs, and behind him he heard her scurry into the kitchen. Her fear of him pleased Vincent; in fact, it was the basis of their relationship. When he'd brought Polly to the cottage from the workhouse twelve years ago, ostensibly to care for his mother who was ailing and see to the house, he'd chosen a girl he could easily bend to his will. His mother had died slowly and painfully, since the poison he'd used had to be given in small quantities to remain undetected, and by the time she'd passed away Polly wouldn't so much as breathe unless he gave the word. Orphaned and placed in the workhouse as a baby she had been trained not to think for herself since a child but to obey unquestioningly, and he had taken full advantage of this.

He had first taken her on the evening of the day of his mother's funeral, and once he had found he could subjugate her as he wished, had given free rein to the strong unnatural desires he'd previously kept for the women in the brothel he'd frequented. The indignities he heaped upon her were never spoken about between them; in fact, he rarely spoke to her at all. She did not – and never had – receive a wage; her reward for her services as his 'housekeeper' were a roof over her head and being fed and clothed.

The bedroom was as warm as toast when he opened the door, the fire in the small black-leaded grate heaped high with glowing red coals. Every item of furniture in the room was of superior quality, from the James I carved oak tester-bed, wardrobe and chest of drawers, to the pair of leather armchairs with padded arms which stood either side of the window with an oak wash-stand between them. Anyone entering the room could have been forgiven for thinking it was that of a gentleman, and one of some standing to boot.

Once Polly had entered with the water and left again, Vincent did not immediately begin his toilette. After taking off his greatcoat he walked across to the beautifully wrought cheval mirror in a corner of the room, standing and surveying his reflection for more than a minute. He was thirty-four years of age and he wasn't an unattractive-looking man. His hair was still thick and strong, and although the alcohol he consumed nightly was beginning to show in his heightened complexion, his body still hadn't turned to fat. He earned a great deal of money and furthermore he'd decked this place out like a palace. Any lass from the village should consider herself fortunate if he asked for her in wedlock. *Wedlock.*

The word caused his heart to thud like a piston, the strength of it causing him to lift a hand to his chest. He continued to stand for a few moments more before beginning to undress, and he found his hands were shaking as he undid the buttons of his white linen shirt.

A mile or so away in the house in Cross Streets Constance was already in bed. When they had returned from the colliery she'd pleaded a headache after forcing down a few mouthfuls of her grandma's mutton broth, but the ache wasn't in her head. It was in her heart.

She lay curled under the faded blankets, the stone hot-water bottle comforting on her cold feet as she reviewed the events of what had been the worst day of her life.

When news of the disaster had broken that morning, she and her grandma had accompanied her granda to the pit gates. Art Gray had been on the late shift so he hadn't been caught in the fall, but being an experienced rescue worker he'd known he'd be needed. She and her grandma, along with most of the village, had gone to find out how bad the accident was, and once her worst fear had been confirmed and she knew Matt was one of the trapped men, she'd remained at the pit gates with the other folk waiting for news of loved ones. Neighbours had brought bowls of hot broth and warm drinks, but the cold had eaten into bone and sinew; she didn't think she'd ever be warm again.

Tilly hadn't joined them until she'd finished work at the post office, but once there had made her presence felt. Listening to her, you'd have thought she and Matt were betrothed at least. Mind, it was Tilly Matt had picked up in his arms and kissed . . .

The memory brought forth a little moan, quickly stifled even though her grandparents couldn't hear from down in the kitchen.

She shouldn't have broken through the crowd and run to Matt like that. When she thought about it now it made her face burn with embarrassment, but at the time wild horses couldn't have prevented her. Had he thought her forward? And what had his mam and the rest of them thought? Tilly, especially.

Tilly knew how she felt about Matt. This time she didn't moan out loud but buried her face in her lumpy flock pillow. She'd seen the knowledge in Tilly's face today, and if looks could kill she'd be six foot under right at this minute. All her efforts to steer clear of them when she knew they'd be together in case she gave herself away had come to naught. The Heaths' house had always been her second home, but now everything had changed. She couldn't bear it, she *couldn't*. What was she going to do? What *could* she do?

It was another two hours before she heard her grandparents come upstairs, and she was still wide awake. Her grandma put her head round the door, saying softly, 'Constance, lass?' but when she pretended to be asleep the door was closed and she was alone.

As was her custom, she'd cocooned herself under the blankets in the icy room so only her nose was exposed to the air, but after half an hour, when she'd judged her grandparents would be asleep, she crept out of bed, pulling her old faded dressing-gown over the flannelette nightdress her grandmother had made her. Without making a sound she went down the stairs to the kitchen, feeling her way in the blackness.

The kitchen was lovely and warm. The fire in the range was banked down for the night with damp slack, but Constance knew her grandma would soon have it blazing again come morning. The fire was kept going day and night. The only time it was ever allowed to go out was before the chimney sweep called. Her grandma could sort out the cinders, take out the ash, clean and blacken the range and all without burning so much as the tip of a finger. The range fire, and the huge iron oven it heated, was the pivot of the home, and Constance had grown up thinking it was the best place in the world to be. Like her granda always said, a good fire kept body and soul together no matter what else was happening around you.

Although she didn't feel like that tonight.

Constance plumped down in her granda's armchair at the side of the range, tucking her feet under her. Looking into the muted glow of the fire, she soaked up the warmth as the tears ran unchecked down her face.

After seeing Matt with Tilly today, she knew she had to face the fact that her grandma was right. Matt was going to ask for Tilly sooner or later – probably sooner, the way he'd kissed her. And she would be expected to be glad for the pair of them, to dance at their wedding and say what a bonny bride Tilly was. And in due course, when Tilly's belly swelled with Matt's bairn, she'd have to bill and coo over the baby when it was born. And that bairn would be the first of many; you only had to look at Tilly to see she'd have them like shelling peas, as her grandma said.

Wiping her eyes with the back of her hand, she sniffed a few times. If only she could get away, leave Sacriston for good, or at least for a number of years, but her grandma would never countenance her going. In her class at school there had been eight of them who'd turned thirteen before Christmas. The five boys had gone straight down the pit, but Betsy Kirby and Rose McHaffie had gone into service at big houses miles away – Betsy as a kitchenmaid and Rose at a smaller establishment as the under-housemaid. There were no jobs in the village for girls; securing a position like Tilly had done in the post office was rare, and almost inevitably girls left their homes for a life in service, returning on their half-day or day off once a month if they were near enough to make the journey. When she had mentioned what Betsy and Rose were doing, her grandma had first told her she thought she'd got a job lined up for her helping out in the kitchen at the Robin Hood Inn in Durham Street. When that hadn't materialised her grandma had gone to see her teacher, Miss Newton, and since Christmas she'd been helping with the little ones. She didn't get paid for this, but her grandma insisted that if she was patient, a job of some kind would come up in the village eventually. But she didn't think her grandma believed that, any more than she and her granda did.

Constance liked helping in the infants' class. She'd found she could manage even the naughtiest children like the Finnigan twins, but she couldn't do it for ever. She didn't *want* to do it for ever: it was only right she earned her own living.

She recalled the superior little smile which had played round Tilly's mouth at Christmas when the other girl had heard what she was doing, and, like then, she squirmed with humiliation. She was as bright as Tilly any day – brighter, in fact – but she didn't want to make her grandma sad. And her grandma would be sad if she left Sacriston. She had understood that already, even before her granda had had a little word in her ear. Besides, what reason could she give for wanting to go? Not the true one; she'd rather die than admit to that.

It was hopeless. Staring into the red glow underneath the mountain of damp coaldust she looked into a future stretching away in endless days and nights of misery. She wanted to shout and scream against it, to bang her fists on the floor and kick with her heels like the Finnigan twins did in one of their tantrums. And scratch Tilly Johnson's eyes out.

A little whisper came unbidden in the back of her mind. It reminded her how she'd prayed that day. She had promised God that if He spared Matt, if He allowed him to walk unscathed from the pit and feel sunlight and fresh air on his skin again, to see the blue sky and hear the birds sing, she would be content for the rest of her life, even if he loved Tilly and not her. And she had meant it, she had, but when he had kissed Tilly like that . . .

A bargain is a bargain. The whisper came again, stronger. Constance wrinkled her face against it, even as she knew she was fighting a losing battle. All the dreams she'd had, everything good and exciting about the future had been tied up with Matt before Tilly had come along. She had never imagined a life without him at its centre. She had been stupid, so stupid – no wonder he still saw her as a silly little bairn. But she wasn't a bairn. Not any more. Not after today, for sure.

She sat up straighter, her spine stiffening and her mouth pulled tight. And it was only bairns who cried for the moon. She had to get on with things and not wear her heart on her sleeve, not in front of her grandma or anyone else. Today had shown her clearer than anything else what was going to happen, and she couldn't do a thing about it. He would ask for Tilly and she would say yes. And in one way Constance hoped it would be soon, because this waiting for it to happen was unbearable.

Chapter 4

Constance was spared hearing the news of Matt and Tilly's betrothal from the happy couple themselves. Having gone down with a bad cold the day after the pit accident she had the perfect excuse to stay home the following Saturday afternoon, but when her grandma returned from the Heaths' in a state of high excitement, she knew immediately what had happened.

Her granda had been snoozing in his chair in front of the fire and she'd been working away on the clippy mat she and her grandma were making, the box of bits of old clean rags at her elbow on the kitchen table. Once the mat was finished it would replace the one in front of the range and the old one would be taken upstairs to one of the bedrooms. This one had lovely coloured patterns in it and would brighten up the kitchen no end, but she wasn't thinking of the clippy mat when she looked at her grandma.

'Well, what do you think then?' Mabel's face was bright, and without pausing, she went on, 'Matt's asked young Tilly to marry him. Went to see her da and did it properly, by all accounts.'

'And what did young Tilly say?' her granda put in, his face deadpan after he'd given a sly wink at Constance.

'She said yes, of course.' Mabel's voice carried a touch of indignation, for who wouldn't say yes to Matt Heath? 'And they're after setting a date for the autumn. They've already been to see Father Duffy, they'd just got back when I got there this afternoon. Middle of September, they thought, and we're invited.' She beamed at them as though this had been a surprise.

Perhaps because she had prepared herself for this moment over the last little while, Constance found she was able to smile back and say quite naturally, 'I bet Aunty Ruth is pleased.'

'Oh aye, they all are, although likely Ruth'll be at a bit of a loss when Matt goes, him being the last one. I know I felt the same when your mam got wed.'

The pain was killing her but no vestige of it showed in her face or voice when she said lightly, 'And then I was dumped on you and you had to begin all over again.'

In a rare show of affection her grandma reached out and touched her cheek. 'Lass, you've bin a blessing from the day you were born and that's the truth. Am I right, Art?'

Her granda nodded, his eyes soft. 'Never a truer word.'

How could she ever leave them and go into service? The tiny hope she'd kept hidden in her heart as an antidote to this day flickered and died. She couldn't. She owed them so much, and they weren't getting any younger. Her granda was still fit and healthy now, but there would come a time when he couldn't work and she would be the breadwinner. But doing what?

As though her grandma had heard her thoughts, she sat

64

down at the table next to her, her voice low as though someone might be listening when she said, 'Your Aunty Ruth had a quiet word with me this afternoon, hinny. There'll be a job going at the post office when Tilly's wed and she's asked Tilly to put in a good word for you with the postmaster. She gets on well with him, always has done, and he thinks a bit of her so there shouldn't be a problem if she recommends you. What do you think of that then? Working in the post office, lass. Imagine.'

The steel jaws of the trap finally snapped shut. Knowing she'd cry if she tried to speak, Constance squeezed her grandma's arm and attempted a smile.

Her grandma must have been satisfied with the way she was overcome with wonder at the news. Patting her cheek once more, she rose briskly to her feet and after divesting herself of her coat and old felt hat which was going green with age, Mabel walked over to the range and put the black kettle on to the centre of the glowing fire. 'We'll have a nice cup of tea and some of that fruit loaf I made earlier to celebrate,' she said happily, her smile beatific, although whether they were celebrating the news of the coming nuptials or the prospect of Constance's job at the post office, her two listeners weren't sure.

It was only a few days later that the event occurred which changed the direction of Constance's life for ever. She had been helping Miss Newton clear out a store cupboard in the seniors' classroom once all the children had gone home, and Miss Newton had put something to her. She had, the teacher said, been thinking for some time that Constance could do very well for herself. She understood the circumstances in which Constance was placed – this was a tactful way of saying she knew there was no spare money at home – but had Constance considered becoming an uncertified teacher? It wasn't the same as a qualified teacher, of course, but it was something, wasn't it? And she would receive a salary, that was the thing. Miss Newton would do all she could to help her, she had emphasised, and she was sure Constance was up to the task. She had such a gift with the children and it would be a great pity if this wasn't put to good use. It would take some time, of course, but it wasn't essential Constance brought in a wage immediately, was it?

No, Constance had assured the teacher, her eyes shining. It wasn't. But what exactly was involved and how would she go about it? How old did she have to be and how long would it take?

They had talked some more and by the time Constance left the school premises it was dark and snowing hard. Her mind full of the conversation she'd just had with Miss Newton, she didn't notice the tall dark figure standing a few yards away at the corner of Church Street. Consequently when Vincent spoke she started violently and would have fallen but for his hand shooting out to steady her.

'I – I didn't s-see you,' she stammered, taking a step backwards so his hand fell from her arm. She knew who he was, everyone in the village knew Mr McKenzie, the weighman, and every miner's child grew up thinking of him as the devil incarnate, but she had never spoken to him until three days ago. He had been walking along Front Street when she had left school on Monday evening, and had shocked her by smiling at her and saying hello. She had muttered something in reply and scurried away covered in confusion, conscious of his eyes burning into her back. She had thought it a chance meeting and had put the matter out of her mind before she'd reached home, but then he had been there the next night and this time had struck up a conversation with her and she had found herself walking with him until she'd reached Cross Streets.

He terrified her. She swallowed, her heart pounding. And it wasn't just the stories she'd heard about him in the Heaths' kitchen when Matt had vented his spleen about the 'keeker' as the men called him. Exactly what it was that frightened her she didn't know, because he was very well-dressed and he wasn't ugly, but there was something in his eyes . . .

'You're late leaving tonight,' he said quietly, confirming her fear that he had been waiting for her. 'Keeps you at it, does she, Miss Newton? Bit of a slave-driver?'

'No. No, she's not – not like that. She's nice. She just—' Constance stopped abruptly, suddenly aware that she'd been about to share her momentous news with Mr McKenzie, of all people.

'Just what?' His eyes narrowed as he stared into her face.

She shrugged, and as she began walking she prayed desperately that he wouldn't walk with her. He did.

'Just what?' he said again, but in a tone of voice she knew meant he was determined to get an answer.

For the life of her Constance couldn't think of anything to say but the truth. 'Miss Newton thinks I could train to be an uncertified teacher.' She kept her eyes on her boots as she walked. 'It wouldn't be for a while, of course.'

'Uncertified teacher?' The way he spoke, she could have said something immoral. 'What's she doing putting ideas like that in your head? You're bonny, you don't want to end up an old maid like Miss Newton. You'll be after getting married and having a family before too long. Take no notice of her.'

It wasn't the response she'd expected. It didn't occur to her to point out that she could follow the course Miss Newton had suggested and still get married. Instead she spoke out what was on her heart. 'I shan't ever get married,' she said flatly.

'A bonny lass like you? Don't be silly.'

She didn't reply to this. She'd said too much as it was.

After a moment, he said, 'I knew your mother many years ago. She was beautiful too, just like you.'

There was a funny little shake in his voice now and it unnerved her to the point that she felt like running away. And then she wished she had when she'd had the chance as he caught hold of her arm, forcing her to stop and face him through the whirling snow. 'Have you got a lad, Constance?' he asked softly.

She blinked away a snowflake which had landed on her eyelashes. She didn't like him touching her, and something of this was reflected in her voice when she said, 'Of course not, I'm only thirteen years old. No one has a lad at thirteen.'

'You look older than that. You look like your mother did when she was sixteen, seventeen even.'

His eyes were covering her face and she wanted to pull herself free, to fight him if necessary, but she told herself she was being silly. He had only talked to her, after all. And she mustn't forget he was the master weighman. He could make things impossible for her granda if she offended him. If even half the stories about him were true, it was enough for her to know his power was absolute. Looking down at her boots again, she muttered, 'Well, I'm thirteen and my grandma wouldn't hear of me having a lad for a long time, but I don't want one anyway so it doesn't matter.'

He was silent for a moment, then his voice came slowly, almost thoughtfully, but with a harder note in it than he'd used thus far. 'And is this decision anything to do with Matthew Heath getting betrothed to the Johnson wench at the weekend?'

Taken aback, her eyes shot to his face. He couldn't know, no one knew. So surprised was she, the truth was written all over her countenance.

'I saw you with him that day at the pit gates. You've allowed him liberties, is that it? And he's let you down?'

'No.' She was still so shocked by him guessing how she felt about Matt that her voice carried no weight.

'That's it, isn't it?' His hands had tightened on her arms to the point he was really hurting her. 'Damn it.' His face had darkened; now he was growling the words at her. 'Like mother, like daughter.' He shook her and she had to clutch at him or lose her footing on the icy ground. 'What did you let him do? Has he taken you down? Tell me.'

'*Stop it!*' She was struggling violently, panic-stricken and afraid, and as she did so the shawl which covered her head and was tucked in the collar of her coat slipped about her shoulders. At the sight of her golden hair, soft tendrils of which curled on to her forehead and cheeks, he seemed to go mad.

Pulling her against him, he crushed his mouth down on hers, her head going back so far she thought her neck would crack. Now Constance fought in earnest but her frenzied efforts had little impact on the hard male body. Although she was tall for her age, she was slender and finely boned. Vincent was a man in his prime and big and broad; the muscles he had developed in his years before becoming weighman had not yet turned to fat.

The snowstorm had driven everyone inside and the street was deserted; there wasn't even the odd child or two playing out. He had stopped her a hundred yards or so before the grid of streets wherein was home and safety, and now her terror increased as she felt him begin to manoeuvre her off the main street and into an alley which led to a piece of waste ground the colliery were due to develop for housing.

His mouth had left hers, but now one large hand was clamped across her lower face, stifling her screams but also her air supply. She felt herself going faint and limp, and strangely, as she stopped struggling, this seemed to check his madness. He paused a few feet into the alley, removing his hand as he shook her slightly, saying, 'I'm sorry, I'm sorry — you're all right, aren't you? Look, I didn't want it to be like this. I don't want to hurt you. I want . . .' He shook his head. 'Just tell me, and I want the truth, mind: have you and Heath been carrying on?'

He was still holding her arms and she hated herself for the pleading note to her voice when she said, 'No, no, I told you. I swear it.' Her breath caught in a sob. She didn't understand this. He didn't know her, so why was he behaving like this?

'You swear it? On your grandmother's life? He hasn't touched you? He hasn't done anything he shouldn't?'

She shook her head and his eyes moved from her mouth to her hair and then back to her mouth. 'I can find out if you're telling me the truth. And I don't like being lied to.'

'He hasn't touched me, he hasn't done anything. No one has.'

His hands tightened on her arms again but not roughly now. Thickly, he said, 'I'm the first?'

Help me, please help me, God. He was going to hurt her, she knew he was going to hurt her. Her lips trembling, she whispered, 'I have to get home, they'll be worried.'

'Your mother played me for a fool.' He straightened away from her but still didn't let her go. 'You wouldn't do that, would you? I can offer you more than any man in the village and it would all be above board, legal and proper, once you're old enough. You'd want for nothing.'

Dumbly she stared at him, barely able to take in what he was saying. He was the weighman and to her eyes he was old, as old as the fathers of the girls she'd gone to school with, and even before this night something about him had made her flesh recoil.

'Do you understand what I'm saying?' His hands dropped to his sides but she knew if she tried to run he would grab her. 'I want you and I'm prepared to wait but I won't be messed about, be very sure about that. You're mine.'

Again his voice had that funny little quiver in it that made her skin crawl, but instinct told her to say anything he wanted to hear. 'I – I understand.' She didn't dare move a muscle in case it inflamed him again.

'And you're willing? You're willing to be my lass?'

'When – when I'm old enough,' she said faintly, repeating his own words back to him.

He rubbed his hand hard across his mouth, his eyes unblinking as they searched her face. She knew he was

71

weighing her up, wondering if he could trust her. She didn't know what he was going to do next but her legs felt so weak she didn't think she could walk, let alone run. He had to believe her. Something outside of herself guided her tongue: 'You'd have to come and see my granda though, he's a stickler for doing things proper.' She forced a note of pertness into her voice. 'You'd have to ask him when it's time, but until then it's best it's a secret.'

He stared at her a moment more, then his jaw relaxed. 'Young as you are, you've got it all worked out, haven't you? But aye, it'll be a secret. Our secret. Till you're old enough.'

'You live in the big cottage at Fulforth Wood, don't you?'

'You know where I live?'

She nodded. 'Everyone knows where you live.'

The flattery worked. 'Is that so?' He seemed to swell a little. 'And you'd like to live in that fine house, would you? Be mistress of it? It's even bonnier inside, I promise you.'

Again she nodded before saying, 'My grandma, she'll be worried. I have to go or else she'll come looking for me.'

The snow was lying thick on her bare head and as his hand came out to brush it off she cautioned herself to remain perfectly still. When his fingers moved down to her cheek she couldn't stand it though, stepping back a pace as she pulled the shawl over her hair again. 'I'm late, I have to go.'

To her amazement he didn't protest, merely taking her arm and leading her out of the alley into Front Street once again. She wanted to break free of him and run, but warning herself that would be foolish she steeled herself to walk with him. They passed one woman with two little bairns a minute or so later but Constance kept her head down.

He didn't speak until they came to where she had to turn off the main road. Then he stopped, his grip on her arm forcing her to look at him. She expected him to reiterate his warning about other lads, or worse, try to kiss her again, but he surprised her once more by mumbling, 'I'll be good to you, I promise. You'll want for nowt. I've got plenty put by and you can live like a lady: fine clothes, anything you want.'

Now she was so close to home the urge to take to her heels was almost overwhelming. Trying to stop her lips trembling, she stepped away from him and he let her go without protest. 'I must go.' She turned, waiting for his hands to grab at her but as she stumbled away they didn't come. Then she was flying down the street despite the treacherous snow and ice underfoot and she didn't look back to the tall dark figure watching her go.

When she burst into the kitchen her face was streaming with tears and she was calling her grandma's name in a voice which caused Mabel to drop the humpty-backed rabbit pie she'd just taken out of the oven. It was almost five minutes later before Constance could speak clearly enough for Mabel to understand what had happened, and then only after Constance had insisted the back door was locked and bolted.

As Mabel held her child in her arms – and this was the way she'd always thought of her precious Hannah's daughter, as her own bairn, different from her other grand-children, loved as they were – her shock and revulsion had an element of relief running through it. He hadn't forced her, she hadn't been taken down. When Constance had arrived home late and in such a state she had thought the very worst.

Now she pressed Constance down into Art's armchair after one last hug, saying, 'I'll make us a sup tea, hinny, and then I want you to tell me everything again and slowly. Exactly what he said from the minute you saw him – and don't miss anything, especially that bit about your mam. I remember Vincent McKenzie from when he was a little lad and he followed your mam about like a puppy – she couldn't turn round but he was there. But this . . .'

With the second, more detailed telling, Mabel's fear for her granddaughter increased. Vincent had been a strange little boy and a troubled youth; she remembered the times she'd warned Hannah about him but her lass had just smiled and said he was lonely. Hannah had been kind, too kind maybe, but Mabel knew for a fact that her lass hadn't led Vincent up the garden path as he'd claimed. And now here he was attacking Constance and frightening her half to death whilst saying he wanted her as his wife once she was old enough. Art would go barmy when he was told – and with Vincent being the weighman . . .

She mashed another pot of tea after salvaging what she could of the rabbit pie, and all the time her mind was ticking over. Vincent had a housekeeper but the lass kept herself to herself. She flitted in and out of the shops in town like a shadow and didn't say a word to anyone. There were those in the village who thought the girl was more than his housekeeper, but this was just supposition. Nevertheless, the lass looked scared to death and that wasn't healthy, and this thing with Constance . . . It was unnatural, depraved, wanting the daughter because she looked like the mother. Dear gussy, Art would go for him, she knew he would, and then there'd be hell to pay. They could lose everything. But the man had to be warned off, there was no doubt about that. But would he take any notice? That was the thing.

Constance was looking more like herself now although her eyes were red and puffy, but it was when she rolled up the sleeves of her calico dress and said, 'Look, Gran, what he did,' and Mabel saw the livid bruises staining the white flesh that the idea came to her. She balked against it at first, painfully conscious of the sacrifice it would demand from her, but the more she fought against it the more she realised it was the only possible answer. It would serve to protect Constance but also guard them against Art losing his job and thereby their home.

Her mind made up, she wasted no time. 'Hinny, I want us to have a talk before your granda comes in.' She sat down at the kitchen table, patting the hardbacked chair beside her. 'Come here, lass. And stop trembling – you're safe now.'

Constance left the armchair by the range and when she was sitting so close to her grandmother their knees were touching, Mabel said quietly, 'It's best your granda doesn't know about this. He'll go and see Mr McKenzie and who knows what might happen. He's a devil, McKenzie. Everyone says so.'

Constance nodded her agreement. She didn't need to be told this. Vincent McKenzie was the weighman and that said it all.

'But we can't have you troubled by him again, and if you stay here he'll be after you. Now me sister Ivy who lives down in Durham, her eldest lass Florence took herself off further afield twenty-odd years ago and has done right well for herself. She's cook in a great big house where there's umpteen servants inside and out and all sorts. I can ask Ivy to write her lass and ask if she knows of anything going. There might be a vacancy somewhere she's privy to.'

Constance stared at her grandmother. 'Leave the village?'

'I don't see anything else for it, lass. If it'd been anyone but McKenzie, your granda could have given him a good hiding and put the fear of God in him, but McKenzie's got the ear of the manager and the owners. No, we have to get you away.'

'But what'll you tell Granda?'

'I'll bide me time till I've heard from our Ivy, and then if her lass can help I'll say Ivy's written with news of a good job and you'd be daft to miss it. In the meantime I'll tell Miss Newton you're down with a chill and won't be in for a while. If Ivy can't help there'll be other places somewhere wanting a servant, but I'd rather you be placed in a house her lass recommends and where you'll be treated fairly. It'll put me mind at rest.'

She was going to leave Sacriston. She wouldn't have to endure seeing Matt get wed or Tilly preening herself every time they met. For a moment even Vincent McKenzie was blotted from her mind.

But there were her grandparents. Ashamed of her self-ishness, she said quickly, 'There must be some other way, Gran.'

'There's not, me bairn. I wish there was but there's not.'

Constance had never seen this much sadness in her grandmother's eyes. It aroused such a depth of remorse in her that she burst into tears, and her grandma only made it worse when she put her arms round her shoulders, murmuring, 'You'll be all right, hinny, never fear. The only thing that matters is getting you away from that man's clutches, you see that, don't you? There, there, don't cry like that. It'll all work out for the best somehow.'

Florence Banks, Ivy's daughter, wrote directly to her aunt twelve days later. One of the scullerymaids in the establishment where she was cook had been sent packing, along with the footman who'd got the girl into trouble, which meant she was short-handed. Her mother had highly recommended Constance – here Mabel had silently blessed her sister who hadn't set eyes on Constance since she was a babe-in-arms – and for that reason she had obtained an interview for her with the butler, Mr Rowan. Constance was to present herself at Grange Hall on 1 April at three in the afternoon. If she suited she could stay on and begin her duties immediately.

It was a short letter, but one which caused sheer panic in its recipient. Grange Hall was situated near Harrogate in Yorkshire which could be the other side of the world as far as Mabel was concerned, for she had never ventured further than the outskirts of Sacriston. And the next day was the last one in March. However would Constance make the journey? Should she go with her? What would happen if the butler didn't give Constance the position, and how would she get home again? And – now the moment had come upon them – what would Art say to all this? What if he refused to let Constance go?

In the event, just before Art got in from the pit, Mabel had a surprise visitor who settled most of her anxieties in one fell swoop. She and Constance hadn't been long returned from seeing Miss Newton, or at least Constance had spoken to the teacher and Mabel had waited outside the classroom at her granddaughter's request. When the knock had come at the back door Constance had turned as white as a sheet, and Mabel had to admit her stomach had turned over as she'd gone to see who was there.

'Ivy!' Her startled face had transformed into one of relief as she'd drawn her sister into the house. 'Well, I never. Come in, lass, come in. Whatever's brought you here?'

'Our Florence wrote and told me she'd written you about the job at her place and I knew you'd be in a two-an'-eight.' Ivy smiled at Constance over Mabel's shoulder as she hugged her sister. Ivy was a good few years younger than Mabel and had scandalised her family by running off with a travelling farrier who'd passed through the village when she was fifteen years old. In spite of dire predictions of shame and ruin, the man had married her and they'd settled in Durham where he'd gradually built up a thriving business. Ivy considered herself far removed from the country bumpkin she'd once been and which she still felt her sister was, but she was a kind soul, and on receiving her daughter's letter had made post haste to Sacriston to see if she could help.

Once Ivy had become acquainted with Constance and the three of them were settled at the kitchen table over a pot of tea, she explained the reason for her visit. 'I can take Constance to Grange Hall and see she's all right. I've been once or twice to see our Florence over the years and stayed the night in her room, so it won't be a problem.'

Mabel was staring at her sister in awe.

'I've come in our horse and trap,' Ivy said casually, thoroughly enjoying herself. 'If we leave tomorrow after a bite Constance can stay at our place overnight and then we'll make an early start in the morning once it's light.

Now . . .' She bent closer to them both. 'What's this all about then? Why the need to get her out of the village and why isn't Art in on it?'

Mabel told her everything, finishing with, 'I always knew he was sweet on my Hannah but the lass wouldn't have it. Said they were just friends. But he wanted her all right, and now . . .' She waved her hand expressively at Constance.

'The dirty devil.' Ivy was all agog. This was better than the stories she read in *The People's Friend* each week. 'Well, you'll be safe with our Florence, hinny,' she said, turning to Constance and patting her arm. 'Don't you fret.'

Constance smiled at her great-aunt, but said nothing. In truth Ivy had overwhelmed her with her fine clothes and air of prosperity. And fancy her having her own horse and trap like the gentry. She bet news of her great-aunt's arrival had been all round the village before they'd so much as opened the door to her. It was the first time in living memory a horse and trap had been tied up in their back lane, that was for sure. When Miss Newton's brother and his wife had visited last year in a carriage and pair it had been talked about for weeks.

The thought of Miss Newton straightened her mouth. She hadn't told her grandmother what Miss Newton had proposed the night Vincent McKenzie had manhandled her. The news had been lost in the furore of that first evening and when she had thought of it later she'd decided it would do no good to bring it up. It couldn't happen now, so what was the point? She refused to acknowledge, even to herself, that it was the fear her grandmother might change her mind about her leaving Sacriston if she knew which had kept her silent. And so she had insisted on seeing Miss Newton alone today. It hadn't been a pleasant meeting. Miss Newton couldn't understand why she was leaving to work in service – 'throwing away any chance to better herself' was the way she'd put it – and she couldn't explain to the teacher why she had to leave. But Vincent McKenzie apart, she needed to leave the village.

She had seen Matt once since she'd come down with her 'severe chill' and been confined to the house. This had been two days ago. When Mabel had arrived at the Heaths' for the second Saturday afternoon running without her, Matt had left the others and popped round to see her. Her granda had gone with his pals to watch a football match and so she had been alone in the house when he'd called. She had forgotten to lock the back door once her grandfather had left and when Matt had walked in after a perfunctory tap, she'd gasped with fear before she saw who it was.

'Hey, it's only me.' He'd grinned at her, pulling out a chair and sitting down at the kitchen table where she was kneading dough. 'Who were you expecting?'

'No one. You made me jump, that's all.'

'Your grandma says you're still under the weather.' His brown eyes surveyed her thoughtfully. 'You certainly look different, but . . .' His voice trailed away, then he said, 'I know what it is. Your hair.'

She continued kneading the dough although she knew her cheeks had turned scarlet. 'I've put it up, that's all.' She and her grandma had decided that if Florence turned up trumps and found her a position somewhere, the older she looked, the better. Anyway – as her grandma had said – she'd left school now. So there was no reason to continue to wear her hair down like a bairn. And certainly the thick golden coils at the back of her head had put two or three years on her instantly. She felt different too. She had always been taller than her friends and in the past this had caused her to feel awkward and gangly. Now, with her hair piled up and her long neck exposed, it was as though she had found herself within her own skin. She felt nice, womanly.

Matt was still looking at her and he wasn't smiling any more. 'It suits you. You look . . . older.'

'Thank you.' There was a note in his voice she couldn't fathom but it made her feel terribly shy. Clearing her throat, she mumbled, 'I'll get you a cup of tea but I must finish this first. It's had one proving already.'

'I'm in no rush.' He stretched his long legs, taking off his cap and hooking it over the back of his chair before raking a hand through his thick brown hair.

Constance was aware of his gaze but she concentrated on dividing the dough into her grandma's greased loaf tins. Placing them on the fender with a piece of clean muslin over each tin, she scraped her hands free of the dough, saying, 'They can warm there,' through the silence which had fallen.

It was an uneasy silence. *Matt* seemed uneasy, which was a first. Normally he was teasing her or ribbing her about something or other, or else asking her about her week. But then he knew she'd supposedly been ill, so perhaps he thought there was nothing to say. Which was true enough.

'I'll put the kettle on.' She glanced at him as she spoke and his eyes were waiting for her. She'd always loved his eyes. Not so much because of their colour or even his black lashes which were thick and long for a man, but it was the softness in their depths, the kindness, and the way fine lines radiated from their corners when he smiled, which was often. She watched him compress his lips for a moment before they formed words, and then he was speaking hesitantly.

'I've hardly seen you in the last little while. Oh, I don't mean since you've been bad, but before then. Times was when you'd never be out of Mam's kitchen.' He smiled but it didn't cause the fine lines to crinkle.

The longer she looked at him the more she ached inside, and it was to combat this weakness that she moved quickly, saying, 'Things have changed since Christmas when I left school,' as she placed the kettle on the fire. 'I have to help Miss Newton clear up once the bairns have gone home and we talk about what has happened during the day and what we're going to do the next day, things like that. It's usually too late to call in your mam's when I leave.'

'Do you like working at the school?'

'Oh aye.' She'd spoken from the heart and too eagerly in view of what might happen in the coming days.

'You're good with bairns. Me mam was saying the same thing the last time you were at ours.'

She'd kept her back to him while they'd been speaking; now she felt compelled to turn and look at him again. His eyes never seemed to have left hers. She felt nervous and slightly afraid, but not in the way Vincent McKenzie had made her afraid. 'Was she?' she said weakly. 'That was nice of her.'

He nodded. 'You can do no wrong as far as Mam's concerned.'

She wrinkled her nose. 'My grandma's the same about you.'

For the first time since he'd come into the kitchen they smiled normally at each other with the old easy warmth, but the moment was deceptively natural. Almost immediately their shared gaze intensified and lengthened, and now there was a note of bewilderment in Matt's voice when he murmured, 'Constance?'

The knock at the back door and Tilly's voice as she'd called, 'Hello?' on thrusting it open had acted like a bucket of cold water over Constance's head, much as Ivy's did now as her great-aunt brought her back to the present.

'Don't you worry, hinny,' Ivy said fondly, her plump face flushed with the excitement of what she'd heard. 'We'll have you far away from him in no time. He won't be able to find you, believe you me, and even with the most ardent of men, out of sight is out of mind. They aren't like us, constant and true. Not the majority anyway.' She cast a glance at her sister. 'Your Art and my Seamus being the exceptions that prove the rule, of course.'

Constance stared at her great-aunt before her eyes turned to the sad, torn countenance of her grandma. She laid her head on her arms and began to cry, slow painful tears. The dream wasn't hers to share. It was Tilly's; he'd made it so. She must leave Sacriston. It was settled.

Chapter 5

'What do you mean, she's gone?' Vincent ground his teeth as he glared into the thin, precise features of the school-teacher in front of him, and something of his desire to put his hands round her scrawny neck and squeeze it until her eyes popped must have shown in his face because Miss Newton had backed away until she was pressed against the classroom wall.

'I'm only repeating what I was told, Mr McKenzie. Miss Shelton came to see me and said she was leaving the village for a position in service, and I understand her great-aunt collected her and they left yesterday morning.'

'You told me she was recovering from a chill.'

'Which is what *I* was told.' Miss Newton had recovered her poise and with it her courage. Her nostrils flared, she bit out, 'I suggest you take this matter up with her grandparents, Mr McKenzie. Not myself. I am not responsible for the girl.'

'And you have no idea where she has gone?'

'She did not divulge her intended whereabouts and I did not press her. I confess I was disappointed by her decision.'

Disappointed. For a moment a red mist swam in front of Vincent's maddened eyes. He'd been sewn up like a kipper. All the time he'd been telling himself to proceed circumspectly the little scut had been making plans to skedaddle.

But no, he told himself in the next moment. It wouldn't be the lass who'd instigated this, it'd be the old couple who were behind it. Hannah's mother had never liked him, even as a bairn – she'd never said but he knew. And Art Gray was a miner. What miner had any time for the weighman? They all hated him. The lass must have let on what he'd proposed and this was their answer. In spite of all he could give her, the fact she'd be sitting pretty and want for nothing the rest of her life, they'd rather force her into service than have her associate with him.

'Mr McKenzie, the children will start to arrive soon. I must ask you to leave.'

For answer Vincent surveyed the bristling figure a moment more and then turned away without a word. He had made up his mind the night before that if Constance wasn't at the school in the morning, he would go round to the house and demand to see her. It had been a full two weeks since she'd supposedly been taken ill, but no chill he'd ever heard of lasted that long. If she was still sick he would fetch the doctor to the house himself and ascertain what was wrong. If she wasn't sick . . .

He strode down the path of the school, an impressive figure in his fine clothes and polished leather knee-high boots, but inside he felt like a young lad again – humiliated, debased and in a sea of aloneness. *They wouldn't get the better of him.* His face set, he walked towards the colliery, passing St Peter's Church and the graveyard before walking over

Blackburn Bridge. He didn't turn into the colliery gates, however, he wasn't due in for another hour. Instead he continued along Edmondsley Lane, and he didn't pause until fields stretched either side of the roadway and the only sound to be heard was the birds twittering in the hedgerows.

He would find her. He gazed unseeing over the rolling meadows where patches of white here and there indicated the last of the snow. He would find her and bring her back and to hell with them all. There weren't too many big houses round about, and the old 'uns wouldn't want their precious ewe lamb so far away they couldn't visit her and she them. And this great-aunt the dried-up crone of a schoolteacher had spoken about, he'd find her and all. With some persuasion, gentle or otherwise, he'd get the whereabouts of Constance out of her. They wouldn't beat him; he wasn't a boy any longer to be scorned.

There were primroses and wood anemone scattered in the grass verges either side of the lane; the arrival of spring was late this year but new life was blooming nonetheless. The air was icy cold still but the morning was bright and a beam of sunlight through the trees picked out the delicate white flowers of the anemone which appeared to dance in the slight breeze. He gazed down at the pure ethereal beauty and then savagely ground the flowers under his heels before almost immediately stopping and dropping to his knees where he attempted to lift their broken heads, cradling them in his big hands. He groaned, the sound coming from the depths of him as he stood up, his hands going to his face. He leaned against the stout trunk of an oak tree, the tears dripping through his fingers as he gave vent to the sobs tearing him apart.

* * *

Constance had been travelling all day. Her bottom was sore from being bumped up and down on the hard wooden seat of her great-aunt's trap, and the many ridges and pot-holes in the roads and lanes had rattled her bones and jarred her head. They had left Ivy's house in Durham before dawn in order to arrive at Grange Hall for three o'clock, but once they had reached the swelling moorland and wooded valleys which made up the wide landscape of Yorkshire, the beauty of Constance's surroundings had caused her to forget her aching body.

Although the snow had all but gone in Durham it was still banked up either side of the roads on some of the high fells here; to the right and left of the horse and trap, a white wilderness spread out with just the odd isolated farm dotted here and there.

Constance didn't think she'd ever inhaled such pure air, and its quality was all the more enhanced after spending the night in the town. Not that her aunt's house wasn't bonny, she told herself quickly as though the thought had been a criticism, and as clean as a new pin. And her uncle had turned out to be a jolly fellow the size of a brick outhouse, his bright red face and massive muscled arms a by-product of his work. He had shown her round his huge smithy with evident pride, and she had even stroked two of the horses waiting to be shod, although she was fright-ened of their teeth and hooves, but overall the busyness of the town and the smell and dirt of the crowded streets had repelled and overwhelmed her.

They had eaten the bread and cheese her aunt had packed for their lunch sitting in the trap watching a water-fall cascade into a rocky stream beneath it, the fast-melting snow sparkling in the sunlight, and then travelled on. There were drystone walls everywhere carving man-made patterns into the landscape, but as they drew closer to the outskirts of Harrogate where Grange Hall was situated, the scenery – magnificent as it was – ceased to work its magic and keep Constance's mind from the ordeal in front of her.

It had been agreed that, should she have to face the ignominy of making the return trip with Great-Aunt Ivy, she would stay with her in Durham until she could obtain work. But she didn't want to go back to the city with its filthy, muck-strewn roads and pavements, numerous snotty-nosed, barefoot urchins and constant din which went on day and night. She hadn't slept a wink the night before for the noise outside her window; even at two in the morning there'd been carts trundling over the cobbles and people shouting and carrying on. Her aunt had said she'd get used to it and wouldn't notice it after a time, but she didn't want to get used to it. She had to get the job as scullerymaid, she just had to. She wouldn't mind how hard she worked or what she did if they'd give her a chance.

The horse and trap arrived at the gatehouse to the estate at exactly half-past two. The gatekeeper came through a narrow side gate and enquired as to their business before opening the huge black wrought-iron gates that stood eight foot high with the family crest covering half of one of them. Ivy appeared to take it all in her stride, thanking the man in a dignified fashion before following the long winding drive which led to the huge turreted house in the far distance. The drive was wide enough to take three carriages side by side, but as they grew nearer it divided, a narrow road snaking away from the main one. Ornamental privet hedges, sculpted trees and meticulously tended gardens stretched away as far as the eye could see and Constance's mouth had fallen into a gape: She had never seen such splendour.

Ivy had taken the narrow road and now Constance became aware that they were effectively hidden from view from the house by a row of densely planted evergreen trees which had been cut to provide an impenetrable screen of green. 'Close your mouth, hinny,' Ivy murmured quietly at the side of her, a touch of laughter in her voice. 'They'll think you're simple if you look like that. And don't forget what I've told you. You don't talk unless you're spoken to, you proffer no opinions about anything, and you keep in mind that as a scullerymaid you're the lowest among the servant hierarchy.'

Constance's mouth snapped shut and she nodded, her stomach churning. Ivy had told her the family were very well-to-do and employed a large staff of indoor and outdoor servants, but she had found the pecking order of their ranking difficult to remember. The house steward was responsible for the overall running of the household and was at the top of the tree, she knew that. And after the steward came the butler and Sir Henry Ashton's personal valet and the housekeeper, but the pyramid-like structure of lesser servants under these exalted ones was confusing. The cook and coachman and lady's maid were near the top, along with the nanny, but then there were footmen and housemaids and nurserymaids and kitchenmaids and grooms, along with gardeners and stable-boys and others she couldn't recall. And all for a family of three, although she understood that Sir Henry Ashton's wife was expecting their second child. They already had a daughter who was four years old.

The horse and trap emerging into a stableyard, Constance now realised that the road they'd taken had skirted round the back of the house. Ivy was pointing in the opposite direction to the house as she said, 'Beyond the stableyard are the glass-houses and walled fruit and vegetable garden – you'll likely be fetching bits and pieces from there if you're set on. And there's a peach-house, a vinery, a rose-house and the dairy, of course, and a mushroom-house and thatched fruit-house and—' She caught sight of the girl's terrified face. 'Oh, don't worry, hinny. Give it a week or two and it'll all be second nature,' she said quickly.

As she had been speaking, a young stable-lad had scurried up to them. Ivy smiled at him as she climbed down from the trap. She handed him the reins, saying, 'I'm Mrs Banks, the cook's mam. You're expecting us, aren't you? See the horse has a good rub-down before you settle him for the night, he's had a long journey. I'll be leaving in the morning after breakfast so I want him ready for eight o'clock.'

Constance was full of admiration for the way her aunt was handling herself, but the stable-lad didn't seem to share her awe. He grinned at them cheekily, winking at Constance as he said, 'Oh aye, I know about you. You're the new scullerymaid.'

'Not yet she isn't.' Ivy's voice was sharp and she wasn't smiling any longer. 'And I'll thank you to see to the horse.' Taking Constance's arm she ushered her across the stableyard and through an arch which led into another courtyard beyond which was the house itself. 'You don't fraternise with the likes of that one, do you understand me, Constance? Everyone will be well aware of your

90

family connection with Florence, and anything you do or say will reflect on her. She has a high position here and has always conducted herself with absolute decorum. I expect you to do the same.'

Constance couldn't have answered if she wanted to. She was concentrating on remaining upright on the slippy cobbles beneath her feet, but fully aware the moment was upon her and she was about to enter Grange Hall. If she secured the post of scullerymaid, this place would be her life for the forseeable future. If she didn't . . .

But she wouldn't let herself think of failure. Her granda had always said if you wanted something badly enough, you could make it happen. She didn't know if she agreed with that, but Grange Hall was another world and one so far away from Sacriston she wouldn't be able to run home when the ache in her heart became overpowering. Already she was so homesick she felt chewed up inside and she wasn't foolish enough to think it would get better in the next little while. She wanted to see her grandma and granda, to soak up the sweet normalness of their lives in Cross Streets. She wanted to sleep in her own bed and hear the owl that came and perched on Mr O'Leary's roof each night at exactly eleven o'clock, come rain or shine. But Sacriston held other folk too, and here she wasn't thinking of Vincent McKenzie but a tall, laughing-eyed lad with hair the colour of hazelnuts and the pert miss who had stolen his heart. They all seemed to think the world of Tilly back home, but she would never like her and she'd rather work her fingers to the bone and suffer whatever befell her here than have to pretend to be glad for Matt and watch them together. The way Tilly had sailed into the kitchen and dragged him off with hardly a by-your-leave at their last meeting had been downright rude, and he'd gone with her with barely a protest. That's what had hurt.

'Here.' Ivy stopped outside the kitchen door and adjusted her niece's hat, brushing Constance's coat and pulling it straight. She was carrying the carpet bag which held the sum total of Constance's personal possessions: a change of clothes along with her Sunday best frock, her hairbrush and some spare pins for her hair, the little New Testament Miss Newton had presented all the children with when they left school and the linen pads with ties she used for her monthlies. The bag was not heavy.

Ivy gazed into the deep blue eyes looking at her so anxiously, and not for the first time reflected that such beauty in one of Constance's class was not a good thing. It made the girl noticeable, made her stand out, and following on from this thought, she said, 'Your grandma has told you that men, lads, will take advantage of a lass if she lets them, hasn't she, but now you're here you've got to be even more on your guard. If you get set on there'll come a time when you might come to the attention of visitors to the house. Male visitors. Do you understand what I'm saying, hinny?'

'I — I think so.'

'If that should happen and the man won't take no for an answer, you open your mouth and yell wherever you are. That'll show him you mean business. Some . . . gentlemen think servants are fair game for a spot of dalliance and that's been the ruin of many a poor lass, I'm telling you. And there'd be no help if there were consequences, you can be sure of that. You'd find yourself dismissed without a reference and then the only place would be the workhouse for you and the baby. So however charming or persuasive the gentleman is, just remember you'd mean less to him than his favourite dog or horse. They don't see us as real people, the gentry. That's when they see us at all. All right, hinny?'

Constance gulped and nodded. If anything could have made her feel more terrified than she already was, her aunt's little talk had done the trick.

'That's a good lass.' Ivy smiled fondly. 'Come on then.'

Ivy's knock at the door was answered by a young girl with a pimply face wearing a dress with the sleeves rolled up and a huge holland apron. Her hair was plaited and put up neatly under a cap and she had on her feet the ugliest thick boots Constance had ever seen. 'We're here to see Mr Rowan,' Ivy said, then pushed past the girl, adding briskly, 'Come along, Constance,' and as they stepped into a room which to Constance's gaze seemed endless, Ivy called, 'Hello, Florence, we've arrived at last.'

'Mother.' A small round woman who was as fat as she was tall rose from a rocking chair placed at an angle to a monster of a range and came towards them. The kitchen was full of other girls of varying ages who all seemed to be busy working and who carried on with what they were doing with just a quick glance here and there at the newcomers.

Constance watched her aunt embrace her daughter and then Florence turned to her. She didn't smile or say hello, merely eyed her up and down, before saying, presumably to her mother, 'She doesn't look very strong.'

'She is. And willing. She's a hard worker, is Constance.'

'Aye, well, she'll need to be. There's no room in my kitchen for malingerers.'

'She'll pull her weight, have no fear.'

They were talking as though she wasn't there, but bearing in mind her aunt's warning to say nothing unless she was spoken to directly, Constance remained silent.

'Sit yourself down there.' Florence pointed Constance into a corner of the room where a long wooden settle without any cushions stood. Ivy she drew closer to the fire, saying to one of the kitchenmaids working at the enormous table, 'Make us a pot of tea, Agnes, and fetch out that fruitcake we had yesterday. It's a while till tea and you must be peckish, Mother?'

Constance sat down, biting on her lower lip. Everyone was ignoring her, even her Aunt Ivy. She took the opportunity to gaze at her surroundings. The kitchen was bigger than her grandma's whole house, so large and lofty it seemed incredible there was so much space just for a kitchen. Through an open doorway at one end she could see a scullery and that looked huge too. The lower parts of the walls were covered in glazed tiles and the floor was stone slabbed in the kitchen, wooden duckboards standing on the floor round the table where the girls were working, probably to lift their feet off the cold stone. Three enormous dressers stood against the walls holding jugs, copper moulds, a staggering array of dishes and utensils and many objects Constance had never seen before. Furthermore, she didn't have a clue as to their purpose. Pin rails holding metal dish covers were positioned near each dresser, and against one was a tall pestle and mortar.

Even as she watched, the young girl who had opened the door and who wasn't dressed as nicely as the kitchenmaids with their neat white frocks, smaller aprons and tiny pancake of a cap, came to the pestle and mortar carrying a large lump of meat. The mortar looked to be made out of part of a tree trunk with a marble basin inserted into the top, and the pestle was a stout wooden pole with its bulbous base resting in the marble bowl and its top secured to the wall by a metal ring. The girl gripped the pestle with both hands after placing the meat in the basin and began to pound up and down with all her strength. Constance gazed at her, fascinated. The girl was so small and skinny and the pestle looked so heavy.

The kitchenmaid, Agnes, had made the tea in the biggest teapot Constance had ever seen. Everything seemed larger than life here. After pouring Florence and Ivy a cup and taking it to them with a piece of cake, Agnes placed a mug near everyone else although no one stopped working. When she brought the tea to Constance, Constance smiled her thanks. 'I didn't know if you took sugar but I put a spoonful in anyway,' Agnes murmured, returning the smile. 'And don't look so scared. You'll be fine. If Gracie' – she indicated the girl pounding at the meat – 'can do the work, I'm sure you can. She's the other scullerymaid,' she added by way of explanation. 'And she's not very bright.'

Constance just had time to whisper, 'Thank you,' before Agnes returned to her post at the table, but the little exchange warmed her far more than the hot tea. Suddenly the kitchen wasn't such a strange and hostile place.

A footman walked into the kitchen at five to three from the scullery and his tone was deferential as he spoke to Ivy's daughter. 'Mr Rowan is ready for the girl now, Cook.'

Florence rose from her chair, brushing cake crumbs from the front of her dress. Constance had stood up too and now Florence beckoned her. 'Come along, girl. Don't stand there dilly-dallying.'

As she followed the liveried footman and the cook into the massive scullery, Constance realised there were only two ways into the kitchen: one, the door she and Ivy had first come through, which led out into the courtyard, and this other, which took them across the scullery and out into a passageway leading to a back flight of stairs.

She only had time for a quick glance round the room in which presumably she'd spend most of her working hours if she got the job, but it was a dark, dismal place. There were several sinks dotted round the walls, some made of wood and some of stone, and a huge floor-to-ceiling plate-rack. Three rough tables stood in the centre of the space and a boiling copper took up one corner. The one and only window was tiny.

There was no chance to see any more, but as they walked down the passageway towards the stairs, Florence waved her hand at doors as they passed them. 'These are the storerooms. This one's the dry larder holding bread, pastry, milk, butter and cold meats. That one's the meat larder. This one's the wet larder for fish, and the vegetable store's between them. The last one is the salting and smoking store where we also store the bacon. It'll be one of your jobs to cut sufficient rashers of bacon for the house and staff for the week every Monday morning. There's a pastry room off the dry larder.'

They had almost reached the stairs when Florence said shortly, 'This is the housekeeper's still room and private quarters, but that needn't concern you,' as she nodded at the door on her left. 'And here' – as she turned to the right of the passageway where the footman had just knocked on the last door – 'is Mr Rowan's pantry and private quarters. You keep your eyes lowered in his presence and only look at him to answer if he speaks to you, is that understood? Now stand up straight, girl, and don't slouch.'

The footman had opened the door for them and was standing to one side, but as the cook sailed past him he winked at Constance, mouthing, 'Good luck.'

Constance didn't dare smile back. Her aunt had regaled her with stories about footmen and servant girls; they were to be avoided as much as gentlemen. She stepped out of the dark-brown-painted passageway into a sitting room of some considerable comfort, and the contrast made her forget the cook's instructions to keep her eyes on the floor. The room was small but cosy, the two armchairs either side of the fire and the bookcase along one wall homely and the wooden floorboards polished, with a bright thick clippy mat in front of the hearth. Another door, which was closed, led to the butler's bedroom and pantry, the place where in a pair of lead sinks all the tableware too valuable to be trusted to the ministrations of the scullerymaids was cleaned, and where a fire-proof safe held items of value the master and mistress wanted keeping under lock and key. Ivy had filled her in on all this, along with the fact that the butler, the house-keeper, the master's valet, the lady's maid, the nanny and the cook – this last had been said with some pride – ate their meals with the house steward in his room where they were waited on by the steward's boy. The rest of the servants ate in the servants' hall, a room with long scrubbed tables and benches which was situated next to the steward's room on the next floor.

The butler had risen to his feet as they had entered. Now he indicated an armchair as he said, 'Please be seated,

Mrs Banks,' as he took Florence's arm and helped her sit down.

'Thank you, Mr Rowan.'

Once Florence was sitting down, the butler also resumed his seat and now they were both staring at Constance. After one swift glance at the butler Constance remembered her manners and lowered her eyes to her feet.

'So this is your aunt's granddaughter. How old did you say she is?' The butler addressed himself to Florence, his voice precise.

'Thirteen in the December just gone, Mr Rowan.'

'She looks older. And she's a good worker?'

'So I've been assured, Mr Rowan. So I've been assured.'

'Well, in all matters appertaining to the kitchen, you know I trust your judgement, Mrs Banks.' There was a pause, and then: 'You, girl. You're aware of your good fortune in being recommended for this position by Mrs Banks?'

Constance looked into the thin bony face staring at her. 'Yes, sir.' At least she could answer with genuine enthusiasm.

'I hope so. You're a most fortunate girl. Most fortunate.'

Constance dropped her gaze again but not before the incongruity of the two figures sitting in the armchairs struck her. They were like the nursery rhyme about Jack Sprat and his wife which Miss Newton told the little ones, she thought with a touch of nervous hysteria. The picture she'd held up in her book had shown a woman so rotund her tiny feet didn't look as though they could support her, and a man so thin he was skeletal.

'You will receive a wage of eighteen pounds a year, along with your board and lodging and uniform. Mrs Banks will detail your duties. Do you have any questions?'

Hundreds, but Constance knew better than to ask. 'No, sir. Thank you, sir.'

Florence had stood up again, so apparently the interview was over. It had lasted all of two minutes and for this she had got herself into a right state? Seeing him had obviously merely been a formality; it was clear Florence had the say in everything to do with the kitchen and its staff as the butler had intimated.

Outside in the passageway once more, Constance followed the waddling figure of Florence back to the kitchen. Ivy was sipping another cup of tea as they entered and she didn't seem surprised that Constance had got the job.

'Agnes?' Florence called the kitchenmaid over. 'See to it Constance is given her uniform and show her where she'll sleep and put her belongings. Run through what will be expected of her while you're about it.' Turning to Constance, she said, 'Agnes is first kitchenmaid and you will answer to her if I am not here. She has been with me for fifteen years and knows how I like things done. My other girls are Teresa, Cathleen, Maria and Patience.' Each kitchenmaid bobbed their head as she spoke. 'And Gracie is the other scullerymaid,' Florence added, looking over at the small figure still pounding away at the meat. 'Put your back into it, Gracie. I want that beef fine enough to push through a sieve.' Looking at her mother, she shook her head. 'Drives me mad, that one.'

The next few hours flew by in a whirl of confusion for Constance. After she'd been given her uniform from the laundry store next to the housekeeper's quarters, along with a pair of the hideous boots Gracie was wearing, Agnes led her up the back flight of stairs. They climbed three floors to the attics which were icy cold, and there lines of pallet beds stood under the rafters with boxes beside each one holding the occupant's meagre belongings. It was a dismal place.

Agnes led her over to one at the far end of the attic. 'This was Dolly's, the girl you're replacing,' she said. 'You know what happened to her? With the footman, I mean?'

Constance nodded. 'My aunt told me.'

'Carrying on with any of the male house-servants is strictly forbidden, but they'll try it on so watch them. They sleep on the floor below us but you never pass through the door leading into their billets whatever they might say.' Agnes stared at her. 'And they'll say plenty to you, I'll be bound. Once you reach a certain age, walking out with one of the outside staff is allowed, as long as you confine yourself to just walking out, if you know what I mean. The head gardener and the gamekeeper have cottages on the estate, but the rest of the garden staff and the grooms and stable-boys and what-have-you sleep above the stables or in the building between the stableyard and the greenhouses.'

Constance nodded again. She'd made up her mind she'd steer clear of all the male staff; she wasn't remotely interested in having a beau, ever.

'Now as to your duties, I'll try and tell you everything – but ask me if you're not sure over the next days, all right?' Agnes smiled. 'And don't look so scared. Cook's bark is worse than her bite. She prides herself on running a good kitchen and if you work hard you'll find her easy enough to get on with.'

Constance smiled back weakly. She did so hope so. Remembering something that had puzzled her, she said,

'When I was in the butler's room he called her Mrs Banks but I didn't think she was married?' Her aunt had never mentioned it anyway.

'She isn't, but it's respectful to address someone in Cook's position as Mrs. Anyway, that won't concern you. We call her Cook, it's only those of the same standing who can address her as Mrs Banks. Mr Rowan, on the other hand, is Mr Rowan or sir, but it's doubtful you'll speak to him.'

Her belongings deposited in the box next to her bed, Constance quickly changed into her uniform. The dress and apron felt as ugly and stiff as they looked and the boots weighed her feet down.

'You and Gracie start work at six o'clock in the morning in winter and six-thirty in the summer. You finish when you finish.' Agnes wrinkled her nose sympathetically here. 'If there's a dinner party you'll still be washing pots and pans at midnight. You'll mostly be in the scullery cleaning and scouring all the pans and things, and washing the scullery and kitchen floors. Plucking the poultry and skinning the game is part of your job and Gracie'll show you how, but be careful how long you leave the birds hanging. Feathering is easier when it's been hung a while but too long and it won't only be the feathers that drop out.'

At Constance's wrinkled brow, Agnes added significantly, 'Maggots.' She shuddered. 'Gracie doesn't mind them so she'll leave a bird ten days sometimes, by which time it's heaving.'

Constance was aghast and her face reflected this.

'If you don't like them, then be careful to watch the fat that scums the side of the sinks. You have to scrape it off by hand and put it in boxes for the woman who buys it at the back door for making soap, but the maggots will

101

get in that quicker than you can blink in the summer. Best to clear it every other night then.'

Agnes paused for breath. 'You and Gracie wait on table in the servants' hall and once everyone's finished, you clear away and set the places again. Breakfast's eight o'clock in the summer and half eight in the winter. Lunch is at eleven and the main meal of the day is half one. Tea's at five and supper's at nine o'clock. Once breakfast is over the upper staff join us in the servants' hall for morning prayer which Mr Howard, he's the house steward, takes. On Sunday mornings we attend the estate church with the family. You're allowed every other Sunday afternoon off and a full Sunday once a month, but you're still expected to attend church in the morning.'

Agnes had turned and led the way out of the attics as she had been speaking. As they descended the stairs she pointed to a heavy green-baize door. Constance had noticed one on each landing. 'These doors lead to the main house and you must never open them, not ever. If one of the family or any guests caught sight of you there'd be ructions and Cook would have a blue fit. None of us kitchen staff must be seen.'

Constance stared at the back of Agnes's neat head. 'When do we go into the main house then?'

'We don't. I've been here fifteen years and I never have. Only Cook does on occasion when the mistress wants to discuss a special menu or a dish she's had when she's been out visiting. If you should happen to be outside in the yards or fetching stuff from the glass-houses or dairy and you see any of the family or guests, you make yourself scarce till they've gone.'

Agnes continued to reel out further instructions until

they reached the kitchen once more, but Constance found she couldn't take them in. Her head was spinning, her cap kept slipping down over her forehead and she felt as if she was walking in seven-league boots. The earlier feeling of warmth and comfort brought about by Agnes's kindness had evaporated, and now she felt lost and lonely and bewildered, and not a little afraid of what was expected of her. If it wasn't for the thought of Tilly and Matt she would run out of here this very moment and make her way back to Sacriston – which had now taken on a heavenly aura – even if she had to walk every mile of the way, she told herself wretchedly. She didn't belong here, she'd never fit in. There were so many dos and don'ts, so many pitfalls, and she didn't think Florence – or Cook as she must be called – liked her.

Ivy looked up as she followed Agnes into the warmth of the kitchen. 'All right?' her aunt asked brightly. 'All settled in?'

'Yes, thank you.' Her voice sounded very small.

'That's a good lass. You've landed on your feet here, hinny, and no mistake. Your grandma and granda will be tickled pink when I tell 'em.'

Constance stared back wanly. Her grandma and granda wouldn't be tickled pink. Her granda's face had been pulled tight when he'd said goodbye on the morning she left and he'd looked ten years older, and her grandma had cried so much she'd been unable to speak. A great wave of desolation and guilt washed over her.

Florence's voice, coming at her now, startled her. 'As you've changed, there's no time like the present to get started, girl. There's a pile of dishes six foot high in the scullery for starters, and I hope you're a bit more nimble on your feet and quicker with your hands than Gracie. Drive you to drink that one would,' she added, turning to her mother. 'Been here nearly a year and I'm still wiping her nose for her.'

Constance glanced at Gracie who was still wrestling with the pestle and mortar. She must have heard what the cook had said but she gave no indication of it.

Her heart in her boots, Constance went to do battle with the dishes.

Chapter 6

The wedding had been a merry one. After the service, which had gone without a hitch, the wedding guests had made their way to the Johnsons' house where a fine spread had been waiting for them, courtesy of the womenfolk of the two families involved. The laughter and ribald nature of the proceedings had increased as the afternoon had gone on, ably abetted by the copious amounts of home-made beer and blackcurrant wine the guests had imbibed.

Tilly, dressed in white, felt her face was stiff with smiling, but what else was she supposed to do on her wedding day? The day that was the happiest of a lass's life. And she was happy, she would have been ecstatic but for the night ahead which was hanging over her like the Sword of Damocles. Matt had been wavering before that little chit had skedaddled to pastures new. She had known it the afternoon she'd caught them in the kitchen, and in the following days he'd been withdrawn, even cold towards her. And then Constance had vanished without a word to anyone, and Tilly had pretended she hadn't known how upset Matt had been.

She glanced at him across the crowded room. He was talking to the girl's grandparents, but she'd ceased to fear they would tell Matt where Constance was. For some reason she was unable to fathom they'd told no one where Constance had gone, just repeating how an aunt had heard of a wonderful job further south and it had been an opportunity Constance couldn't ignore. But she knew where the girl was. She had seen Constance's name and address on the letters her grandma posted to her regular as clockwork, but that was post-office business and it suited her to keep quiet. With Constance out of the way Matt had gone along with the marriage. She was safe.

Unconsciously her hand went to her stomach under the white satin. Rupert had assured her he knew what he was doing, that there'd be no consequences to their lovemaking, and – fool that she was – she'd believed him. Her mouth tightened. But she'd missed two monthlies on the trot and already her body felt different. Not only that, but the last couple of mornings she'd felt queasy and yesterday she'd come over all queer when her mam had dished up tripe and onions for their dinner. Just the smell had had her heaving. Her mam and da had put it down to wedding nerves, but she'd known for sure then that these particular wedding nerves weren't going to go away.

'It's a bonny wedding, lass, and you look a picture.'

She turned to see Matt's brother smiling at her. 'Thanks, George.' Unconsciously her gaze returned to Matt.

'He's like a dog with two tails, as well he might be.'

The forced joviality didn't fool her. Matt wasn't like a dog with two tails, more like a dog that had lost one. He'd been the same for weeks, months, and in spite of Rupert

106

and her desire for respectability she'd almost got to the point where she was ready to tell him to sling his hook before . . . Again her hand touched her stomach. And after that she'd had no choice.

No one must know. No one. But was she going to be able to fool him, not once but twice? Initially he had to believe he was the first and then that she'd fallen on her wedding night and the baby, when it came, was early. And Matt was no young lad wet behind the ears. He'd had his fun before he'd taken up with her. Mary Fairley had all but thrown herself at him, and Peggy Lee had already got herself a name before he'd walked out with her for a while. He knew his way around, did Matt.

But she could fool him. She again looked at her new husband. She had done so far, hadn't she? And once tonight was over she needn't worry any more. Crying out that it hurt, a few tears and pretending to be shy, that'd do it. And from this day there would be no carry-on with Rupert. Here she conveniently ignored the fact that the postmaster hadn't come anywhere near her since she had told him about the baby, not even meeting her eyes when she had said her farewells on leaving the post office for the last time the day before. As she had expected, Matt had been adamant he was the sole breadwinner once they were wed.

They would be all right. Again she reassured herself. And at least they weren't starting off living with the in-laws as so many couples did. Matt had been paying the rent on a house a few doors down from his mam for the last four weeks and they had been lucky to get it. They'd furnished the front room and their bedroom already, there was only the spare room to do and that could wait a bit. She'd keep things nice for him and be a good wife. Everything would work out.

Across the room Matt was telling himself the same thing. It was done now. He was a married man. He had a wife. And nothing could have come of that other thing, he knew that. Constance saw him only as a brother, she always had done. He would have frightened her to death if he'd behaved in any other way. And she was so young, little more than a bairn. He didn't know what had got into him that day in her grandma's kitchen but at least he hadn't made a chump of himself by saying anything. And then in the next day or two she'd disappeared into the blue with this aunt and without even saying goodbye. That had told him all he needed to know. It had felt like a punch in the stomach when he'd heard.

He took another long pull at his tankard of ale. Around him the laughter was loud, the talking and joking vying with the sound of children's cries as they darted around this room and the kitchen in some game of their own making.

His mother must have used a packet of starch on his shirt alone, the way the collar was chafing his neck. He tried to ease his sore flesh by pulling the rock-hard material away from his throat but to little effect. The unnatural feel of the stiff linen and his Sunday suit added to the overall unsettled feeling which had gripped him for months, even though he told himself over and over again he was a most fortunate man. Tilly was a bonny lass and she loved him, even with his moods over the last little while. He hadn't been easy, he knew that, but he'd make it up to her in the coming days. They had their own place where they could shut the front door and to hell with the rest of the world. Tilly'd had some savings and he'd had a bit and she'd made the place right bonny. She had taste, he'd give her that.

'This is your wedding day, man.' Andrew spoke in his ear. 'And you look like you've lost a bob and found a farthing.'

Andrew had a knack for catching him on the raw and today was no exception. Telling himself to go easy, Matt smiled. 'I'm not surprised, the way this shirt's scraping the flesh off my bones. Mam was determined I'd look the part, no doubt about that.'

'Aye, she always was a bit handy with the starch. Olive knows not to use above a thimbleful or else she gets it thrown back at her. Start as you mean to carry on, that's my motto.'

Matt made no comment. It was well-known within the family that Olive wore the trousers, although she did it so discreetly Andrew never seemed to catch on.

'Tilly looks bonny the day, you're a lucky man.'

Again Matt said nothing. Tilly and her mam had been working on 'the dress' for months; it was one of the things which had made him feel the noose was tightening round his neck. How could he say he wanted to call things off when her own da had told him it was impossible to move in their front room without treading on patterns and pieces of material, and that Tilly and her mam talked of little else?

'Driving me to drink, lad, I can tell you,' Tilly's da had said, tongue in cheek, a couple of weeks ago when they'd sat talking over a pint in the Colliery Inn one evening. 'I don't know who's the more worked up, Tilly or her mam, but it's got so I hardly dare open me mouth. Take today, for instance. The lass was having another of these "fittings" – that dress has been on and off more times than I've had hot dinners – and all I said was, trying to be helpful, like, was that I thought she'd put on a bit of weight in the last week or two because it was pulling a bit round the' – he indicated his chest. 'By, you'd have thought I'd confessed to some crime or other. Tilly went off the deep end and then her mam had a go at me. I was glad to get out of it and I shan't go back till I'm three sheets to the wind neither. Women, they're another species, lad. Another species.'

'Mam says you're not taking a day or two off then?' Andrew swigged at his glass of beer. 'Straight back to work on Monday?'

'Can't afford to lose more than one shift,' Matt said shortly. It was true; the furniture had taken every last penny but Tilly had wanted nice things and, feeling as he did, guilt had caused him to give in to her every whim.

'Aye, well, mebbe that's no bad thing, the way things are with the strikes an' all. You never know when we're going to be out for three months or more like we were two years ago. Get the shifts in while you can, that's what I say, and put a bit by for a rainy day. There's going to be a few of them coming up if you listen to the fighting talk of some of 'em in the union. Old Enoch Murray was claiming there's nigh on sixty-five thousand in membership now, that's a force to be reckoned with and the owners know it. But like I said to him, you corner a rat and it gives no quarter.'

Matt moved restlessly. The last thing he wanted on his wedding day was Andrew going on about the unions. Not that he didn't agree with him, he did. When the

Independent Labour Party which had formed last year had sent its national organiser, Tom Taylor, to Durham he'd gone to listen to him, and his socialist teaching and ideas had struck a chord in every miner present. But change would carry a price. Taylor had said that an' all, and it wouldn't be the owners in their fancy houses who'd pay it but the people who could least afford it, ordinary working-class men and women.

'. . . be a long hard fight and a bitter one, you mark my words.' Andrew was still talking.

Matt glanced at his brother. 'I'd better do my duty and thank folk for coming.'

'Aye, aye man, you do that.' But then, before he could turn away, Andrew caught his arm. 'What's up?' he said quietly, and for once there was no thread of mockery or provocation in his voice. 'You haven't been yourself for weeks. That fall when we were stuck underground a while put the wind up you? Because we all feel the same, to a greater or lesser degree. You just have to work through it till it gets better, that's all.'

Matt stared at him. Andrew had always been the joker, the clown, the brother who had pulled his leg until he'd wanted to hit him on occasion and who could wind him up quicker than you could say Jack Robinson. For years now he'd got used to thinking of Andrew as a pain in the backside, and yet he could see from his brother's face that he was genuinely concerned. Contrition brought a thickness to his voice when he said, 'It's not that, not really. To be honest I think it's a mixture of things all come at once. The fall, getting wed, wondering if we'd get a house in time – Tilly had set her heart on starting in her own place, you know what women are.'

111

'Oh aye. We started off in Olive's mam's front room if you remember and Olive couldn't rest till we were out of there.'

'It'll be better now the big day's over and we're settled.' Matt forced himself to smile. 'Tilly's been in a two-an'-eight for weeks and it rubs off, you know what I mean?'

Andrew nodded, satisfied. Matt wondered what his brother would have said if he'd told him the truth. But then what was the truth? He was damned if he knew any more. He punched Andrew lightly on the arm. 'You're out of ale, man. Go and get a refill before it runs out. And Tilly's mam'll be bringing out the sandwiches and cake in a while.'

'I'm still stuffed from earlier but I won't say no to a drop more beer.'

He hadn't seen Tilly approach but as Andrew left she took his arm, smiling up into his face. 'Hello, husband.'

'Hello, wife.'

She giggled, leaning against him so he put his arm around her waist. The top of her head came to his shoulder and her veil billowing out from the comb of fresh wild ox-eye daisies her mother had gathered that morning and threaded through the comb was slightly scratchy against his face.

'I've had two glasses of wine,' she whispered, 'and I feel a bit tipsy.'

'I've had several glasses of ale and I feel tipsy too.'

She giggled again. 'It's been a nice wedding, hasn't it?'

'Aye, it has.' The September day had conspired to add its blessing by providing a humid warmth devoid of any breeze as the wedding party had walked home from the church through dusty streets. The north-east had been experiencing an Indian summer for the last two weeks, and for days the old-timers had been predicting a storm to end the hot spell. Tilly had been convinced the weather would break the day before the wedding, and now Matt murmured, 'You needn't have worried about it raining, need you? I was right. Let that be a lesson to you to take heed of your husband.'

He was feeling better now. Tilly was his wife and this was the start of their new life together. That's how he had to think from this day on. Any 'what ifs' had to be put aside; they had no place in his marriage. He loved Tilly, and he would grow to love her more as they settled into married life. That was the natural way of things.

To seal the thought, he bent his head and kissed Tilly full on the lips. As he felt her mouth immediately respond to his, his resolve strengthened. He had promised to love, honour and cherish this woman and she was a good lass. Everything would be all right from now on.

A heavy twilight blanketed the still air later that evening as the newlyweds walked through the shadowed streets of the village to their new home in the company of Matt's parents and a couple of other wedding guests who lived close by. Constance's grandparents had left the festivities earlier, and Tilly had been glad to see them go. She intended to make sure they saw little of the Grays from this day forth.

Matt whisked her up into his arms amid cheers from the others when they reached their front doorstep, and both of them were laughing as he carried her across the threshold. He kicked the door shut but still held her against his chest

113

as he kissed her long and deeply, and then he carried her upstairs.

He set her on her feet by the high double bed they had purchased from the village carpenter who had his premises next to the smithy in Plawsworth Road. Tilly had insisted on a new bed although he'd had a bonny secondhand one in the back of the cavernous room where he worked which took up the whole of the bottom floor of his house. 'It's going to be the beginning of our life together and I don't want to start it where someone else has been,' she'd pleaded when he'd pointed out how much money they could save in buying the other bed. 'I don't mind the wardrobe and anything else being secondhand, but not the bed.'

Tilly's mam had made them a magnificent patchwork quilt as a wedding present, but now he pushed it aside with scant ceremony, revealing the coarse linen sheets scented with tiny muslin bags of lavender. 'Come here,' he said softly, sitting down.

She came to stand in front of him, her eyes bright as he began to undress her. Her wedding dress had a row of small satin-covered buttons from the V of the bodice to several inches below her waist, and as his work-roughened fingers which already bore evidence of his occupation in the tiny blue indentations beneath his skin fumbled to release them, Tilly gave one of her throaty giggles. 'More haste, less speed, lad,' she murmured provocatively.

When the dress pooled at her feet she stepped out of it and Matt undid the strings of her waist petticoat. She now stood in the full under-petticoat which she'd made as part of her trousseau. It was a fine, delicate thing, edged with lace, and her bloomers were of the same material.

Her skin, glowing with health, had a slight sheen to it and her voluptuous breasts were pushed high above the laced bodice. She had made the undergarments with the wedding night in mind, knowing it was the most important night of her life. She had to captivate Matt, bewitch him. He mustn't be allowed to think . . .

Still seated on the edge of the bed, Matt surveyed his wife. Through the tide of rising passion that had turned his body as hard as a rock, he was conscious of a faint feeling of shock at Tilly's attire. Then he told himself not to be so daft. Tilly had done this for him, perhaps all lasses did the same on their wedding day. Whatever, there was no reason for him to think that she looked like a floozy. Aware she was waiting for him to respond, he said thickly, 'You're bonny, lass. Beautiful.'

Quickly he began to undress and Tilly watched him for a moment before reminding herself of the part she was playing. Walking round the side of the bed she climbed under the sheets, wriggling out of her bloomers. She had already decided an innocent maiden probably wouldn't take off the petticoat and so, covertly now, she watched Matt continue to disrobe.

He was a grand-looking man. His body was better, more muscular and well developed, than Rupert's, but then it would be, Matt being a miner. She knew she was going to enjoy this side of married life. Rupert had once said she was like a man with regard to the sating of her bodily needs, and although she had pretended to be offended she'd secretly agreed. From puberty she'd known the fires which burned in her didn't seem to burn in other girls. Hence her dropping into Rupert's lap like a ripe plum. And he hadn't been slow to take full advantage of her.

Tilly's mouth pulled tight for a moment and then she schooled her features into what she hoped was a shy smile as Matt slid in beside her, as naked as the day he was born.

Matt didn't speak as he drew her into his arms and held her close. His attitude was one of restraint despite his huge arousal. 'You're beautiful,' he whispered again after a few moments. 'And I'm glad we waited now. It makes it more special. You're not frightened of me, are you? I'll be gentle, I promise.'

Experiencing a rare feeling of shame, Tilly snuggled against him for answer. After tonight she could be herself, but for now she had to be careful.

The room was warm and the shadows deep. As Matt began to kiss and caress her Tilly's passion rose to meet his. It had been some time since Rupert had touched her and she had felt the enforced celibacy keenly. Before she had told him about the baby their intimacy had been a daily occurrence, most of the time.

It was another ten minutes before the marriage was consummated. Matt lay on top of her for a few seconds more and then heaved himself away. He sat on the side of the bed, his back to her, and he didn't move or speak.

Tilly held her breath. After a few moments, her voice small, she whispered, 'Matt? What's wrong? What's the matter?'

Matt's shoulders tensed but he didn't trust himself to look at her right at this moment in time. Not without doing something that would have him sent down the line. All this time – *all this time* – she'd been making a monkey out of him. This was no pure maiden lying in the bed. The abandonment she'd shown and the things she had encouraged just might be explained away by saying she was a naturally warm and giving woman, even how her hands and tongue had pleased him could – at a stretch – come under the same thinking, but once he had taken her he had known. He'd only had one virgin in his life and that had been Amy Croft. They'd both been fifteen years old and the hormones had been raging, and one hot Sunday afternoon when they'd taken a walk near Findonhill Farm to watch the haymaking, more than haymaking had gone on. But even if he'd never had Amy he would have known Tilly was no virgin. She'd been with a man.

'Who?' His voice could have come from the depths of a cavern. 'Who was it? Or was there more than one?' He swung round as he spoke, catching her unawares, and the look on her face before she brought indignation to bear was all the confirmation he needed. It made her play-acting all the more infuriating.

'What are you accusing me of?' She hitched herself into a sitting position, her back against the wooden headboard. 'I don't understand.'

'You understand all right.' He had never had the urge to strike a woman in his life but now he had to ball his hands into fists at his side to prevent himself doing just that. 'You've been with someone. Who was it? I want his name.'

'I haven't. How dare you say that? You're the first.'

'Tell me, Tilly. I'm warning you, don't try my patience.'

'You're mad, there's been no one but you.'

He wasn't mad. And she hadn't been with the man just the once either, his gut instinct was telling him that. Was it before she'd taken up with him? It had to be. But he didn't think she'd had a serious suitor before him. Obviously he was wrong. What else was there he didn't know?

Suddenly he grabbed at her, shaking her shoulders until her head bobbed like a rag doll. 'Tell me his name or so help me I'll shake it out of you. You've lain with someone, you've been used.'

When she brought her hands up and pushed him so hard he fell backwards, he was amazed at her strength. She was kneeling on the bed now, hissing, 'Don't you lay your hands on me. I'm not having any of that. And I tell you again, there's been no one but you. You can go on all you like but that's the truth.'

'You're lying.' His face was suffused with rage.

'I'm not lying.'

She was lying. She'd played him for a sucker with all her talk about keeping herself for the wedding night and he'd been duped into believing every word. Had she thought he might guess if she went with him before she had the ring on her finger? Well, she would have been right.

He ground his teeth together, glaring at her as he bit out, 'I was straight with you, I didn't pretend I hadn't sown a few wild oats. You could have told me at any time over the last year.'

'Oh aye, and it was all right for you to have a bit of fun with those lasses, was it? Never mind you left them and went on to the next obliging fool. It's one rule for you and one rule for a lass in your book, is it? Like all men.'

Immediately she knew her temper had led her to say something that further damned her in his eyes. 'So that's how you think? That a lass can act that way, the same as a lad?'

'Of course I don't. I don't. And I haven't.'

'You've lied to me. All these months you've lied to me whilst acting the virtuous maiden. Does he know? The one who had you? Has he been cocking a snook an' all?'

He'd taken her aback, and in the split second before she regained control he read the truth in her face.

When he pounced on her again she fought him with fists and feet, but even before her knee made contact with his groin he was telling himself to get out of the room. He wanted to hurt her, really hurt her, and the madness she had accused him of earlier was there in the red mist before his eyes. Stumbling over to the wardrobe, he pulled out one of his working shirts and his trousers. His mother had insisted on washing them after his last shift the day before and dried them ready for him to drop off at the house first thing that morning with his other clothes and bits and pieces, before he went home to get ready for the service.

Tilly said nothing as he pulled them on, but as he went towards the door her voice came to him, trembling and low. 'I'll never forgive you for this and you're wrong, do you hear me? I haven't been with anyone else. I swear it.'

Without a backward glance towards the bed, he growled, 'Shut up or so help me I'll come over there and shut you up.'

Once on the landing he stood for a moment, breathing easier as the pain in his loins where she'd kneed him began to subside. It was quite dark now and the landing was in blackness, but all the houses in the Cross Streets were identical and he had no trouble walking down the stairs and into the kitchen.

The kitchen felt strange; at home the range would have been emitting a warm glow and the faint smell of food would be in the air. As yet they hadn't lit the range but it was black-leaded to within an inch of its life. Tilly and her mother had spent hours scrubbing and cleaning every inch of the place when they had first picked up the key from the agent.

Barefoot, he walked over the stone flags and stepped down into the tiny scullery, opening the back door and standing on the threshold where he gazed up into the sky. The humidity was fierce and the stars were hidden by stormclouds. Even as he watched, the first fat raindrops began to fall, bringing with them that distinctive smell peculiar to rain on parched earth.

He closed his eyes, his teeth grinding into his bottom lip, hardly able to take in the enormity of what had happened. And she had insisted the *bed* couldn't be second-hand. What had she said? Oh aye, she didn't want to start their life together where someone else had been. Damn it. *Damn it.*

What was he going to do? What *could* he do? She was his wife. They were married before the sight of God and man, besides which he'd be the laughing stock of the village if he left her and the truth came out. He'd never live the humiliation down, it'd follow him to his dying day. No, she'd sewn him up like a kipper. But how could they live together after this?

Who the hell was the man? His mind brought up and rejected one name after another until his head was throbbing, and all the time the rain got heavier until it was a solid sheet, drumming on the roof and hurtling down on to the slabs in the backyard so violently it shot several inches into the air again.

He'd stood there for a full fifteen minutes before he

allowed Constance into his mind, but when he did so the pain she brought caused him to groan out loud.

Was there ever such a fool as him? he asked himself bitterly. Such a blind, stupid fool? He'd known that day in her grandma's kitchen; it was as if he'd been seeing her for the first time, and he'd been bowled over by the sheer wonder of her.

And now the agony of mind that was tearing him apart was less to do with the betrayal by the woman he'd taken as his wife, and more the loss of a golden-haired child-woman whom he'd been too proud to seek out and bring back home.

Chapter 7

Constance had been at Grange Hall for six months, the first few weeks of which she had described to herself as hell on earth. Gradually though she had begun to understand the routine, cope with the overwhelming tiredness that often saw her falling on her bed fully dressed at midnight and waking while it was still dark to begin her duties, and even make friends among the other girls. One thing that had helped her begin to settle was realising that Florence's brusque attitude towards her wasn't personal; she was the same with everyone. Florence ruled 'her' kitchen with a rod of iron and all the girls both admired and feared her. Being a senior servant, her word was absolute and she gave no quarter, but she wasn't a spiteful woman, merely a perfectionist. And as Constance became accustomed to the working of the house, she understood that a cook's position in an establishment such as Grange Hall was a privileged one with a very comfortable way of life.

All the plain cooking and the cleaning and scouring of the kitchen, scullery, larder, passages and kitchen utensils were done by the kitchen- and scullerymaids. When Florence cooked the morning pastries, jellies, creams and more fancy dishes, Agnes prepared all her ingredients and one of the other kitchenmaids waited on her. As the most junior member of the kitchen staff, Constance took a cup of tea and a plate of biscuits up to Florence's private quarters every morning at seven o'clock, before Cook got up to supervise the making of the dining-room breakfast for the family. And every afternoon, unless there was a dinner party to prepare for, she took her ease, either in her room on the floor beneath the attics or in the kitchen where she could keep an eye on her staff.

The evenings were always hectic – five or six perfectly presented courses had to arrive in the dining room piping hot and at exactly the right moment – and this was the only time Florence was known to lose her temper. And Florence in a temper was something to be feared and avoided at all costs. Consequently the kitchen staff's nerves were fraught, come nightfall.

It was in Constance's second week at Grange Hall that Agnes explained to her about Cook's 'perks', after a rag and bone man had knocked on the back door and money had changed hands between him and Florence. It appeared that all the rabbit skins, feathers and bones were bought by the rag and bone man and the money went into Florence's pocket, along with the proceeds of the sale of dripping to itinerant traders who resold it to shops or at cottage doors. There were other perks too, along with beer money to help Cook cope with the heat of the kitchen, especially in the summer.

'Most cooks leave their family with enough money to buy a nice little cottage somewhere and live comfortably in their old age,' Agnes had whispered as she supervised Constance's first attempt at plucking a pheasant. 'I was thinking of that once, before me and Cuthbert started walking out.'

Cuthbert was the second gamekeeper, the son of the head gamekeeper, and he and Agnes had been courting for ten years. It was evident Cuthbert would have been happy for this state of affairs to continue indefinitely, but after some pressure from Agnes who, at twenty-eight years old, was conscious she wasn't getting any younger, they had agreed to get wed at Christmas. A cottage was under construction for them close to the head gamekeeper's, a concession by the master who often went shooting with Cuthbert and his father, and who didn't want Cuthbert to move on elsewhere for a position as head gamekeeper.

The days were long, especially when the summer came and the dining hours of the family got later. Any time off due to her Constance spent sleeping in the early weeks, but as her body and mind adjusted to the exhausting grind she sometimes went for a walk on her half-days in the company of Patience and Teresa whose free time corresponded with hers. They were both lively, intelligent girls and the three of them got on well, although Teresa – being very aware of her position as second kitchenmaid under Agnes – sometimes tried to lord it over Constance.

The highlight of Constance's week was the letter from her grandma. This arrived from the post office in a leather mail bag which went to Mr Rowan, and he then passed letters for the kitchen staff to Cook. It was not unknown for Florence to demand to know who the writer was, should she suspect one of her staff had an admirer, and then veto any further correspondence accordingly.

Constance's last letter from home was under the lumpy flock pillow on her bed, her grandma's large round writing smudged with Constance's tears.

It was a bonny wedding, her grandma had written, *and Tilly looked a picture. Your Aunt Ruth and Tilly's mam did us proud, I've not seen such a fine table for many a long day. It was such a shame you couldn't be there, hinny, but needs must, and you're better where you are.*

Constance knew the letter off by heart now and as she stood peeling the sack of potatoes the gardener's boy brought to the kitchen door every morning, she told herself fiercely that she wasn't going to cry any more. Matt and Tilly were wed. It was done. She had known it was going to happen and now it had.

She looked across at Gracie who was sitting on a stool plucking several teal. The small freshwater ducks looked so pathetic once they were featherless; she hated plucking or skinning anything and always plumped for peeling the potatoes or the huge barrel of vegetables they got through each day if she could. Gracie was feathering into a deep bucket to try to prevent the feathers floating about, but every so often she gave a sneeze as the fine down irritated her nose.

Agnes and the other kitchenmaids, even Gracie, seemed perfectly happy working in the kitchen, but Constance couldn't bear to think this would be her life for years to come. She knew that was ungrateful and that she had been lucky to be taken into service at Grange Hall, but sometimes she longed to take off her apron and heavy thick boots and leave the house and just run and run for miles in the wild and beautiful countryside surrounding the house. Every hour, every minute here was ruled over by

Cook. The natural freedom the children of the village had always taken for granted was now, in hindsight, an infinitely precious thing.

She'd tried to explain how she felt to Teresa and Patience on their last walk, but the pair of them had looked at her in amazement. 'But look at the food we eat,' Teresa — who was already turning into a roly-poly — had protested. 'Where else would you have as much as you want? I'd never tasted ice cream or meringues or French pastries before I came here. Had you?'

Constance had to admit she had not.

'And the master and mistress aren't stingy like some. Look at Christmas, we all had a present and a party in the servants' hall and a supper and a ball on Twelfth Night. The master led off the dancing with Mrs Craggs and the mistress with Mr Howard.'

'The master danced with Mrs Craggs?' Constance repeated in astonishment. Mrs Craggs, the housekeeper, was a dour individual with iron-grey hair and a moustache any man would be proud of. As Cook had her kitchen- and scullerymaids, so Mrs Craggs had her own parlour- and housemaids. Under her direction, besides seeing to the smooth running of the house, they worked in the stillroom off the housekeeper's quarters. Constance had never stepped inside this exalted place, but she understood from Agnes that the room held a range and a confectioner's oven, and here Mrs Craggs and her staff bottled fruit, made jam, crystallised fruits and flowers from the estate and created sugared novelties.

The housekeeper's rooms also had cupboards from floor to ceiling, and in these were stored preserves made from the fruit off the estate and pickles, spices and sugar. She also had charge of the soap and candles for the house, along with bulk goods such as flour, rice, dried fruit and tea and coffee. Every Monday morning Agnes would take Cook's order for the week to Mrs Craggs, and later in the morning two of the housemaids would deliver it to the kitchen.

The three of them had continued on their walk, with Teresa and Patience describing the fun they'd had at the ball and how Mr Rowan had whisked Cook round the floor, but nothing that had been said had changed Constance's mind about the future. She didn't want to work her way up from scullerymaid to kitchenmaid and then further up the ladder until she reached the dizzy heights of first kitchenmaid like Agnes, only leaving her employment to take the job of cook elsewhere. When she heard the housemaids' chatter at mealtimes, their lives on the other side of the green-baize doors seemed so much more interesting. They got to see the family and all the goings-on in the house, and although their work was hard and often laborious, the house was filled with beautiful things, and interesting people came and went. If she was destined to stay in service and have her liberty curtailed, she would far rather be there than in the kitchen.

She knew better than to make her views known, however. If Cook caught wind of how she was feeling her life wouldn't be worth living. Mrs Craggs and Cook had never got on, according to the other kitchenmaids, and going over to the enemy would be the worst sort of betrayal. Not that she would ever have the opportunity anyway. Her fate had been sealed when she'd been taken on as a scullerymaid. Her destiny was on the wrong side of the green-baize doors.

Having finished the last of the potatoes for the day, Constance started on the vegetables. The sky had been blue and high first thing when she and Gracie had fetched the milk, cream, butter, cheese and eggs from the dairy. Flocks of birds had been calling and swooping as they gathered together before they went off to warmer climes for the winter, and it had reminded her that September was nearly over. This time last year she had still been at school, she had been happy. And now . . .

She paused, looking towards the small narrow window. Now she was a scullerymaid at Grange Hall.

Chapter 8

Vincent's patience was wearing thin. When Constance had first left the village he'd had no doubt that he'd find her within the month, three at the most. But both she and this aunt of hers had disappeared into thin air. He had been convinced the old couple wouldn't want the girl to be more than a few miles away and that even if they discouraged her from visiting them, they would go and see her after a while. But to date they hadn't budged and although there'd been the inevitable gossip about Constance's sudden departure, it had been just that – gossip. All his enquiries had drawn a blank, and even when he'd gone to the expense of hiring the man who had traced one of the owners' daughters when she'd run off with some ne'er-do-well the year before, it had proved fruitless.

He glanced again at the letter which had come that morning. He was very sorry, Mr Robson had written, but it wouldn't be right to continue to take payment when there was no inkling of a lead in this matter. Maybe his client should face the fact that the girl in question had gone to parts unknown, maybe even abroad, and resolve to put the matter behind him?

'Abroad,' Vincent muttered in disgust, screwing the paper into a tight ball and throwing it at the wall. He had returned home an hour before and, having finished his dinner, was sitting in his armchair by the fire with a glass of brandy at his side. Since the hot spell had broken the weather had become colder, and October had been ushered in with a sharp nip in the air the week before.

Constance had not gone abroad. He stared into the flickering flames of the fire. He'd bet his life on that. But where the hell was she? As far as he could ascertain, her grandparents had kept mum on her whereabouts even with their nearest and dearest. Damn their eyes.

He finished his brandy in one gulp and stood up, too restless to continue sitting by the fireside. He needed to clear his head and decide how to proceed from here if Robson wasn't going to come up trumps, because he *was* going to find her. He didn't believe for one minute she'd left willingly. Since he'd had time to mull it over he was sure her grandparents had forced her to leave with the aunt they'd brought in. What young lass would give up the chance of a life of ease for the drudgery of service? No, Constance had told them of his intentions and they'd reacted like the ignorant scum they were, driven by fear of what their neighbours would say if their granddaughter married the weighman.

Pulling on his greatcoat he left the house without a word to Polly who had come into the kitchen doorway as he opened the front door. He rarely spoke to her if he could avoid it.

As it banged behind him, Polly stood quite still for a

moment. Then, as though the air had gone out of a balloon, her body relaxed and she walked slowly into the sitting room, staring at his empty chair and the glass on the table beside it. Her gaze moved to the window and she wondered how long he'd be gone.

Did he know how much she hated him? Her chin gave a nervous jerk. No, she doubted if he even thought she had feelings beyond fear of him. And she did fear him; she was terrified of him, and with good reason. When she had first come to the cottage, she had thought she was the luckiest lass in the world. The comfort and colour and warmth had been dazzling after the grim confines of the workhouse. She thought she'd landed in heaven.

She gave a bitter 'Huh!' of a laugh, picking up the brandy glass and taking it into the kitchen.

She had thought him handsome in those days. She had even day-dreamed about him secretly when she'd been about her duties. At what point she had come to realise his devotion in always taking his mother's dinner-tray to the sick woman and feeding her himself wasn't what it seemed, she didn't know. Perhaps it had been simply a feeling of unease at first that she couldn't place. And then he'd been laid up with a bad dose of influenza and there had been three days on the trot when she'd seen to the older woman. By the second day Mrs McKenzie had been able to sit up and feed herself, and by the third the terrible sickness and pain that had her calling out most of the night had ceased.

When, on the fourth day, Vincent had literally dragged himself into the kitchen, his mother had gone downhill again. And Polly had known, even before she came across him stirring some white powder into a bowl of soup she'd

131

prepared one night. He always sent her into his mother's bedroom to see to her pillows and get her ready for dinner before he carried the tray through, but this particular night she had waited in the hall and then returned to the kitchen on the pretext of changing her soiled apron for a clean one. By then she'd felt she had to know for sure.

He had looked at her, that was all. But there had been something in his eyes that had sent terror into her soul. She had already been a little afraid of him, he was such a cold, distant man, but that in itself had been attractive in a strange sort of way. She had gabbled a few words about the clean apron, and he had told her he'd bought a tonic to add to his mother's food, and the moment had passed.

Later that evening, when he had been sitting reading the paper in front of the sitting-room fire, he had called her into the room.

There was a sad case in the newspaper, he'd said softly. It appeared a couple had taken in a workhouse scut as servant, and the girl had abused their kindness by telling all sorts of stories about the master. When the man had accused the girl of stealing from them and explained that was why he'd had to discipline her, which had caused her to lie about him, the baggage had been put away for a long, long time.

He had raised his eyes at this point and looked at her, the same look he'd given earlier in the kitchen.

That was what always happened with workhouse vermin if they were foolish enough to bite the hand that fed them; the magistrates knew who to believe in these cases. His voice had been quiet, even gentle. One could kill such a girl and get off scot-free.

132

From that night, her fear of him had grown into a dread which could cause her to shake in her shoes, but it wasn't until the night of his mother's funeral that hatred and deep revulsion had been born in her. She had known that she was paying, and would go on paying, for not speaking out and trying to save Mrs McKenzie. With her death, demons had been released in her son.

She sank down at the kitchen table, gazing dully round the room. It was bonny. The whole house was bonny, but for years now she would have gladly traded living here for the hard life in the workhouse.

According to the matron's records, she had been about six months old when she'd been found in a rented room next to the dead body of her mother. Neighbours had told the authorities that her father had been lost at sea some weeks previously, and that the couple had been relative newcomers to the area. Certainly no family had come forward to claim her. And so she had been taken to the workhouse nursery. She had been clothed and fed by the guardians, and as she had grown it had been repeatedly drummed into her that she had much to be grateful for. She had sometimes lain in her narrow iron bed at night, shivering in the icy cold dormitory under the thin grey blankets as she listened to the snores and coughs of the other inmates, and imagined a life in which there were no paupers' uniforms, no infirm wards with their screams and cries and creeping stench, no punishment and beatings, and no labour mistress and matron. And now she knew what such a life was like.

Polly shook herself mentally. She didn't know where Vincent had gone or how long he would be, but she'd better get on with the evening chores so he had no excuse to pick fault when he returned. However late he was, she knew better than to go to bed before him. She had only done that once in the days after his mother had died, and there had followed such a night of torment after he had come and dragged her from her room to his, that she hadn't repeated the mistake. Since then she had waited to see if he expected her to service him or not.

Service him. She shut her eyes for a moment against the phrase Vincent used for what went on in his bedroom. She had been a virgin when he had first forced her, but even that time she had known that the things he had done to her hadn't been normal between a man and a maid. It had been as though he was punishing her. And that had never changed. But she had never angered him, never crossed him in any way, so why? Why?

She stood up, walking into the scullery where the evening's dirty dishes were waiting. Determinedly, as she'd done many times in the past, she made her mind go blank and mechanically now, like a wind-up doll, she set about washing the pots and pans.

There was the sharp scent of an early frost in the cold air once Vincent had left the cosy warmth of the cottage. It was going to be another hard winter. All the signs were there. Already the leaves were falling from the trees in their droves, and that morning he'd seen flocks of birds gorging themselves upon the fruits and berries and seeds in the hedgerows and fields, as though they knew the autumn was going to be a short one. They could be snowed in for weeks again.

He frowned darkly, the rage that had gripped him when he'd read Robson's letter increasing. By now he'd imagined Constance would be back where he could see her and touch her. He had pictured her visiting the cottage and becoming acquainted with each room, and the two of them taking tea together before he took her back to her grandparents'. He would court her, as he had wished to court Hannah, and as soon as she was old enough he would make her his wife. That had been the plan. Instead, he was in no-man's land and it was driving him mad.

With no conscious plan of where he was going, he followed the road to the crossroads, and there he stood hesitating for a moment. To the right were open fields and Barrashill Wood, and beyond that the villages of Nettlesworth and Kimblesworth. These were small compared to Sacriston, although Kimblesworth Colliery had a workforce of 600 men and boys. Once he had left the village, this road would be dark and lonely, but it wasn't this which made him pause. He often walked at night and the blackness held no fear for him. The cosh in his coat pocket was protection enough, that and his fists and feet, and he felt more at one with nature in the darkness. He knew the place where a vixen had had her den and a litter of little ones, and deep in Barrashill Wood there was a spot where badgers came to play in the moon-light. But tonight it wasn't the animals that were on his mind but a need to be near Constance in some way.

As he walked through the village there was no one about. It was cold and dark and the middle of a working week. Folk would mostly be in bed by now, since morn-ings started early in a mining community. When he reached the Cross Streets, he hesitated again. Everything in him wanted to make his way to the Grays' back door and take the old couple by their throats until they told him where Constance was. To choke it out of them.

He smiled grimly to himself. Wouldn't the neighbours love *that*! It'd set the tongues wagging with a vengeance. He'd be the butt of every wit who hated him, and that was all of them.

He walked on, past the school on his left and the rows of silent streets to his right, but as he drew level with the Colliery Inn the door opened and Art Gray stepped down into the street. For a moment surprise froze Vincent's tongue. For months now he had watched the older man coming and going to the colliery, hoping to catch him alone. He had even followed him home a few times, but Gray had always been in the company of other miners and he'd had to keep a good distance behind them. He knew Constance's grandfather frequented the Colliery Inn but it would be more than his life was worth to step inside there, besides which Gray would have his pals around him. But not tonight. Tonight he was alone.

'Hello there. It's a cold one.' He kept his voice low and he could see the amazement in the other man's eyes that he had stopped and spoken. 'Been having a bevy or two to warm the cockles?'

It was some seconds before Art said flatly, 'Just a couple.'

'Here, wait on.' As Constance's grandfather made to turn away, Vincent caught his arm. 'I want a quiet word.'

Vincent could read the old man's mind as Art turned his head and glanced back towards the door of the inn. He didn't want to be seen talking to the weighman. If he was suspected of trying to curry favour, the other men would make his life hell. But neither could he refuse the man who held his livelihood in his hands and had the power to make it so he earned less than nothing if he chose.

Vincent watched him squirm for a moment or two before saying, 'I was taking a walk. Walk with me.' It was an order, not a request, and he walked on knowing the man had no choice but to obey.

They had passed Church Street and St Bede's Catholic Church and were approaching the graveyard and Blackburn Bridge, the village some distance behind them, when Vincent spoke again.

'Where's Constance?' he said softly. 'Where did you pack her off to?'

The other man's footsteps stopped. Then Art was hurrying to catch him up, actually grasping hold of his arm as they reached the bridge. 'What did you say?'

They faced each other. It was very dark now they were away from the built-up area of the village, but the sky was clear and the moonlight showed Art's bewilderment. Vincent stared at him, sure he was playing a part. 'I asked you where Constance is, and if you know what's good for you, you'll tell me. I can make your life not worth living, don't forget that, and I'm done playing games.'

'Playing games? I don't know what you're talking about – and why would you want to know where the bairn is?'

'You know full well.' Vincent's voice was a growl.

'The devil I do.' Art was bristling like a terrier dog.

'So why have you and your wife kept her whereabouts to yourselves, eh?'

Art moved one lip tightly over the other. McKenzie had hit on the one thing that had bothered him about

137

the bairn taking this job at Ivy's lass's place. That and the fact it all seemed to have come about in the blink of an eye. One minute the bairn had been as happy as Larry working at the school with Miss Newton, and the next she'd been adamant she wanted to spread her wings and fly off down south. And when he'd questioned why it all had to be done so quickly, Ivy had added her two penn'orth and said opportunities like the one her Florence was offering didn't come up that often. There were jobs in service all right, she'd said, but working for the Ashtons was a step above. And then Constance had said she didn't want anyone knowing where she was, and Mabel had backed her, and when he'd asked why, there'd been some garbled story about the lass wanting to find her feet, and if folk like the Heaths and others knew, they'd want to write and keep in touch. Well, he'd said, what was wrong with that? But the pair of them had made up their minds, and when Constance had got tearful and insisted she didn't want the worry of having to tell folk how she was getting on, he'd succumbed. He only wanted his granddaughter to be happy, after all. But he hadn't understood it.

As Art stared into the glowering face of the man he'd watched grow up, the lad who had always been hanging on their Hannah's coat-tails at one time but who had grown up into a morose, spiteful individual who'd taken on the contemptible job of weighman, a thought – an impossible thought – was hovering at the back of his mind. Slowly, he said, 'Why do *you* think we've kept quiet about where the lass is?'

'I told you, I'm done with playing games. She told you I wanted her and you couldn't dispatch her quick enough, could you?'

'You want her?' Art was glaring now, his rage equal to Vincent's. 'She's nowt but a bairn and you say you want her, and you old enough to be her father!'

'I should've been her father.' Vincent thrust his face close to Art's. 'But you and that wife of yours didn't think I was good enough for Hannah, did you? I know, I know. And so you threw her Shelton's way and she played the whore with him. But I won't be crossed again. Constance is mine and I'm going to have her, with or without your consent, old man. Now are you going to tell me where she is, or do I have to beat it out of you?'

'You could try.' Art was a small man, and slight. He looked like David squaring up to Goliath but he had no sling or stones up his sleeve. 'But I'd rather see my lass dead than with midden scum like you. I felt sorry for you as a lad, do you know that? With a da like you had and a battleaxe of a mam, you didn't have much on your side, but my Mabel was right. She always said you were bad. Something inside wasn't normal, she said, and she warned Hannah time and time again to keep away from you, but my bairn was too warm and sweet, too kind to see the evil in folk.'

What followed happened so quickly Art had no time to avoid the blow. Vincent had reached in his pocket while the other man was talking and now he brought his cosh full force across Art's head, the crack as wood hit bone sickening. For a moment Vincent stood poised over the crumpled figure but Art was quite still. Then he bent down and inserted a hand in his jacket. He was still breathing.

Vincent straightened, his eyes peering in every direction. The night was quiet and peaceful; in the far distance an owl hooted and somewhere in the village a dog barked.

He had to finish the job. Having come this far, he couldn't run the risk of Art talking; besides which, if her grandfather died Constance would come home for the funeral. A bolt of excitement made his heart pound faster. It was clear that alive, Gray wasn't going to help him, but dead he might well serve a purpose.

The burn was higher than it had been for a while after the recent storms, he noted as he lugged the inert body down the bank, positioning it face down in the icy water. He stood for a few moments in case the shock revived Art, but when this didn't happen he rearranged his legs so it looked as though he'd stumbled and fallen into the water from the bridge. Lastly he checked Art's heartbeat once more. There was none. The burn had done its job.

Satisfied, he climbed the bank and continued walking away from the village along Edmondsley Lane. He would skirt round the back of the colliery and make his way home across the fields and woodland. He doubted he would run into anyone the night but there was always the chance if he went back through the village. He nodded to the thought, breathing in the frosty air and beginning to whistle to himself as he strode on. Soon he would see Constance again – and this time she would not escape him.

Constance did not come home for her grandfather's funeral. She did not know of it until a full month after he was buried, because Mabel had decreed it so. Ivy travelled to Grange Hall to break the news, and although she did it as gently as possible, the shock to Constance was great.

Florence had allowed her mother to take Constance up to her private quarters on the floor below the attics, and this in itself had alerted the girl to the fact that something was badly wrong.

'But . . . but how? When?' Constance stared at her great-aunt. They were sitting in Florence's two armchairs which were either side of the fireplace. 'Was it an accident in the mine?'

'No, lass, it weren't the mine, not this time. Your granda had had a drink or two and it would seem he didn't go straight home; whether he wanted to clear his head or not it's not known, although by all accounts he'd not had more than he usually did, but . . .' Ivy stopped; the grief in Constance's face was paining her. 'But anyway, he went for a walk in the dark and slipped off Blackburn Bridge into the water. They said he banged his head and was knocked unconscious, and being face down . . .'

'He drowned?' Constance's fingers were pressing her mouth.

'Aye, hinny, he drowned.'

'But why didn't me grandma write? I would have come home.'

'She knew you would, which is why she didn't tell you. That man, that McKenzie fella, was on her mind. She said you couldn't do owt so what was the point in stirring all that up again? And she was right, lass. When you've had a chance to think about it you'll see that. You couldn't have done nowt, now could you?'

Constance wiped her eyes, her voice shaking as she said, 'But the house? Has she been turned out?'

'Oh don't you worry your head none about your grandma, hinny. Your aunties were fighting each other to have her live with them, but beens as Beryl moved to Kimblesworth when your Uncle Jacob died and she met

Percy, your grandma's opted to live with Molly so she can stay in the village. There's only your Aunt Molly and Uncle Edwin at home now the bairns have grown up, and the three of 'em get on just fine. Molly an' your grandma'll be company for each other when Edwin's at work. I said for her to come to us, but she wouldn't; like I said, she wanted to stay where she knows everyone and everyone knows her. It's only natural, I suppose.'

'My granda never has one too many, not like some.'

'Aye, I know that, hinny.' Ivy didn't add here that Mabel had said the very same thing and that her sister wasn't convinced about the circumstances of her husband's demise. There was something funny about all this, Mabel had said. She knew it in her water. But a woman's water wasn't sufficient reason for further investigation regarding a man's death, not when the individual concerned was merely a miner and a miner who had been drinking at that.

Constance stared down at her fingers twisted together in her lap. She could hardly take in that her granda had gone and she hadn't been able to say goodbye. The accident, the funeral, her grandma leaving the house – it had all happened and she hadn't known a thing about it. Before this moment she had always held on to the fact that if things got too bad here, if she really couldn't stand it a minute more, she could go home to her grandparents. But she had nowhere to go back to now; her home had gone.

She took a deep breath. Cook had been kind in letting them use her room but she knew better than to take advantage and linger. Ivy had inadvertently chosen a day when the family were giving a large dinner party. Already the atmosphere in the kitchen was so tense the air crackled. She would have to do her grieving when she was alone

142

in bed tonight; for now, she must get on with what was required of her.

She stood up, her face chalk-white and her eyes red-rimmed. 'I'd best get back downstairs, Aunt Ivy. Do you want to stay here and I'll bring you a tea-tray shortly? It's busy in the kitchen.'

'Aye, Florence let me know I hadn't picked a good day to turn up,' Ivy said wryly. 'That's a good idea, hinny. I'll be out of the way up here. I can talk to Florence later once I come down for a spot of supper when the dinner party's done.'

After Constance had closed the door to Florence's room behind her, she stood on the landing without moving for a moment or two. Her granda, her lovely granda. And her grandma having to move in with Aunt Molly. Her grandma would have hated getting rid of the furniture she and Granda had collected so painstakingly over the years. They hadn't had much and what they did have wasn't of the best, but her grandma had been proud of it nonetheless. But there wouldn't have been room at Aunt Molly's for more than a few keepsakes.

Hot tears were stinging the backs of her eyes but she blinked them away furiously. Squaring her slender shoulders, she lifted her chin. Her grandma would be making the best of things and that's what she had to do. She would give her Aunt Ivy her wages to date to take to her grandma; her grandma would be happier if she was paying her way at Aunt Molly's and the sale of the household furniture wouldn't have brought much. And she'd ask her aunt to tell her grandma that she'd send her more every month from now on. She couldn't do much for her grandma stuck here, but she could do that at least.

This was the start of a new life. It had probably been so when she'd first come to Grange Hall in the spring, but it hadn't felt like it at the time. But now, now it did. And she would give ten years of her life or more if she could just slip back in time to a year ago when she was happy. To see her granda puffing his pipe in front of the fire, her grandma humming to herself as she bustled about the kitchen, and Matt— Oh Matt, Matt . . .

PART TWO

Through the Green–Baize Door

1900

Chapter 9

It was the dawn of a new century and Britain was celebrating.

According to the newspapers, the extent of Britain's imperial powers had never been greater. 'The Empire, stretching round the globe, has one heart, one head, one language and one policy,' stated one positively euphoric reporter, conveniently ignoring the matter of the Boer War which had begun a few months before. But then no one was in any doubt that the fight with the 'stubborn breed of Dutch peasants who had revolted against the just and noble sovereignty of our glorious Queen' would soon be over, and that Britain would be victorious.

Everyone knew that the previous century's unparalleled success and expansion would continue, bringing more wealth and prosperity to Britain's citizens. Or to its upper classes at least, which was all that mattered. Was not the Master and Servant Act, which entitled only the employer to give evidence in a court of law and not the employee, a clear guideline by those who knew best of the great divide between the upper classes and the working class?

And, it had to be said, muttered politicians and magistrates alike, the working class often had none of the sensibilities which differentiated noble man from lowly beast.

As for the trade unions – troublemakers and agitators the lot of them. What good did it do to incite ignorant men and women to refuse to do an honest day's work for an honest day's pay? Keir Hardie with his Socialist prattling and the whines of the Independent Labour Party were damaging the well-being of ordinary men and women, not helping them.

For Constance, whose life revolved around the goings-on in the kitchen of Grange Hall, such views and statements held little interest. She didn't have time to reflect on her lot, she was too busy, and in the little free time she had she would rather read Mr Thackeray's *Vanity Fair* or something by Jane Austen than a newspaper. They at least gave her hope that one day, maybe, her life might consist of more than kitchen duties, even though she was now third kitchenmaid.

When Agnes had married her Cuthbert and become pregnant almost immediately, Teresa had taken her place as head kitchenmaid. Patience, Cathleen and Maria had each taken a step up the ladder and when Florence had promoted Constance to fifth kitchenmaid she had been overjoyed, even though she'd felt sorry for poor Gracie who – Florence had said – was born to be a scullerymaid and would die one. Within four years Teresa had left to become a cook in a small establishment in York, taking Patience with her – something Florence looked on as an act of betrayal and had waxed lyrical about for weeks. Constance got on well with Mirabelle and Clara, the two new kitchenmaids beneath her, and life in the kitchen of

Grange Hall was not unpleasant, merely repetitious and humdrum.

Try as she might, Constance found she just couldn't get excited about a perfect salmon mayonnaise au Gridoni or a Charlotte Russe. She appreciated that Florence was an excellent cook, she was in awe of some of the dishes that went through to the dining room and by keeping her eyes and ears open she had quickly learned the French names for these, and what sauces and accompanying dishes were needed − but she didn't long to be a cook like Cathleen and the others did. She now earned twenty-four pounds a year, most of which she sent to her grandma to enable her to contribute to Molly's household expenses and have the odd little luxury for herself, like the Tiger Nuts and Everlasting Stripes that her grandma had always enjoyed.

She had seen her grandma three times in the last six years since she'd left Sacriston, thanks to Ivy and her intrepid horse and trap. On each occasion Ivy had made sure her visit coincided with Constance's free Sunday. Constance had relished the hours with her beloved grandma, but after the time had come to say goodbye and she had waved the two sisters off, she'd felt acutely homesick for days.

She had made it a point of conscience never to ask after Matt when she corresponded with her grandmother, but Mabel mentioned him often. Through her, Constance had heard when Tilly had given birth to a little girl seven months into the marriage. Supposedly premature, her grandma had written, but the baby had been a good weight and like no premature bairn she'd ever seen. Still, they wouldn't be the first betrothed couple to jump the gun and all was

149

well that ended well. They'd called her Rebecca and she was the spitting image of her mother.

There had followed a period of two or three years when her grandma had written about what Rebecca was doing and saying, and how the child was progressing. By all accounts she was a bright little girl. Gradually though, more by what was unsaid than said, Constance got the impression all was not well with Matt's marriage. Then, just a few weeks ago, her grandma had written to say Ruth had confided she was worried about Matt. He'd become withdrawn since his marriage, non-communicative, and he was getting worse with time. Constance had found that hard to imagine. Matt had always been outgoing and sociable, not exactly the life and soul of the party but certainly affable and friendly.

Her fingers stilled on the plate of hors d'oeuvres she was arranging. To celebrate the new century the Ashtons had invited both sets of in-laws and other family members and friends to stay for a few days over the New Year, and it had been one big dinner party after another. The kitchen staff were exhausted.

But Matt wasn't her problem to worry about, she reminded herself for the umpteenth time since receiving her grandma's letter. She hadn't seen him for years and of course men changed with the responsibility of a wife and family, it was only natural. It didn't mean he and Tilly weren't happy together. And even if they weren't, they were married. End of story.

'You finished, Constance?' Florence bustled up, her face as red as a beetroot. Her critical eyes surveyed the pimentos, brilliant red and green foreign pickles, startling white and yellow slices of egg, pink curls of tongue and tiny rolls of cured ham, and black trails of truffles. She nodded approvingly, handing the plate to one of the housemaids who was waiting at the entrance to the kitchen.

Without being told, Constance went over to help Cathleen transfer the two enormous saucepans of soup – one thick and one clear – into the warmed soup tureens. Both soups had been started two days before. The consommé had been cooled, had the layer of fat removed from the top, then reheated and cleared by dropping in eggshells and egg-whites so any bits of meat would rise with them to the top of the pot. Once the soup had been allowed to cool again it was reheated and the performance repeated. This time the meat stayed on the surface for an hour and a half before being skimmed off. After soaking a cloth in boiling water to ensure the stock passed through quicker, it was strained into the saucepan it would be reheated in for serving. Making the thick soup was an equally lengthy business, and because Florence was adamant that the quality of the soup revealed the calibre of the cook, everyone was on tenterhooks until she expressed her satisfaction that all had gone well.

Several more courses would follow the soup. The menu for the evening was pinned to the wall so there was no excuse for anyone to say they didn't know what was required of them. A saddle of beef with vegetables and salad was next, followed by a sorbet – pineapple ice with rum. Then the roast. Tonight it was rabbit and the animals were served on two enormous platters in a crouching position, complete with tails and by courtesy of judiciously placed skewers, with their heads on and ears erect. A choice of two sweets followed the roast, a tall and elaborate jelly with fruits inside, and an opaque blancmange. A savoury was next. This evening it was *marrons en mascarade*, Sir Henry's favourite, and the braised chestnuts coated with a savoury stuffing and then half with grated ham and half with grated cheese was one of Florence's specialities. Then more ices would be served to clear the palate for dessert – pineapples in ornamental beds of leaves, dishes of grapes with silver grape scissors, and strawberries and cream, along with the housekeeper's crystallised fruits, sweetmeats and nuts.

Constance knew she'd be lucky to be climbing the stairs to the attic before midnight, and the two scullerymaids wouldn't fall into their beds until well after one o'clock in the morning. Every member of the kitchen staff was now longing for the next day when the guests were due to depart and normality would be resumed. And not just the kitchen staff. Listening to the chatter in the servants' hall, the nanny and the nursemaids were exhausted too. As well as their usual charges – Miss Charlotte who was ten years old, Miss Gwendoline who had been born the year Constance had arrived at Grange Hall, and Master Edmond, the long-awaited son and heir whose third birthday had been celebrated shortly before Christmas – they'd had the care of several children of the guests who had apparently all run riot.

'Bedlam, it's been,' Katy, one of the nursemaids, had muttered to Constance when she had flopped on her seat in the servants' hall the day before. 'And of course they're all over-excited, it being the Christmas holidays, which doesn't help. Master Edmond's a handful at the best of times, but this week . . .' She'd rolled her eyes expressively. 'If he'd been one of my little brothers, he'd have had a good slap by now.'

'But Master Edmond is *not* one of your little brothers,' Betty, the head nursemaid, had said sharply. 'He is the master's son and don't you forget it, Katy Mallard. A good slap, indeed! You let Nanny Price hear you talk like that and you'll be out on your ear without a reference.'

She'd glared at the unfortunate Katy who'd looked suitably chastened, but only for as long as Betty looked at her. Then she had whispered in an aside to Constance, 'He put a worm in Nanny Price's pocket yesterday and he knows she's mortally afraid of them. Screamed like a two year old, she did. And how he got it with the ground so hard, I don't know. He's a little devil, that one. You never know what he's going to do next.'

Constance had caught the odd glimpse of the family over the years when Cook had sent her on errands to the glass-houses or dairy, but she had always made herself scarce as soon as she could. Sir Henry and his Italian-born wife Lady Isabella were a handsome couple, she as dark as he was fair, and the two girls were pretty in a fairly nondescript way. Edmond was as fair as his father, and a sturdy little boy. Katy had told her they had been forced to take him out of his infant dresses when he'd yelled the place down, and now he strode around in little breeches and a waistcoat like his father, and thought himself the bee's knees.

Constance had found it amusing, although Katy hadn't been laughing. Master Edmond reminded her of the Finnigan twins, who had been in Miss Newton's class and who had been characters with minds of their own. They'd tried her patience but she had to admit she'd found them more interesting than the bairns who did everything they were told and wouldn't say boo to a goose.

Once the soup tureens had been dispatched, the rest of the courses flowed as smoothly as a well-oiled machine. Abe Rowan and Florence worked well together. As butler he stood silently behind the master's chair and kept a careful eye on the table. As each course progressed he judged the appropriate time to ring the dining-room bell and signal the kitchen, thus ensuring there was no delay between courses. Essential in such an eminent establishment.

It was nearer one o'clock than midnight when Constance and the other kitchenmaids finally dragged themselves up to bed, leaving Gracie and the second scullerymaid still scouring pots and pans with sand and salt in the dark, dismal scullery. As one, they fell into their pallet beds just as they were, drawing the thin blankets up over their heads to combat the freezing cold. In the moment before Cathleen blew out the candle, thus plunging them into pitch blackness, Constance thought, However will I get up in the morning? But then in the next instant she was fast asleep.

Constance did get up in the morning. They all did. And when Florence walked heavily into the kitchen some time later after Lotty, the second scullerymaid, had taken up her tea-tray, she voiced what her staff were thinking when she said, 'Thank the powers-that-be they're all going home this morning. I'm dead on me feet and that's no lie.'

But before the guests left, breakfast had to be served, and that in itself was no mean feat. Just the fancy breads alone had had Constance and the other kitchenmaids rising even earlier than normal to get them underway. French and Vienna bread rolls, muffins, oat cakes, crumpets, breakfast cake, bannocks, wholemeal rolls and scones, and all baked fresh that morning. Add to this the rissoles, kedgeree, cold meats, hot meats, broiled eggs, omelettes and the inevitable porridge and choice of several preserves, and it was no wonder they all scrambled up to morning prayers breathless when the footman sounded the gong, pulling on clean aprons and straightening their caps as they went. After breakfast they dived back down to the kitchen to begin sending up the myriad dishes which had been kept warm for fifteen minutes.

It was mid-morning by the time both family and guests, and the servants, had finished eating. Then all the dirty dishes were cleared and once the scullerymaids were tackling them the rest of the kitchen staff had a cup of tea before they started on the preparations for luncheon.

Constance and the other kitchenmaids were sitting at the table too tired to talk as they finished their tea, but once Florence had drunk two cupfuls straight down with hardly a pause, she rallied her troops. Rising ponderously to her feet, she didn't have to tell them to get to work. No one would dare to remain seated when Cook was standing. Everyone knew what they had to do but as Constance went to fetch a clean white cloth and lay out the spoons and knives and other equipment needed for the game pie Florence was about to make, Florence said, 'Leave that, Constance. Maria will see to it. I want you to nip to the mushroom-house and bring me back a basketful, and a jug of cream from the dairy while you're about it. That one they sent over first thing went at breakfast.'

Constance didn't have to be told twice. Any excuse to venture outside for a few minutes was welcome. Sunbeams rarely strayed into the kitchen for, in an attempt to keep it cool in the heat of summer, its windows faced north.

Today, although bitterly cold, the weather was bright and sunny and she had been longing to feel the fresh air on her face if only for a moment or two. It always lifted her spirits.

Quickly changing her apron for a clean one – an unwritten rule even for a quick errand like this one – Constance made her escape. It had snowed steadily over Christmas, but in the last day or two after a brief thaw, everything had frozen solid, as hard penetrating frosts had made themselves felt. Brilliant sunsets and rosy dawns spoke of clear high skies, and as Constance hurried across the courtyard which the outside staff kept clear of snow even in the worst of the weather, she breathed in the sharp frosty air with delight, taking it deep into her lungs.

Passing through the archway into the stableyard, she ignored the low wolf-whistle Ray McGuigan, one of the grooms, sent her way. She'd rebuffed numerous advances by some of the outside staff since she'd been at Grange Hall, along with the odd surreptitious suggestion by one or two members of the indoor staff too. Now their overtures were without expectation and friendly; they knew she wouldn't respond and she knew they knew.

Nevertheless she sped across the yard towards the door in the far wall which led to the kitchen gardens, not because of Ray and his harmless flirting, but due to the fact that a stable-lad might bring out one of the horses for exercise. She thought the master's horses were beautiful, their glossy coats and noble heads were a sight to behold, but she was very aware of their lethal hooves and huge sharp teeth too. Midnight, the master's favourite stallion, was known to be a temperamental beast; on one of her half-days when she'd visited Agnes in her cosy little cottage, Cuthbert had come in full of the fact that Midnight had kicked one of the stable-boys straight through the wooden divide into the next stall.

Passing through the garden door, she shut it carefully behind her. To her left was a long line of glass-houses, to her right were the vineries, the nectarine and early- and late-peach-houses, the thatched fruit-house and the mushroom-house and the potting sheds. Beyond these lay the walled fruit and vegetable garden.

The gravel scrunched under her feet as she made her way to the mushroom-house and she experienced the feeling she always felt when out of the house – pure joy. She wished, she so wished that women could be allowed to work in the gardens. It would be the next best thing to working with children as she'd done before she left Sacriston. Here things were nurtured and cared for, you could see their development and growth. When she thought of the produce which had been sent to the kitchen over the last day or two – artichokes, chicory, asparagus, sea-kale, endive, celery and dandelion, not to mention the items from the fruit store – she so envied the head gardener and his staff.

After collecting her basket of mushrooms she retraced her footsteps. The dairy was situated at the far end of the stableblock and stockyard, and was closer to the kitchen. The jug of cream was a large one and needed both hands to steady it, and so with the basket slung over her arm she left the dairy, her breath a cloud in front of her in the brilliant icy air.

She was never very sure of the order of events which followed. One moment she was looking across the stable-yard and seeing Bruce Travis, one of the stable-lads, leading

Midnight across the cobbles. The next, the shrill cries and shouts of children had her attention as a group of them came hurtling into the yard from the direction of the narrow road which skirted the house, the road Ivy had taken when bringing her to Grange Hall six years ago. From there everything became blurred. She had an image of the stallion rearing up on its hind legs and of Bruce letting go of the reins and falling, and of Master Edmond – tiny and frozen with fear – straight in the path of the magnificent beast with its flailing hooves and maddened eyes. Instinct, the same instinct which would have taken hold if the child in front of her had been one of the Finnigan twins, caused her to drop the jug and basket and race forward.

She had reached the child and scooped him into her arms before she felt the tremendous blow, but even then instinct demanded she curl her shape round that of the child's as they were flung halfway across the yard, to protect him from the impact. They landed. The breath left her body and she thought, So this is what it's like to die. And then . . . nothing.

Chapter 10

Henry Ashton wouldn't have described himself as an emotional man, certainly not since he had fallen in love with Isabella and discovered – for the first time in his hitherto very English upbringing – what passions could burn in the depth of another human being. Isabella was fire against his ice, that was the way he liked to look at their union. She felt deeply about even the smallest thing, and wasn't afraid to say so. He adored that about her. He adored everything about her. He adored his daughters too, but after his son had been born and he had looked at the miniature recreation of himself, his heart had been swamped with a love so fierce and powerful it had terrified him. It still did, if he was truthful.

When he had seen his nieces and nephews and his youngest daughter running pell-mell after his son in some noisy game of their own making – and not a nursemaid in sight – he had been panicked, he admitted it. And he had been right to be panicked. If he lived to be a hundred he would never forget the sight that had confronted him as he'd rounded the corner of the stableyard. The horse, and in front of it, his son. And he knew he was too far away to save him. That there was nothing he could do.

'Darling, he is fast asleep and he will remain so until morning. Doctor Jefferson was adamant there will only be slight bruising to show for this escapade.' Isabella put her hand on her husband's arm, her voice gentle. The day had been an exhausting one. First, the accident as everyone had been leaving which had necessitated the doctor being summoned, not only for their son but the servant girl, and then the inevitable delay before their guests had departed. And Henry had been quite unlike himself, rampaging about the house and dismissing the nursemaids on the spot like that. She was sure he would have dismissed Nanny Price too but for the fact that she had been dealing with Charlotte who was in bed with a stomach upset and feeling very sorry for herself after being awake all night.

'Escapade?' Henry shook his head. They had just retired to the drawing room after dinner, but neither of them had been able to eat more than a bite or two. 'He could have been killed today, Bella. But for this kitchenmaid, it is almost certain he would have been mangled under Midnight's hooves.'

Isabella shut her eyes tightly for a moment. 'I know. I can't bear to think of it. Don't say any more, Henry.'

'He is only three years old but he has the whip hand with Nanny Price. Do you realise that? And those dim-witted nursemaids were worse than useless. I swear they were frightened of him.'

'He's high-spirited, that's all.'

'That is not all and you know it. He has the Ashton determination and stubbornness, along with your father's conviction that he is always right.' They exchanged a smile.

Isabella's father was a very wealthy Italian aristocrat who was as inflexible as he was powerful in his own country, and he had a view about anything and everything which he wasn't shy about expressing. He was also a warm, generous and intelligent man who loved his only daughter very much, and Isabella knew Henry was fond of him. In small doses. Very small doses.

'Do you think this girl, Shelton, will be all right?' Isabella's voice shook a little. 'It appears she is only twenty years old, Henry.'

Henry wasn't at all sure she was going to be all right, but Isabella had been upset enough for one day. 'Of course, it's just a matter of time. The broken arm will heal and once she is fully conscious and recovered from the cuts and bruises and cracked ribs, she'll be as right as rain. Don't worry, Bella.'

Isabella nodded. They had done all they could, she told herself. When Dr Jefferson had expressed his doubts about the wisdom of attempting to move the girl to hospital, they'd had two of the footmen carry her upstairs to the room adjacent to Nanny Price's in the nursery suite which the two nursemaids had occupied until earlier that day. And the private nurse who had arrived within hours to take care of her had been highly recommended by Dr Jefferson.

'We owe her so much, Henry,' she said. 'So much. She didn't think of herself. She was so very brave.'

'Indeed she was.' If the girl recovered, something would have to be done for her. He'd had a word with the butler and ascertained that the girl was of exemplary character. The cook had given a good report about her too. It appeared she had been with them for six years and in that time there had not been a breath of impropriety connected with her, despite the fact she was the prettiest little thing he'd seen for a long time.

A knock at the door preceded the butler entering with the coffee they had decided to take in the drawing room rather than the dining room. After pouring them both a cup, he did not leave immediately but stood by the chair and coughed.

'Yes, Rowan? What is it?'

'It's Cook, sir. She wondered if she might be allowed to see the Shelton girl. There's a family connection.'

'Really? Well, perhaps tomorrow depending on how she is. The doctor was very explicit about no visitors until he gave permission. He's coming again in the morning so we'll know more then. Tell Cook she will be kept informed.'

'Thank you, sir.'

The butler was halfway across the room when a thought occurred to Henry. 'Rowan?'

'Yes, sir?' The butler immediately retraced his footsteps.

'Is Cook informing the girl's family of the situation?'

The butler hesitated. 'She thought it better to wait for a few days, sir. There are no parents or siblings, merely an elderly grandmother who brought the girl up after her parents died when she was a baby. In view of the grand-mother's age Cook judged it best to delay until she had good news to impart.'

'I see. Well, as Cook thinks best.' Henry watched the butler quietly leave the room. He just hoped there was good news. The girl had looked as near death as he'd ever seen anyone look, earlier, and he didn't give much for her chances.

★　★　★

For the next few days it would be true to say that Constance hovered between life and death, but slowly, and due in no small part to the excellent nursing she received from the woman Dr Jefferson had brought to the house, she gained ground. Then came the day when she could sit up in bed propped up by pillows, and the terrible headache and sickness the concussion had caused lessened, although she still slept twenty hours out of twenty-four. It was a full week before she was deemed well enough by Dr Jefferson to have visitors, but when Florence waddled into the room her opening words weren't exactly fortifying. 'Dear gussy, girl, but you do look bad.' Florence's eyes had stretched wide. 'You never did have any meat on your bones but there's nothing left of you now.'

As the nurse gave a disapproving cough, Constance smiled weakly. 'Hello, Cook.'

Florence sat down by the bed, causing the chair to creak in protest. 'How are you feeling?'

'Better.' Although it still hurt even to breathe.

'We're going to have to feed you up, m'girl, I can see that. Now I haven't yet written to your grandmother because' – and here Florence was uncharacteristically tactful – 'I wasn't sure how much you'd want me to say.'

'Oh, I'm glad you didn't, Cook! She'd only worry. I'll write and explain when I'm a bit better.'

'Aye, that'd be best.' Florence glanced round the room which had been the nursemaids' up to the time of the accident. She was pleased to see it wasn't a patch on hers. The two beds and wardrobe and dressing-table the room held were nice enough – functional, she'd say – but there were no frills and fancies, which was as it should be. Nursemaids weren't on a level with herself, after all. But

163

she'd often wondered what their accommodation was like, beens as they were in the main house, so to speak. No doubt Nanny Price's room was a cut above, but that too was as it should be.

Florence only stayed ten minutes but by the time she left Constance was exhausted. She slept the rest of the day, but as an early twilight fell and the nurse closed the curtains against the thick snow which was falling outside, she opened her eyes to see a small figure standing by the bed.

'Hello.' Edmond's round baby face was solemn. 'You're the lady who stopped Papa's horse from kicking me, aren't you? Is your arm better?'

The nurse had turned sharply, saying, 'What are you doing in here?' but Constance smiled at the child. 'My arm's much better, thank you, Master Edmond.'

'Did it hurt a lot?'

'Quite a lot.' She struggled to sit up straighter, wondering how he'd found his way into the room. Elsie, one of the housemaids who saw to the cleaning of the room, had told her the master and mistress had given instructions to Nanny Price that she had to watch the children every moment. When she had protested that that would be difficult without any nursemaids to assist her, the master had reminded her that it was the nursemaids who had nearly got his son killed when he'd been designated to their care. Elsie said that Nanny Price had been weepy for days; she wouldn't be surprised if she applied for another position before long. Needed eyes in the back of her head, she said.

'I don't like strawberries.'

Constance looked into the huge blue eyes staring at her. 'Don't you?' she said, wondering at the change of conversation.

164

'No. The medicine I had to have when Midnight nearly kicked me tasted of strawberries. It was horrible and bright pink.'

Constance nodded. 'I see. I suppose the doctor thought most little boys like strawberries.'

'I don't.' He continued to watch her as he said, 'I spat it out over my bed.'

She forced herself not to smile. 'Do you think a big boy would have done that or taken his medicine like a man? Like your father would have done?'

This was clearly an argument which he'd not heard before. He frowned. 'I'm a big boy.'

He was certainly an extremely articulate and intelligent one for his age. When she had discovered that much of the Finnigan twins' bad behaviour was due to boredom and had persuaded Miss Newton to let her give them sums and reading books far above their age, much of their naughtiness had disappeared overnight. 'So next time you have to take any medicine, you'll swallow it straightaway – even if you don't like it, just as your father and the big boys do?'

Edmond considered this for some moments. Then he nodded slowly and very seriously. 'Yes,' he announced firmly. 'I will.'

'I will hold you to that, Edmond.'

The dry voice from the doorway caused the nurse to bustle forward, her voice prim as she said, 'Why, Sir Henry, I didn't see you there.'

Henry didn't glance at the woman. He appreciated that she was good at her job but he didn't like her. His eyes still on his son, he said, 'Nanny Price is looking for you, Edmond. It is time for your bath, is it not?'

Edmond's lower lip thrust out in a decided pout. 'I don't like—' He looked at Constance as she shook her head. His fair brows coming together, he said, 'Do you like baths, Papa?'

'Of course I do. I like them very much.'

'Did you like them when you were a boy?'

Henry's lips twitched. 'Not much, but I trusted that my father and mother knew best. We cannot always do what we would like to do, merely what is expected of us. Our duty.'

'And is it my duty to have a bath?' Edmond asked solemnly.

'Absolutely, and with good grace.'

'Oh, Sir Henry, you've found him. I left him for two minutes to see to Miss Gwendoline's toilette, that's all.' Nanny Price was breathless and her colour was high as she came up behind Henry in the doorway. 'He was supposed to be undressing.'

At the sight of the nanny Edmond's face took on a pugnacious expression that was comical. There was clearly no love lost between the nanny and the child. Nevertheless, he allowed himself to be led away, turning before he left the room and saying to Constance, 'May I come and see you again tomorrow?'

Constance was at a loss as to what to say. It was Sir Henry who answered. 'Yes, you may – if you behave yourself and don't run away from Nanny Price again.'

The small face that was a miniature of the older one smiled. 'I won't,' he said.

Sir Henry didn't follow his son and the nanny as Constance had expected. Instead he came further into the room. She had vague memories of this cultured male voice asking the nurse how she was now and again, but it was lost in the fog of the first few days after the accident. Now she was covered in confusion. This was the master, the god-like creature whose sensibilities would be offended by the mere sight of a kitchenmaid, and he was not only looking at her but speaking to her.

'I'm told you are on the road to recovery?' he said pleasantly.

'Yes, sir. Thank you, sir.'

'I rather feel it is my wife and myself who should be thanking *you*, Shelton. But for your courage and quick thinking my son would not now be suffering the thing he hates most, a bath. Although he may regard that as a mixed blessing.'

He obviously expected her to smile but she was so overwhelmed it was beyond her. Stammering, she said, 'It – it was nothing, sir. Anyone would have done the same.'

'Now that I doubt.' He paused. 'You have a way with him, with my son. And yet I understand from Cook that you have no brothers or sisters?'

'No, sir, but – but I helped Miss Newton, the schoolmistress, with the bairns – with the children, sir, before I came here.'

'And you like children?'

This time the answer was without hesitation. 'Yes, sir.'

'But you didn't seek a means of employment which would allow you to work with them?'

Constance's head was still aching and faintly muzzy; she couldn't think clearly enough to deflect what could be an awkward line of questioning inasmuch as it might reveal why she left Sacriston. And so she spoke the truth. 'Miss Newton was going to help me become an uncertified teacher, sir, and I would have liked that, but the job of a kitchenmaid came up through my Great Aunt Ivy, Cook's mother.'

'I see.' And Henry thought he did. It took time to train to become a teacher, certified or uncertified, and no doubt the grandmother had been tempted by the thought of immediate financial gain rather than the vague notion of the possibility in the future. To test his theory, he said quietly, 'And your grandmother wanted you to come here?'

'Yes, sir.' Suddenly realising he might have taken her words as a criticism, she added quickly, 'It was a grand opportunity, sir. I'm aware of that.'

He made no comment to this. His voice even quieter, he said, 'You are tired – rest now. It is early days. I'll leave you in Nurse Harley's capable hands.' He left, shutting the door behind him after smiling very kindly at her.

Nurse Harley made a little 'Huh' sound in her throat. 'Very much the Lord of the Manor, that one,' she said as though to herself before plumping up Constance's pillows.

Constance lay back, shutting her eyes. Considering she had slept all day she was deathly tired, but Dr Jefferson had said that would soon pass. And her arm and cracked ribs were paining her tonight. But still, it was lovely to be in this bonny room after the attics, and sleeping in a proper bed with so many blankets she was as warm as toast at night. Dr Jefferson had said it would be seven or eight weeks before her injuries healed, but she supposed Cook would find her jobs to do that she could manage with one hand once she was back on her feet. She would miss this room though. She wouldn't have wished for Master Edmond to have such a fright or for herself to be kicked by the master's horse – she was still black and blue all over, and everything ached when she moved a muscle – but at least she had seen a little of what life was like on the other side of the green–baize door. Not quite in the way she would have liked though.

She smiled to herself, a wry smile, and in a few moments was fast asleep once more.

It was a week later, a full two weeks after the accident, when Constance was summoned to the drawing room. Nurse Harley had been gone some five days but Constance was still residing in the nursemaids' room, although every day she expected to be told she was returning to the kitchen and the attics. Edmond had become a regular visitor, either in the company of his eldest sister, Charlotte, who was a grave, sedate young girl, or with Nanny Price.

Constance found the times with the nanny present a strain. Nanny Price clearly didn't understand her young charge. Charlotte was easy to handle and Gwendoline, although a little more lively than her sister, was also malleable and obedient to the nanny's instructions. Edmond was neither. He ran rings round the poor woman and delighted in making the simplest request by her into a major confrontation. Although the nanny maintained a stiff exterior in front of Constance – as befitted a senior member of staff with a mere kitchenmaid – it was obvious she was at her wits' end more than once. And the little monkey knew it. Constance had seen Edmond's eyes gleam with glee as Nanny Price resorted to chasing him round the room when it was time to go and he refused to budge.

Ivor Gilbert, the same footman who had winked at Constance the day she had arrived at the house for her interview with the butler, came to fetch her from her room.

Since she had risen from her sickbed she'd dressed in her ordinary clothes each day rather than her kitchenmaid's uniform, spending most of her time sitting in a chair by the window which looked out over the front drive. At his knock, she put down the book she had been reading and stood up, her heart pounding faster. Elsie had told her the master and mistress would see her downstairs at three o'clock when she'd brought her luncheon tray earlier, and since then Constance's stomach had been turning over with apprehension. She had expected to be told to return to her duties in the kitchen this week by Cook or Mrs Craggs; she couldn't imagine why the master would want to see her. Ivor smiled at her when she opened the door, his gaze falling on her arm in its white cloth sling for a moment. 'Hello, lass, it's nice to see you on your feet again,' he said warmly, his eyes lingering on the beautiful face in front of him. 'We all thought you were a goner, you know. There was a right do in the kitchen. Cook was in tears and in a state for days on end.'

'Was she?' Constance was touched and not a little amazed.

'She heard the commotion and came outside to see what was happening and saw you lying on the ground with Master Edmond, and Bruce trying to get Midnight back into his stall. She thought you'd gone then and there. Cathleen gave her a couple of cups of tea laced with brandy for the shock, and she was so tiddly she put sugar in the soup rather than salt. Luckily the master and mistress were so upset they sent back course after course untouched that night anyway.'

The picture he'd painted was so funny Constance couldn't help smiling.

'That's better,' said Ivor softly. 'You looked scared to death when you opened the door, and there's no cause to be frightened. Everyone knows you saved Master Edmond's life. Now come on, we mustn't keep the master and mistress waiting.'

She followed him into the narrow corridor she had glimpsed when folk had opened and shut the door during the time she had been confined to the room. Unlike the nursemaids' room, which had bare floorboards, the corridor was carpeted but dark, illumination coming from several lamps in brackets which were fixed head height on the wall. There were a number of doors leading off on the same side as the nursemaids' room, and as they passed these, Ivor said, 'This is the children's school and day room; this is the nursery bathroom and closet; this is Miss Charlotte and Miss Gwendoline's room, and this is Master Edmond's. This last one is Nanny Price's bedroom and sitting room, and there's an interior interconnecting door to Master Edmond's room from hers.'

As they came to the end of the corridor Ivor opened a door and they stepped on to a galleried landing. Constance stopped dead, looking about her in wonder. She felt as though she had emerged into another world, a fairytale world of colour and light and space. The thick gold carpet under her feet, the gold frames of the huge pictures on the walls, the dark wood tables set at intervals along the landing with great bowls of hot-house flowers scenting the air; it was all magnificent, unbelievable.

But she didn't have time to stand and gape. Ivor was already waiting for her at the top of the massive winding staircase that led down to the ground floor, and as she hurried to his side, he murmured, 'Mr Howard will see

171

you in to the master and mistress, he's waiting in the hall.'

Constance nodded but said nothing. In all the time she had been at Grange Hall the house steward hadn't so much as acknowledged her existence. Even on the social occasions which took place in the servants' hall – the suppers and balls at Christmas and Twelfth Night and May Day – Mr Howard had kept his distance with the junior staff. Constance had often thought he'd be a perfect match for Mrs Craggs; the pair of them were cold and forbidding, with eyes that looked straight through you as though you didn't exist.

The hall was a larger version of the galleried landing with couches and small tables dotted about its vast expanse, but she didn't have time to take much in. Ivor hurried her along to where the house steward was waiting, resplendent in his coat and tails. The expression on his face did nothing to alleviate her nerves.

'Come along, come along.' Granite-hard eyes inspected her from head to foot. 'The master and mistress are waiting.' She had clearly committed a crime of momentous proportions in not appearing a minute or so before. 'And don't fidget, girl. The master can't abide fidgeting.'

Ivor knocked on the drawing-room door and then opened it, standing aside as Mr Howard led the way into the room. If she had thought the hall magnificent, the drawing room was more so, but the swift impression she received of walls filled with paintings and gold-framed mirrors, gleaming furniture and floor-to-ceiling windows framed by heavy blue drapes was brushed aside as the house steward turned and, with a hand on her shoulder, pressed her forward. Sir Henry was sitting in an armchair to one side of the biggest fireplace Constance had ever seen, and Lady Isabella reclined on a couch with a small dog on her lap. They were both smiling, but Constance was too nervous to notice.

Sir Henry had accompanied his children a few times when they had come to her room in the afternoon, but Lady Isabella only once. On that occasion she had expressed her thanks for Constance's swift thinking and action on the day of the accident, said she hoped she would soon recover from her injuries, and left shortly afterwards. Elsie had told her one day that Lady Isabella was not of a strong constitution, and the lady's-maid had told Nanny Price who had told her head nursemaid who had presumably told Elsie, that the doctors had warned Sir Henry and Lady Isabella that a fourth confinement could be disastrous. As it was, Lady Isabella had to rest most afternoons, whether there were guests staying or not, and some days remained in her rooms until evening. It was something to do with her heart, Elsie had whispered.

Constance thought of this now as she looked into the pale, beautiful face of the woman lying on the couch, remembering just in time to bob a curtsy to her and then to Sir Henry. She was so overawed by her surroundings that the etiquette which had been drummed into her since arriving at Grange Hall had deserted her for a few moments which would never do, especially with Mr Howard watching.

'Ah, Shelton. How's the arm?' Sir Henry nodded at the sling. 'And the ribs, of course. Damned painful, cracked ribs.'

'All right, thank you, sir.'

'Good, good. Not too painful?'

'No, sir. Thank you.'

'Capital, capital. Now you're probably wondering why Lady Isabella and I want to speak to you.' He didn't wait for her to comment but went on, 'We are greatly in your debt, Shelton, but of course you know this. Now my wife and I have a proposition to put to you, one which you may wish to think over for a day or two. As you know, the children's nursemaids were dismissed' – for a moment an expression crossed his face which made Constance swallow – 'and at present Nanny Price has her hands full.'

He smiled and Constance forced her mouth to move in response.

'This state of affairs cannot continue. My daughters are one thing, they are older than Edmond, of course, and a large part of their day is taken up with Miss Lyndon, the governess who comes daily to instruct them in all matters appertaining to becoming young ladies.'

Constance knew about Miss Lyndon but she had never seen her. The servant grapevine had informed her that the governess was the daughter of the rector of the parish, a refined and well-educated young woman who was also unfortunately as plain as a pikestaff with a deformity in one leg which required her to wear a surgical boot. Whether it was this which had persuaded her to take up the occupation as a governess no one knew, but it was generally agreed that Miss Lyndon had been most fortunate to acquire a post so close to home which meant she was still able to live at the Rectory and was therefore not restricted by the rules of the house in her free time.

'Edmond, as you have probably already gathered, is not like his sisters. He is very high-spirited and inquisitive, and the combination is a little much for Nanny Price.'

Behind her Constance heard Mr Howard shift his feet slightly. She knew exactly what he was thinking. It wasn't right for the master to make an observation about one of the senior servants which might be construed as criticism to one of such lowly rank as herself. She wasn't sure if Sir Henry had also cottoned on, but when he next spoke it was to the house steward, and his voice was sharp. 'That's all for the moment, Howard, and before you go bring that chair over here for Shelton to sit down.'

Constance didn't dare to look at the house steward as she sat down on the small cushioned chair he provided a moment later. But it wasn't as if she'd asked to sit down, was it, she reassured herself. She knew no one could do that in front of the master; it was unheard-of. Nevertheless, she was grateful for Sir Henry's thoughtfulness. Her arm was paining her and her ribs still ached from contact with Midnight's hooves; just the walk down to the drawing room had taken it out of her more than she would have thought possible.

'I understand you worked with the local schoolmistress in your village before you left to come here?' Lady Isabella addressed her, her Italian accent noticeable.

Constance inclined her head as she murmured, 'Yes, my lady.'

'And you enjoyed working with children?'

'Yes, my lady.'

'How many children were you in charge of?'

Constance hesitated. 'I wasn't exactly in charge, my lady.' She didn't want them to get the wrong idea. 'I helped the teacher, Miss Newton. There were about thirty most days.' She didn't mention here that some of the mining families rarely sent their children to school if they were needed at home or could earn a wage in the summer working in farmers' fields picking turnips or scaring the crows away. 'I looked after the infants, the little ones.'

'And were they well-behaved?'

Again Constance hesitated. It probably wouldn't look very good if she said they weren't, but her innate honesty led her to say, 'Mostly, my lady, except for the Finnigan twins.'

'The Finnigan twins?'

'They were two little boys from one of the poorer families, my lady. The family were Irish and there were a lot of them.'

'And they were disobedient, these twins?'

'They could be right little devils. Oh, beg your pardon, my lady, I mean they were . . .' Constance searched for a word, her face red, '. . . high-spirited. But—' She stopped, aware she had been in danger of talking too freely, which the master and mistress would find disrespectful.

'Yes, but?' Lady Isabella queried.

'It was only because they were bored most of the time, my lady. They were bright, see, but being the youngest in a family of eighteen' – Lady Isabella blinked – 'no one had any time for them. And so they thought of things to amuse themselves.'

'And how did you overcome the problem of the Finnigan twins?' Sir Henry's wife asked, a brightness in her eyes which indicated amusement. 'If you did, indeed, overcome it, of course.'

It was obvious, wasn't it? 'I set them the same sums as the older ones had and helped them learn to read, my lady. Miss Newton was a lovely lady and she had lots of books she'd bought for the school out of her own pocket. At first she thought Moses and Aaron—'

'Moses and Aaron?' the other woman interrupted her.

'The family were devout Catholics, my lady, and all their bairns – their children – had Bible names, mostly New Testament, but I think they'd run out of them by the time the twins came. Anyway, Miss Newton thought the twins would tear or dirty the books, but they didn't.'

'I'm glad to hear it.' Lady Isabella appeared to be struggling. She coughed, holding her handkerchief to the lower part of her face for a few moments before she said, her voice shaking slightly, 'And did you find the – the Finnigan twins hard work?'

'In a way, my lady, but I liked them. The things they came out with . . .' Again Constance stopped. Her tongue was running away with her. 'They were interesting,' she finished weakly.

Lady Isabella turned to her husband. 'You were right,' she said cryptically. 'Perfect.'

Sir Henry nodded. Leaning forward, his hands on his knees, he stared at Constance. 'How would you like to take the place of the nursemaids? Not to see to Miss Charlotte and Miss Gwendoline, Nanny Price can be responsible for them, but Edmond needs the sole attention of someone, and I rather think that someone is you. He has taken to you, that's the main thing, and you have a way with him. Rather than a nursemaid, your position would be that of an under-nanny, which would necessitate a higher salary. Shall we say . . . seventy pounds a year?'

Constance's eyebrows moved upwards and her eyes opened wide but she couldn't speak. She was aware they were doing this because she had saved Master Edmond from being trampled, but seventy pounds was as much as a fully experienced nanny could hope for. She had seen a post advertised just the other day in the *Yorkshire Chronicle* which Cook had been reading.

'The position would also mean you would accompany Master Edmond when we visit my family for two months in the summer.' Lady Isabella was speaking again. 'You would also come with us in the spring when we take the waters in Bath, and in the autumn when we visit a branch of Sir Henry's family in Scotland for the shooting and fishing. You are not averse to travelling?'

Italy. Lady Isabella's family had an estate in Italy. And to see Bath, and Scotland. Aware they were both looking at her, she whispered, 'Sir, my lady, thank you, thank you.'

'You are decided? Good, good.' Sir Henry rang for the house steward. 'Once your arm is mended you may take up your duties, but in the meantime you might like to acquaint yourself with the workings of the nursery suite on an informal basis. Nanny Price will answer any questions you may have.'

'And we will have to see about a uniform for you,' said Lady Isabella as Mr Howard knocked and opened the door. 'And a suitable wardrobe for those times when you are off-duty, especially when travelling abroad. I shall give Mrs Craggs the necessary instructions.'

Constance rose to her feet. The sudden change in her circumstances was too much to take in. With tears in her eyes, she whispered again, 'Thank you, sir. Thank you, my lady.' In a daze she allowed the house steward to lead her from the room, and it was only when she was in the hall that she realised she hadn't made a final curtsy.

When the door closed behind Constance, Isabella

glanced across at her husband. 'Moses and Aaron,' she murmured, a gurgle in her voice, 'because they had run out of New Testament names.'

'And they were right little devils. Oh, beg your pardon, my lady. High-spirited.'

They looked at each other a moment more before bursting into laughter.

Chapter 11

Mabel Gray was sitting in Ruth Heath's kitchen, Constance's letter in her hand, but she was experiencing a curious feeling of deflation without really knowing why. When she had received her granddaughter's amazing news that morning she had been beside herself, and it being a Saturday had hardly been able to contain her impatience until she was due to visit Ruth after lunch. But in the event, the telling of Constance saving her employer's son's life and her rise to under-nanny and all that entailed had been something of an anti-climax. Perhaps it had something to do with the fact that Matt and Tilly and Rebecca had been there when she arrived. Although everyone had oohed and ahhed – everyone except Tilly, that was – somehow she'd sensed their heart wasn't in it. She hadn't made mention of the most extraordinary thing of all either, the seventy pounds, not with the men being in the middle of another strike and money so tight.

Perhaps Ruth sensed how she was feeling because now Matt's mother leaned across the kitchen table and squeezed her arm as she said, 'You must be proud, lass, of what your

Constance did. And they must think a bit of her to give her such an opportunity. Travelling, you say, and to Italy an' all. Who'd have thought it? Matt had a notion he'd like to take off to foreign parts when he was a lad, isn't that right, Matt?'

Tilly had been bending forward looking at a picture Rebecca had drawn on her slate as Ruth had spoken. As she straightened she made a little sound in her throat which could have meant anything, but which caused Matt to look daggers at her. Answering his mother, he said flatly, 'I don't remember.'

'Oh aye, full of it you were for a while. Your da picked up a picture book from one of the mining galas about Egypt and lost civilisations, moth-eaten old thing it was even then, but you pored over that book until it fell to pieces. Made up your mind you were going to be an explorer.'

Tilly made the sound again. 'Didn't get very far, did you?'

The bitterness in Matt's voice when he said, 'No, more's the pity,' was embarrassing, and when the back door opened in the next moment and Andrew and Olive and their brood walked in, Mabel heaved a silent sigh of relief.

There was no disguising the fact that Matt and Tilly couldn't stand the sight of each other these days, and Matt had no time for the bairn – Ruth had told her that. Which was a shame because Rebecca was a nice little thing and the very image of her mam. Although Tilly brought the bairn round to see her grandparents and the others every Saturday afternoon, Matt rarely accompanied them, but then with there being no football due to the weather, she supposed he hadn't got an excuse not to come today.

Ruth, her voice overloud, was urging her to tell her news to the newcomers, and when she did their reaction

181

was warm and genuine. But it was too late. She felt all at sixes and sevens now. She'd get back to their Molly's when she could. Their Pearl was bringing the new baby round – she could use her granddaughter as her excuse and she was longing to see her great-grandson anyway.

When, after a decent interval, she got up to go she was surprised when Matt stood up too. 'I'll see you along the back lane, Mrs Gray. It's frozen solid out there and there's places it's treacherous.'

They didn't speak until they were out of the backyard. Then Matt took her arm as they began walking over the icy ridges and glassy puddles, and said quietly, 'When you write back to Constance, tell her I'm pleased for her, would you, Mrs Gray? And glad she wasn't hurt too badly, of course.'

'Aye, I'll do that, Matt, although between the two of us I think she was hurt more than she's let on to me or she'd have written sooner. And it's funny Florence didn't let me know. Still, all's well that ends well and it looks like she's landed on her feet, sure enough. She's always made light of slaving away in that kitchen but I know she wouldn't have chosen that sort of work if—' Mabel stopped abruptly, aware that she'd said too much.

'But . . .' Matt's brow wrinkled. 'She wanted to go into service, didn't she? You said—'

'Aye, I know what I said, lad, but to tell you the truth there was a reason she had to leave.'

'A reason?' Matt stopped walking, turning Mabel round to look at him. 'What reason?'

'Oh, it's nowt, lad. It's done with now.'

'What reason, Mrs Gray?'

'There was a man who was bothering her, that's all.'

'A man?'

'Oh, don't look like that, lad. Nowt happened. But he was the type who wouldn't have given up and he'd frightened her. We thought it was best for her to get away.'

'Who was it? What's his name?'

'I'm sorry, Matt, but I can't tell you that.'

'Mrs Gray—'

'No, Matt, I can't.' Her tone was final. 'It wouldn't be right.'

'So he still lives in the village?'

Mabel pulled her arm loose and began walking again so he was forced to do the same. Her head down, she said quietly, 'We dealt with it as we saw fit, and as I said, it's done with.'

She had said a man. Not a lad, a man. Matt felt sick.

'So that was why she went so suddenly without saying goodbye to anyone and why you've never said where she is?'

'It was for the best, lad, believe me. He'd scared her half to death and I think he'd got it in him to be a nasty piece of work. She was best out of it.'

Names were flying round his head and being dismissed with equal speed. 'You should have told me. I'd have sorted him out.'

'We didn't even tell her granda, lad. Like I said, I reckon he could be violent, and you never know with a man like that. Least said, soonest mended.'

If she came out with one more platitude, he'd scream. Constance had been forced to leave, she had been frightened and intimidated by some swine, and he hadn't known. He'd just continued on his merry way and all the time—

'If you tell me his name —'

183

'– there'll be hell to pay,' Mabel finished for him. 'And what good would that do? It's in the past now and best left there. And it's done the lass a good turn in the long run. She wouldn't be where she is now if she'd stayed in Sacriston. She'll get to see a bit of the world, experience all sorts of things any other lass would give her eye-teeth for. It's a grand place where she is, Matt, and even if she came back here tomorrow, what is there for her? She's outgrown us,' Mabel finished, a touch of sadness in her voice now.

They had reached the end of the lane and a few desultory flakes of snow were being blown in the arctic wind. Mabel shivered. 'You get back to your mam's, lad. I'll be fine from here, and I'll be sure to give Constance your best wishes when I write.'

She turned after patting his arm and Matt watched the small stout figure clothed in black until it disappeared round the corner and was lost to view.

Constance. Oh, Constance, Constance. He leaned against the wall of the last house in the terrace, his hands in his pockets and his cap pulled low over his eyes. If only he'd had the gumption to follow his heart all those years ago, who knows what might have happened? That afternoon in her grandma's kitchen, something had passed between him and Constance, something indefinable, but she had been so young and he'd been hooked up with Tilly, and then like a will-o'-the-wisp she'd taken herself out of his life. And maybe she hadn't felt like he felt anyway.

He took off his cap and raked his fingers through his hair before pulling it on again.

Excuses. Excuses, excuses, excuses, damn it. He was good at those. Why hadn't he thrown Tilly out on the street the day she'd told him she was expecting a baby? He'd known it wasn't his, and not just because they'd only come together the once, on the wedding night. The 'upset tummy' she'd had for weeks and which she maintained had been brought on by nerves after his treatment of her, the subtle but distinct change in her figure when she was in her nightdress, the fact she hadn't gone running to her mother with tales of his cruelty in ignoring her very existence day after day, all spoke of one thing. She'd been in the family way when she'd walked up the aisle and she had known it. And now she had to maintain the illusion of togetherness.

No one believed the premature baby story. Rebecca had been a plump and bonny seven-pounder, nothing like the scrawny little scrap Andrew's Toby had been when he'd been born six weeks early. No, everyone had known but of course they'd all assumed the baby was his, that they'd jumped the wedding night a mite early as more than one engaged couple did. Nothing had been said directly to him or Tilly, but he could imagine the conversations that had gone on behind closed doors. 'They're not the first and they won't be the last.' 'Well, what can you expect when the sap's running high and they know they're going to be wed shortly?' 'At least he did the decent thing and married the lass, but then who wouldn't jump at the chance of marrying a bonny lass like he's got?' And so on and so forth.

Oh aye, he'd walked round for weeks after Rebecca's birth knowing what folk were thinking and hearing the edge to their words of congratulation. And Tilly, no matter how he'd ranted and raved in that first couple of days after she'd told him she was expecting, she'd looked him straight in the face, her eyes never flinching from his, and maintained the baby was his. She'd even had the gall to say the 'premature' birth was a result of the mental suffering he'd inflicted on her since the wedding night. He hadn't touched her since that night and nor would he. She had his name but he was damn sure she wouldn't have any other part of him. Just to look at her now made him sick.

Many was the time he'd wonder what his brothers would say if he told them he'd only had her the once. But they wouldn't believe him. No one would believe him. Why would any man be such a fool as to work and provide for a bairn that wasn't his and a wife that was little better than a whore, just to save face? They'd say he was barmy, a candidate for the asylum, and they'd be right. But although his guts writhed every time he walked into the house, he'd rather be sliced open and have them spill out on the ground than anyone suspect the truth.

He heaved himself off the wall and began walking slowly back towards his mother's backyard. Who was this bloke who'd had Constance so scared she'd taken off and left everything and everyone dear to her? And Mabel, she'd worshipped the ground the lass walked on. Why hadn't she made a stand rather than lose her? It didn't make sense, but then women's logic was beyond him at the best of times. How had Tilly thought she had a chance of fooling him that he was the first and the father of Rebecca? But perhaps she hadn't cared, once the ring was on her finger. He had been the simpleton she'd fastened on when she'd decided she wanted a meal-ticket for life, and in truth she'd known him better than he'd known himself. She'd banked on the fact that he'd keep quiet rather than be known as the buffoon who'd let himself be duped. Aye, she'd had his measure, all right.

'Da, I've been waiting for you.'

Rebecca came running towards him when he was halfway down the lane, and when she nearly went head-long on a piece of ice he caught hold of her arm, his voice harsh when he said, 'What's your mam doing, letting you out here without your hat and coat? You'll freeze to death or break your neck.'

Subdued now, the child answered, 'I slipped out to wait for you without Mam knowing. If I'd got my coat she'd have twigged.'

As Matt looked down at the small head he sighed inwardly. Rebecca was a miniature replica of her mother, and if Tilly loved anyone she loved her daughter. He, on the other hand, had never made any secret of the fact he had little time for Rebecca, but such are the quirks of nature that the child adored him and would escape her mother's presence whenever she could. More gently now, he said, 'Look, it's beginning to snow and here's you in your clean Saturday pinny with your hair in a ribbon and you're going to get wet. Come on out of it.'

When a small hand crept into his as they walked along he didn't remove it but it held no joy for him. If Tilly hadn't fallen for a bairn he doubted she would have gone through with marrying him; they'd had one row after another in the weeks leading up to the wedding day – most of which, he had to admit, had been down to him. Looking back, he could see she had known he didn't love her, even before he'd fully realised it himself, but she'd stuck with him because she'd needed a patsy to pin the label of da on for her child.

Times he'd searched Rebecca's face for a clue as to who had fathered her, but she was Tilly to a T, it was as simple as that. Outwardly, that was. In nature she had none of her mother's brashness. Although she was as bright as a button the child was shy, reflective even. His mam always described her as having an old head on young shoulders and she was right.

When they reached the backyard Matt braced himself for entering the house. The family get-togethers he had once loved he now loathed and avoided whenever he could; they brought the strain of living a lie to the fore, and ofttimes he sensed his family's sympathies were all with Tilly. She was bonny and amiable and kept the house clean and himself and the child well fed; his own mother had said that to him a few months ago when she'd asked him what was wrong between his wife and himself. Whereas he was seen as a morose individual who didn't know on which side his bread was buttered; his mother had said that an' all when he'd told her to mind her own business.

'I've done a picture for you on my slate.'

Rebecca brought him back to himself and he looked down at her as he opened the back door and they stepped into the scullery. 'Oh aye?' he said without any real interest.

'It's of a bird flying in the sky, flying high above the rooftops and all the people far below.' Her fingers were still resting in his and her small face was solemn. 'And there's another bird, a little one, with it. They – they're together.'

For a moment, a brief moment, the gnawing loneliness that was always with him these days lifted. His fingers closing more tightly round Rebecca's, he said softly, 'Come and show me, hinny.' And he opened the kitchen door.

Chapter 12

In the five years that had passed since Constance had been promoted to under-nanny her life had changed beyond recognition. Sir Henry and Lady Isabella had been as good as their word and she had travelled with the family to Italy each summer to stay at Lady Isabella's father's country estate on the eastern shore of Lake Garda. The Morosini family also had magnificent townhouses in Florence and Rome, but Lady Isabella preferred the beauty and tranquillity of the Garda estate where the children could run wild in a way they were never allowed to do in England, and where each day she seemed to increase in strength and vitality.

On Constance's first trip, the vibrant colours of Italy had dazzled her: the azure sky, cobalt sea, golden sunshine day after magical day, silver olive trees and green vines, and white marble. The villa itself was a splendid sixteenth-century fairytale castle of a place, built in pinkish terracotta bricks with turrets and spires which perfectly complemented the richness of its interior decoration. The villa was shaded by huge chestnut trees, and a terrace which ran the length of the three-storey building overlooked the lake and a shallow harbour for fishing boats.

All the children's meals were eaten al fresco on the terrace, and over the summer Gwendoline and Edmond turned nut brown, although Charlotte, already beginning to think like a little lady, wore a big straw hat to shade her complexion and carried a parasol when she was outside.

For the rest of her life Constance was to look back at those wonderful summers as an awakening of a part of her she hadn't been aware existed but which changed her irrevocably. Sir Henry and Lady Isabella liked to expose the children to culture and history, so although a great deal of the time was spent swimming and fishing in the lake and sailing in the company of Roberto, the Morosinis' boatman, other days were devoted to visiting churches and cathedrals, art galleries, and ancient buildings and amphitheatres. One evening Edmond was left in the care of the Morosini bevy of servants and Constance accompanied Charlotte and Gwendoline and Nanny Price, along with members of the family, to Verona for a performance of *Romeo and Juliet*. Constance had had no idea what to expect, but when they reached the Piazza dei Signori and the production began, she was entranced. Italy itself entranced her. Each time they had to leave to return to England she felt like crying along with the children.

Her new life hadn't been all plain sailing at first though. Sir Henry had made her position as one of the upper servants very clear to Mr Howard and Mrs Craggs, but that didn't mean they had to like the fact that a mere kitchenmaid was now one of their elite circle. Surprisingly it was Nanny Price – with whom Constance had expected to be at odds – who proved to be her greatest ally, along with Florence, who bathed in the reflected glow of Constance's act of heroism, being 'family'. The fact that Constance had, in one fell swoop, taken Edmond off the nanny's hands, was the main cause of her favour with Enid Price at first, but then due to Constance's willingness to learn and her unassuming manner, the older woman began to treat her kindly for herself. Eventually Estelle Upton, Lady Isabella's personal maid, and Sidney Black, the valet, included Constance in their conversation at mealtimes in Mr Howard's room, but the house steward, along with Mrs Craggs and Mr Rowan, stubbornly refused to do more than acknowledge her presence. She hadn't come up the hard way, Mr Howard was heard to mutter to Mrs Craggs and the butler. She hadn't earned her stripes, and he, for one, didn't agree with elevating a mere slip of a girl to such dizzy heights.

Constance knew exactly how the three felt. She could hardly fail to notice their disapproval, but with Enid and Florence backing her and Estelle and Sidney on her side she ceased to worry about it after a while. The master and mistress were for her. She knew it and the rest of the household servants knew it, and in the long run that was all that mattered. Master Edmond could be a bit of a handful at times and she longed to see more of her grandma – Ivy had brought her a few times since Constance had been promoted but it was never enough – but on the whole she was happier than she had ever expected to be away from the village and Matt. Indeed, that life – and even Matt too – had faded into little more than a pleasant memory. The girl who had fallen so hopelessly in love was a different being from the woman she was now. Grange Hall was real. Travelling to Italy and Bath and Scotland with the family was real. Sitting in with Mr Wynford, the young tutor who was employed to prepare Edmond for preparatory school when he was a little older, was real. Already she knew a smattering of Latin and French, and she had been able to converse sufficiently well in Italian to make herself understood since her second visit there. Mr Wynford had informed her that she had a natural aptitude for languages. Some people had it and some didn't, he'd told her, and she definitely had a propensity that way.

She glanced at him now as she listened to Edmond stumbling through his French verbs. He was a nice young man, good-looking in a slightly foppish sort of way, but when he had asked her to call him Nicholas when it was just the two of them and Edmond in the room, she'd known she had to make it clear she wasn't interested in him in 'that' sort of way. It wasn't that she didn't like him or find him interesting, she could listen to him for hours when he was talking about literature and the Classics, but there was no spark. Nothing that made her heart beat faster.

She glanced out of the schoolroom window. The day was hot, the odd fluffy white cloud sailing in the blue sky. Green velvet lawns, bathed in sunshine, stretched away into the distance, neatly manicured flowerbeds and sculpted trees adding to the charm of the grounds. Through the open window the sweet heavy scent of full-blown roses drifted into the room now and again on the warm breeze. The outer walls of Grange Hall were covered with the carefully cultivated flowers, along with rare honeysuckles and other creepers in bloom.

Constance stretched surreptitiously. They had only recently returned from Italy after their two months at the

Morosini villa, and it wasn't only the children who found it hard to adapt to being home, especially when the weather seemed determined to remind them of long hot days watching the wild birds on Lake Garda and eating fish drawn straight out of the water and cooked to perfection by the Morosinis' excellent chef.

Not that she was complaining, she told herself in the next moment. Not a bit of it. She was only too aware that the kitchen staff would be toiling away in the bowels of the house with barely a shaft of sunlight falling on them, whereas shortly she and Edmond would be free to take a walk in the grounds until teatime.

When the schoolroom door opened and Estelle beckoned her, Constance made her apologies to Mr Wynford, told Edmond to be a good boy until she returned and then followed Estelle into the narrow corridor. 'Lady Isabella wants to see you in the drawing room,' Estelle said quickly, 'and Connie, your aunty is with Cook in the kitchen. I think it might be bad news from home.'

Constance didn't wait to hear any more, fairly flying down the corridor and on to the landing. There she remembered herself and forced her feet to walk down the winding staircase when she really wanted to run, but none of the senior staff would behave in such an undignified way. When she tapped on the door and entered the drawing room, Lady Isabella was standing in front of the fireplace and Constance saw immediately that she was troubled.

'Come in, Shelton, and sit down.' Lady Isabella sat down herself as she spoke, indicating a chair opposite hers with a wave of her hand. 'Has Upton told you your aunt has arrived unexpectedly?' And without waiting for an answer: 'Yes, yes, of course she would have done. I'm afraid your aunt's the bearer of grave news. It appears your grandmother is seriously ill.'

Constance's body slumped for a moment before she pulled herself straight. Seriously ill. That meant she was still alive. For a moment she had thought the worst.

'Your aunt is prepared to escort you home at once. I understand she is partaking of some refreshment but then she will be ready to leave. And you must stay as long as you are needed, my dear. I know that is what Sir Henry will say when he returns from Town. I'm sure seeing you will do your grandmother good.'

'But – but Master Edmond, my lady?'

'He will miss you, of course, but you have trained him well.' Lady Isabella smiled and Constance forced herself to smile back. 'Nanny Price will see to him, and Miss Charlotte and Miss Gwendoline will do their part – they are very good with him. You may tell him that you are leaving for a short time and why, but I suggest you give no specific date as to your return or he will be counting the days as only he can. Please give your grandmother my best wishes and tell her we hope she will soon be fully recovered. And Constance' – it was the first time Lady Isabella had called her by her Christian name but Constance was too het-up to notice – 'please take this to help with any expenses you might incur.' She pressed a small velvet purse into her hand.

A little dazedly, Constance murmured, 'Thank you, my lady, but there's no need . . .'

'It's a trifle, that's all. Now go and collect your things and I'll have your aunt's horse and trap brought to the front steps.'

Even in her deep anxiety Constance knew such an

action would cause Mr Howard to become apoplectic. 'Thank you, my lady, but I'll go to the kitchens and say goodbye to Cook before I leave, if that's all right, and go from there.'

'As you wish, my dear, and do try not to worry too much on the journey home. It may not be as serious as your aunt fears.'

Once Constance had left Lady Isabella, she sped up to the schoolroom to make her goodbyes to Edmond and Mr Wynford, then she hastily threw a few necessities into her big cloth bag, changed out of her uniform into a summer dress and jacket and hurried down to the kitchen. The normal bustle and chatter was subdued, and Florence was sitting with her arm round her mother's shoulders when she entered. Constance looked at her great-aunt's red-rimmed eyes. 'It's bad?' she said weakly, her heart pounding.

Ivy nodded. 'A stroke, hinny. Out of the blue, so your Uncle Edwin said. One minute she was laughing at something or other Molly had said, and the next . . .' She shook her head. 'Molly sent Edwin to tell me and asked if I'd bring you as soon as I could. I left straight away, and if you're ready we'll go now.'

Florence stood up, fetching a basket one of the kitchen-maids had just placed on the table. 'There's food and drink for the journey,' she said quietly, handing it to her mother before awkwardly patting Constance's arm. 'Try not to worry, lass.'

Funny, that's what Lady Isabella had said. *Try not to worry.* But how could she *not* worry? Constance thought as she and Ivy walked across the courtyard and into the stable-yard where the horse and trap were waiting.

The birds were singing in the trees bordering the drive as the trap bowled out of the grounds, the flowerbeds a mass of scarlet, crimson, blue, yellow and orange – a picture, as her grandma would have said. How could her grandma be so ill on such a beautiful day as this one? Fear gripped Constance, stark and gut-wrenching. It was such a long journey back to Sacriston – what if they weren't in time? What if she didn't get to say how much she loved her grandma? She hadn't said it enough.

They had been travelling for some time and the sun's rays were losing much of the fierce heat of the day when Constance remembered Lady Isabella's purse which she had stuffed into the pocket of her jacket. She drew it out, pulling the cords apart and reaching inside. It contained a number of large white pound-notes. A trifle, her employer had said. She was so kind, Sir Henry too, and on her visits to Italy the Morosini family had made far more of her than they would a normal servant. On her first stay at the villa five years ago, Lady Isabella's father had taken her aside and personally thanked her, most profusely, for saving the life of his grandson, and he'd had tears in his eyes.

She blinked, knowing she mustn't let herself break down. Suddenly her new life was unimportant; she'd gladly give it up and everything that it held for a few precious minutes with her grandma. Life had a way of bringing you back down to earth when you least expected it, she thought wretchedly.

Chapter 13

Everything was the same. The Boer War had started and finished since she'd been away; Queen Victoria had died after forty years of mourning her beloved Prince Albert, and Edward VII had been crowned King; there had been earthquakes and assassinations and famines in all parts of the globe, and yet Sacriston was unchanged. Constance stared at the silent houses as the horse clip-clopped down Front Street in the dead of night. And then, when they passed the Cross Streets and continued into New Town before turning into Blackett Street, she bit hard on her lip. Things *were* different. The home she'd known for the first thirteen years of her life had other folk living in it now, her granda was gone and her grandma . . . Oh, her grandma.

The horse was weary. When Ivy tied the reins to a lamp-post he gave a soft whinny as though asking where his stable was. 'All right, Ned, don't fret.' Ivy briefly stroked the velvet muzzle. 'I'll see to you in a minute, old lad. There's a nice stall left open for you at the smithy tonight, it's all arranged.'

Molly opened the front door before they had a chance to knock. Constance stared into her tear-ravished face and couldn't say a word, so great was her fear. And then Molly was drawing them inside, saying, 'She's sinking fast but it's as if she's been waiting for you, lass. We told her you were coming and she knew – even the doctor said she knew. Come on up, hinny, don't delay.'

Constance didn't delay. The door to the second bedroom was open and Edwin was sitting by the bed, but he rose immediately to his feet, saying, 'Look who's come to see you, Mam. Didn't we say she was coming? Well, here she is.'

Constance moved to the bedside, her eyes fixed on the small figure under the covers. It had only been three months or so since she'd last seen her grandma. Ivy had brought her to Grange Hall shortly before they had begun packing for Italy in the middle of June, but in that short time she seemed to have shrunk to half her size, and her face wasn't her face any more. Knowing she had to hide her horror and distress as best she could, Constance knelt by the bed and kissed the contorted mouth gently.

'Grandma, it's me, Constance. I've come home and I can stay and look after you. I love you, Grandma.'

One side of her grandma's face was so twisted the eye was closed, but as Constance spoke the other eye opened and looked straight at her. Then the hand on that side made a feeble movement and immediately Constance took it in hers, holding it against her chest as she whispered, 'I'm not going to leave you, Grandma. I'm here now. Aunt Ivy is here too. I'm going to stay until you're better, all right? I love you, Grandma. I love you so much.' Putting her arms round her, she pressed her cheek to that of her grandmother's, murmuring all the time, 'I love you, Grandma, I love you. I love you all the world.'

It was only when the crick in her neck forced her to straighten after a minute or two that she realised what had happened. Death had smoothed out the distorted features and brought peace to the face that was utterly her grandma's again. She looked as though she was sleeping, and for a desperate moment Constance tried to believe that was so, but even before Molly's broken voice whispered, 'She's gone, hinny, she's gone. I told you she was waiting for you,' she knew.

'*She's* back.'

'What?' Matt had just got in from a double shift and he was dog tired. Too tired to play any of Tilly's games. All he wanted was a wash, his dinner and bed, in that order.

Tilly had got the bath ready for when he walked in and now he sat down in the warm water, his knees on a level with his chin. He had kept his drawers on, as his father had always done and as he'd been brought up to do when there were women and bairns about, but his work trousers, shirt and jacket were on the floor in the scullery where they'd remain until Tilly took them outside to bang the worst of the coaldust out of them ready for the next shift. Lathering himself with the blue-veined soap which never gave of its foam easily, he'd begun to wash himself before she said again, '*She's* back. Mabel Gray collapsed the day before yesterday. A stroke, your mam said, and she died last night, and that aunt who lives Durham way went and fetched her.'

Aware of her eyes tight on him, he made himself

continue with what he was doing but it was a moment before he could say, 'Constance, you mean?'

'Aye, Constance. Of course Constance. Who else?'

'Did she see her grandmother before she passed away?'

'So Molly said. She went round to see your mam this morning so she didn't hear about Mrs Gray second-hand.'

Matt nodded. He was surprised how the news of Mabel's death had affected him. He hadn't seen much of Constance's grandmother in the last few years, but he felt a sense of loss as though one of his own family had died. 'When's the funeral?'

'Next Monday.' Tilly handed him the bucket of warm water.

Matt stood and sluiced himself down with it to get rid of the black scum from the surface of the bathwater, and then picked up the towel warming on the clothes horse next to the range along with a fresh pair of drawers. He then went upstairs to get dressed while Tilly disposed of the bathwater and hung the bath back in place on its peg on the scullery wall. Once in their bedroom he sat down on the bed, his head spinning. Constance was here. His heart was thudding so hard against his ribcage it actually hurt. He'd dreamed of seeing her again one day so many times that he couldn't actually believe it, now that day had dawned. But he was sorry about Mabel Gray, really sorry. She had been a nice woman and a good friend to his mam, who would be very upset.

Mechanically he stood up and opened the wardrobe, taking out his trousers and shirt and clean socks.

It had been eleven years since she had left. She would have changed, as he himself had done. What would she think when she looked at him now? He stared at himself in the thin long mirror attached to the back of the wardrobe door. His whole body was a pack of hard tight muscle, but it was the 'buttons', the healed-over wounds on his shoulders and arms and hands that had coaldust in them and were quite blue against his white skin that caught his gaze. All the miners had them and they'd never bothered him before, but suddenly he was seeing himself through her eyes – the man he had been before she went away and the man he was now – and he found himself wanting. There was grey in his hair now and lines on his face which hadn't been there eleven years ago. He was thirty-four years of age but he looked older, a good deal older.

He pulled on his clothes, so many thoughts and emotions tearing at him he felt physically sick. Once dressed he steeled himself to go downstairs.

Rebecca had come in from school while he'd been upstairs, and as he walked into the kitchen she flashed him a quick smile but said nothing. She'd clearly picked up on the fact that something was wrong; likely she thought they'd had another row. That was the only time Tilly and he normally spoke – to row. The rest of the time they existed in a state of mutual loathing which took the form of cold silences and monosyllabic utterances when absolutely necessary.

He smiled back at the child who was so like her mother in looks, but sweetness itself in nature. He didn't know quite when she had wormed herself into his affections, but for some years now he'd acknowledged that his life was the richer for her being in it. Quietly, he said, 'How did the competition go?'

Rebecca had informed him the night before that her teacher had asked them all to write a story about a myth- ical creature with magic powers for homework, and that

201

there would be a small prize for the best one. Before she'd gone up to bed she'd shyly shown him what she'd written. The creature had been something between a dragon and a bird which could fly to a land beyond the sun, and carry with it anyone who was tired of life on earth.

It had bothered him. It still did. For a long while he had known that Rebecca was aware of how he and her mother felt about each other, and he felt that the story, along with her drawings centred mainly upon birds flying high in the clouds and winging their way far above civilisation, was a statement that the child was not happy. He'd said as much once to Tilly, suggesting they should make an effort to be civil in front of the bairn, but she'd been so vitriolic in reply he'd had to accept that the time for civility between them had long since passed.

Rebecca's smile widened as she bent down and rummaged in her schoolbag, bringing out a small slim volume bound in leather. 'It's a book of poems, Da.'

'You won?' He beamed at her, genuinely delighted. 'Well done, hinny. I told you it was a cracking story.'

'Aye, and Miss Newton read it out loud to everyone. I didn't want her to but I couldn't very well say no.'

'You won, you say?' Tilly entered the conversation, her voice sharp. 'You didn't say when you came in.'

Some of the light died in Rebecca's face. 'You were busy.'

'Let's see.' Tilly took the book from her daughter, flicking over a few of the pages before handing it back. 'It's not new.' Her voice was disparaging.

'No, it was Miss Newton's when she was my age. Her da – her father – gave it to her. It's a collection of poems for children.'

Rebecca's voice was flat now, and as Tilly turned to the range and took a covered dish from the oven, Matt leaned across and took the book before Rebecca could put it away. 'It's grand,' he said softly. 'You've got bits from Wordsworth, Shakespeare and Tennyson in here, lass, to whet the appetite for more. And Longfellow's "The Song of Hiawatha", that's a canny piece I remember from school.' He began to recite:

> 'At the door on summer evenings,
> Sat the little Hiawatha;
> Heard the whispering of the pine-trees,
> Heard the lapping of the waters,
> Sounds of music, words of wonder . . .

'We all had chunks of it to memorise, and some of the bairns couldn't do more than a few lines, but I learned the whole thing, I liked it so much.'

Rebecca came to stand by his knee, her eyes shining, and quoted:

> 'By the shores of Gitche Gumee,
> By the shining Big-Sea-Water,
> Stood the wigwam of Nokomis,
> Daughter of the Moon, Nokomis.
>
> 'Dark behind it rose the forest,
> Rose the black and gloomy pine-trees,
> Rose the firs with cones upon them—'

'All right, all right,' Tilly interrupted Matt, placing a steaming plate of shin of beef and black pudding with sliced potatoes in front of him. 'It's dinnertime in case you hadn't caught on. Put that book away, Rebecca, and sit down.'

The child did as she was told but once they were all eating, she reached out and touched Matt's arm. 'Da?'

'Aye, hinny?'

'I didn't know you liked poetry. Mam doesn't so I must get it from you, mustn't I?'

Matt looked into her eyes and saw the need there. 'Aye, lass,' he said softly. 'You get it from me.'

They had finished their dinner. Rebecca was in the front room doing her homework and Tilly was clearing the dirty dishes from the kitchen table. When Matt drained his cup of tea and placed the cup on the saucer before standing up, Tilly stopped what she was doing and watched him as he pulled on his cap and jacket. 'Where are you going?'

'You told me Mrs Gray has just died. Mam'll be upset.'

'So you're going to your mam's?' she said, hands on hips.

'Is there anything wrong with that?'

'No, if that's where you *are* going.'

Matt stared at the tight, sour face of his wife and it came to him that he wasn't the only one who looked older than his years. Conscious of Rebecca in the next room, he said quietly, 'Mam will expect me to show my face. You know that as well as I do.'

Tilly said nothing to this and he had stepped down into the scullery and had his hand on the back-door latch when she spoke again. 'I shall ask her tomorrow. Your mam, I'll ask her.'

'You do that,' he said, without turning.

'When you arrived and when you left.'

His shoulders stiffened as he looked at her. 'Why the hell should you care where I go or what I do?'

Her set face contracted but her eyes were as hard as granite and they burned with her hate of him when she said, 'I don't, but I won't be made a fool of. Just you remember that.'

His voice was even quieter than it had been in the kitchen, but his words came firm and were weighted with bitterness.

'You're one on your own, I'll give you that. How you've got the gall to come out with that to me of all people, I don't know.'

'I warn you—'

'Well, don't.' The sudden movement he made checked her voice although she knew he wouldn't raise his hand to her. 'You've got no right to tell me what to do, none whatsoever.'

'I'm your wife. That gives me the right.'

'A few words spoken over a couple in church and a bit of paper doesn't make a wife in my book. You've never been my wife.'

'How dare you. How *dare* you say that?'

'How dare *I*?' said Matt, his words hard and clipped. 'Let me make something plain once and for all, Tilly. You're nothing to me, less than nothing. You have no rights, no claim on me as a husband as far as I'm concerned, and we both know why.'

'You're cruel.' Her face was white. 'Even if what you think was true, and it's not, the way you've been all these years would have far outweighed my crime. You're heartless, vicious.'

'If I am it's because you've made me so.' His voice was full of contempt. 'But I don't see what you've got to complain about. You got what you wanted – a ring on your finger and a licence to say you're a married woman with her good name intact. I'd say that's better than the workhouse any day, because likely that's where you would have ended up.'

'There're many times over the last years I've thought anything, including the workhouse, would be better than being married to you. If you knew the times I've thought of leaving you.'

'Then it's a pity you didn't go, isn't it?'

'I hate you.' Her voice quivered with anger. 'I really hate you.'

'So you've said before.' His voice held a note of deep weariness in it now, partly because in a secret recess of his mind he had to acknowledge there was an element of truth in what she said. Her punishment had exceeded the wrong she'd done him. He had begun to think this way shortly after Rebecca's devotion to him had melted his heart towards the child, but by then the state of war which existed between him and Tilly had been too fierce and bitter for withdrawal. Maybe if she had been honest with him at some point, confessed and asked his forgiveness, there might have been some hope for them. But how could you forgive someone who was adamant they'd done nothing to merit blame? Even God Himself expected repentance and remorse. Not that he was setting himself up on a par with the Almighty. Since his marriage he'd barely crossed the church door and he knew Father Duffy thought he was on the path to hell and damnation. Tilly, on the other hand, went to Mass every week, taking

Rebecca along with her, as befitted a good wife and mother.

This last thought caused his mouth to tighten and he turned from Tilly's glare, opening the back door and stepping out into the warm September evening. This time she made no effort to detain him and he shut the door quietly behind him.

Inside the house Tilly remained where she was for a full minute. She'd see her day with him. By, she would. Mr High and Mighty. If it hadn't been for the fact her belly was full with Rebecca she'd have left him in the early days of their marriage, run off somewhere far away from Sacriston where the shame and scandal of such an action wouldn't reach her. She could have done it. She nodded mentally to the thought.

But she had stayed. And what had happened? Slowly he had taken her child from her. Oh yes, he had. She inclined her head as though someone had refuted this. At first he had wanted nothing to do with the baby. Oh, he'd put on an act when they were visiting his mam for a while, but eventually he'd stopped doing even that. He'd wanted no say in anything to do with Rebecca, and in a funny sort of way she hadn't minded. Rebecca had been hers, all hers, and her daughter's dependence on her had helped negate the terrible feelings that burned her up as night after night she'd lain in that bed next to Matt, her body aching for release, knowing he didn't want her. She disgusted him, that's what he'd said when she'd tried to make it up with him. She was repulsive to him.

Slowly she released her fingers which were bunched into fists at her side. Walking back into the kitchen she made a pot of tea but all the time thoughts were racing round her head. It had been subtle, the way he'd turned Rebecca against her. She hadn't seen it happening. But one day she'd woken up to the fact that the child adored him, worshipped him even. There was no one like her da as far as Rebecca was concerned. *Her da* . . .

Tilly's lip curled even as she blinked away hot tears. What she'd give to be able to tell Rebecca her da was a white-collar worker, someone with a proper education, not a dirty, ignorant miner scratching away in the bowels of the earth like a filthy animal. No, she didn't mean that, she told herself in the next moment. Her da was a miner and his da before him, and they were good, upright men – decent men.

She shut her eyes, swaying back and forth as she sat at the table and then, taking a hold of herself, she poured a cup of tea and forced herself to drink it scalding hot. It helped restore her equilibrium and she poured herself another cup, holding it between her hands as she stared pensively across the room. She didn't doubt Matt would go and see his mother, not after the things she'd said before he left, but would he go round to Molly's too? Her stomach churned sickeningly, even as she asked herself why it would matter if he did. When she could find no logical answer within herself to this, she repeated the words she'd flung at Matt: *I won't be made a fool of.*

'Has Da gone out? I didn't hear him go.'

Rebecca was standing in the doorway, her homework book in one hand. Tilly nodded. 'Aye, he's gone to Grandma Heath's. I'm afraid Mrs Gray passed away yesterday and your grandma'll be upset. Your da's gone to see if there's anything he can do.'

'Oh, poor Mrs Gray. I liked her. She told me about

how Da had rescued her granddaughter from the fire before I was born. He was a hero, she said. He saved Constance Shelton's life.'

It was too much in view of the evening's events. Her voice stiff, Tilly said, 'I think anyone would have done the same in your da's position. He happened to be there, that's all.'

Rebecca's chin went up a notch. She didn't speak, she didn't have to. Her eyes were very expressive.

Tilly's face tightened. 'Have you finished your homework?'

'I was going to ask Da something, but it'll wait until tomorrow.' Rebecca's tone stated very clearly that she had no intention of discussing whatever it was with her mother.

Her da, always her da. 'Then I suggest you get yourself to bed after you've packed away your things.'

It was another hour before her bedtime but Rebecca didn't argue. With one last telling look she swung round and flounced off, her brown plaits bobbing as she tossed her head.

Tilly pressed her hands either side of her nose, struggling for control. She wanted to race after her daughter and box her ears, but the way she was feeling she knew she might not stop at that. Besides which, it wouldn't really be Rebecca she was hitting.

She was nothing but a skivvy in this house. As her anger cooled, despair took its place. She washed and cooked and cleaned and each day was the same. She couldn't stand it any more. If he didn't come straight home from his mam's, if he went to Molly's place then she'd go and see Rupert about that part-time job he had offered her a while ago. She'd started speaking to him again recently – for years he'd treated her as just another customer when she'd gone into the post office, and pride had forbidden her to press for more. Then at the beginning of the summer she had met him while she was doing her shopping and he'd stopped to chat. She'd been cool with him that day, but the next time she'd gone into the post office he'd left his assistant in charge and followed her outside. She'd known his wife was ailing, it was common knowledge Nancy Wood had taken to her bed and declared herself an invalid after her seventh bairn had been born at the beginning of the year, but when he'd suggested she might like to put in a few hours' cooking and cleaning for them she hadn't known how to take it at first. He would pay her well, he'd entreated. Very well.

Rebecca's feet padding up the stairs broke into her thoughts, then her daughter's bedroom door opened and closed and all was silent once more. For a moment Tilly considered going up and making her peace with the child, but just as swiftly she dismissed the notion. If Rebecca wanted to sulk, then she could; she was sick and tired of her moods.

Her mind returning to the matter in hand, she recalled Rupert's words. It appeared his wife's mother had taken the bairns in hand. He took them to her every morning and she brought them home at bedtime, he'd told her, so there wouldn't be any childcare involved, just preparing a main meal for the evening after he'd locked up downstairs, and seeing to the house and any laundry. He would have got someone in before, he'd murmured, but he hadn't wanted a stranger in the house. And she wasn't a stranger. His eyes had been soft with the look that had used to thrill her when she'd been young and foolish.

When he'd begun to say how much he had missed her, she'd stopped him with a sharp movement of her hand. She would think about his offer and let him know, she'd said coolly, but if she agreed to help for a few hours a day it would purely be a business arrangement. But even as she'd spoken she had known she wanted him.

That had been a few weeks ago and she hadn't mentioned anything to Matt because she was sure he'd create merry hell if she suggested working outside the house, besides which she had taken a perverse pleasure in making Rupert wait for an answer. But the more the notion had played in her mind, the more she'd liked the idea of earning her own money and having some independence, although she wasn't sure if the furore it would cause at home would be worth it. But if he hotfooted it to Molly's tonight to see that little scut she'd have her answer.

Her chin lifted, much as Rebecca's had done earlier.

Chapter 14

When Matt left his mother's house and stepped into the backyard, the moon was riding high in a black sky, the heat of the day still evident in the warm lazy air and the smell of the privies which were due for clearing out by the scavengers with their cart and long shovels. Once in the back lane he walked purposefully and without hesitation: wild horses couldn't have kept him from seeing Constance. When he had told his mother that he intended to call round and pay his respects, she'd been all for it.

'Oh aye, lad,' she'd said at once, patting his arm. 'They'd appreciate it, I'm sure, and Constance would like to see you again. She's took it hard, her grandma going like that, and I daresay she's regretting going away, but then that was her choice. Still, I did feel sorry for her this afternoon when I popped round. She barely said more than a word or two the whole time I was there.'

That didn't surprise him. His mother could talk the hind leg off a donkey when she got going, and Molly was the same.

When he reached Blackett Street the air was sweeter.

It was the last street in the New Town development and backed on to open fields, and the heady scent of freshly cut hay wafted on the faint breeze from the surrounding countryside. Normally he would have stopped for some minutes and taken great gulps, filling his lungs to the brim. After the stench and dust of the mine, such moments were precious. Tonight though, his senses barely registered the gentle perfume.

He was going to see her. After all these years he was going to look at her again, listen to her voice, touch her hand maybe. His mother had said she thought Constance was somewhat changed, but when his father had laughed and pointed out that the lass had been little more than a bairn when she'd left the village twelve years ago, she hadn't said anything more. He'd wanted to ask her exactly what she'd meant but the chance had passed. Anyway, he'd see her for himself soon.

When he reached Molly and Edwin's doorstep it took him three tries before he could bring himself to follow through and sound the door-knocker. The few seconds before the front door was opened seemed like hours, but then Molly was peering at him and saying, 'Matt, is that you? Come in, lad, come in. Why didn't you come round the back? We thought it must be Father Duffy about the funeral. He said he'd call by this evening but he sent a message to say he'd been held up.'

'I just called to say I was sorry about your mam . . .' He found he was talking to thin air. Molly had disappeared down the hall, obviously expecting him to follow, and he could hear her saying, 'It's all right, Ed, it's only Matt. You needn't put your jacket on. It's not the Father.'

When he reached the kitchen doorway, he said again,

'I just called to say how sorry I was,' to Molly who was facing him. 'It must have been a terrible shock for you.'

'Thanks, lad. It was a shock, I admit it, especially because she hadn't really had a day's illness in her life to speak of, but now I've had time to think, I know it was the way she would have wanted to go. She had a horror of lingering. But here, come and sit down, lad, and take the weight off. Can I get you a cup of tea? And I bet you can manage a bit of fruitcake.'

Edwin was sitting in a high-backed wooden chair with thick flock cushions, his slippered feet resting on the shining steel fender in front of the range, but otherwise the kitchen was empty. She wasn't there. For a moment Matt's disappointment was so keen he couldn't speak. Then he nodded. 'Thanks, Molly.' He smiled at Edwin who inclined his head in reply without taking his pipe out of his mouth, and then pulled out a chair and sat down at the table which had a vase of wild flowers in the centre of it.

'I can't really believe she's gone yet.' Molly bustled about, making the tea and fetching a big fruitcake to the table. 'It's a blessing Constance is here − it'll sort of ease me into it, if you know what I mean. We used to have a crack or two, Mam an' me, an' never a cross word. Edwin'll miss her too, won't you, lad?'

'Aye.'

'They used to have some right old debates about this and that when he got home from work. Great one for reading the paper and keeping up with what was going on, was Mam. And she was all for the suffragettes. Edwin thinks the lot of 'em ought to be put away, isn't that right, Edwin?'

'Aye.'

'Meself, I don't read much. I mean, it's all doom and gloom in the papers, isn't it, and there's enough of that in daily life without going looking for more. That's what I always say, isn't it, Edwin?'

'Aye.'

Matt found it difficult to imagine the stolid Edwin rousing himself enough to engage in a 'debate' about anything. Getting a word in edgeways must be an accomplishment with Molly around.

'You'll have a shive of cake, won't you, lad? And help yourself to sugar.' Molly poured him a cup of tea and placed it in front of him before cutting a large wedge of fruitcake.

Matt opened his mouth to thank her, but the words were never voiced as the sound of footsteps coming down the stairs brought his eyes to the doorway. His heart pounding fit to burst he waited, and then there she was. So beautiful she took his breath away. He rose clumsily to his feet, his voice gruff as he said, 'Hello, Constance.' He knew he'd gone red but he couldn't help it.

'Hello, Matt.' She came fully into the kitchen, the light shining on the golden coils of her hair which she wore in a smooth chignon. 'It's been a long time.'

She was dressed plainly in a dove-grey dress with a neat lace collar, but he sensed it was an expensive plainness. There was a poise about her, a polish, and the words her grandmother had spoken years ago came back to him. *'She's outgrown us, lad.'*

His voice stilted, he said, 'I came to pay my respects and say how sorry I am about your grandmother. She was a good woman.'

'Yes, she was.'

'Come and sit yourself down, lass, I've just made a fresh pot of tea.' Molly drew out one of the hardbacked chairs from around the table and as Constance came forward and sat down, Matt couldn't take his eyes off her face. He could see what his mam had meant about Constance having changed, and yet in another respect she was just the same, not that that made sense.

Clearing his throat, he said, 'How long are you planning to stay?' as he took his seat again.

'Just until the funeral's over. They're very good, Sir Henry and Lady Isabella, but I wouldn't want to presume.'

So she worked for a Sir and a Lady? 'Aye, your grandma said they thought a bit of you but then they would, you saving their lad an' all.' He knew his eyes had lingered on the soft curve of her lips a mite too long, but he couldn't help himself.

'Constance has been telling us a bit about Italy, haven't you, lass?' Molly plumped herself down beside her niece. 'Your grandma did enjoy getting them picture cards you used to send her when you were there, tickled pink she used to be. It looks right bonny.'

Constance's eyes were on the cup in her hand, her cheeks flushed. 'It is bonny.'

'You're a lucky lass and no mistake. Most folk I know haven't been further than their own backyard. Isn't that right, Matt?' And without waiting for a reply: 'And here's you been the other side of the world and seen goodness knows what.'

Quietly, Constance said, 'It isn't really the other side of the world, Aunt Molly, and — and there's nowhere like home.'

Matt stared at her bent head. She *was* the same. Sweet to the core. How could he have been so incredibly, so monumentally foolish as to not see what was under his nose all those years ago? The conflict that had warred in him for over a decade brought his guts twisting. She'd never change. Not his Constance.

And then something of what he was feeling was challenged when Constance raised her head, her voice pleasant but cool when she said to him, 'How are Tilly and Rebecca, Matt? Rebecca must be . . . what? Eleven years old, I suppose.'

He had to swallow before he could speak. 'They're fine. Rebecca is doing well at school, they tell me she is very bright.'

'Does she know what she wants to do when she leaves school?'

It wasn't a question any of the folk in the village would have put to him. When a lass left school there was no personal choice involved in what she did thereafter. Until she got married she helped at home or went into service or got some other job until a ring was put on her finger. Her question stretched the divide between them. Stiffly, he said, 'We haven't discussed that yet.'

'And Tilly? She's well?' Constance said politely.

'Well enough.' It sounded too abrupt even to his own ears.

'Good. Give her my best regards and tell her I hope to see her before I leave. Will she be coming to the funeral?'

He doubted it but now was not the moment to say so. His voice even stiffer, he said, 'Of course.'

A knock at the front door brought Molly to her feet

217

again. 'That *will* be the Father this time.' She cast a glance at her husband. 'I've lit the fire in the front room.'

It was clearly an order and Edwin obeyed it by silently pulling on his jacket over his shirt-sleeves and knitted waistcoat. 'You won't mind if we leave you for a while?' Molly was already at the door leading into the hall. Father Duffy coming to the house was an event equal to that of the doctor calling, and both of those gentlemen were accorded the esteemed front room which was only used on high days and holidays. 'Constance, pour Matt another cup of tea when he's finished that one. There's plenty in the pot and that cake needs eating up.' So saying, she bustled to answer the door, Edwin trailing after her.

After an awkward pause when he had never felt so self-conscious in his life, Matt finished his cup of tea. He didn't object when Constance silently refilled his cup although he didn't really want more. He had always prided himself on being any man's equal, be they one of the gaffers or an ordinary pitman like himself. He'd upset his mother one day when he was still living at home by saying Father Duffy was just a man like himself and he wouldn't doff his cap to him or anyone else. Caused ructions, that had, but he'd stood by what he'd said. But now . . .

'I saw your mother today. She told me all the family news.'

She had said mother not mam, and although her voice carried the warm northern burr it always had, it came to him that her speech was different, uppish. Not in an artificial way, he'd have felt better if she was putting it on, but he knew that wasn't the case. He supposed mixing with the family like she did, something of their way of talking and carrying on was bound to rub off. He had to

moisten his lips before he could say, 'I can imagine. I bet
you got the i's dotted and the t's crossed about everything
that's gone on for years and then some.'

'I like your mother.'

She spoke as though he'd criticised his mam in some
way. With the anger came a perverseness which prompted
his tone to take on the pitmatic as he said, 'Aye, me an'
all, she's a canny little body, is me mam.'

Constance looked into her cup again and he felt at a
complete loss as to what to do or say next. He felt he'd
been boorish and that made him angrier still at her –
she'd put him in the wrong somehow. Well, she could go
back to her high-and-mighty going-on and good riddance.
That's what he said, he told himself bitterly. He wasn't
ashamed of what he was.

'I've missed the village.' Her great azure eyes met his
across the table and his heart bounded with a force which
nearly choked him. 'Especially in the early days when I
was working in the kitchen. Not that there's anything
wrong with working in a kitchen,' she added hastily, and
he knew she'd sensed how he was feeling, 'but I felt so
shut in – claustrophobic, you know?'

He nodded although he hadn't heard the word before.

'Sometimes I started work in the dark and finished
when it was dark and I hadn't been outside once. I – I
thought about how you must feel, all the miners. Not that
you can compare working in a kitchen with being down
the pit.' Her eyes dropped from his. 'At least I could see
the sky through the window.'

'Your grandma told me about why you left.' Her head
shot up, her eyes wary. 'Not when you first went, but after
you'd saved the little lad – she told me then. Why – why

didn't you say anything to me? Surely you knew I wouldn't have let anyone bother you? I'd have sorted it – you could have stayed.'

She bit on to her lower lip for a moment. 'No one knew.'

He asked the question which had been there like a thorn in his flesh for years. 'Who was it? What's his name?'

'She didn't tell you?'

'Not his name, no.' There had been relief in her voice. After all these years, was she still frightened of this man? Of what he might do? That was crazy. 'Who was it?' he asked again.

'It doesn't matter, it's so long ago now.'

'If it doesn't matter you can tell me his name.'

She shook her head. 'Please, Matt, leave it.'

The tone of her voice had been such that he felt he was being put in his place, and it washed over him afresh that Constance the woman was very different from Constance the girl. He also knew he loved the woman as he had never imagined he could love anyone, and the knowledge roughened his voice when he said, 'Constance, you left the village because of him, he drove you away from' – he had been about to say 'me' and caught himself just in time – 'your grandma and granda and changed the course of your life.' *And mine. Because if you had stayed I would have finished with Tilly and waited for you. I would have.* Something had happened that day in her grandma's kitchen which had been fundamental.

'But it's turned out all right.' Again she met his gaze and her eyes, luminous with unshed tears, belied her words.

'Has it?' He reached across the table and took one of her hands. Her fingers were cool and delicate in his; he felt as though if he tightened his hold they would break, so fragile they seemed in his callused, work-roughened hands. The emotion that ripped through him was so fierce it stopped his breath, and for aeons, countless ages, they stared at each other.

The front-room door opening and Molly's voice calling, 'Constance, lass?' brought her hand jerking from his. In the next moment Molly appeared in the doorway. 'The Father would like a word with you, lass,' she said busily, 'and I'm just going to make some fresh tea and sand-wiches, as the Father's a mite peckish. You'll stay an' all, won't you, Matt?'

'No thanks, Molly, I'd best be off.' The thought of sitting in Molly's front room with the priest and making polite conversation with Constance present wasn't an option.

'Aye, all right, lad.' Molly smiled at him before saying to Constance, 'Go on, lass, don't keep the Father waiting.'

'Goodbye, Matt.' Constance's voice was little more than a whisper and she didn't meet his eyes. 'Thank you for coming.'

''Bye, Constance. I'll call again tomorrow when things are sorted and find out about the funeral.'

'You do that, lad.' It was Molly who answered as Constance disappeared into the hall without replying. 'You're welcome any time, you know that.'

When he arrived at the house the following evening, he found that Constance had gone to bed early with a headache. Molly and Edwin told him she hadn't been well all day and had stayed in her room most of the time. The funeral was the day after tomorrow, Molly said. Constance had wanted it to be over and done with as soon as possible, and Father Duffy had been able to accommodate them and so . . . Her tone made it clear she didn't agree with the rush.

Matt had had a cup of tea and left, but he hadn't gone home straightaway. Instead he'd walked into the first of the fields beyond New Town, sitting amid the bristly corn stubble left by the farm labourers' sickles, his arms draped over his knees.

All day the thought of seeing her again had been like a shining light in a dark place. He hadn't known which end of him was up, and on the way round to Molly's he'd been hard-pressed not to run. And what had he found? She had a headache.

He made a guttural sound deep in his throat. She was avoiding him, the same as she was avoiding this man who'd been the cause of her leaving the village. Molly had told him Constance hadn't set foot outside the house since she'd arrived back, and he dare bet she wouldn't venture beyond those four walls until the funeral. She was frightened of this bloke, that was obvious.

He needed to tell her how he felt, to bring it out into the open. He flung himself back on the sun-warmed ground, looking up into the black sky glittering with stars. He had to explain about Tilly, the sham that was his marriage. There was so much she needed to understand. But . . . did she really want to know?

The doubts and fears that had tormented him since he'd seen the polished young woman she'd become washed over him. She had the sort of life that came once in a blue moon for a working-class lass, she'd be a fool to give that up. Not that he had any hope she would consider doing that for him; why would she? He was a miner. The pit and all it entailed was the only life he knew. And he was married. Married with a bairn. Hell, why had he come to see her again anyway?

Because he hadn't been able to keep away.

He groaned, rolling over on to his face and startling a young rabbit at the edge of the field that had come out to feed upon the lush herbage of early autumn at the perimeter of the hedgerow. What was he going to do? What *could* he do?

Nothing. The answer brought him sitting up again as he stared into the darkness. He could do nothing. Even if Constance had feelings for him, and he didn't know for sure that she did, nothing had been said. He couldn't ask her to give up everything and run away with him. It was unthinkable. She would be branded a scarlet woman and her name would be mud, and what could he offer her in recompense? Himself?

The sound he made now was the final straw for the rabbit. It dived for its burrow, quivering and afraid.

Matt shook his head at himself, tired and weary suddenly in both mind and body. What would it be like to be dead? If you believed in the hereafter Father Duffy spoke of, every Catholic was to be welcomed at the Pearly Gates and every Protestant went straight to the other place, but he wasn't so sure. Maybe you just slept, a deep and dream-less sleep with no worries and no rows and no memories, no regrets about what could have been.

Enough of that. He heaved himself to his feet and drew in a long slow breath. He was thinking like a skittish slip of a lass. He was done in; he hadn't slept above an hour or two last night even after the double shift, and he'd put in another full day today. That was all it was. A good night's sleep and he'd be back on an even keel. He had to be.

He dusted some dried grass and stubble from his trousers and jacket, taking off his cap and running his hand through his hair before placing it on his head again.

The streets were quiet as he walked home. Darkness had sent the bairns indoors but the odd window was open as he passed and sounds from within filtered through: a woman laughing; bairns squabbling; the smell of dinner cooking. He felt a loneliness so intense as to be unbearable and for once he was actually glad when he stepped into his backyard.

Tilly was letting down the hem of one of Rebecca's summer dresses when he entered the kitchen. She didn't look up or speak but he didn't expect her to. Taking off his boots he pulled his slippers on and sat down in his easy chair to one side of the range, opening his newspaper.

It was then she said, 'Didn't stay long, did you?'

Without lowering the newspaper, he said quietly, 'I told you, I wanted to find out about the funeral, that's all.'

'Sent away with a flea in your ear more like. I hear our Constance is quite the little lady now, too high and mighty for a pit-yakkor.'

The abusive term for pitmen didn't bother him, he'd heard far worse from her, but the fact that she'd hit the nail on the head caught him on the raw. Warning himself not to give her the satisfaction of seeing she'd riled him, he said even more quietly, 'Don't talk such rubbish, woman.'

'Rubbish, is it? And I suppose it's rubbish that you've been round to see her two nights on the trot?'

He lowered the paper, saying with elaborate patience, 'I went to offer my condolences yesterday. Molly has lost her mam and Constance her grandma, if you remember? And tonight I asked about the funeral arrangements because I want to be there. Are you coming? You were invited.' He didn't say by whom.

'I'd rather walk on hot coals.'

'I take that as a no then.'

'You think you're so clever, don't you? The big fellow. But you're nowt, Matt Heath.'

He flung the paper down as he rose. 'I'm not in the mood for this, Tilly. I'm going to bed.'

'Are you in the mood to hear I've been offered a job and I start tomorrow?'

'What?' He stopped and stared at her.

'Aye.' She had stood up too, hands on hips and her head thrust forward. 'Rupert Wood wanted someone to help out in the flat above the post office now his wife's so poorly, a bit of cooking and cleaning and such, and beens as I used to work for him before we got wed, he asked if I might be interested.' Her tone was openly defiant. 'Five shillings a week, he said, for a few hours each day 'cept Sunday.'

Everything about her proclaimed she expected to have to fight him on this. She knew as well as he did that it lowered a man's prestige if his wife worked outside the house. She could take in washing or ironing, mind other folks' bairns, bake and sell cakes and pies, work as a seamstress making clothes and mending others, do jobs for a pittance compared to what she'd earn doing the same work in a factory or shop, but as long as she was in the home, her husband's rightful place as breadwinner was protected. He worked with men – good, upright men who loved their wives and families – who would guard

225

this male authority to their last breath. No gentle emotions or kindly instincts must be allowed to weaken it. And even though the wife might work half the night at whatever she did, the bairns and house and everything in it was the woman's responsibility. A man would let the clothes go rotten on his back before he'd wash them, and starve rather than cook a meal. As for changing a child's nappy, he'd as soon cut his own throat.

All this went through Matt's mind as he stared into Tilly's belligerent face. And he was a man of his own people, through and through. It would never have occurred to him to think any differently; he'd imbibed such customs and conventions along with his mother's milk. And maybe if she'd put this forward a week ago, even a couple of days ago, he wouldn't have countenanced it. His eyes narrowed with his confusing emotions. He couldn't have put into thoughts, let alone words, the jumbled-up feelings he was experiencing, but somehow after seeing Constance again there was an element of pity in his dislike of his wife which hadn't been there before. He'd withheld himself, body, soul and spirit from her, and of the three he knew it was the first that had affected her the most. There was a passion and desire in Tilly as strong as any man's.

Not that he could have done any differently, he told himself. He'd been angry and hurt on their wedding night, but maybe in the months that had followed he might have been able to come to terms with the fact she'd lied to him. But once he knew she'd married him with her belly full of another man's bairn any spark of sexual desire had gone, and it had never been any different. But she'd wanted him. Even now, hating him as she did, he knew if he lifted his little finger she'd come running.

Quietly, he said, 'Do you want to take this job?'

Her voice was like her face, sharp and hard, and he read in her eyes that she thought the question was double-edged when she said, 'I would like to earn my own money and receive some thanks for what I do, aye.'

He knew she was telling him he wouldn't see a penny of what she earned, but that didn't bother him. He'd been supporting the three of them for the last eleven or so years and he could continue to do so without any help from Tilly. His family wouldn't understand, and he'd get some stick from his pals down the pit when the news got out, but strangely that didn't bother him either, although before this day he would have expected it would have. Like a bolt of lightning it came to him that for a long time now he'd realised he'd tied himself into a loveless marriage through pride and fear of what folk might think of him if they knew the truth. He was a damn fool, because other people didn't matter a jot. But he'd ruined his life finding that out.

He didn't actually *care* if Tilly worked for the postmaster and his wife, that was the truth of it, and if he didn't care, why should he stop her? And he sure as hell didn't have to answer to his family or pals or anyone else for his decision.

Tilly was staring at him and he could see she was bracing herself for the explosion she was sure was coming. Still speaking very quietly, he said, 'You'd still see to the bairn's needs and your duties here? Run the house like it's always been run?'

For a moment she didn't reply. 'Aye,' she said, slowly and flatly. 'Of course I'd do that.'

He nodded. 'Good.' He continued to the door, stepping into the hall before her voice caused him to turn.

'You mean I can do it? You don't mind?'

'Does it matter what I think one way or the other?' She made no reply and after a long pause, he said, 'No, Tilly, I don't mind. As long as you look after things here, I don't mind.'

She made a little sound that jerked her head as she emitted it, and in answer to it, he said, 'What's the matter? I've said I don't mind, haven't I? That's what you wanted, isn't it?'

Their eyes met and held, and what he read in hers caused him to feel uncomfortable enough to say, 'Damn it, there's no pleasing you, woman. I've said you can take the job, what more do you want?' before he turned his back on her and made for the stairs.

Tilly watched him go. She remained in the kitchen doorway for some minutes more before turning and walking over to the chair she'd occupied before Matt had walked in. Rebecca's dress lay where she'd thrown it and now she picked it up, burying her face in the cotton in an attempt to stifle the sobs that were tearing her apart.

Chapter 15

It was the middle of the night but Constance was wide awake. She hadn't been able to sleep properly since she had arrived back in Sacriston, and it wasn't only the death of her grandma that had her tossing and turning in an agony of mind.

She'd done the only thing possible in pleading a headache and staying out of Matt's way, she told herself for the umpteenth time. And if she'd offended him, she was sorry, but every minute she was with him there was the possibility she'd give herself away. He'd been kind and friendly last night. He'd always been kind and friendly to her and it wasn't his fault she loved him, but her love had her reading too much into what he said and the way he looked at her, because she wanted to believe he cared for her as she cared for him. Which was wrong. He was a married man.

Molly had told her she didn't think Matt and Tilly were happily married. 'It's not a match made in heaven, lass, that's for sure. Your grandma didn't think so and neither does Ruth Heath from what she's let on to your grandma over the years. Still, you make your bed and you have to lie on it. And there's the bairn to consider. She's a grand little lass, Rebecca, and she thinks the sun shines out of her da's backside. Always has done. Followed him about like a puppy when she was younger.'

Constance had forced herself to smile. 'That's nice.'

'Aye, although he didn't want much to do with her when she was first born. Mind you, my Edwin was like that. He was always worried he was going to drop 'em when they were little. All fingers and thumbs, he was. Said they gave him the willies.'

Knowing she shouldn't ask, she'd said, 'But Matt and Tilly are all right on the whole?'

Molly had shrugged. 'All I know is Mam didn't think things were right. But then marriage isn't a bed of roses for anyone. Me an' Edwin have had our differences but you work through them. You've got no choice, have you? Once that ring's on your finger it's for life an' that's that.'

Constance had nodded. She knew one of the Ashtons' friends had recently acquired a divorce because she had heard them talking about the scandal which had ensued, but such a thing was unheard of among ordinary men and women, even those who weren't Catholics.

'I mean, our Daisy's husband can be a bit handy with his fists,' Molly had gone on, 'and Edwin had to go round and give him a taste of his own medicine which seems to have done the trick. Mind, like I said to her, she needs to stand up for herself. Wait till he's asleep and give him a bashing, that's what I'd do.'

'But Matt doesn't hit Tilly?' she'd asked, shocked.

'Ee, no, lass. Whatever put that idea in your head? No, no, nothing like that as far as I know. They're just like lots of other couples round here. No worse and no better.'

And that had been the end to what had been a depressing conversation.

Marriage shouldn't be like Molly had described, indeed, what she had seemed to think was normal. Constance sat up, swung her feet out of bed and padded across to the window, opening the curtains wide. The moonlight lit the recently harvested fields beyond Blackett Street nearly as brightly as day, and she could see beyond Cross Lane right to the wooded area in the distance. The view was softer in the moonlight, gentler. You could almost imagine that the voracious entity that was the pit, which ate men and lads whole and spat out their bones, didn't exist. For eleven years she had lived in dread of opening one of her grandma's letters and reading that the pit had got Matt. She still dreaded it; she supposed she always would. But she'd have gladly put up with that constant fear if she could have been his wife and had his bairns.

She loved him as much as ever. She shut her eyes tightly before opening them again. She had tried to pretend to herself over the last years that she was over him, but she'd never be over Matt. Just seeing him last night, hearing his voice, watching the way his mouth moved had made her weak at the knees. She didn't know why and she couldn't explain the attraction he held for her; she supposed he was nothing special in the world's eyes, but everything about him made her blood race. And she'd felt there was something there on his side too yesterday, the same as that long-ago afternoon in her grandma's kitchen.

She leaned her forehead against the cold glass of the window. But she'd been wrong then. He had married Tilly and they'd had a bairn together. That was reality. All her silly imaginings and fancies were just that. Silly. And even if Matt and Tilly weren't happy, even if they were the most unhappy couple in the world, it was nothing to do with her.

The glass was smudged with her tears and she took her handkerchief out of the sleeve of her nightdress and rubbed the window. As she did so, she gave a start, leaping backwards into the room, her heart thudding. Someone was out there. Someone had been spying on her, she'd swear to it. Down in the hedgerow dividing the fields nearest the houses, she'd definitely seen the figure of a man.

Biting down on the knuckles of her clenched hand she edged to the side of the window and peered out round the curtain. Bathed in moonlight, the view mocked her with its peacefulness. Her legs trembling, she continued to watch for a full ten minutes but nothing stirred.

She must have been mistaken. A trick of the moonlight combined with her reflection in the glass, that was all it had been. Nevertheless, she continued with her vigil for a little longer before returning to bed, and it was another hour before she fell into a restless, troubled sleep.

Vincent didn't move from his spot in the hedgerow until the subtle fingers of dawn began to spread across the sky. He'd known there was little hope of seeing her again after that one time when she had obviously caught sight of him, but he still hadn't been able to tear himself away. He drank the last of the half-bottle of brandy he'd brought with him for company and stretched before standing up. It wouldn't be long before the early-morning shift would be turning out and he needed to get home and have a wash and change before then.

He glanced across the stubble fields where a large loose flock of lapwings were already having breakfast, picking off the plentiful supply of grubs and beetles disturbed by the harrow. They had risen early; their plaintive cries had been echoing for at least an hour before daybreak. The old wives would have you believe the birds were departed human spirits who could find no rest and were doomed to wander the earth seeking absolution, bringing down evil upon all who heard them, but he liked them. He liked all nature, but there was an element to the lapwings' melancholy cries that touched something deep in him. He admired them too. In the breeding season he'd spend hours watching them perform their spectacular display, flying high and then plunging towards the earth with spinning movements, as if mortally wounded, their wings vibrating and causing a loud, thundering noise.

He'd come across a couple of youths a few summers ago – ne'er-do-wells, by the look of them. They'd netted and captured a good number of lapwings and had been busy cutting out their hearts, brains and eyes to be enclosed in necklaces which they sold, saying it would profit the wearer against forgetfulness, kidney trouble and the slow workings of the body. Another old wives' tale. To see the remains of the beautiful dark plumage shot with iridescent specks of metallic turquoise and the blood and bones had sent him fair mad. Even their own mothers wouldn't have recognised them by the time he'd finished with the lads. He'd buried their bodies where no one would find them, along with the remnants of the birds.

Casting his eyes back towards the village he stared at

Constance's window. He hadn't expected to see her, he had just wanted to be near her once he'd heard she'd returned because the grandmother had died. He had to get her alone, to talk to her and let her know he understood she'd been sent away against her will and that his offer of marriage still stood. The heady excitement that had kept him warm all night sent his blood pulsing through his veins like spiced wine. The old woman and man had gone now. There was nothing stopping them. Once she understood that he'd tried to find her, that he'd left no stone unturned in his attempts to track her down, she wouldn't blame him. But he didn't want to say what he had to say in front of the old 'uns' daughter.

He did not allow himself to acknowledge here his fear that Constance wouldn't want him. She *had* to want him. For years now he had carried the image of her in a pocket of his mind, and when the weight of her absence had become unbearable, he'd taken out his frustration and blind desire on Polly, but it had never sufficed. Never met the need in him.

He tucked the brandy bottle in the deep pocket of his jacket after tipping it against his tongue to get the last drop or two. He knew he was drinking too much. The ghosts that came and paraded in front of him every time he closed his eyes at night could only be obliterated by brandy, and the amount he had to drink to be able to sleep had increased with the years. But that would change once he had Constance.

Brushing his clothes down with the flat of his hands, he stepped out into the field, giving a mental apology to the birds as they rose screaming into the air. The rising sun had yet to sweep the dew of dawn from the fields and chilliness stabbed the fresh autumn air, but Vincent didn't feel it. The funeral was tomorrow and then his life could begin afresh. Nothing mattered except Constance. His position as weighman, the cottage – he was willing to leave it all if she wanted to put the village behind her and start again where there were no wagging tongues. He had enough money to take her wherever she wanted to go.

She would understand tomorrow. He would make her understand.

Polly stood hidden at the back of the crowd at the graveside. The funeral service had been short but sincere; you could tell Father Duffy had liked Mabel Gray, but then she had too. Mrs Gray had been one of the few women in the village who always spoke to her if she saw her when she was out shopping, and not just a 'good morning' or 'nice day' but a proper conversation. She suspected Mrs Gray had felt sorry for her, but she hadn't minded this – why should she? She felt sorry for herself.

A little breeze swept over the graveyard, rustling the leaves in the trees which bordered it. She could see Vincent on the far side of the cemetery but she had been careful to stay out of his sight. She hadn't asked permission to come to the funeral in case he refused it, but she didn't want to incur his wrath if she could avoid it.

She could see Mrs Gray's two daughters and their families; they were weeping, and so were some of the neighbours and friends. Mrs Gray would be really pleased if she could see what a send-off she'd had; there wouldn't be one person in the whole wide world who would cry if *she* popped her clogs, Polly reflected. And that girl who'd come home for the funeral was beautiful but sad-looking, but then she supposed she would be. It must be awful to lose someone you loved.

As the grave-diggers began their work of filling in the hole, folk began mingling and Polly prepared herself for the moment she could slip away unnoticed. Probably because it was such a lovely warm day, no one seemed in any hurry to leave. A group had gathered round the two daughters, and a row of folk were looking at the posies and wreaths at the head of the grave; a number of bairns were running up and down the cemetery paths.

Polly edged her way towards the gate, taking care to stay hidden as she did so and keeping an eye on Vincent. She saw the bonny lass was standing slightly apart from the rest of the family with two or three bairns hanging on her hands; she was talking to Mr and Mrs Heath and one of their sons, the youngest one. As she got nearer she heard the girl say, '. . . today, with Aunt Ivy. We'll stay overnight at her place and then go on in the morning. I've been away long enough.'

She was within a few feet of the group now and again she thought, By, but that girl's beautiful. Fascinated, she stared at the heart-shaped face, the deep blue eyes and golden hair. Polly's fingers unconsciously went to her own skin which bore the scars and blemishes of the acne she'd suffered years before as she took in the pure milk and roses complexion in front of her. She wondered what it would be like to wake up every morning and look in the mirror and see that face staring back at her.

It was as the Heaths made their goodbyes and the girl bent down to hear something one of the bairns was saying, that Polly realised with a stab of panic that she didn't know where Vincent was. Glancing round, her eyes swept the crowd and then she saw him coming straight for her. Without hesitating she darted behind a laurel bush and crouched down, fiddling with her boot as though she was tying the laces. With luck, he wouldn't notice her.

When she heard him speak she wondered for a moment if it *was* Vincent. His voice was deep and soft, with a quality she couldn't put a name to because she was unable to associate tenderness with the man she knew. 'Hello, Constance,' he said.

'H–hello.'

'I've been waiting to talk to you.'

Peering through the leaves of the bush, Polly could just make out that the two of them were alone, since the bairns had obviously run off to join the others. She saw the girl glance around before she said, 'I have to go, there're people I need to thank. Everyone's been so kind and I don't want to miss anyone.'

'I searched for you.'

'What?'

'When they sent you away, I looked for you for months. It was because of me, wasn't it? They didn't want you to marry the weighman but I don't have to do that job any more. I've got plenty put by, Constance. More than enough for us to make a new life somewhere and for us to live in clover. I'll sell the cottage and we can buy a place wherever you like. You can furnish it – you'd like that, wouldn't you? And—'

'What are you talking about?'

Polly saw the girl back away and as she did so Vincent caught her arm.

'Us,' he said. 'I'm talking about us. We made plans,

don't you remember? We talked about how it was going to be.'

'No, we didn't. Let go of me.'

'What's the matter?' There was a note of almost childish temper in his voice, like the moment before a bairn threw a tantrum. 'Look, you don't have to worry about the old folk any more, they're gone. You're free now, aren't you? And the rest of them don't matter. I've waited for you for years—'

Again she broke into his pleading, pulling her arm free as she said, 'I didn't want you to wait. I never wanted you to wait.'

'You said you'd marry me. I know it wasn't your fault they made you go away, but there's nothing stopping us now.'

'I didn't say I'd marry you, I never said that. I don't want to marry anyone. I've only come back for the funeral, that's all. Now leave me alone and go away.'

'You don't mean that, and you don't have to worry about folk—'

She cut him off. 'I do mean it.'

'No. Wait, Hannah.' Again Polly saw him clutch at her.

'My name's Constance, not Hannah, and if you don't let go of me, I'll scream.'

The girl's voice had been shaky but now it was angry, and although Polly was so close she could have put her arm through the bush and touched Vincent, she couldn't hear what he said next, so low was his voice. But she heard Constance when she said, 'Well, I'm sorry but I don't love *you*. I hardly know you and you don't know me either, so how can you say you love me?'

When Constance walked away Polly still didn't dare

move. Vincent was standing with his back to her staring after the girl and even when Constance left the cemetery in the middle of a big group of family and friends, he still remained where he was. It wasn't until Father Duffy came up and tried to engage him in conversation that he walked away, his face grim and tight.

Once she was sure it was all clear Polly emerged from her hiding-place and joined the last stragglers leaving the graveyard. Outside the low stone walls she looked about her. No one had spoken to her, not even Father Duffy, but she was still glad she'd come and not only to pay her respects to the woman who had shown some kindness to her. She had been thirteen years old when Vincent McKenzie had brought her to the cottage from the workhouse: she was now thirty-seven, and apart from his physical needs, she knew as little about her employer now as she had done then. He was capable of great cruelty – the way he'd watched his mother die inch by inch was always at the back of her mind – and even though she hadn't been with a man other than him she knew the depravity he subjected her to wasn't natural, but Vincent himself was a mystery and one she'd been content to leave well alone. But here he was declaring himself in love with Mrs Gray's granddaughter, that beautiful young lass with the face of an angel.

Polly began to walk swiftly; she knew a short-cut to the cottage down Staffordshire Street and past the coal depot where the wagonway ended, and then over the fields to Fulforth Wood. She had to get back before Vincent came in and realised she'd been out. The mood he'd be in, it wouldn't take much for him to go for her. It never did at the best of times.

She was sticky and hot by the time she got home, but to her great relief Vincent wasn't there. She'd left their dinner – a thick rabbit stew – gently cooking in the oven, and there was stottie cake fresh from her baking that morning to go with it, so once she had changed into her old skirt and blouse she was free to go outside and work in the vegetable plot at the back of the cottage; although she didn't regard it as work, not on a day like today when the sky was a cloudless blue and the air was sweet with the smell of the ripe juicy blackberries which grew in the hedgerow bordering the garden from the wood.

Once she was sure it looked as though she had been in the garden for a while, she sat back on her heels and thought about what she'd heard at the funeral. Him, Vincent, thinking he could have that beautiful young lass, that she'd look the side he was on. Polly's thin lips curled back from her teeth at the thought of it. He must have been mad to imagine such a thing, especially the way he was now.

When she had first come to the cottage she had thought him handsome in an austere sort of way, 'a fine figure of a man' as one of the girls at the workhouse had said when they'd seen him waiting in the vestibule while she collected her things from the dormitory. Even ten years ago he had still been presentable, but since he'd started the drinking his face had gone red and flabby, and his belly had swelled. He still had a good shock of thick hair, she'd give him that, but it was grey and brittle-looking, and when he took off his hat indoors it stuck up from his head like horns either side, except where it had been flattened. And it might well be horns because if ever there was a devil in human form, it was him.

Polly closed her eyes for a moment, tilting her head backwards and letting the hot sun beat on her eyelids and colour the world golden. Since he'd taken to the bottle his demands on her were less though – sometimes two or three weeks would elapse between the nights he called her into his room, although every evening she lived in dread of it.

She had long since ceased to pray that he would die, although in the early days she had lived in hope that one or more of the men who hated him would wait for him one dark night. But, 'the devil looks after his own'. One of the women at the workhouse used to say that, when she was grumbling against the hardships the matron used to heap upon them, like giving them broth with all the consistency of dishwater while the matron and her crew sat down to lamb or beef with roast potatoes and a nice pudding to follow. They had used to laugh at old Beattie but she'd been right, although the matron wasn't a patch on Vincent for heartlessness. And now he wanted to get his hands on Mrs Gray's granddaughter. Imagine, a dirty old swine like him touching a lovely young lass like her.

But Constance had certainly told him what was what. She'd sent him away with a flea in his ear, and good on her.

Polly opened her eyes, pulling her straw bonnet more firmly on to her head as she continued with her weeding. She suspected she might well suffer as a result of Constance's treatment of Vincent but she was glad nonetheless, and not only for the lass's sake. She would have hated for Vincent to get what he wanted.

Constance left Sacriston with Ivy that same day. Ivy had stabled the horse with the blacksmith overnight and

Constance arranged to meet her at his premises in the late afternoon. She was terrified that if she left from the house, Vincent would be watching. Now she thought about it, she was convinced it had been him hiding in the hedgerow the other morning, and for that reason she exited Molly's house by the front door rather than the normal back way, keeping her eyes peeled as she walked the dusty streets to the smithy in Plawsworth Road south of New Town.

She had told Ivy what had occurred with Vincent at the cemetery and why it was necessary to leave quietly, and when she reached the smithy the horse and trap were waiting. Ivy was all of a dither until they had left Sacriston behind them, constantly turning in her seat to check the road behind and peering to the left and right until it seemed as if her head was rotating on her neck. Constance felt the same but she tried to keep calm. Nonetheless she was glad of the reassurance of the long heavy stick her aunt had secured from somewhere and slid along the back of the seat where they sat.

It was only when they were well on their way to Durham that Constance allowed herself to dwell on her last goodbye to Matt. He and his parents had come back to Molly's along with family and other friends for a bite to eat after the funeral, and although Molly's front room and kitchen and even the backyard had been full of folk talking and eating and drinking, she had known exactly where Matt was at every moment. She was glad Tilly hadn't accompanied him but she was disappointed not to meet his daughter. It would have been painful, knowing Rebecca was part of Tilly and him, but she would have liked to see her nonetheless.

He had already spoken to Molly and Edwin before he'd taken her aside, looking uncharacteristically smart in his Sunday suit. When he'd reached for her hand her fingers had quivered in his for a moment before she could control them, and his brown eyes with their thick lashes hadn't been smiling. They'd stared at each other for a moment before he'd said, 'I'm sorry your grandma has gone, lass. She was a fine woman with a big heart and she'll be missed. I'm sorry you're not staying longer too.'

Considering how she was feeling inside, her voice had been remarkably steady. 'I'm afraid I can't.'

'Aye, I know, I know.' His eyes had covered her face before he'd murmured, 'Do you ever wish you could go back in time and change things, Constance? See clearly what you'd missed first time round? I do.'

As his eyes had done, now hers followed the bone formation of his face. From somewhere – she still didn't know where – she had found the strength to gently remove her hand from his and say lightly, 'My grandma always used to say hindsight was like bairns, a mixed blessing.'

He had smiled for a moment. 'As always, she was right.'

She had feasted her eyes on him one last time and her voice hadn't reflected her inner turmoil when she'd said, 'Goodbye, Matt. I hope everything goes well for you in the future.'

And then he had kissed her. Just a fleeting touch of his lips on her cheek, but for a brief wonderful moment she'd been close to him, close enough to smell the faintly astringent soap he used and the barely discernible odour of pipe tobacco which clung to his clothes. It was like coming home.

'You all right, lass?' Ivy brought her back to the present

with a jolt as she patted her arm. 'Not long now. My, it's been a day and a half, hasn't it? But I tell you one thing, lass. If ever you needed proof you did the right thing in getting away from the village, you had it today. Your grandma always used to say there was something funny about that Vincent, even when he was a lad trailing after your mam. But to expect you to take up with him like that, it isn't decent. You're well rid of that one. Still, with your grandma gone there's nothing tying you to Sacriston any more, is there?'

'No,' Constance agreed dully. 'No, there isn't.'

'You can get on with your own life – and what a life, eh, lass? Your goings-on have been the talk of the village for years. Who'd ever have guessed you going into service as a scullerymaid could lead to such things. But you deserve it, lass. Saving that little bairn an' all. Aye, you deserve it. But still, you're a lucky girl and no mistake. A very lucky girl.' Ivy smiled warmly at her. 'What do you say, lass?'

Constance moved her lips in a smile. 'Yes, I'm lucky, Aunt Ivy. Very lucky.'

PART THREE

Roots

1910

Chapter 16

Constance stared in open amazement at Sir Henry Ashton before looking to Lady Isabella, who said, 'Oh my dear Shelton, don't look so shocked. Surely you sensed this might happen one day, and by your own admission there is little to hold you in England.'

'My wife's health is so much improved here we really can't put off the move any longer.' Sir Henry glanced at his wife as he spoke, his voice soft.

'No, no, I see that, sir, my lady. Of course I do.' Constance nodded as she spoke. The three of them were sitting in easy chairs on the terrace of the villa at Lake Garda. Below them in the harbour Edmond was helping Roberto gut the fish they had caught earlier, and she had been standing looking on until a maid had summoned her to the terrace where her employers were sitting enjoying a glass of wine as the sun set. Edmond was now thirteen years old and her duties within the family had changed once he had gone away to boarding school three years ago. During termtime she became Miss Charlotte's and Miss Gwendoline's personal maid–cum–chaperone, Nanny Price having retired some years before, but in the holidays when the boy was home it was accepted that he would claim much of her attention, simply because he liked being with her. But now Sir Henry had rocked her world. The Ashtons were going to live permanently in Italy and the move would be accomplished before the winter; moreover, they fully expected she would accompany them.

Lady Isabella now leaned slightly forward, her voice hushed although there was no chance of anyone hearing them: 'Miss Charlotte would like to get married from here and they intend to set a date for early next summer. There are some pieces from England she wishes to have for her own house.'

Charlotte had become engaged the year before to a distant cousin from a branch of the Morosini family in Florence. She and her sister were staying with her fiancé's parents for a few days, but Edmond had asked to remain at Lake Garda where he could fish and swim to his heart's content.

Thinking of her charge, Constance said, 'But Master Edmond's schooling, my lady?' Like most of the young boys in the circle in which the Ashtons moved, Edmond's place at public school and university had been mapped out shortly after he was born.

Lady Isabella's voice was a little stiff when she replied, 'There are excellent establishments here in Italy which equal anything England has to offer.'

'Oh, of course, my lady. I didn't mean . . .' Constance's voice trailed away. She didn't know what she meant, only that the thought of leaving England for ever made her feel she couldn't breathe properly. But Lady Isabella was right, there *was* little to hold her to the country of her birth. Since Ivy had fallen and broken her hip four years ago, her visits to Grange Hall had stopped, although she enclosed a little note for Constance now and again when she wrote to her daughter. Molly wrote with news from home once in a blue moon, the last time being eighteen months ago or more. By her own admission Molly hated putting pen to paper. She was a talker, not a writer, she'd declared more than once.

'Think over what we have said,' Sir Henry said into the silence which had fallen. 'Lady Isabella and I think very highly of you, but the decision has to be yours, of course. However, we would be sorry – very sorry – if you feel you cannot leave England.'

'And not just us, I think.' Isabella smiled archly. 'Signor Menitto will also be disappointed.'

Constance knew her cheeks were burning as she excused herself and left the couple, who were smiling benignly at her.

Giuseppe Menitto, the family's estate manager in Lake Garda, had made no secret of his regard for her over the last few years and persisted in his attentions even though she'd made it clear she looked on him only as a friend. The trouble was, she liked Giuseppe. She had grown to like him more and more the better they'd become acquainted. But liking wasn't love.

At forty-five, Giuseppe was fifteen years older than her but being tall and lean and very fit he didn't look a day over thirty-five and was handsome in a rugged, Latin sort of way. Altogether a very masculine man. His position as estate manager was a powerful one, and he was wealthy enough to enjoy a good standard of living, owning a large house complete with housekeeper and maid. But besides all that he was a kind and gentle man, a true gentleman, and charming.

Constance smiled to herself as she walked down the wide stone staircase to the basement of the villa where a door opened on to more steps leading to the shore of the lake. Oh yes, Giuseppe was charming all right. She had teased him the other night when they had walked together along the shoreline that he could charm the birds out of the trees, and he had agreed with her, saying any true Italian was the same.

She paused with her hand on the door knob. If she left England and came to live here, Giuseppe would ask her to marry him, she knew that. And she also knew that they would have the Ashtons' blessing. She would live in a beautiful house with servants of her own, and Giuseppe's considerable extended family of sisters and brothers and nieces and nephews would accept her as one of them because she was Giuseppe's choice. She would be able to have children of her own, become a wife and mother. The ache in her heart which grew stronger with each year that passed caused her to press her hand against her chest. She longed to hold her own child in her arms, to have a baby to love and cherish. And Giuseppe wanted a large family: from what she'd seen, all Italians were the same. Her children could grow up healthy and strong in this safe, tranquil place, blossoming in the sun like precious flowers.

Again she gave a rueful smile at the poetic path her thoughts had taken. But it was true. It was all true. The chemical works and iron foundries, the stinking factories and mines of the north-east of England were as far removed from this place as heaven is to hell. This morning she had woken up to find her room bathed from floor to ceiling in a brilliant orange glow, the sunshine having been filtered through the sail of one of the boats out on the lake. She had pulled back her curtains and sat gazing over the still and limpid water for some time, not really thinking of anything, just being.

It would be madness not to embrace what could be the perfect life because of someone in England who had probably forgotten all about her by now. Someone who had loved and married another girl, who'd had a bairn by them. Someone who wasn't and never could be hers. She would always be grateful to Matt for saving her life, maybe she'd always love him in a private room in her heart, but she was thirty years old and she wanted more in life than caring for other people's children and living in someone else's home. And that wasn't wrong, it was natural.

The heartaches of the past, along with the spectre of Vincent McKenzie, who still featured in the odd nightmare from time to time, would be banished if she made her home in Italy. And Giuseppe was a good man. She liked and respected him and she would grow to love him. There was nothing not to love.

She opened the door and walked out on to the top of the steps, but she didn't immediately descend. Instead she stood looking over the water which the setting sun had turned into a blazing lake of red and gold. She could be content living in this spot, she told herself, as the warm wind caressed her face. Giuseppe had told her that in the morning the wind called the *Vento* blew from the north whilst in the afternoon it was the *Ora* from the south, but it made no difference to her. Even when the winds whipped up the waters of the lake into violent storms they were nothing like the bone-chilling savage winds of home. Everything was gentler here, softer.

Edmond turned and saw her, raising his hand before returning to his grisly work with Roberto. His blond hair had already been bleached a couple of shades lighter since they'd been here, and Constance was insistent that he wore a long-sleeved shirt when he was out sailing with the boatman, for fear he'd be burned by the hot Italian sun. She loved Edmond dearly and she knew the boy didn't regard her as a servant but more as one of the family. If she married Giuseppe she would be able to stay close to Edmond and the rest of the family and still share in their lives to some extent.

'Come and see, Constance!' Edmond shouted to her, beckoning. He had never called her Shelton as his parents did. 'We've plenty for dinner tonight. Cook will be pleased.'

'I'm coming.' She began to walk down the steps, the tumult that had arisen in her mind when Sir Henry had first spoken to her quietened. She had made her decision.

Chapter 17

Tilly felt sick with fear. She had felt sick for weeks, and not just because of the physical effects of the child growing in her belly. When her monthlies had stopped she hadn't been able to believe what her body was telling her at first. Rupert had said he'd be careful, he *was* careful, so how could this have happened to her? She'd prayed for a while that it was an early onset of the change – she was in her late thirties, after all, and her mother had told her once that she'd stopped having her monthlies before she was forty. But then the sickness had begun, not much at first but now she felt ill every time she ate and the weight had dropped off her – everywhere except her belly, that is.

She put her hand to her stomach and Rupert, who was sitting at the side of her, said, 'All right, lass?'

All right? No, she wasn't all right. How could she be all right knowing what she was about to do? But she had no choice. When she'd told Rupert about the baby he had said he'd make arrangements for her to see someone who could get rid of it. It had been cut and dried as far as he was concerned. And now here they were in this squalid little house in Chester Le Street, five miles from the village. There was a midwife, Rupert had told her. She was well-known. For the right price she would see to things and no questions asked. She hadn't asked how he knew about the woman; she didn't care.

'It'll soon be over.' Rupert put his hand over hers but she jerked it away.

He didn't care about her, not really. Everyone and everything came before her, she thought bitterly. His wife, his bairns, his position as postmaster and his comfortable going-on; she was bottom of the list. When she looked back, Rupert had ruined her life and yet she'd still started up with him again. She must have been mad. But she had been lonely. She'd wanted to be loved.

'I hope she's not much longer, I told Mrs Clark I'd be back before eleven,' Rupert said after another two or three minutes had ticked by. He'd arranged for one of the neighbours to come in and sit with his wife while he took care of some 'post-office business' with the post-master in Chester Le Street, using that as the excuse to borrow Miss Newton's horse and trap for the evening. Tilly had told Matt she had to work late, and Rupert had picked her up some distance down Edmondsley Lane north of the pit once he'd closed up the post office for the night.

As though on cue, the door to the front room where they had been shown by a slovenly-looking girl opened, and a big, stoutly built woman bustled in. 'Sorry to have kept you waitin', dear,' she said to Tilly, her gaze encompassing Rupert for a moment. 'One of my ladies had her baby a mite early. I'm Mrs Hammond, Ethel Hammond. Nice to meet you both.'

'Mr and Mrs Irvin,' Rupert responded, holding out his hand. 'How do you do?'

Ethel's keen sharp eyes surveyed the man in front of her for a moment. If he was this woman's husband, she was a monkey's uncle. Still, it was no business of hers. 'Well enough,' she said, shaking his hand briefly. 'Now I understand you have a problem, dear?' she added, turning back to Tilly. 'A health problem if this pregnancy continues?'

Not knowing what Rupert had led the midwife to believe, Tilly said simply, 'I can't have this bairn.'

'I see, dear.' Ethel nodded slowly. 'Well, you come upstairs with me and I'll see what's what, all right? Your husband can wait here. My lass'll get you a cup of tea shortly,' she added to Rupert.

As the woman disappeared into the dark hall Tilly glanced helplessly at Rupert. She didn't want to do this but the prospect of telling Matt she was expecting again was more frightening than anything waiting for her upstairs. Rupert inclined his head at the doorway in a gesture which said, Get on with it.

On leaden feet she followed the midwife up the narrow wooden stairs. There was a strong smell of cabbage and unwashed bodies permeating the air and she was struggling with all her might not to retch. Once on the tiny landing that held two doors, one of which was closed, she stepped into the room the midwife had entered. To her surprise it was cleaner than the rest of the house. The bare floorboards had been scrubbed and bleached until they were a light brown and the walls were white-washed. A long trestle table stood against one wall with a straw mattress and folded grey blankets on it, and in a corner of the room another much smaller table held a wooden bucket, a washbowl, strips of towelling and carbolic soap.

Ethel placed the black bag she had been carrying on this table as she said, 'Take off your bloomers and hop up over there, lass, then we'll take a look at you. You've had bairns before, I take it?'

'One. She – she's coming up for seventeen.'

'Just the one?'

Tilly nodded as she scrambled up on to the long table by means of a three-legged stool standing beside it.

'Was that by choice or because it simply didn't happen?'

'My – my husband didn't want any more bairns.'

'And you? What did you want?'

Tilly was sitting up and now she looked at the midwife who was busy scrubbing at her hands with a nailbrush and the soap. 'That didn't really come into it, what I wanted. It's – it's a long story.'

'Lass, if I had a bob for every time I've heard that I'd be a rich woman,' Ethel said quietly. 'The bloke downstairs isn't your husband, is he?'

Tilly shook her head. 'No, he isn't.'

'Is the bairn his? The bloke who brought you here?'

'Aye, yes.'

'An' there's no chance you could pass it off as your husband's?'

A tear seeped out and down Tilly's cheek. 'If there was I wouldn't be here,' she whispered. 'My husband and I, we haven't – I mean for years he hasn't wanted . . .'

'Don't upset yourself, lass. I get your drift. And this other one, he's married an' all, I take it?'

'Aye.' Tilly's head had drooped but now she raised it as she said, 'I'm not a bad woman, I'm not. I've only ever

256

been with the two of them, my husband and – and Mr Irvin.'

Again Ethel said, 'Don't upset yourself, lass,' even as she thought, And if that's his real name I'll eat my hat. She smiled kindly at Tilly. 'Lie down now, lass. I need to examine you and see how far gone you are for meself, to make sure. It'll be uncomfortable, I warn you now.'

It was uncomfortable and it seemed to go on for ever. Tilly was sweating with the pain by the time the midwife walked over to the smaller table and washed her hands. She pulled up her bloomers under the blanket Ethel had thrown over her, but her legs were trembling so much she didn't attempt to get down from the trestle table.

The midwife seemed to take a long time drying her hands. When she eventually came to stand by the makeshift bed, she stared down at Tilly for some moments before she said softly, 'Lass, you're not expecting a bairn.'

Tilly struggled into a sitting position, wincing as she did so. 'What? I must be. My monthlies have stopped and everything.'

'There's no bairn in there. How long has it been since your monthlies have stopped?'

'They – they haven't been right for a long time, maybe a couple of years. That's why I didn't worry when they stopped altogether, not at first anyway. Then I started to feel bad.'

'And when was that? That they stopped completely?'

'Four months ago, nearly five now.' Tilly stared into Ethel's face and something in the midwife's expression made her breath catch in her throat. 'What's the matter with me?'

'Go and see a doctor, lass. I'm only a midwife.'

'No.' As Ethel made to turn away, Tilly clutched at her arm. 'Please, tell me. There's something wrong, isn't there?'

'Lass, I know everything there is to know about delivering babies but like I said, I'm no doctor.'

'Please.' The blood had drained from Tilly's face, leaving it chalk-white. 'If I'm not having a bairn, what's wrong with me? You know, don't you? Please tell me.'

Ethel stared at her, chewing on her lower lip. Then she seemed to come to a decision. 'You've lost weight?'

'Aye, but that's because of the sickness.'

'And that started when?'

'I've been having queasy spells for months, years even, but the last five months I haven't been able to keep much down. And – and that's when my belly got bigger. So I thought . . .'

'I think you've got some kind of growth in there, lass, but it's not a bairn.'

'A growth?' Tilly was staring at the midwife but not seeing her. For the moment she was only capable of listening to her words and repeating them.

'Aye, but a doctor'll tell you better than I can.'

'It's – it's serious?' And then Tilly shook her head as she said, 'Of course it's serious. It is, isn't it?'

There were many who would describe Ethel Hammond as a tough old bird, and rightly so, but they would have been surprised how tender her voice sounded as she said, 'Mebbe, lass, but I can't say for sure. Look, you take a minute or two to rest up and I'll get you a cup of tea. I'll send your bloke up, shall I?'

'No.' And then Tilly moderated her voice as she repeated, 'No. Thank you, Mrs Hammond, but no.'

The midwife nodded. 'As you like, lass. I'll go and get that tea.'

Alone, Tilly lay down again, pulling the thin blankets over her. She was shivering, shaking, but she lay as still as her limbs would let her. There was no bairn. What she had thought was the worst thing that could have happened to her had turned out not to be the worst after all. She was sick. If Mrs Hammond was to be believed, and there was no reason for the midwife to lie, she had been sick for a long time without knowing it. Unconsciously her hand went to the rounded swell of her stomach before she brought it sharply away. There was no baby but a monstrous something feeding off her, and it was growing. She curled into a little ball, too terror-stricken for the relief of tears as she stared dry-eyed at the white-washed wall. She was going to die. She had read it in Mrs Hammond's eyes.

Matt was bone weary. Another strike was on the cards at the pit, there had been a wave of them all over the Durham coalfield in the last few years. He supported the union – who wouldn't, when their sole aim was to improve working conditions and safety, along with seeing that their members got a decent wage – but any enforced idleness brought home the fact that his life wasn't worth living. Not that he wanted to end it like the poor devils who'd been crushed and burned to death at West Stanley last year, or the Glebe Colliery the year before that. Hell, no. But he was tired of what had become merely an existence.

He stretched his legs before standing up and throwing his newspaper on the kitchen table. It had been full of reports that the cotton workers were preparing to strike, in sympathy with the Welsh miners and the dockers who'd been out since the beginning of the month. It was clear to everyone that the Shipbuilding Employers' Federation were digging in for a long fight after they had taken the step to instigate the national lock-out. Things were already getting nasty in certain areas of the country, with rioting and the ensuing violence. The next thing would be the troops being sent in to help the police, which would inflame the situation like a red rag to a bull. He had seen it all before.

Glancing at the wooden clock on the mantelpiece above the range, Matt saw it was eleven o'clock. Eleven o'clock and Tilly still not home. He could have done with her here tonight, in view of young Larry making a surprise appearance and the resulting scene with Rebecca after he'd given the lad short shrift. It was rare he and Tilly saw eye to eye on anything, but for once they were singing from the same songsheet over this.

Thoughts of Rebecca caused the frown on his face to deepen. For the first time in his life he was at loggerheads with the lass and it didn't sit well, but the idea of her keeping company with Larry Alridge had made him see red when she had broached the matter at the weekend. Rebecca was sixteen, for crying out loud. She had all the time in the world for that sort of thing, once she was a little older. And Larry coming to see him tonight to request his permission to start courting Rebecca didn't cut no ice either. She might have been working in the village shop since she'd left school, but she was still nowt but a bairn, whereas Larry at seventeen was ready to start sowing some wild oats. But not with his Rebecca. He had been seventeen once. He knew how it was with lads.

He was standing wondering whether to go up to bed or make himself a cup of tea when the back door opened and Tilly walked in. He glanced fleetingly at his wife and was turning away when his eyes shot back to her face. 'What is it?'

When she gave no answer but stood looking at him, he was about to shrug and make himself scarce when some inner prompting caused him to remain where he was and say, in a far softer voice than he normally used when talking to her, 'Tilly, what's the matter? Has something happened?'

To his amazement she didn't fire back with one of her caustic retorts. Instead he watched her reach blindly for a chair and pull it out from the table, and it was only when she was seated that she whispered, 'I have to talk to you.'

'Yes?' His brows were drawn together. This was a different woman from the one who had left the house earlier.

'Sit down. Please,' she added, when he didn't move. 'Please sit down.'

This wasn't like her usual histrionics. He looked hard at her. Then he slowly walked to the table and sat down on the edge of it, mainly because it had come to him that she didn't look well.

'I – I've been to Chester Le Street tonight.'

'Chester Le Street? What are you talking about? You told me you had to work late because Nancy Wood's mother's ill and couldn't see to the bairns.'

She didn't comment on this and her face could have been made out of plaster cast when she said stiffly, 'I went there to see a midwife because I thought I was expecting a bairn – Rupert Wood's bairn. I thought it was a case of history repeating itself.'

For a moment the enormity of what she'd said didn't dawn on him; it was as though he was transfixed by her words. Numbly, he said, 'What did you say?'

'I thought I was pregnant again by Rupert.'

It was the 'again' which brought him to life. Rage as hot as molten metal surged through him, taking the numbness with it, and he sprang forward, grabbing her arms and yanking her to her feet as he shook her so violently her head bobbed like a rag doll's. 'You dare to sit there and tell me that, as if it's nothing. You and him, all this time.'

When she went limp in his grasp he thought for a moment she was feigning. It was only when her head lolled and she slipped to the floor that he realised the faint was real. Anger was blinding him and he could, without the slightest compunction, have put his hands round her throat and throttled her where she lay. Her and that little runt of a postmaster, it was unbelievable. And him with a sick wife and umpteen bairns. When he had thought about Rebecca's father he'd always imagined it to be a young lad like himself. For years he had stared into the other men's faces at the mine, looking for a flicker in their eyes which would have told him they were the one. And he'd let her take up her whoring for a second time. He'd allowed her to go and work for that conniving so-and-so because at bottom he'd felt sorry for her. Aye, and a bit guilty, he admitted it. But he needn't have bothered, need he. No, by hell he needn't.

The urge to do her harm was so strong he didn't trust himself to touch her, but when after a minute or two she still hadn't come round he felt obliged to pick her up off the stone flags. He carried her over to the settle and placed her on it, positioning one of the flock cushions under her head. As he did so it came to him she was little more than skin and bone. When had she lost all that weight? And her skin, it was a sickly-looking colour.

Her eyelids flickered as he stood staring down at her and when her eyes opened he didn't turn away. He said the obvious: 'You passed out.'

She shut her eyes again, but when a tear slid down her ashen face he said gruffly, 'I'll get you a drink.'

'No, no, I need to talk to you.'

'You can talk to me, but over a cup of tea. I need one if you don't.'

She said no more, lying as still as a statue as he boiled the kettle and made the tea. He put plenty of sugar in hers and when he took it to her she swung her feet down on the floor and sat up, taking the cup from him as she mumbled, 'Thank you. I need to explain—'

'Drink that first, all of it.'

She looked like a little old shrunken woman sitting there, and so desolate and alone he found the anger was evaporating, even as he reminded himself she'd made a fool of him for the second time. But then again – he hadn't wanted her, so could he really blame her for going elsewhere? How many times had he seriously considered seeking relief for the torment his body had put him through over the years? Too many to count. He'd even got as far as the doorstep of a whore-house he'd heard about in Lanchester, the next village west of here, half a dozen times but had found himself unable to take the final step and go in. It hadn't been the fact he was a married man or anything Father Duffy preached from the pulpit which had stopped him, nor yet any finer feelings about right and wrong or paying for it. He had simply known he would never be able to look Constance in the face should they ever meet again, and it was this which had sent him walking home on leaden feet, telling himself he was every kind of fool.

When Tilly finally put the cup down on the seat beside her, he said quietly, 'How long has it been going on? Or perhaps I should ask if it ever stopped?'

'It did stop,' she said quickly. 'When we got wed it was over, I swear it, and for years it remained like that, but when I went to work for him again . . .' She looked down at her hands gripped together in her lap, the knuckles showing up like bleached bones. 'I've no excuse, Matt. I know that.'

'Do you love him?'

'No.' It was definite. 'I thought I did once, when I was a young lass, but no.' She drew in a long breath, raising her head and glancing quickly at him before looking down at her hands once more. 'You probably won't believe this, and I don't blame you, but before I thought I was − was pregnant, I'd told him I wanted nothing more to do with him in that way. I'd finished it, once and for all.'

'Why didn't you tell me − in the early days, I mean? Admit you'd tricked me into marrying you? Why did you keep up the pretence even after you knew I knew?' It was something that had puzzled him for years.

Colour suffused her thin cheeks then ebbed almost immediately. 'At first I was frightened.' She gulped, her hands twisting in her lap before becoming still once more. 'And I thought if I kept to my story you just might believe me. Stupid, I know. But after a while it wasn't that, but because—'

'Because what?'

'I – I realised I loved you and I knew you would never love me if I told you the truth.'

Matt put a hand to his mouth and rubbed it slowly, pulling his lips first one way and then the other. Dear gussy, what a mess they'd made of things. What an unholy mess.

'I knew you wanted Constance. You did want her, didn't you?' And then before he could reply she went on, 'Not that that matters, not now, but at the time I imagined if I told you about Rupert you'd go looking for her. I hated you and I loved you and . . .' She shook her head. 'And time went on and I couldn't back down, I suppose.' She leaned against the high wooden back of the seat, her voice but a whisper as she said, 'I couldn't believe you'd keep it up, the not touching me, not after how you'd been when we were courting. I thought you'd come round eventually.'

There was something nagging at the back of his mind and then he realised what it was. 'You said you thought you were expecting again. You're not then? There's no bairn?'

'No, there's no bairn,' she said flatly.

'So why tell me? Not just about tonight but any of it?'

'The midwife examined me.' Her voice expressed a kind of terror. 'She said I'm ill, that I need to see a doctor. This' – she touched her stomach and for the first time he noticed a roundness that was at odds with the thinness of the rest of her – 'is a growth. That's what she said.'

He stared at her. 'Don't be daft.'

'I haven't felt right for a long time but in the spring it got worse. I – I think she's right.'

'Why the hell didn't you go and see the quack before?'

265

'I don't know. Some days I didn't feel so bad and then I'd tell myself I was all right. Other times I put it down to – to women's trouble. I thought it would pass.'

'You thought it would pass.' He repeated her words.

'You know me, I don't like doctors,' she said defensively. 'If you're not sick before you see them you are after, the things they put in your head, and all to sell you a bottle of medicine that's coloured water, like as not.'

'Tilly—' He stopped abruptly, and when he next spoke the note of exasperation was gone. 'You're seeing Doctor Fallow tomorrow. He might be young but that's to his advantage. He's fresh out of medical school apparently and full of all the new-fangled ideas and advances that are happening.'

She didn't reply immediately, and when she did speak it was to say very quietly, 'I'm frightened, Matt.'

Again he stared at her in the dim light from the oil lamp in the middle of the kitchen table. It was probably a trick of the shadows but her eyes looked lifeless, like a corpse's in her white face. He wanted to say there was nothing to worry about, but it wasn't a night for useless platitudes. He wondered how it was that his anger had vanished, to be replaced by a wish to comfort as he said softly, 'Do you want me to come with you?'

The look of surprise on her face heaped coals of fire on his head. Still more were added when she murmured tremblingly, 'Would you? Would you come?'

He nodded. The need to say he was sorry for how he had behaved towards her over the years was strong, but under the circumstances it would smack too much of the hypocrite. Anyway, as his mam was fond of saying, actions speak louder than words. He would see her through this, however it turned out. He owed her that at least. He owed her a lot more but it was too late to turn back the clock, and maybe he wouldn't act any differently if it was possible, being the pig-headed man he was.

His voice even softer, he said, 'Come on, lass. Let's get you to bed. You look all done in.'

Chapter 18

Two months later, on a bitterly cold November day when the cavalry were called to ride out to restore order in Welsh coalfields, Tilly Heath died. According to Dr Fallow, the disease had gone into her liver, which had precipitated her sudden end. And this, the young doctor said privately to Matt, was actually a blessing in disguise. He had seen people linger on for months in unbearable pain and anguish, and Tilly had been spared that.

Matt knew the doctor meant well but he had looked into the dead face of his wife and his heart had cried out in protest, a remorse gripping him that was comparable with nothing that he had felt in his life before. Even the torments of his love for Constance paled before this terrible regret and guilt. He had made Tilly's life miserable for sixteen years.

True, he had provided for her and unlike some men he knew he had never asked her to account for every penny of the housekeeping he gave her each week, or quibbled if she bought this or that for herself or Rebecca. Indeed, compared to most of the women hereabouts she had lived very comfortably. With having only the one bairn it had been rare they had had to scrimp and save or go without, and he had often worked double shifts to make sure they had money put by for the rent and food should he fall ill for a bit or one of the strikes drag on. But that was just material wellbeing. And right now it didn't mean a jot.

He had been holding Tilly's hand and talking to her when she had slipped away in the middle of the night, although according to the doctor she had been unable to hear or feel anything since she'd fallen into a coma two days before. Nevertheless with his conscience crying loud he had sat in a chair by the bed every moment when he wasn't at work, dozing now and again but most of the time pouring out his heart in a way he had to acknowledge he would never have done if she had been conscious. He had cared for her the best he could since the morning after her visit to Chester Le Street. Dr Fallow had confirmed the midwife's diagnosis and Tilly had gone rapidly downhill. It was as though in knowing what was wrong, her body had given up.

And now she had gone. It was too late to make amends, too late to start afresh. He had known she wanted more bairns in the early days and he had deprived her of that, along with so many other things.

Rebecca cried when he woke her in the morning with a cup of tea and told her the news, and she continued crying for most of that day. When she was still crying the next day after a sleepless night, Matt called Dr Fallow to the house. The doctor spent a few minutes alone with Rebecca and then came downstairs to where Matt was waiting in the kitchen.

'I've given her a strong sedative. She should sleep for a good few hours once it's taken effect, but you might like to have a chat with her in a moment before she goes to sleep. It's only natural she is upset about her mother, but I feel there's something more bothering her – something she needs to get off her chest. Are the two of you close?'

'Yes. No.' Matt shook his head to clear his mind. 'What I mean is, we were up until a while ago. There's a lad she likes and who likes her, it caused a bit of bother as her mother and I didn't think she was old enough to start courting. But aye, I'd say me an' the bairn are close.'

Dr Fallow placed a gentle hand on his arm. 'Rebecca is a young woman, Mr Heath, not a child. And young women can be emotional, very emotional. It might be as well to remember that when you speak to her.'

Matt saw the doctor out, then stood in the hall for a moment, looking up the stairs. He'd got Tilly laid out in the front room and Rebecca beside herself upstairs. What had happened to their humdrum going-on? And that about Rebecca being a young woman; what had the doctor meant by that? He didn't think she could be . . . His heart stopped and then raced so fast the blood thundered in his ears. No, no. Rebecca was a good girl.

But bonny, bonny as a summer's day, and lads would always be lads. Maybe they'd all but thrown her into Larry Alridge's arms by taking the stance they had? And with Tilly being so poorly he hadn't had time to concentrate on anything else over the last couple of months. Come to think of it, Rebecca had flitted about the place like a silent little shadow when she hadn't been taking a turn with her mam, once she was back from the shop.

He took the stairs two at a time but stopped on the

tiny landing to compose himself before he tapped on the door. Her dull, 'Come in,' had him swallowing against the panic gripping his vitals.

'Doctor Fallow said he's given you something to help you sleep.' He smiled a brittle smile. She looked so small lying there in the narrow iron bed as though in contradiction of Dr Fallow's statement that she was a young woman. But the doctor was right. Rebecca would be seventeen soon and Tilly had already been seduced by that piece of scum in the post office by then. She had been barely fifteen when he had first taken her. *Fifteen*. Matt had wanted to go round and smash the postmaster's face in when Tilly had told him that. And him acting the respectable pillar of the community!

Matt sat down on the chair by the side of the bed, reaching for Rebecca's hand which remained limply in his. 'Doctor Fallow thinks there's something more than this with Mam bothering you, lass. Is he right? You can tell me, you know. Whatever it is.'

For answer she shut her eyes and fear swamped him. It was a moment or two before he could trust his voice to sound normal. Then he said softly, 'Is that a yes or a no, hinny?'

She mumbled something, and when he bent his head and asked her to repeat herself, there was a long pause before she muttered, 'I – I don't want to talk about it.'

'So there is something?'

Slow, painful tears fell over the dark lashes of her lower lids and she jerked her hand free, turning over on her side away from him. 'I said I don't want to talk about it.'

He drew in a long slow breath, searching for the right words. 'Is it anything to do with Larry?' he asked quietly.

'What?' Her voice, though muffled, carried a note of surprise.

'Larry Alridge. I wondered if you'd had an argument or something, or if he'd upset you?'

'Larry?' She turned back to him, scrubbing at her eyes with the sleeve of her nightdress. 'I've hardly seen him since Mam was took bad, although he's walked me home from the shop a few times. He's waiting till my seventeenth . . .'

Relief robbed him of speech. So it wasn't that. Thank You, God, thank You. Aware of her eyes on him, he nodded, as though the question had been of little significance. 'Then what is it?'

'I can't – I mean –'

When she burst into tears again he dropped on to his knees by the bed and gathered her into his arms and he soothed her quietly. 'There, there, hinny, come on. We'll get through . . . What?' He put his ear closer to her face to catch her spluttering words.

Straightening, he raised himself to sit on the side of the bed, still with her head against his chest. 'Don't fret, hinny. Of course your mam knew how much you loved her,' he said gently. 'Where has all this come from?'

'But that's just it, Da.' She twisted round, raising her streaming eyes to his. 'I don't think she did because *I* didn't know till she was poorly. We – we never got on, me and Mam. You know we didn't, and I was horrible to her at times. I – I didn't like her. I loved her but I didn't like her. She used to say I always saw your side of things and she was right.'

She buried her face in his chest and above her head Matt shut his eyes. The sins of the parents crippling the children. From a tiny bairn she'd been made to choose between them. Not by him. Oh no, not by him. That was one thing he could say in absolute truthfulness in his defence. But he had been part of the cold war which had damaged this child. And whatever Dr Fallow said, that's what Rebecca was. A child. His child. It might not have been his seed that brought her into being, but no bairn from his loins could be more his.

'Listen to me, lass.' He had to lie now, and lie convincingly if she wasn't going to be weighed down with guilt for years, maybe the rest of her life. 'Your mam did know you loved her.' As she moved restlessly, he put her from him and looked into her face, his hands holding her upper arms. 'Do you know what she used to say to me? "That lass is a carbon copy of me, that's why we come up against each other all the time. But it says a lot if you can fight but still love each other."'

She was quieter now, looking at him, and warming to his theme he went on, 'Your mam used to say the pair of you would never see eye to eye on anything. She used to laugh about it, hinny, after some disagreement or other. She liked to think you were a chip off her block, that's how she put it. But she never, ever, doubted you loved her. That I do know.'

'You – you can't be sure.'

'Oh aye, I am. Here . . .' He reached for the small white Bible Rebecca had been given after her Confirmation, which was kept with a few other books on the shelf above the bed, and placing his hand on the cover, he said, 'I swear she knew you loved her, hinny, and that she loved you. Before God, I swear it. All right?'

'Oh, Da.'

Her relief was palpable; the weight had been lifted and that was all that mattered. For a moment he thanked the God he'd just sinned against that she was still young enough to accept the gesture as confirmation of the truth. 'Now go to sleep with an easy mind, lass. All right? If your mam was back here tomorrow, and well and fit, the two of you would still carry on in the same old way, and to tell you the truth I think she enjoyed it. She was always proud of the fact you'd got a bit of what she called spirit.'

Her smile was absolution for the lies which had tripped out of his mouth, and when she said, 'Da? Will you stay with me until I go to sleep?' he nodded.

He sat stroking her forehead as she drifted off almost immediately, and he made sure she was deeply asleep before he went downstairs. It was midday on a Thursday morning. Normally he'd have been at work and Rebecca would be at the shop and Tilly— He put a hand to his brow. He couldn't think of Tilly.

The kitchen was as warm as toast but he didn't want its comfort. Knowing that nothing short of an earthquake would rouse Rebecca for a good few hours, he bolted the back door and pulled on his coat and cap before leaving by the front door which he locked behind him. He needed to walk. He would go stark staring mad if he didn't leave the house for a while and that coffin lying on trestles in the middle of the front room.

The last glories of autumn had faded away and it was a dank, bitterly cold landscape that greeted him as he made his way to Plawsworth Road, turning left into Cross Lane after a while. Open fields stretched either side of him and the season's dreary hue matched his mood. There had been a sharp frost the night before and the ground was still frozen, the stark, bare trees and grizzled countryside shrouded in a slight mist. Within the empty fields crows glided, emitting their cackling cries, and a number circled noisily overhead as he walked.

When he reached the Cross Lane Bridge he stood for some minutes, gazing blankly in front of him. Three-quarters of a mile away his da and brothers were grubbing away down a big black hole, as he himself would be doing tomorrow, he thought dully. And all the tomorrows following it. He looked at the blue marks on his hands full of the coaldust he'd take with him to the grave, and felt a moment's piercing bitter-sweet relief that he didn't have a son to follow him down the pit. That was one anxiety he hadn't been called to bear, being responsible for taking another human soul into that hell-hole.

He pulled his muffler closer round his neck as the chill wind blasted his ears, but his lungs expanded as he sucked in the clean cold air. George and Andrew had never felt like he did about the pit, he knew that. They hadn't been able to wait till they left school and went down like their father, and in spite of their carping and daily grumbles about working conditions and such, he knew neither of them would have wanted anything else. He found that incomprehensible.

Even now, after twenty-six years of being a miner, he still had moments when, deep underground, his bowels seemed to come loose and shake, and he wanted to throw up. The desire to get out, to escape the millions of tons of rock above him would be so strong he would have to shut his eyes and press his arms against his chest to quell the panic. He hadn't noticed it so much before that first fall umpteen years ago when he'd still been courting Tilly, but after that the fear in him had grown until some days it was a battle to get into the cage and begin the descent into what he privately termed Hades.

He'd tried to bring up how he felt with George and Andrew once when the three of them were having a drink in the Colliery Inn, but they'd looked at him with such blank bewilderment he hadn't pursued the matter. George had his canaries in a shed in his backyard with an outside wire enclosure attached so they could fly out and sit in the sun when they wanted to, and Andrew had his whippets and his darts, and they were content. As long as they had a few coppers for a drink and their baccy, they didn't ask for more. He wished he could feel like that.

He should have died instead of Tilly. The sudden thought startled him and caused his eyes to narrow.

Tilly had wanted to live. Although her body had given up the fight, her mind and spirit had been strong. Whereas he felt it was more painful to carry on than to slip into a place of . . . what? Endless joy for some and endless torment for others, if Father Duffy was to be believed, or maybe – just maybe – the Hereafter might be a place of eternal, dreamless sleep. Whatever, it was infinitely preferable to anything in the here and now.

Tilly had known how he felt about Constance. He took his cap off, raking his hand through his hair and enjoying the touch of the icy wind on his scalp before he pulled it on again. And the knowledge had hurt her because of the feeling she'd apparently had for him. He couldn't, as yet, term this feeling love because there was only so much remorse he could shoulder at one time, but the truth of what she had told him had been plain to see in her face since she had known she was dying.

The waste, the futility, the pointlessness of it all swept over him anew and he drove his clenched fists against the solid oak handrail of the bridge. It was only when his knuckles were dripping blood that he could focus on the pain rather than the blackness in his mind.

He had to get control of himself. There was Rebecca, she needed him. She'd just lost her mam and he couldn't go to pieces. He'd acted a part all his married life and most folk had been none the wiser; he could do it now he was a widower. And once the funeral was over he would pay a visit to Rupert Wood and show him what he thought of a man who'd carry on with a young lass who worked for him. Tilly had begged him not to go, and rather than upset her he had fallen in with her pleading, but she had gone now and he'd see the scum got a little of what was due him. He owed it to Tilly as well as to himself.

The grey November light was briefly illuminated by the flash of a pheasant's iridescent plumage in the far distance as it strutted out of the hedgerow and made its way across a frozen ploughed field. He watched the bird until it took fright at something or other and rose squawking into the sky, and then he saw what had disturbed the bird as the reddish-brown body of a fox slunk into view. It crossed the field rapidly, and once it had reached the safety of the hedgerow, it howled a sharp triple bark. Matt knew what that meant. When he'd been a young lad working in the fields at the weekend for Farmer Todd, the farmer had taken a shine to him and would often spend his lunch-hour talking to him about the farm and the countryside. Farmer Todd had said November was the time the dog fox sought out a vixen to be his partner.

Once the pair had enlarged a rabbit burrow, they'd make a den for protection against the worst of the winter, and the cubs would be born at the end of March. Sure enough, a moment later an eerie, wailing scream rang out – a female answering the dog fox's call.

Job done. Matt smiled bitterly to himself. For supposedly dumb animals they certainly had the advantage over the human race in matters of the heart. He called, she answered – and a few months later there'd be four or five more foxes in the world. No long-drawn-out courtship, no pretence, no lies. And no getting it wrong and living the rest of your life regretting the loss of something you never had in the first place.

Oh, to hell with it! He straightened, stuffing his smarting hands in the pockets of his trousers. He had no one to blame but himself for the way his life had turned out, and he hated whingers. He would carry the weight of Tilly to his grave, but that was something he would have to come to terms with. It was either that or go under, and he couldn't afford that luxury, not with Rebecca depending on him.

Nevertheless, as he looked across the bleak, empty countryside, it reflected what he could expect of the future and he shivered, his footsteps heavy as he turned for home.

Chapter 19

'But I don't understand, Shelton.' Isabella Ashton was clutching her husband's arm as she spoke, her evident agitation confirmation of just how upset she was. Isabella had been brought up to believe one should never show one's emotions in front of the servants, even one as close to the family as Constance was. 'It is all arranged. We leave next week.'

'I know, my lady.' Constance stood wringing her hands in the middle of the drawing room at Grange Hall. This room, along with others in the house, showed signs of the exodus which was to take place shortly. In the hall, a number of trunks and cases stood ready to be shipped to Italy the next day. Some had already gone the week before and more would follow, once the family had left. The servants who were to remain in England and who were being kept on by the friends of the Ashtons who had bought Grange Hall, had a list of instructions to observe before the new family took up residence after Christmas.

'Then what has changed your mind?' Isabella's voice was calmer and she motioned for Constance to be seated as she sat down herself. Sir Henry remained standing in front of the fireplace where a roaring fire glowed and crackled. It was the last day of November, and outside the window the grounds were frozen solid with the thick white frosts which had held the north in a relentless grip for a week. 'I thought you had made your decision and were looking forward to coming with us?'

'I was, my lady, and it's not that I don't want to come, not really, but . . .' Constance's voice trailed away helplessly. How could she explain that one letter had turned all her plans upside down? She hadn't heard from Molly for months and then this morning a letter had come. She had been busy packing Miss Charlotte's trousseau all morning – Charlotte had insisted on buying everything she needed in London and hadn't trusted any of the maids to take sufficient care with the exquisite and wildly expensive items of clothing – and so she hadn't opened the letter until lunchtime. It had begun with the usual apology for not writing sooner and then listed how each member of the family was doing, but it was the postscript which had caused her heart to race.

Molly had written in her large round handwriting:

PS: Nearly forgot to tell you. Tilly Heath, Matt's wife, passed away at the beginning of the month, poor lass. Growth of some kind in her belly and her only thirty-five. He's took it hard, well, you would, wouldn't you, but the funeral was well attended and at least he's got Rebecca to see to things in the house. Like I said to Edwin, you never know what's round the corner.

She had read the words over three times, a tumult of emotion surging in her breast, not the least of which was guilt for the immediate stab of wild elation that Molly's news had brought. But it was awful, awful for Tilly to have died. She had never wished for that, not once, and as Molly had intimated, Tilly had been a relatively young woman. She had sat clutching the letter to her, and when she raised her eyes it was to see Florence staring at her. 'What's up, lass? Bad news from home?'

'Some— someone's died. A woman I know.'

Florence had clucked in sympathy. 'A friend of yours?'

'Not exactly, but she was only five years older than me so it's a bit of a shock.' She couldn't explain, not right now. Ridiculous, but she couldn't have spoken Matt's name.

She had reached for her cup of tea then and Florence had taken the hint and said no more, but once they'd left Mr Howard's room, Constance had gone to Charlotte's quarters to stand staring at the swathes of tissue paper and the filmy wedding veil made of gossamer-thin French lace which she still had to pack.

Nothing had changed, not really, and yet everything had. Italy was still the sensible choice to make; Giuseppe had made it quite clear before she had left how he felt, and she knew she could expect a proposal of marriage if she made her home in Italy. She could look forward to a life of ease and comfort in that beautiful country, a life with children and grandchildren to enrich her days. If she stayed in England there was no guarantee that Matt would ask for her, none at all. He was grieving for his wife and could do so for many years. Even if he still had some feeling for her it might not be the same, and all the time she was getting older and the chance of children was fading. In Italy she would be surrounded by people who loved her. She would see Edmond grow up, and Charlotte and then perhaps Gwendoline marry. She would still be a part of their lives. She was sure of a future full of blessing and love. It would be madness to give all that up. Absolute madness. That was what she had told herself.

Lady Isabella's voice brought her back to the present when she said quietly, 'What is it, Constance? What's happened?'

It was only the second time Isabella had addressed her by her Christian name, but like the first time they were both too het-up to notice. Constance stared into her employer's dark eyes. She couldn't tell her the truth. How could she say she had received news that the wife of the man she loved had died, and so she was going home hoping that one day in the future he would ask for her? It wasn't decent. Helplessly, she murmured, 'I'm so sorry, my lady, but now the time is near I realise I can't leave. Italy is wonderful and I know my life there would be equally wonderful and I'll probably regret this for the rest of my life, but . . .' Again she couldn't go on.

'Roots.' Sir Henry spoke for the first time, and as his wife and Constance stared at him, he repeated, 'Roots. That's what's at the bottom of this. Not everyone can leave the country of their birth, but you do understand there will not be a suitable position for you with the Stewarts, Shelton? Mrs Stewart has her own lady's-maid and as yet they have no children.'

'I understand that, sir.'

'But Edmond will be heartbroken.' Isabella's voice caught in her throat. 'And he has so many new circumstances to contend with already. A new school, new friends to make . . .'

Constance could not reply to that, but as her colour rose

it was Sir Henry who came to her rescue again. 'He will survive, m'dear. There is going to be much to occupy him, and young boys are very resilient. This will be character-building in the long run. It won't do him any harm.'

Lady Isabella's glance at her husband told him exactly what she thought of this male logic.

He turned to Constance again. 'There is one thing I would ask of you, Shelton, and that is to take a little more time to think this over. We leave next week but there is no reason why you couldn't follow at a later date, if you change your mind. There will be no cause for you to leave here until the New Year, when the Stewarts take up residence.'

She couldn't give them or Edmond false hope. 'I won't change my mind, sir. I'm sorry, I'm truly sorry.'

'Ah well, so be it.' Sir Henry walked across to his wife and put his hand on her shoulder. 'You have every right to do as you wish, and the last thing Lady Isabella and I would want is for you to be unhappy. We are very aware that but for your courage all those years ago, our son could have been killed or maimed, and our lives would have been very different. Isn't that so, m'dear?'

He squeezed his wife's shoulder and it seemed to bring Lady Isabella to life. 'Yes, oh yes.' She smiled a little tremu-lously. 'It is so. And my husband is right. We want you to be happy.'

'Thank you.' Constance was blinking hard but still the telltale moisture seeped from the corners of her eyes. She didn't want to leave them and she knew if the letter hadn't come she could have made a life for herself in Italy. But the letter had come – and now the pull of home was so strong she could almost taste it.

'Where will you go when you leave here?' Isabella asked softly. She had seen the tears. 'Is there family you can stay with until you decide what you want to do?'

She hadn't had time to think things through, but she knew she wouldn't stay with Molly, kind though her aunty was. Nor could she live with Ivy; Durham was too far away from the village.

'There is family, yes, my lady, and I know they would be happy to have me, but I think I would like to rent somewhere of my own with a garden.' She had always imagined a house with a garden when she had been growing up in a sea of backyards.

'Why not buy somewhere?' Sir Henry smiled at her. 'That way, you are beholden to no one.'

Buy? She had never thought of buying, but why not? The Ashtons had paid her handsomely over the years and once her grandma had gone she had saved most of it. There were hundreds of pounds in the old carpet bag on top of the wardrobe in her room, more than enough for her to buy a small cottage and live comfortably for a few years until the future sorted itself out, one way or the other. And she would like to be her own mistress. A dart of excitement pierced the turmoil and sadness. To be able to rise when she wanted to, eat when she chose and go where she wished.

She smiled back at him. 'Yes, I could do that, sir. I've plenty saved but I wouldn't know how to go about it.'

'Don't worry your head about that, Shelton. I can give you the name of a solicitor who will take care of things for you. With whom do you bank?'

'I'm sorry, sir?'

'Your savings? Which bank are they deposited with?'

Constance stared at him blankly. 'I – I keep my money in a bag, sir. On top of the wardrobe.'

'On top of the wardrobe? In your room here?'

'Yes, sir.'

'Good grief.' But Sir Henry rallied almost immediately. 'I can see we need to have a chat, but that will wait until another time. Miss Charlotte is anxious for you to assist her with the remainder of her packing.' Looking down at his wife, he added, 'Is there anything you wish to say to Shelton, m'dear?'

'Only that we will miss you.'

Constance looked into the great dark eyes, and fresh tears spurted. 'Oh, my lady.'

It was the morning of the family's departure and Sir Henry had been as good as his word. Over the last days he'd spent time with Constance in his study and she now had a better understanding of what was needed to survive financially out in the big bad world. Her savings had been deposited with a trustworthy building society in Chester Le Street – since Sacriston and the other villages thereabouts did not boast more than a post office – and she had the name of a good solicitor in the town. Moreover, Sir Henry had engaged the services of an estate agent in the area to look out for a suitable cottage close to the village. She had also become conversant with the house telephone over the last week, a dreaded appliance which only Mr Howard and Mr Rowan had hitherto answered, and which filled the rest of the staff – Constance included – with apprehension. However, Sir Henry had insisted this means of communication was fast coming into its own and that over the next weeks before she left Grange Hall for good, she would have need of it, if only to discuss with the estate agent what he had found for her. It had been decided that Constance would spend Christmas at Grange Hall and leave in the middle of January, shortly before the new owners took up residence.

The servants who were remaining at the house, Florence included, were lined up in the hall to say goodbye to the master and mistress and the family after breakfast was finished, but Sir Henry called Constance into the drawing room once they were ready to leave. Charlotte and Gwendoline were doing a tearful tour of the house where they had been born, saying goodbye to each room, and Edmond was down at the stables making an equally tearful goodbye to his favourite horse, so it was just Sir Henry and Lady Isabella waiting for her.

'Remember what we have said, Shelton. If you would like a holiday in the sun you would be very welcome at any time.' Sir Henry smiled kindly at her. 'There will always be a place for you.'

'Thank you, sir, my lady.' But she wouldn't. She felt she had burned her bridges in that regard. She had written to Giuseppe explaining her changed circumstances and it wouldn't be fair on him to make an appearance, even temporarily.

'My wife and I have taken the liberty of making a small deposit into your new bank account.' Sir Henry handed her a piece of paper. 'Here is the receipt.'

Constance stared in disbelief at the noughts on the paper. Two thousand pounds. *Two thousand pounds.* It was a fortune, riches beyond her wildest dreams. 'I – I don't know what to say.' She looked at them helplessly. 'Thank you. Thank you, Sir Henry, my lady, but it's too much.'

'What price a son?' Sir Henry said gruffly, clearly embarrassed. 'And frankly, I've seen certain gentlemen lose as much in one evening on the roll of a die. If you invest it wisely, and the solicitor I recommended will know the people to help you there, you will have a steady income for life. It will mean you living fairly frugally, of course.'

Frugally? Constance stared at the receipt. Hardly. Oh, how her grandma would have loved this, although it would have been all round the village in two minutes flat. She hadn't expected anything, they had been so good to her already . . . She gulped hard. 'Thank you,' she said again. 'I can't believe it.'

'Let's hear no more about it.' Sir Henry's voice was suddenly brisk. 'It is little enough but it will smooth the way. Ah, here they are,' he added as the door opened to admit Charlotte and Gwendoline. 'And still in tears, I see. I fear it is going to be a long journey to Italy.'

The next hour was difficult, especially when Edmond clung to her as though he would never let her go, insisting he would write to her every week and demanding that she did the same. But then the family were gone, along with Mr Howard, Sidney Black – Sir Henry's valet – and Estelle Upton – Lady Isabella's personal maid.

Constance had been charged with packing the last of the family's clothes and personal belongings and seeing that they were sent on, among other duties, but when she wandered into Edmond's room she stood looking out of the window until lunchtime. She felt deeply disturbed even though she knew she had done the right thing – the only thing possible – once she knew that Matt was free again. Nevertheless, she was aware that she had placed herself in an almost impossible position.

The heavy blue-grey sky promised snow, and the frozen grounds outside the warmth of the house intensified the strange feeling that had taken hold of her once the Ashtons' carriages had drawn away. Here, in England, she was in no-man's land, she thought sadly. Her years sitting in with Edmond when he had his lessons before he left for boarding school meant she was educated far above what the village school had been able to offer. She knew some Latin, could speak Italian very well and had a good understanding of basic science and chemistry and other subjects. Charlotte and Gwendoline had delighted in teaching her to play the piano and paint on glass and do tapestry – accomplishments they themselves, as wealthy young ladies, had learned from a young age. And that was fine for them, right and proper, but she wasn't a young lady with a titled background. She was just a lass from the north-east who, due to pure chance, had been lifted out of her ordinary environment into an extraordinary one.

Her gaze wandered to a line of hazel bushes near the house, naked except for dainty grey tassels that trembled in the bitter wind.

She felt like that inside – trembly. Trembly and afraid. In Italy her new accomplishments would have fitted perfectly the role of wife to the Morosinis' estate manager, but here she was neither fish nor fowl, as her grandma used to say. The folk she had grown up with – people who had been kind to her and who'd liked the grand-daughter of Mabel Gray whose parents had been lost so tragically, would call her an upstart. Oh yes, they would. She nodded in emphasis to the thought. And all the more so because before, when she'd simply been the 'poor Shelton bairn' – as she'd heard more than one well-meaning neighbour refer to her in the past – they had been able to feel sorry for someone less fortunate than themselves. Oh, she knew how her people thought, and it was only in the last ten years when she had been brought to the perimeter of the privileged world of the Ashtons and looked on in wonder, that she'd realised the working class was every inch as snobbish as the upper classes, perhaps more so.

She sighed, brushing a strand of hair from her face before bringing her hands in front of her as she stared down at their smooth soft prettiness, her nails clean and well-shaped. Not one of the women in the village would have hands like this, except perhaps the schoolmarm. When she had been at home her hands had been sore and chapped most of the time from helping her grandma with the household chores and washing and so on, and when she had first come to Grange Hall her duties in the kitchen had left them so angry and chafed they had cracked and bled no matter how much goose fat she had rubbed in them at night.

She had changed. Inside and out. Even her use of grammar and the way she expressed herself was different. But one thing was the same and would always remain so: her love for the tall, brown-eyed man who had caught her in his arms as a young lad when her father had trusted him to catch her. The years between, Matt falling in love with Tilly and fathering a child with her, and all her experiences here at Grange Hall and the travelling and wonderful things she had seen and heard, were as nothing compared to that love. Circumstances couldn't touch it or change it.

She didn't know why she loved him as she did. She

closed her eyes, picturing his face. But at the oddest times, often when her whole being was wrapped up in staring at a beautiful sunset or the view across Lake Garda or listening to Charlotte who played the piano with the skill of a virtuoso, there would come into her body an ache to see him, an ache so strong it would rob her of the joy of the moment and bring the taste of ashes to her mouth. Stupid.

She opened her eyes once more. And it *was* stupid, to let her need of him spoil such times, but she couldn't help it. She had railed and fought against it, prayed against it, attempted to bring logic and reason to bear, but to no avail. Matt was her Achilles heel. A fleeting smile turned up the corners of her mouth as she imagined his reaction if he ever heard that. But it was true. She wanted to be near him. Even if she featured as nothing more than a friend in his life, she wanted to be near him. No, she *needed* to be near him.

She straightened, smoothing her hair and stiffening her shoulders. And she wouldn't apologise for the person she'd become when she went home to live among her old friends and neighbours either. She accepted them as they were. They could accept her.

And Vincent McKenzie? The voice in the back of her mind brought to the fore the name she'd been trying to ignore since deciding on returning home. Her stomach turned over and she pressed her lips together. If – and she didn't know this for sure, since he might have accepted that she wanted nothing to do with him – but *if* he tried to press his attentions on her again, she would go and see the Constable. She would *not* live in fear of that man. But she wouldn't be silly either. There was nothing wrong with protecting herself and she would see to it she had the means. She was acquainted with firearms; she had looked on when Sir Henry had taught Edmond the finer arts of shooting, and although she had, of course, never participated herself, she had seen how to fire a pistol. She would buy one once she was living alone and keep it in a safe place. She hoped she would never have to use it to threaten anyone, but just knowing it was there would help her sleep better at nights.

She glanced at the pocket-watch pinned to the front of her dress. Lunchtime. She would feel better once she had eaten. She had always known the day she said goodbye to Edmond and the rest of the family would be a disturbing one. But all that to one side, her course was set. It had been set from the moment she had read Molly's letter.

Christmas was a subdued affair at Grange Hall. Normally the house was full with friends and family of the Ashtons, and Florence would have been cooking for days. The servants had a little get-together which was pleasant enough, but everyone was wondering what the new master and mistress would be like and how they would be affected by the changes. They knew the Stewarts were a young couple recently married and at present on their honeymoon, and that in this they were fortunate. Had the new owners been older they might well have brought their own servants with them. Mrs Stewart's father was a powerful and influential politician in the House of Lords, and Mr Stewart the only son of a hugely wealthy individual who – according to the titbits of information which had filtered down to the servants – owned half of Scotland. Constance thought this might be somewhat exaggerated, but as it pleased the rest of the staff to believe it so, she said nothing. It wouldn't affect her one way or the other anyway, since she would be gone before they arrived.

By Twelfth Night, when the main servants' ball took place, everyone was a lot happier. Just after Christmas a package had been delivered to the house by a special courier from Scotland. It had contained generous monetary gifts for each of the remaining staff, from Mr Rowan down to the scullerymaids; Christmas boxes from the Stewarts. Everyone agreed this boded well for the future. And so on 5 January, when Florence brought out the King's Cake – remembering the visit of the three Magi to the babe in Bethlehem – the staff were merry after an evening of feasting and dancing and drinking copious amounts of ale and wine.

At midnight, when Epiphany began, everyone drank to the Christ Child and the party ended. Constance went to her room but not to sleep. Tomorrow she was leaving Grange Hall. The estate agent Sir Henry had engaged had done a thorough job, and through him she had agreed to buy what he described as a pretty cottage near Findon Hill, south-east of Sacriston. The agreement was she would inspect the property with him the following day, and if she liked it funds would be transferred. If not, she would rent the cottage for a month or so while he continued his search for her.

Sir Henry, with kind forethought, had left instructions that Fred Weatherburn, the coachman, would drive her to her new home when the time came for her to leave. Constance didn't know how she felt about arriving back so grandly – it would confirm her position as an upstart, that was for sure – but the weather was harsh and the journey long, and she would be glad of travelling in the Ashtons' very comfortable carriage. Although it wasn't the Ashtons' now, she reminded herself, as she lay in bed watching the moon surrounded by scudding clouds through the window. It was the Stewarts'. Everything had changed and there was no going back – and in a strange sort of way that was comforting. For right or wrong, her path was set.

She snuggled deeper under the covers. The room was icy cold but she had a stone hot-water bottle at her feet and a thick eiderdown on top of the many blankets piled on the bed, and she was as warm as toast.

Should she have told Molly of her plans? But if she had, likely Molly would have let it slip to someone or other that she was coming back. Molly was a love but she couldn't keep a secret to save her life. And she wanted to settle in and establish herself before she saw anyone. Before she saw Matt. She needed to be in control.

Control. The word mocked her. When had she ever been in control of her feelings where Matt was concerned? Nevertheless, if she could have a few days to find her feet she'd feel better. The estate agent was due to meet her at the cottage after lunch, which meant an early start the next day, but once she was there she could begin to take stock. He had promised he would see to it that the cottage was warm for her arrival and that there was food in the cupboards. He'd been extremely helpful in every regard, and was certain she'd fall in love with the house he'd found.

Her heart began to race at the thought of the next day before she told herself to calm down. She needed to sleep. Everything would pan out. She had done the only thing she could have done by returning home to Sacriston once she'd received Molly's letter. And it didn't matter if no one else in the world understood that. She did.

With this last thought came peace. In a couple more minutes, she was fast asleep.

PART FOUR

The Third Chance
1911

Chapter 20

Rebecca sat in her grandmother Heath's kitchen watching her knead dough. It was Monday afternoon, her half-day from the shop. Her long working week – from seven o'clock sharp in the morning until eight at night from Tuesday to Saturday meant that most of the daylight hours were spent indoors, and on a Monday afternoon in the summer she often went for a walk before calling in on her grandma. Today though, with the deep snow and raw wind, she'd been glad to make her way straight to Ruth's warm kitchen.

She had arrived at nearly three. Mr Turner, the owner of the village shop, was crafty, her da said, insisting her half-day began *after* her half-an-hour lunch-break at two. Mr Turner always saw to it he was busy out the back in the shop's storeroom doing this, that or the other on a Monday at two o'clock, which meant she nearly always worked in the shop rather than ate her lunch till two-thirty, and even longer some days. Like today. He'd been measuring out sugar from the big barrel into little blue bags to be sold in the front of the shop, and hadn't wanted to stop till they were all done.

Not that she minded, not really. Mr Turner wasn't a hard taskmaster and Mrs Turner was lovely, always slipping her bits and pieces to take home. She'd brought her latest hand-out, a bag of bacon bits to her grandma today. She knew the old couple were struggling. Since the strikes towards the end of last year her granda, a dyed-in-the-wool union man, had found his pay savagely docked by the weighman, Mr McKenzie, along with other miners who had got under the owners' skins. But for the help of her da and uncles, her grandparents would be starving on what her granda brought home. But other people were having it harder.

Only last week her da had come home beside himself after hearing that one of his pals had hanged himself from a tree in Barrashill Wood. He'd been another militant union man and after the last strike the colliery hadn't taken him back. When the family had been turned out of their cottage they had moved in with one of the man's sisters, but that had meant eight of them living and sleeping in the sister's front room, and apparently the sister had a big family of her own to feed. One morning the man had said goodbye to his family, the way he always did when he was leaving to see if he could pick up a day's work doing odd jobs for folk, or failing that collecting firewood which he'd tie into small bundles and sell round the doors, and he hadn't come back. It had been his eldest boy, a lad of nine, who had found him. She knew the family by sight. All the bairns were as skinny as rakes and their teeth looked too big for their mouths.

'You're a sobersides today, hinny. Owt the matter?' Ruth paused in her kneading, surveying her granddaughter's round pretty face. 'Not fell out with that lad of yours, have you?'

Rebecca shook her head. ''Course not, Gran.' She hadn't been able to believe it when her da had relented and said she could start walking out with Larry at Christmas. Larry had told her her da had taken him aside one day at the pit and given him a talking-to about treating her right and being respectful before he'd given them his blessing, but she didn't mind that. Neither had Larry. And now when Larry came round theirs he and her da got on all right.

'What's up then?' Ruth's voice was soft. 'Missing your mam?'

'No. Yes. I mean I *am* missing Mam, 'course I am, but it's more that Da's . . .' Her voice trailed away. 'Oh, I don't know, Gran.' How could she explain? If she said her da was different since her mam had died, her grandma would say that was only to be expected and it was early days. And she knew that herself. But it was the *way* he was different. It wasn't just that he was sad and weary, it was more that he was drained of emotion. Empty. He put on an act for her, and when Larry came or they saw her grandparents he tried even harder, but she knew it was just that – an act. She had never seen him like this before; not even in the past after one of her mam and da's rows when things had been awful for weeks had he looked so . . . dead. It frightened her. And after her da had told her about his pal she'd been even more frightened. People did awful things when they lost all hope.

'He'll come round, lass. It's early days.'

There, she knew that's what her grandma would say. Woodenly, she murmured, 'Aye, I suppose so.'

'Losing your mam like that was bound to hit him hard. When you've been married to someone for umpteen years you grow together and when one is taken . . . Well, it's not easy, lass. It takes some adjusting to. And the wife is the homemaker, after all.'

Rebecca said nothing. She had noticed that since her mother had died, since she had become ill, in fact, she seemed to have acquired sainthood in everyone's eyes. Even her grandma insisted on speaking as though her mam and da had been the most happily married couple ever, and yet her grandma knew well enough this wasn't the case. She and Larry had discussed this and he was of the opinion that superstition came into it – 'an irrational fear of speaking ill of the dead' was the way he'd put it. He had also said that mis-directed reverence could be a dangerous thing when it blurred reality. She loved talking to Larry. He wasn't like a lot of the lads hereabouts whose only interests were football and beer. He loved books. Half his wage went on books, and not just stories but books on astronomy and philosophy and the natural world. He and her da had been having a conversation about lost civilisations yesterday when he'd come for Sunday tea, and the way man's desire to conquer and rule others meant that wars would never cease. She'd found that a bit depressing, to be honest.

'Don't worry your head about your da.' She came out of her thoughts as her grandma put a doughy hand on hers. 'He'll be all right in a while.'

No, he wouldn't. Her love for her father told her so. From when she could toddle she had adored him and wanted to be near him every moment she could, and she knew this had been one of the things which had caused the divide between herself and her mother. But it hadn't mattered. She could have done without her mother as long as she had her father. But now, somehow, he'd gone away. He was still around physically, but something had died. And yet he hadn't loved her mother; until recently, she hadn't even thought they liked each other. She didn't know what to do. She was no consolation to him; she couldn't help him. Forcing her fear to the back of her mind, she smiled at her grandma and changed the subject. Her grandma had enough on her plate and she didn't want to add to her worries.

By four o'clock it had started to snow again and it was so dark her grandma had lit the oil lamps. Rebecca was putting on her hat and coat when a tap came at the back door followed by the appearance of Mrs Mullen, her grandma's next-door neighbour.

'Ee, lass, I didn't know you were here,' she said on catching sight of Rebecca. 'Come to see your grandma then? That's nice.'

Rebecca sighed inwardly. Mrs Mullen was the biggest gossip for miles around, and once she started talking no one could get a word in edgeways. Rebecca would be standing here like a lemon waiting to say goodbye now.

Sure enough, without taking a pause, Mrs Mullen went on, 'I just thought I'd pop in and see if you've heard about Constance Shelton, Ruth? I know you were close to her an' her grandma at one time, and when our Fanny told me the news I couldn't believe me ears. "Are you sure it's her?" I said to our Fanny, and she said her Seth would know the lass anywhere. "Great big blue eyes and the spitting image of her mam", he said. No mistaking her.'

When Mrs Mullen came up for air, her grandma said, 'What *about* Constance, Sarah?'

'She's back. Back here. Well, not exactly here – she's too good for the village now, by all accounts. She's taken Appleby Cottage, the one the other side of Findon Hill where Colonel Vickers used to live. Bonny place, you know? Seth went to deliver a wagonload of coal and logs and said he nearly died when she opened the door. Some house agent from Chester Le Street had set everything up, but he didn't know who the new owner was, and there she stood. Bold as brass. Thanked him and gave him a good tip an' all, like she'd been born to it, he said. You didn't know then? That she had moved into Appleby Cottage? That she was back?'

'No. No, I didn't.'

'That's what I said to our Fanny. "Ruth would have told me if she knew," I said. "She's not one for being secretive for no reason. Open as the day is long, that's Ruth Heath".'

Rebecca hid a smile. It was obvious Mrs Mullen *had* suspected her grandmother had held out on her.

'Likely she'll pay you a call soon,' Mrs Mullen continued. 'Came on Friday from Yorkshire, she said, when Seth asked her, and when he went round the back to the outhouses with the coal and logs, there was a horse in the stable and a bonny trap. This house agent bloke saw to that an' all. Seth found out from Mrs Duckworth whose daughter is married to the smith. So' – Sarah Mullen looked her neighbour full in the face and now there was a note of what could be termed aggression in her voice when she said – 'how does a lass like her come by the means to have all that?'

Rebecca watched her grandmother's face stiffen. 'What do you mean?' Ruth asked with deceptive mildness.

'Just what I say. It was all cloak and dagger, Constance leaving here, don't you think? And no one knew where she went. We only had Mabel's word for it that the lass had gone into service and she's a beautiful-looking girl. When I saw her at Mabel's funeral there were plenty of men who couldn't take their eyes off her.' Mrs Mullen's ample chin settled into her neck.

'I know for a fact that Mabel used to visit Constance at her place and that she was employed as a scullerymaid before she saved the little lad from being trampled by a horse,' Ruth said coldly. 'After that, the family were grateful to her and no wonder. And Mabel was a friend of mine. A very good friend.'

'Oh aye, I know, lass. I know.'

'I'd as soon believe your Fanny had gone bad than Mabel's lass, and since when was it a crime to be bonny?'

'Now look, Ruth, I didn't mean—'

'You ought to be careful what you insinuate, Sarah Mullen, when a nice lass's good reputation is at stake. And a lass who has friends in high places an' all.'

'Well!' Rebecca watched as Mrs Mullen seemed to visibly swell, but she thought her voice now carried a note of apprehension when she continued, 'I came here in good faith, Ruth, to tell you the news, knowing you thought a bit of the family, and now you accuse me of 'sinuating. Me, of all people!'

'Constance Shelton has been treated like a daughter by that family since she saved the son and heir,' said Ruth, warming to her theme and telling herself a little exaggeration was called for. This had to be nipped in the bud right now. If Constance *was* back to stay, then for the lass to have any hope of a reasonable life, the wagging tongues had to be silenced from the beginning – and who better to start with than the ringleader of any gossip? 'They think the world of her and rightly so. That is where any reward has come from and she deserves it.'

'Aye, well, that's all right then,' Mrs Mullen spluttered, backing towards the door. 'I'd better go and see to me dinner; himself will be back from the pit shouting the odds afore long.'

When the door shut behind her grandmother's neighbour, Rebecca finished buttoning her coat before she said, 'By, Gran, that told her,' laughter in her voice. When her grandma didn't smile back, she said, 'She hasn't upset you, has she?'

Her grandmother had been staring at the door. Now she gave a little start, shaking her head, but the tone of her voice belied her words when she said, 'No, no – I'm all right, hinny.'

'What's the matter, Gran?'

'It's nothing, lass, not really. It just seems strange that Constance didn't let us know she was back, that's all.'

'I'm sure she will. She probably wanted to surprise you, but with the weather so bad it's stopped her coming.'

'Aye, mebbe.' Her grandma didn't sound convinced.

'Da saved her life when she was a baby, didn't he? I've never even seen her, you know.'

'No, I don't suppose you have, hinny,' Ruth said absently. 'Anyway, you get yourself home. It's coming down thicker than ever and you don't want to be out in this.'

Rebecca said goodbye and left by the back door. It was only a few yards down the lane to her own backyard, and she glanced back at her grandma's house before she went inside. She hoped Constance Shelton came to see her grandma before too long. Her gran had clearly been upset that she'd heard about her homecoming second-hand. Blow Mrs Mullen. Her gaze travelled to the house on the far side of her grandmother's. She'd stir up trouble in heaven itself, that woman, as her mam had been wont to say.

Once in the scullery she stamped the snow off her boots and changed into her slippers before entering the kitchen. It had been a rule of her mother's that they all changed their footwear in the scullery, be it rain, hail or shine, and for a moment she stood looking round the dark room before she lit the oil lamp. The banked-down range gave off a muted glow, but even in the faint light the white-washed walls and dresser with her mam's fancy dinner set – used only on high days and holidays – radiated the spruceness she had grown up with. Her mam had liked things spick and span, and even after she started working for Mr Wood she had made sure their own house remained spotless and they came home to a hot meal. Rebecca sat down on a kitchen chair with a little plump. She suddenly wanted to cry.

It had stopped snowing when Matt emerged out of the pit gates, but the fresh fall on top of what had been deep-packed snow made walking treacherous. He hadn't hurried once the cage had brought them to the surface, letting the rest of his shift queue in front of him to give in their lamps and token. When Andrew and George had called to him once they were ready to leave he'd waved them off, saying he'd catch them up. He had no intention of doing so, however. He didn't want to have to talk to anyone tonight.

He'd had one of what he privately termed his 'moments' whilst working on the face today; a time of such blind panic and fear of being shut in and trapped beneath the earth that he'd had to bite the inside of his mouth until the blood ran to take his mind off what was going on in his head.

Was he going mad? Satisfied that his brothers had gone, he began to walk through the clean white world in front of him that was so different from the filth and stench of the pit. Joe Benson had snapped last year, running amok and nearly braining himself when he'd cracked his head on the roof where he'd been working. In the asylum now, Joe was, and his wife and bairns in the workhouse.

He shivered, the contrast to the heat and humidity he'd laboured in for hours and the bitingly cold air outside hard to adjust to. He lifted his face to the black cloudy sky which promised more snow and breathed long and deeply, pulling the icy air into his lungs over and over again.

He needed to get out of the pit before he went barmy. He was sick of working in a black hole surrounded by rats and mice and beetles with feelers as long as bootlaces. He was sick of being reduced to little more than an animal grubbing away, eating his bait along with dust, sweat and grit every day and smelling the stench of human muck and even treading in it sometimes. He wanted— He stopped abruptly, shaking his head like a boxer after a hard blow.

Pack it in, he told himself harshly. Thinking like this only made things worse. He had to get on with it. He had it easy compared to some and he was alive, wasn't he? And with all his faculties. Not like them poor devils who had bought it just before Christmas at the Hutton Colliery near Bolton. Three hundred and fifty men and boys gone in one blast and over a thousand bairns without a da. Nice Christmas present. And that colliery had been held up as one of the safest and best equipped. They were all death traps, every last one of them.

Even the final stragglers had passed him and now he stood on Blackburn Bridge, looking over the sparkling white countryside towards Nettlesworth as the quiet cold night settled around him. There were none of the usual sounds. All the farmers hereabouts had brought their animals in from the fields and nothing stirred.

But there he was wrong. A movement from the lane behind him caught his eye and he turned to see Vincent McKenzie pass him. Their gaze met for a moment, expressing mutual loathing, and then the weighman strode on without a word being exchanged.

The moment of tranquillity broken, Matt followed in his wake, but slowly, his eyes fixed on the big, portly figure in front of him. McKenzie was the most hated man for miles and yet it didn't seem to bother him. Indeed, he openly relished it. Even the owners and the managers weren't detested in the same way. They were of a different class and as such had no link with the miner on the coalface, but McKenzie had been one of them, a working pitman. Matt knew any one of a number of men who would kill him if they got the chance and could get away with it, and it had crossed his mind more than once. Particularly so in the last weeks when he'd had to watch his own father being subjected to

McKenzie's special brand of viciousness. Fourteen shillings his da should have earned last week, and his wage-packet had contained less than half that amount after McKenzie put his oar in.

He'd suffered himself under McKenzie's trumped-up fines when he'd first gone to the coalface, but after his marriage to Tilly, McKenzie hadn't seemed to bother with him much. Likely he'd got it in for other blokes by then. It didn't take much.

He was still thinking about the weighman when he reached home. It was gone half-past ten. He'd been on the afternoon shift from two until ten at night, but Rebecca was waiting up for him. He'd told her many times that she needn't. He'd be happy with cheese and pickles and cold meat for his dinner but she insisted he needed a hot meal when he came in from the pit.

She bounded up out of her chair like a puppy when he walked in, fussing round him while she got the tin bath full and then disappearing upstairs until he called her to say he was dressed again. She had waited to eat with him, and once they were seated at the table with a plate of steaming hodge podge each and between them a plate of stottie cake she'd made earlier, they talked of this and that while they ate. She always tried to make him laugh as she related the happenings of the day in the shop, and she usually succeeded. He looked at her as she cleared their dirty plates and fetched a bread and butter pudding out of the oven, and his voice was soft when he said, 'You're a good lass, none better. Larry'll be a lucky man if he holds on to you.'

She went red with pleasure, hiding her embarrassment by bustling about still more as she dished up the pudding.

'So what time did old tight Turner let you out today then?' Matt asked after a bite or two.

'Oh, Da, he's not tight, not really. And Mrs Turner gave me a big bag of bacon bits that I took round to Gran. There were some whole rashers in there which she'd slipped in when I looked once I got outside, and an end which was an inch thick an' all. She's so nice, Mrs Turner.'

'And you took them to Gran's? Bless you, hinny. I bet that cheered her up. Did you stay and have a bit of a crack with her? She looks forward to that.'

Rebecca nodded. 'But then Mrs Mullen came in just as I was leaving and I think she upset her.'

'Mrs Mullen upset your gran? How?'

'She was full of it, you know how she is sometimes. She was saying that Constance Shelton has come back home. She's got a cottage near Findon Hill and she moved in at the end of last week. I think Gran was upset 'cos she hadn't known anything about it.'

Matt carefully lowered his spoon to his bowl. 'And Mrs Mullen's sure it's Constance Shelton?'

'Oh aye.' Rebecca nodded, taking another mouthful before she said, 'Her daughter Fanny – well, her husband Seth – delivered some coal and logs to Appleby Cottage and he recognised Constance.'

'Appleby Cottage? The Colonel's place?'

'Aye, yes.' Rebecca glanced at her father. 'You all right, Da?' When Matt inclined his head, she went on, 'And Mrs Mullen was saying how did she get the money to buy such a grand cottage – Constance, I mean. And Seth, Fanny's husband, said she's got a bonny horse and trap an' all. Mrs Mullen tried to make out . . . well, that Constance hadn't been working in service but had been doing something else. You know? And then Gran went for her, she really did. She sent her away with a flea in her ear. She said the family Constance has worked for thought the world of her and they'd given her the money. Do you think that's true, Da?'

There was a strained quality to Matt's voice when he said quietly, 'I'm sure it is and I'm absolutely certain Constance would never do anything like Mrs Mullen's nasty little mind conjured up.'

Rebecca's voice was uncertain when she said again, 'Sure you're all right, Da? What's the matter?'

Matt made a huge effort to pull himself together. She was back. Impossible though it was, she had returned home. But Appleby Cottage? He had gone into the kitchen there once as a lad when the Colonel's wife had had a bunch of them picking the apples in the orchard at the back of the house for a few pennies apiece. She'd given them lemonade and a bun each in the middle of the afternoon and they had sat in the kitchen hardly daring to move. It had seemed like a palace at the time. What the rest of the house was like he didn't dare to imagine, but it was big – four bedrooms reportedly, and all under a thatched roof that set off the cottage to perfection. And Constance had chosen to live there.

Aware that Rebecca was looking at him, he forced his voice-box into action. 'I think I feel a bit like your gran to be honest, hinny. Disappointed she didn't let on she was back. Not that she was beholden to us to do that, of course, and no doubt the family know.' He swallowed a mouthful of bread and butter pudding although it nearly choked him before he added, 'This is every bit as good as your mam used to make. You're a grand little cook. I reckon you could put in for a job at one of them big houses as cook and no one would turn you away, not if they had any sense, that is.'

The diversion worked. Rebecca giggled. Her, 'Oh, Da', expressing her gratification of the compliment, meant they finished the pudding in a comfortable silence. Comfortable on Rebecca's side, that was, which was all that mattered. For himself, Matt felt physically ill, the meal he'd just eaten threatening to rise up into his mouth.

Constance was back, and by all accounts with the wherewithal to live as a lady. But hadn't he felt, five years ago at her grandmother's funeral, that she had risen far above him? After that first time when he had gone round to Molly's and talked with Constance in the kitchen, she had avoided him. He didn't want to admit it to himself, but she had. Had he embarrassed her? Damn it, he was such a fool. Why would a beautiful lass like her look the side he was on? The Appleby place and her own horse and trap. She had no need of a common working man, that much was clear. She could have anyone she wanted.

'Da?' Rebecca rose, reaching for his empty bowl as she spoke.

'Aye?' He glanced up at her.

'You could take Gran with you and call on Constance, couldn't you? With you saving her life when she was a baby and all? I think Gran would like that.'

He swallowed. 'She has been away a long time, Rebecca. People change, circumstances change. It's probably better she goes to see your grandma herself when she feels the time is right.'

'But what if she doesn't? Gran's already hurt and—'

'Leave it, lass.' He stood up, reaching for his pipe and baccy.

311

'But—'

'I said leave it.' And quickly, to offset his abruptness, he added, 'It'll all pan out, lass. These things always do. Now it's late. Get yourself off to bed – the dishes will wait till morning. And thanks for waiting up, hinny.' He stretched out his hand and her face lightened as she took it. He pulled her close, kissing the top of her head. 'Go and get your beauty sleep or I'll be in trouble with Larry for turning you into an old hag before your time.'

'Oh you, Da.' She grinned at him, equilibrium restored, and did as she was told, calling, ''Night, Da,' from the hall.

Alone in the kitchen he sat down in his easy chair at the side of the range and lit his pipe, annoyed to see his hands were trembling. He sat there for a long time. And when he finally stood up to go to bed his hands weren't shaking any longer but the trembling was inside him, shrinking the essence of him – the place wherein sat his pride, his self-esteem, his manhood – down to nothing.

Chapter 21

Rebecca knew she shouldn't have done it. If Mr and Mrs Turner found out, she could lose her job – and then where would she be? She'd been lucky to be taken on in the first place, and that was only because Mr Turner had known her mam when she worked in the post office, and had considered her what he called 'a cut above' most of the lasses roundabout. He was a bit like that, Mr Turner. Snobby.

She paused and looked behind her. The village was still in sight but in the distance, and the view wasn't so clear now, masked as it was by trees and the rise and fall of the road. She stood catching her breath; the snow was deep and made walking hard.

When she had opened her eyes that morning after a restless night's sleep she had known what she was going to do. At the shop she'd been purposely quiet as she worked, and towards midday she had rubbed a little flour on her face from one of the sacks in the storeroom and spent an inordinate amount of time in the privy in the backyard of the shop. It had been freezing but it had been worth it because when she'd come indoors again Mrs Turner had been insistent she go home when she said she had a tummy upset.

'You look like death warmed up, child,' Mrs Turner had said anxiously, making her feel awful for deceiving her. 'You go home and go to bed and likely you'll be as right as rain come morning.'

Rebecca bit her bottom lip, her small white teeth gnawing away as she thought, I'll make it up to her, I'll work twice as hard tomorrow. And it's not as if I've ever done anything like this before. She turned and began trudging through the snow again which was banked high either side of the road.

Once she turned off into the thin lane opposite the reservoir, she breathed easier. The lane curved behind Findon Hill and there was less chance of being seen. A farm wagon had obviously trundled down the lane earlier and she walked in the tracks left by its wheels, but even so it was a struggle. She looked up into the pale grey sky, willing it not to snow until she had safely completed her mission and was home again, and warned herself that she had to be back on the main road before dark. Snow was thick on the hedgerows either side of the lane, and the long frozen branches of the trees overhanging the lane formed a canopy of glistening white as she plodded on. It was well over half a mile from the main road to Appleby Cottage, which was situated in a large amount of ground just past the old quarry.

Her legs were aching with battling against the snow when Appleby Cottage finally came into sight, nestling amidst trees and with blue smoke curling from the chimney. Rebecca had passed by the cottage in the summer and then the rustic porch had been smothered in honeysuckle and the small front garden a mass of flowers. She had stood and gazed in wonder at the wallflowers, lavender and sweet william, pinks and roses of every hue, until her father had urged her on in the Sunday-afternoon walk they were taking. It was then he'd reminisced about the Colonel and his wife, telling her about the orchard at the back of the house which led to a little field where the Colonel kept his horse and a cow. There was a yew hedge closer to the cottage, he'd said, as solid as a wall, which sheltered the Colonel's wife's beehives, and another separate enclosed piece of ground where they grew vegetables and had fruit-bushes. But of course the Colonel was old now, the couple had been much more sprightly when he was a boy although sadly they'd never had bairns of their own.

It had only been a few months after that, just before Christmas, that they'd heard the Colonel and his wife had died within days of each other and the cottage was up for sale.

The diamond-paned windows twinkled at her as she opened the rickety gate. Someone had brushed the path leading to the cottage free of snow and the brass knocker on the front door was gleaming bright. Now the moment had come to confront the woman she had heard so much about, Rebecca found she was nervous. What if Constance refused to visit her grandma now she was a grand lady? Worse, she might take offence at her inter-ference and complain about her. Not only would she get into trouble with her da for disobeying him, but Mr and Mrs Turner could get to hear of what she'd been about when she was supposed to be in bed with an attack of the skitters.

She stood hesitating on the doorstep for a few moments, and then a picture of her grandma's face the way it had been when Mrs Mullen had left came to mind. Her heart beating in her throat, she lifted her hand and grasped the knocker.

The sound it made seemed to echo in her head and it increased the feeling that she shouldn't have come. She heard a dog bark inside the cottage and took a nervous step backwards, half-inclined to retreat to the lane and close the gate. But then the door opened.

She knew immediately this must be Constance because the woman staring at her was quite, quite beautiful, fair and delicate-looking, with the biggest blue eyes she had ever seen in a human face. Quickly, she gabbled, 'I'm sorry to bother you and I shouldn't have come, I know that, but I wanted to ask you to visit my grandma. She knows you're here and—'

'You are Tilly's daughter.'

The warm northern voice was reassuring. Rebecca took a breath. 'Aye, yes I am.'

'You're very like her.' Constance smiled. 'Come in, do.' She opened the door wider and as she did so Rebecca saw a great, lanky dog standing behind her. It was skeletal, just skin and bone, and as Constance followed her gaze, she said, 'This is Jake, at least that's what I've called him. He was scrounging around in the outbuildings when I arrived. I think he must have been the previous owners' dog and everyone forgot about him when the old couple died. We've adopted each other. As you can see, I need to feed him up.'

'Is he friendly?' Rebecca liked dogs but this one was huge.

Constance nodded. 'I think he's one of those dogs whose bark is worse than his bite, although he doesn't seem to like men much.'

Tentatively Rebecca edged into the hall and as she passed Jake a long pink tongue came out and licked her hand.

The hall was small but when Constance opened a door which led into an oak-beamed sitting room, Rebecca involuntarily murmured, 'Oh, it's bonny,' as she gazed around her, open-mouthed.

The room was a perfect snuggery and lovely and warm thanks to a large fireplace in which a good fire blazed. This was framed by a carved wooden mantelpiece which would have graced a far bigger residence. Rebecca knew nothing about furniture but she could see that every piece in the room was vastly superior to anything she had seen before, and the thick red curtains at the window and fine shop-bought rugs on the polished floor – shop-bought, mind, and not clippy mats – emphasised the feeling of expensive comfort. The whole of the downstairs of their house could have fitted into this one room.

'It is bonny,' Constance agreed quietly, 'but I'm afraid I can't take credit for it. Everything was left as it was when the Colonel and his wife died and is included in the price of the cottage. Would you like to see the rest of it?'

Rebecca would like, and the cottage's dining room, study and kitchen, along with the four large bedrooms, were equally well furnished and opulent. There was even a bathroom upstairs with a cast-iron bath on little legs in the middle of it and two hand basins on stands with enormous copper watering cans at the side.

In a small room leading off the kitchen, which Constance

said she thought might have been a scullery at one time, the Colonel had installed an indoor privy, the drain of which led under the gardens at the back of the house right past the field where the cow and horse had lived in the summer to a soakaway which disappeared at the edge of the old quarry. This innovation had Rebecca awe-struck. She had heard of indoor privies but never thought to see one. Not in Sacriston.

The Colonel had even provided a flow of water into the house by means of a pump and piping from the stream which ran along the bottom of the garden, but that was frozen over at the moment, Constance told her. But the well at the back of the outhouses and stable yielded water, winter and summer. A washhouse with a boiler and big stone sink and mangle completed the tour, after which Constance left her in the sitting room while she went to make a pot of tea. Rebecca was acutely aware that Constance hadn't referred to what she had said when she'd arrived on her doorstep, but had kept the conversation friendly but impersonal.

She sat nervously fondling Jake's silky ears as she waited for Constance to return with the tea-tray and practised what she was going to say. The dog nuzzled her hand now and again, as if he sensed her agitation. Which he probably did. Dogs were intuitive that way, she thought.

When the sitting-room door opened again she didn't know whether to stand up or remain sitting, and something of her state of mind must have communicated itself to the graceful young woman in front of her because Constance said softly, 'Don't be fearful, Rebecca. I hope you know you're among friends.'

'I'm not fearful, not really. It's just that . . .'

'No one knows you've come to see me?' Constance finished for her.

Rebecca's eyes widened. 'How did you know?'

'I put two and two together. I doubt your father would have been happy for you to take a walk on such a day if he had known.' Constance put the tea-tray on one of the small occasional tables dotted about the room and drew a chair closer to Rebecca's. 'Now, tell me what's worrying you.'

'It's not me.' Rebecca found that after all her thinking she still didn't know where to start. 'It's my grandma and Mrs Mullen.'

'Oh, I remember Mrs Mullen. We used to call her Meddling Mullen when I was a bairn.'

'Did you? Well, she still is. Meddling, I mean. You see, it's like this . . .'

Constance sat looking at Tilly's daughter as she talked. She liked her, she thought with a dart of surprise. Somehow she hadn't expected to. But Rebecca was a lovely lass, warm and sweet with a natural kindness which shone out of her pretty face. And Matt was her father. She waited for the ache which always came with the knowledge that he had fathered a child with someone else, and although it was there it wasn't so painful now she had met Rebecca.

'. . . and so I wondered if you'd mind calling to see her as soon as you can. Just so she knows the two of you are still friends,' Rebecca finished.

'Of course I will. I fully intended to call once I'd settled in over the weekend, but then with the weather being so inclement I'm afraid I haven't budged from the fireside. I'll walk back with you now if you like . . . Oh no, no, that won't do, will it? Not if your visit needs to be kept between the two of us. I'll go tomorrow morning, whatever the weather. How's that?'

Rebecca smiled. This had all gone far better than she could have hoped. Now all she had to do was get home without anyone seeing her. She could say to her da once he came in from the pit that she'd been in bed all afternoon but felt much better.

They sat having tea and cake and Constance told Rebecca all about the Ashtons' estate and life in the big house until the rapidly deepening twilight reminded Rebecca that she had to leave. Constance insisted she and Jake would accompany Rebecca to the end of the lane and along the main road until the lights of the village were in sight, and the three set off together. Jake bounded ahead of them, cavorting in the snow like a puppy and making them laugh as he flung great mouthfuls of snow in the air.

It was dark by the time they reached the place where they had to part but Rebecca didn't mind this. She was less likely to be spotted by someone. As Constance called Jake to heel, Rebecca touched her arm. 'Thank you,' she said awkwardly, suddenly shy again. 'I hope you didn't mind me intruding.'

'You didn't.' Constance smiled at her. 'You were my first visitor and I can't think of a nicer one. I hope we see each other again now I'm back in the area. You must come for tea one day and bring your Larry, and – and your da, of course. Once you and I have met officially, that is.'

Rebecca grinned. 'I'll have to remember I don't know you, won't I? But once you've seen Gran I'll get Da to come and say hello. Perhaps on Sunday afternoon? I could bring Larry too.'

Constance's heart bounded in her chest. 'Please do.' She and Jake stood watching Rebecca until the girl turned and waved just before a bend in the road hid her from view.

Constance looked down at the big dog who gazed back at her with soulful eyes before giving a soft whine. 'I know, she's nice, isn't she, and the last thing we expected was a visitor out of the blue.' She ruffled the wiry hair on the long head. 'I think this is a good omen, lad. Don't you?' Her gaze returned to the dark road. 'Please, God, please let it be a good omen,' she whispered. 'Please let him want me. I don't mind waiting. I've waited years as it is.'

Jake whined again, louder, bringing her attention back to him. 'You're nothing but a cupboard love,' she said softly. 'You want your dinner, don't you, and who can blame you after what you've been through? Come on then, let's go home.'

Rebecca was humming to herself as she approached the house via the back lane. The snow had held off and Constance had agreed to see her grandma tomorrow. And she was lovely. Not a bit uppity as she'd half-expected. And Appleby Cottage – oh, she wished her grandma could see inside. Her eyes would pop out.

Engrossed in her thoughts, she was halfway down the backyard before she realised there was a light in the kitchen. She stopped, her brow wrinkling. Her da was on the afternoon shift, so it couldn't be him, but who else would be in their kitchen? Quickly now she entered the house, not stopping to take off her boots before she opened the scullery door leading into the kitchen. As she did so, her father looked up from where he was sitting at the kitchen table with a cup of tea in front of him.

'Da?' Her voice was high. Something was wrong. 'Why are you home? What's happened?'

'Your granda had an accident.' He raised his hand as she went to speak. 'He's all right, just a broken leg. There was a bit of a fall and he was in the wrong place at the wrong time. We got him up and the doctor's seen him and he's back home with your grandma. He was asleep when I left.'

Rebecca sat down on one of the kitchen chairs as her legs went weak. For a moment she had thought . . .

'I called in at the shop to tell you.'

Her eyes shot to her father's face. She suddenly realised his voice hadn't been the same when he told her about her granda.

'They told me you were home with an upset tummy so I came here. That was at four o'clock. It's now' – he looked at the clock on the mantelpiece above the range – 'gone half-five. Where have you been, Rebecca?'

He knew. She could see it in his eyes. They had lost their usual velvety softness and were gimlet hard. Swallowing, she said, 'I can explain. I had to tell them I was ill.'

'Oh aye? Why was that then?'

'I – I couldn't stop thinking about Grandma and how she'd looked after Mrs Mullen had told her about Constance, and so – and so I . . .' She drew in a deep breath; she had never seen him so angry, not with her anyway. 'I went to Appleby Cottage.'

'Despite the fact I'd specifically forbidden it?'

'You didn't, not exactly. You said you wouldn't go but you didn't say I couldn't.'

'So you thought I would approve of you lying to your employers and skiving off for the afternoon in order to demean yourself by begging Miss Shelton to do your grandma the great honour of visiting her? Is that it?'

Put like that it sounded awful. 'It – it wasn't like that. Constance isn't like that.'

'And you had no intention of telling me about this, had you? Nor your grandma, I presume.'

Rebecca hung her head.

'*Had you?*' he persisted grimly.

'No.'

'Do you understand what you have done? Have you any idea of the position you've placed us in? To go and see a virtual stranger and blackmail her with the past into doing something she obviously had no wish to do. What were you thinking of?'

'I tell you it wasn't like that.' Her voice was harsh now in an effort to stop the tears from falling. 'Constance was lovely and she made me welcome and showed me round the cottage and everything, and it might be grand and beautiful and she might have pots of money but she isn't uppity about it. She wants us to go and have a cup of tea with her Sunday afternoon and she wants to meet Larry and she's going to see Gran tomorrow.'

Before she had closed her mouth on her words she knew she had made a mistake. His face had been red and angry before, now it was as black as thunder. He'd hardly ever raised his voice to her in the past, now it was a bellow as he shouted, 'You say I didn't forbid you to go before? Well, I'm forbidding it now, is that clear? You put all thoughts of visiting her again out of your mind, my girl, or so help me, big as you are, I'll take it out of your hide.'

She couldn't speak, couldn't move, but as the tears spilled over she saw his face change and he became her da once again. Moving swiftly, he came to crouch down beside her chair, taking her in his arms as she shook with her sobbing. He held her until she was calmer, then he stood up, bringing her with him. Cupping her wet face in his big work-scarred hands, he said gruffly, 'I'm sorry, hinny. I shouldn't have gone for you like that but there's things here I can't explain, and you going to see her like that . . . Well, it's made it worse, lass. She was a working girl when she left these parts, but by your own admission she's risen in the world, she's a lady now. And that's good and fine, I'm not knocking what she's accomplished, but it makes things different, lass. Do you see?'

She shook her head slowly. She didn't want to make him angry again but she *didn't* see.

'I'm a miner, lass. You're a miner's daughter and your granda and his granda before him were miners, same as on your mam's side. We get by but that's all we do, and now your granda is going to be laid off for goodness knows how long we're going to be even more strapped because we'll be paying their rent and buying their food until he's able to work again, if ever. The break was a bad one and your granda's not a young man. In truth he should have left the pit a couple of years ago. It might be after the doctor's had another look at that leg in a week or two that he says he won't be able to work again and then they'll have to let the house go because running two houses is beyond me, lass. Then it's either the work-house for them or moving in with us, do you see? It'll mean they have the front room and my wage and yours provides for the four of us.'

'But . . .' She hesitated.

'What?'

'What's that got to do with me going to see Constance?'

Matt closed his eyes for a moment and then opened them as he stared into Rebecca's troubled face for a long moment. 'The Constance I knew had a soft heart, hinny, and from what you've said she still does. We – we don't want charity, all right? Not from her or anyone else. I'll provide for my own.'

'But, Da—'

'I mean it, Rebecca. This is not open for discussion.'

Rebecca stared at him. There was something more here she couldn't grasp, something her mind was dimly searching for. But he meant it. She could see he meant every word. Brokenly, she murmured, 'But I said we'd go, Da. On Sunday, I mean. The three of us. I said we'd go and she was going to get us tea.'

'Well, you shouldn't have.'

'She'll – she'll be waiting, expecting us.'

'Then let that be a lesson to you on promising what's not yours to promise,' he said grimly.

'Da, please. It's not her fault and I'd feel awful.'

'All right, all right.' He raked back his hair irritably as he let go of her. 'I'll go and see her before then and explain that we're not coming but it's a damn awkward position you've placed me in, young lady. Damned awkward.'

'I know.' Her voice was quiet, tearful. 'I'm sorry, Da. I just thought Gran would be so pleased to see her.'

'Aye, and I'm sure she will be. We'll keep the matter of your part in it to ourselves though, all right?'

'Oh yes, that's what Constance and I agreed,' Rebecca said eagerly. 'She was so nice, Da, and beautiful. To think you saved her life all them years ago when she was just a baby.'

Matt turned away. He couldn't take any more of this. He'd known full well where Rebecca had gone the minute he'd got in and found she wasn't here, and it was as well for the lass she hadn't walked in at that moment because he wouldn't have been responsible for his actions. Dear gussy . . . He reached for his cup on the table and drained the last of his tea before saying, 'Put the kettle on, hinny, and we'll have a fresh brew.'

What a day. When the roof had fallen and he'd heard the scream, he'd somehow known it was his da. Flesh calling to flesh. George and Andrew had been the same. Between them they'd got him out and into the cage, but looking at his da's leg then he'd felt the old man's days down the pit were over. And not before time too. For the last year or so his da had left a shift grim and quiet and looking as though he could hardly put one foot in front of the other. He was coming up for seventy; he should be enjoying the little time he'd got left pottering about and sitting and talking with his pals over a bevy come evening, but there were few miners who could afford to stop until they were too broken-down to do anything else – and by then it usually meant they were having all the rest they wanted in a wooden box within weeks. Most of his da's pals couldn't walk more than a yard or two without stopping to catch their breath, and nearly all of them had bad backs and gammy legs and goodness knows what.

Rebecca had taken off her hat and coat and changed into her slippers. Now she put the kettle on and bustled about setting the table. He caught her hand as she passed him, his

326

voice soft as he said, 'You're a good lass, none better.' And he meant it. She tried to look after him and keep the house running smoothly and rarely thought of herself, bless her. 'And I know you did what you did for your gran, but what if Mr and Mrs Turner had found out what you were about? No more jaunts, eh, lass?' He smiled to soften the admonition.

'No more, Da. I promise.'

But the damage was done. He had hoped to avoid Constance over the next little while and, in the unlikely event that their paths crossed, be cordial and polite whilst intimating he had no intention of presuming on their former friendship just because she was now a wealthy woman in her own right. Rebecca's little escapade had put paid to that. Had Constance felt obliged to invite them round on Sunday? He groaned inwardly. Probably. And now he was going to look like a damn fool whatever he did. Dear gussy, what a mess . . .

The next morning, Matt dressed in clean clothes from his underwear up after taking a bath in front of the range once Rebecca had gone to work. He didn't question why he did this. He knew it was all to do with the scent of Constance that had tormented his senses for days after the last time he had seen her. A scent which had nothing to do with the cloying cheap eau de Cologne some lasses favoured and which he'd never particularly liked, and all to do with donning freshly laundered clothes after a warm scented bath, of having clean hair and clean nails.

He inspected himself in front of the thin mottled mirror on the back of the wardrobe door once he was ready to leave the house. He was as clean as soap and water could make him, he thought wryly, walking down the stairs and pulling on his Sunday greatcoat and best cap, both of which were beginning to show the signs of wear. But they would have to do. He looked every inch what he was, a working-class man, and he didn't intend to apologise for it either.

On the walk to Appleby Cottage he didn't allow himself to think about what he was going to say or do. He concentrated on covering the distance as quickly as he could and kept his mind blank. It hadn't snowed again since the day before. The sky had cleared at some point during the evening and a heavy frost had fallen through the night. Now, at half-past nine in the morning, the air was thin and sharp and the blue sky high without a cloud to be seen. In other circumstances he would have enjoyed such a morning in the fresh air.

When he reached the cottage, he didn't pause before he opened the gate and made his way to the front door. He wouldn't have admitted it to a living soul but if he had paused, he felt he would have stood there all morning trying to work up the courage to face her. He brought the brass knocker down hard and immediately a dog answered from within the house, barking ferociously. So she had a guard dog? That was good. One of the things which had kept him awake the last couple of nights was the remoteness of the Colonel's place. He closed his eyes for an instant. *Constance's* place. Admittedly there was a farm at the very end of the lane which finished at Tan Hills Wood, and the odd small cottage scattered about, but none close to Appleby Cottage.

When the door opened he realised he was holding his breath. She was wearing a deep blue dress and her hair was coiled at the back of her head, and her eyes opened wide at seeing him.

'Matt.' Her voice, like her eyes, was warm and welcoming. 'What a nice surprise. Come in, please.' She was holding the dog's collar and as it growled, she added, 'No, Jake. Friend,' before looking at him and saying, 'He's fine, really, but he seems to be wary of men. He's the Colonel's old dog but I think between them dying and me coming he's had a rough time fending for himself, poor thing.'

'Hello, boy.' Matt extended his hand for the animal to sniff and after a moment the big rangy body relaxed.

'Come in,' Constance said again, and as he followed her into the house and she led the way into the sitting room he was aware of a medley of colour on the perimeter of his vision although he couldn't take his gaze off her golden hair.

When she turned to face him their eyes met and held, but hers almost immediately fell away as she said quietly, 'I'm so sorry about Tilly. It must have been awful for you and Rebecca.'

He nodded. 'Yes, it was.' The voice didn't sound like his own; it was stiff, cold.

'Come and sit down by the fire and I'll take your hat and coat. Would you like a hot drink? It's so cold outside.'

He didn't answer this, nor did he move from his spot just inside the room. 'I know Rebecca came to see you yesterday.' He hadn't meant for it to sound so abrupt but having started, he continued, 'She shouldn't have done that. I'm sorry.'

Now it was Constance who stiffened and her voice was cool when she said, 'Really? I take it you mean for some reason other than she should have been at work?'

'She asked you to go and see my mother, didn't she?'

'And what's wrong in that? I was going to go anyway as I told her, once I'd settled in and the weather improved.'

'That would have been up to you but she was wrong to ask.'

'I don't see why.'

He had taken his cap off on entering the house and now he was unaware that he was turning it round and round in his hands. 'You have been away for a long time and things change, people change. I told her that to presume on a past friendship is asking too much. It is up to you who you see and where you go, and she had no right to ask anything of you. She had never even met you before yesterday.'

'Perhaps she thought true friendship is the one thing which never changes. Your mother is my friend. I – I thought *you* were my friend.'

This was killing him. Brusquely he nodded. 'I am.' His gaze moved from her to travel swiftly round the room before coming to rest on her face again. 'But things aren't the same now, you must see that.' She did not reply, and he forced himself to go on, 'Your world is very different to mi— to ours. Your grandma once said to me some years after you'd left the village that you had outgrown us and she was right.'

'My grandma said that?' There was a wealth of hurt in her voice.

'Don't get me wrong, she was very proud of you. She used to tell my mother how you travelled abroad, that you could speak different languages, that you were having an education. Things any other lass from these parts would look on as impossible.'

'But that doesn't mean I'm not still me.'

'I know that.'

'Well, then . . .'

'Constance, you grew up in a mining village. You know what it's like. Most folk don't have two farthings to rub together and there's many a family who duck down under the window and lock the door when the rent man's due. Folk live in fear of the workhouse from the day they're born and with good cause, and the pit's a fickle master. Every so often it demands the blood of those who serve it. But that's how it is, that's how it's always been. The pit owners and the managers and the wealthy on one side; ordinary folk on the other, and a great divide between.'

'And – and you think I'm on the other side to your mam and you and ordinary folk now?' she asked, white-faced.

'Aren't you?' he asked grimly.

'No!' It was a cry of anguish and the dog at her side moved restlessly, growling softly before whining.

'I'd better leave.' He had said way, way too much.

'I'm not,' she protested again. 'I can't help the way things have turned out, the Ashtons being so kind to me and all, but their generosity doesn't make me any different from the girl I was before I left here. I've seen a different way of life and been places, I know that, but I'm still me inside. What do you think I should have done then? Refused to ever be more than a scullerymaid? Is that it?'

'Of course not.'

'You say that, but that's what you're implying.'

He had upset her and all he wanted to do was take her in his arms and make love to her, but that had never been more impossible. 'I'm sorry,' he said quietly. 'I shouldn't have come.'

'Well, why did you?'

'I needed to explain why we can't come on Sunday.'

If it was possible, her face went whiter. 'Don't you mean *won't*?' She gave a brittle laugh. 'And am I banned from seeing your mam too? Are you forbidding me to go round there?'

His voice sharper than he intended, he said, 'Don't be silly.'

'*Silly?*'

He had thought for a moment she was going to cry and he knew that would have broken him, but he had forgotten about her temper. It was rare it had come to the surface when she'd been a child, but when it did it had been generally acknowledged that it was better not to get in her way. But he was in her way now.

'How *dare* you call me silly after you've had the nerve to come here and warn me off from speaking to your family. Anyone would think I was a woman of loose morals, a bad influence, the way you've gone on. And what's my crime? Working hard all my life for genuinely good people who wanted to reward me for what they saw as saving their son's life. It could have been any one of a number of people in the yard that day, but it happened to be me – and you know what? I'm not sorry. If you want me to apologise for the things I've seen and done and experienced over the last ten years, and the money they insisted on giving me when they left England for good, then forget it. I'm me. *Me.*' She dug a finger in her chest. 'And whether I had one pound to my name or one thousand or ten thousand, I'd still be the same. Do you know what you are, Matt Heath? You're an upstart.'

His own temper on the boil, he grated, 'The hell I am.'

'Oh yes, you are. There are many different ways to be an upstart and you've picked the nastiest of all, inverted snobbery. If I had come back home without a penny to my name, you wouldn't have minded Rebecca coming to see me and asking me to call on your mam, but because you're a man, a self-centred, egotistical, *bigoted* man who thinks he's God's gift and an authority on everything, you're determined to think I've changed.'

'Have you finished?'

'No.' The veneer of the last decade had fallen away and, hands on hips, she gave vent to the pain of years which had accumulated to overflowing with his words that morning. She couldn't have said in this moment whether she loved or hated him, she only knew she wanted to hurt him as he had hurt her. 'You're a coward into the bargain. You're worried what people might say if you and Rebecca and her young man were seen coming here, aren't you? Worried they might get the wrong idea, that they'd think you were after a bob or two? At base level, that's what this is all about – what other people might think. You don't care about Rebecca or me or your mam, not really. It's all about you and your stupid manly pride. You obviously wish I'd never come back here. Well, surprise, surprise, so do I. *I hate you!*' And now she felt herself really regress to child-hood as she stamped her foot, beside herself with rage and frustration.

Again Jake growled, glaring at Matt as though he was the one carrying-on, and as the dog's distress got through to Constance, she felt the anger drain away, her voice dull as she murmured, 'It's all right, boy, it's all right. Easy, Jake, easy.'

Matt's face had a stricken look to it but his voice was tight when he stated the obvious. 'I've upset you.'

'Yes.'

'I shouldn't have come.'

'No.'

He turned, but almost in the same movement swung back to face her. 'I never said I wished you hadn't come back.'

Quietly now, she said, 'Not in so many words, no.' She watched his Adam's apple move up and down as he swallowed. He was embarrassed, she thought woodenly, and no wonder. She had made a fool of herself. And yelling at him like that with Tilly only having been gone a matter of months. As if he hadn't enough to deal with. These thoughts reverberated in her head but they were strangely without emotion.

'I – I know my mam would like to see you. When you've got the time, that is. And I'd be pleased if you visited her.'

She nodded, not trusting herself to speak. If she could just hold on to this numbness until he had gone she would be all right. He had said she had changed but so had he. Oh yes, so had he.

And then this last thought was blown asunder when their eyes met. For a fleeting moment it was all there; his need, his longing, his love and desire, like those other moments in time which she'd carried in her heart even as she'd doubted if they'd happened afterwards or whether her love for him had conjured them up in her imagination. He breathed her name but even as she swayed towards him he had stepped through the doorway into the hall, opening the front door and then shutting it behind him.

Constance remained still for a full minute, her ears straining as she listened for his returning footsteps. He couldn't leave like this. He couldn't. If he went now he wouldn't come back again, she knew that.

After a while she sat down and Jake came and put his head in her lap, one paw resting on her knee as though he knew the feeling of aloneness that was in her, an aloneness that was crushing her mind and spirit and bringing such desolation it was unbearable. And it was some more minutes before she put her arms round the furry body and began to cry.

Chapter 22

Polly watched Vincent as he left the house that evening. She knew where he was going because she had followed him several nights ago, certain he was making for Appleby Cottage now he knew the Shelton girl was back. She could pinpoint the very day he found out that Constance had returned because that was the first time he'd left after dinner and been out most of the night. She had known about Constance a day or two before that, but she hadn't let on. However, the day after she'd followed him, she had gone to Appleby Cottage once Vincent had left for work and warned the lass he was watching her.

Polly moved away from the window and walked into the kitchen, and as she began to wash the dirty dishes she was thinking about what Constance had said that day. The lass had been friendly, offering her a cup of tea and thanking her for coming, but she had said she was already on her guard and had taken measures to protect herself, should any unwelcome visitors call. Which was all very well, thought Polly, but the lass didn't know Vincent like she did. But she hoped she'd said enough to make Constance especially vigilant – and there was the dog to give the alarm.

She continued to chew the matter over in her mind, and once the dishes were done and the kitchen was spick and span, she walked into the sitting room with a mug of hot milk and sat in front of the fire. It had been lovely the last few evenings when he hadn't been at home. Normally she sat in the kitchen until bedtime but she was always on edge in case he might come to the doorway and beckon her with one finger as he was apt to do when he wanted her in his bedroom. That was a rare occurrence now, but since the time of Constance's grandmother's funeral when she'd heard the lass tell him what was what, it seemed as if more devils had been let loose in him. A couple of times she'd been in such pain the next day she hadn't been able to leave her bed and thought she was going to die. And all he'd done was look at her with those dead eyes from the bedroom doorway and then gone about his business without a word until she was back on her feet again.

After a while she made herself another hot drink and cut a generous slab of Christmas cake from the half-cake they still had left, bringing it back to the sitting room and toasting her toes on the fender while she ate. Constance was so lucky to have that bonny cottage all to herself without anyone to wait on or see to. How she would love that. To be able to please herself from first thing in the morning until last thing at night was her idea of heaven. And she would have a couple of cats. No, half a dozen to keep her company. She liked cats but Vincent had banned them from the house and garden and threw water at any that ventured near when he was about. He didn't like the way they caught birds and played with them before they killed them. He said they were the only animals he knew that were cruel for cruelty's sake. Him, to call anything cruel! Her lip curled.

She was dozing when the clock on the mantelpiece chimed eleven o'clock. More asleep than awake, she banked down the fire in the sitting room with damp slack before seeing to the one in the range in the kitchen, put out the lamps and made sure the back door was bolted and the front door was locked. Vincent always came in and out of the house by the front door and carried a key. Then she made her way to her bedroom and undressed down to her shift, snuggling under the covers and falling asleep the moment her head touched the pillow.

Vincent had taken up his position a few yards down the lane from Appleby Cottage at nine o'clock, and it was now midnight. In spite of his thick coat and the bottle of brandy he'd swigged at now and again, he was frozen to the bone. He'd burrowed himself a spot in the hedgerow next to the stout trunk of an oak tree, just in case his silhouette should show against the white snow if anyone passed by going to or from the farm near Tan Hills Wood, but he hadn't seen a soul — apart from a pair of wood mice, that was. They'd emerged from their subterranean burrow to forage for whatever they could find in the most sheltered part of the hedgerow, finding a snail each which they'd eaten by nibbling through the shells. He'd watched them for some time until they'd finished their feast and scampered off further afield, and they'd been completely oblivious of his presence. The sleek, quick-witted wood mice were his favourite rodents. He admired their intelligence and the way they gathered and stored food in times of plenty for winter consumption. He'd found a deserted bird's nest once which had contained over a pint of hidden rose hips. But he wasn't here to observe mice tonight.

He shifted slightly. His feet were numb with cold and the crystal-clear air was sharp with the scent of frost. The moonlight was bright and with the reflection of the snow it made the night seem almost like daytime.

How long would it have been before he knew Constance had returned to these parts if he hadn't seen Matt Heath that morning? But he had seen him. He sometimes took a walk round the reservoir in the morning if he wasn't on duty at the pit till the afternoon shift. He liked observing the birds which lived on the banks and in the water, and it was rare he met anyone. That particular morning the snow had been thick but he'd got in the habit of feeding a family of mallards he'd observed since the summer, and he'd known they would be hoping he'd turn up with the weather so bad. Food was scarce, and they had a whole host of other ducks and birds to compete with.

His mission completed, he'd been leaning against the trunk of a tree which was set up high on the bank which over-looked the main road, trying in vain to light his pipe, when a figure had emerged from the lane opposite. Instinct had caused him to duck down. It didn't do for any of the men at the pit to know his habits. One of the reasons he hadn't ended up in a ditch with his head split open was because he was more cunning than they were.

He recognised Matt Heath straight away and his eyes narrowed as he watched the other man pause for a moment and look back whence he had come. What was Heath doing, dressed up in his Sunday best by the look of it, and acting . . . He couldn't find a word to describe how Heath was acting, but it intrigued him. When Heath turned and walked a few paces back down the lane before once again stopping and turning around, it aroused his curiosity even more. It was a full minute before the man seemed to make up his mind about something and then he strode off towards the village, but when he came to the bend in the road which took him out of sight, he again paused and looked back towards Findon Hill.

Once Heath had disappeared, Vincent waited another ten minutes before emerging on to the main road, and then he quickly crossed it and entered the lane. He knew where it led – he knew every inch of the surrounding countryside. Where the badger sets were; where the foxes lay in specially dug-out places, waiting for a rabbit or hare to stray nearby; the hollow trees where bats hibernated; and which tawny owl had territorial rights over which piece of land. When he had come to the Colonel's old place and seen smoke rising from the chimney, he'd paused. Heath's footsteps in the snow had ended at the cottage.

His interest in the identity of the occupant of the cottage had been such that he'd debated whether to go and knock on the front door, but something had stopped him. He'd waited for a while and then left, but within twenty-four hours he'd made it his business to find out who was occupying Appleby Cottage. When he looked back, he had known by Heath's behaviour who it was though. He'd never forgotten the night umpteen years ago and the look on Constance's face when she'd appeared out of the crowd waiting at the pit gates and thrown herself into Heath's arms. Something had been going on even then. Heath might have married the other one but something had been going on with Constance, as sure as eggs were eggs. He should have trusted his instincts, Vincent thought bitterly. Constance looked as though butter wouldn't melt in her mouth but she was cut from the same cloth as her mother. The pair of them had ruined his life with their false smiles and eyes that promised heaven on earth. And look at her now – as shameless as one of the whores he'd visited once upon a time. You didn't get the sort of money she would have needed to buy Appleby Cottage and live like a lady by being in service, not the sort of service the old couple had insisted she was in, anyway. And she'd hardly been back two minutes and Heath was visiting her on the quiet, as well he might. The old wives would have a field day if they knew he was Constance's fancy man, and his wife still warm in her grave.

He ground his teeth, his hands bunched into fists at his side. He'd see his day with the pair of them; he'd make them both suffer, but her most of all. Oh aye, he'd take his time with her, make it last until she was begging him to put her out of her misery. She'd laughed at him for the last time.

A movement on the sleeve of his coat caused him to glance down. A web spider was crawling down his arm close to her intricately woven web in the hedgerow, the fine threads of silk highlighted with a dusting of frost. He carefully raised his arm and deposited her on a nearby twig from which she scuttled out of sight. He stared at the web. It was beautiful but deadly for any unwary insects.

Hannah had woven a web stickier than any spider's, he thought morosely, but unlike an arachnid, her aim had been to torment and frustrate her prey, to make him think she was the answer to all his dreams and desires when really she'd been laughing at him the whole time. Like mother, like daughter.

The lights in Appleby Cottage had long since been extinguished. If Heath was going to make an appearance after his shift he would have done so by now. He'd had several nights on the trot waiting here to catch him, and he didn't fancy another few hours of freezing his vitals off. But he'd surprise him sooner or later. His hand reached inside his coat, feeling for the handle of the kitchen knife he'd brought with him. He wouldn't kill him, not quite. He wanted him to witness everything he was going to do to her before he finished him off.

Vincent eased himself slowly out of his hiding-place, flexing his shoulders and rotating his neck a couple of times before he began to walk home.

'When's Constance coming again to see you, Gran? Did she say?' Rebecca was sitting in Ruth's kitchen having a hot buttered teacake and a cup of tea, and outside the February afternoon was dark and stormy. It was four o'clock but the lamps had already been lit for over an hour, and the whirling snow beat a frenzy against the windowpane. It being a Monday, the first one in February, Rebecca had finished work and brought the latest offering from Mrs Turner – a bag of speckled vegetables and the tail end of a wedge of ham-and-egg pie – straight to her grandma's. Ruth had told her Constance had been round to see her that morning, her sixth visit since she'd moved back.

'Sometime later this week, hinny.' Ruth glanced at her husband who was sitting snoring in his armchair in front of the range, his bad leg resting on one of the kitchen chairs. Quietly she fished in her pinny pocket, bringing out two sovereigns. 'She slipped me these on the doorstep as she was leaving, on the quiet, you know?'

Rebecca nodded. She didn't need to be told her granda wouldn't have liked what he'd have seen as charity if he knew; he was like her da in that respect. He'd protested a bit about the bag of groceries Constance had brought on her last visit, and it was only when Constance had got upset and said she thought he regarded her as family and wasn't family supposed to be able to support each other, and look at all the times she'd been fed in this kitchen as a bairn, that her granda had softened. Men were funny in that respect. She didn't understand it. You couldn't make a meal out of pride and it didn't help with paying the rent either. And why, if you liked someone, did them having money make any difference anyway? Her grandma said Constance hadn't changed one bit.

As though her grandma had followed her train of thought, Ruth said even more quietly, 'Your da's not come round yet then? He's not been to see her apart from that one time?'

'No.'

'It's upset her, you know. She's not said owt – well, she wouldn't, would she – but I can tell. I can't understand him, I can't straight. He thought the world of her when she was a bairn, and what does it matter if she's well set up now? Men! They're a different breed, lass. And what's going to happen to your granda, I don't know. He insists he's going back to the pit but I can't see it meself, not with his leg so bad.' Ruth sighed heavily. Her husband had driven her to distraction since he'd been laid up and he wasn't helping himself by trying to do too much too quickly. Dr Fallow had laid it on the line the last time he'd called. He'd given him a right dressing-down, telling him he'd put his recovery back weeks by his antics. Where was it all going to end? She knew Matt wouldn't see them in the workhouse, but if they moved in with him and Rebecca they'd be a millstone round his neck, whatever he said to the contrary. Sighing again, she whispered, 'I told your da what I thought, about him refusing to see Constance and stopping you from visiting the lass. We had a right two-an'-eight about it.'

'I know, he told me.' Rebecca stared at her grandma. She loved her and had always been able to say anything to her, but she didn't know if she should say what she was about to say. Then, throwing caution to the wind, she leaned forward until her head was almost touching Ruth's and murmured, 'Gran, do you think he likes her? You know, in *that* way? Do you reckon that's why he's so funny about her having money now?'

Ruth surveyed her granddaughter for a moment. 'I have to say it's crossed my mind, hinny. Would you mind if that was so?'

'Mind? No. Why should I mind?'

'Well, with your mam an' all.'

'Oh, Gran.' Rebecca's voice carried a thread of irritation. 'You know how it was between Mam and Da. They never got on, let's be honest. In fact, they couldn't stand each other half the time.'

'Rebecca!'

'They didn't, Gran, and you know it. And . . .' Rebecca paused a moment. There was frankness and there was frankness and she didn't know how her grandma would take this next bit. 'I was born very early after they were wed, wasn't I?'

'*Rebecca.*' Now Ruth was truly shocked. 'You came early – you were premature, that's all. By all the saints, lass, what have you been thinking?'

'That they had to get married because they'd jumped the gun,' Rebecca answered honestly. 'Not because they really wanted to.'

'Dear gussy.' Ruth fanned herself with her pinny.

'Can you truthfully say you've never suspected anything?'

Ruth was at a loss. This granddaughter of hers came out with such things, it would never have done in her day. She stared at Rebecca. Of course she'd had her misgivings. Rebecca had been such a bonny plump babbie for a premature child. She had seen one or two of them in her time and they'd mostly resembled skinned rabbits for the first month or two of their lives, bless 'em. Scrawny arms and legs with their feet and hands looking too big for the rest of them. Rebecca had been a little dumpling – you could never have called *her* underweight.

She swallowed before managing to mutter, 'Ee, lass, you shouldn't say such things. Your da would have a blue fit if he heard that.'

Ignoring this, Rebecca went on, 'And if that was the case, if Mam suddenly found herself expecting, it could well have started them off on the wrong foot, so to speak. Do you know what I mean, Gran? Perhaps they resented it. Both of them.'

Helplessly, Ruth picked up her tea and swigged it down scalding hot. Whatever next?

'That's what I think anyway,' Rebecca said firmly.

'Your mam and your da have always loved you very

much, lass. You know that, don't you?' Ruth managed weakly.

Rebecca nodded. 'Just not each other,' she said sadly.

'Oh, hinny. Don't get upset.'

'Maybe Constance was the person Da was supposed to marry and there was someone else meant for Mam. Larry was saying the other night that he believes we all have several lives mapped out for us, like a crossroads with streets going in different directions, and it's up to us which one we choose. Sometimes it's the right one but sometimes we go down the wrong street, and then . . .' Rebecca shrugged.

Ruth stared at her granddaughter. 'I've never heard such codswallop.'

Rebecca grinned. 'That's what he thinks anyway.'

'Well, I think—'

But Rebecca never got to hear what her grandma thought. There was a terrific thump on the back door which brought her granda shooting up in his chair and cursing when it pained his leg, and then Mrs Burns from two doors down was shouting, 'Ruth, there's a fall, lass. There's a fall!'

And from that moment everything else was unimportant.

Chapter 23

The sound he had hoped never to hear again in the rest of his life was still ringing in Matt's ears. A second after it had started he'd found himself flying through the air and then his head had hit rock and he must have passed out. He lay in the pitch blackness wondering if he still had two arms and two legs, his mouth filled with dirt and his head aching worse than any hangover.

The air was thick with a mixture of grit and coaldust as slowly he rolled over on to his back and then sat up, spitting out as much of the dirt that was choking him as he could. He didn't need to be told that the roof had come down; it was only a matter of how bad the fall was. Nearly all the big pit disasters were caused by gas explosions. It took no more than a hewer's pick to release a pocket, and in the sort of bad weather they'd been having lately the atmospheric pressure was low so more gas would be about, especially firedamp. Bearing in mind that only a few lungfuls of firedamp could kill a man and it was lighter than air, he didn't stand up. He thought the blast had come from behind him, from the direction of the mothergate, and the shift had been moving inbye towards the tailgate.

Matt had been one of the first in the group of men. George had been in front of him, but Andrew and his sons, Jed and Toby, along with George's three lads, had been messing about having an argument about their respective football teams whilst they'd collected their lamps and hadn't been in the first cage to descend. He and George had gone on without them, tired of the argument which was a familiar one and never got anywhere. A bit like the football teams concerned.

He tried to call George's name but his mouth and throat were so caked with dust it took two attempts before he could manage it, and then there was a muffled groan at the side of him. It took another few minutes to establish there were five of them in the pocket of road where the roof still held. It had come down behind and in front of them but the main fall had been behind them where the rest of the shift had been following. George had become silent after this. From what Matt could make out in the blackness his brother was bleeding heavily from a head wound; his hair was matted and sticky, and from his cautious exploration there was a pool beneath his head. Matt had taken off his own shirt and wrapped it round George's head; it was all he could do.

Apart from George there was one other man injured; Reg had been behind Matt in the roadway and one of his legs was pinned beneath a large slab of rock. Matt and the other two, Stan and Monty Griffiths who were brothers, had attempted to lift it off him but they couldn't budge it and had had to admit defeat. The three of them, panting with their efforts, sank down to the floor; the

Griffiths brothers either side of Reg, and Matt next to George who was still silent. Fearfully Matt felt inside his brother's coat and under his shirt for the beat of his heart. It was there but faint and when he patted his face, saying, 'George? George, come on, man, wake up,' there was no answer.

'How is he, Matt?' one of the brothers asked.

'Not good.' He couldn't say any more, he didn't want to start blubbing like a big lassie.

'Don't worry, man. He's a tough old bird, is George. He'll be all right. They'll be coming for us soon.'

Aye, but how long would it take the rescue team to work through the who-knew-how-thick wall of stone and coal and pit-props separating them from life-giving air? And what about the rest of them? Andrew and his sons, George's lads and the others? Had they been burned alive or crushed and suffocated under tons of rock? Sacriston Colliery was like many others in the Durham coalfield. So much coal had been taken out of it and so many long roadways cut, that subsidence was an ever-present danger along with everything else. They all knew it and lived with it.

As he sat in the darkness listening to Stan and Monty's low voices chivying Reg along now and again, Matt wondered why the fear which had been with him at the back of his mind since the last fall wasn't paramount. He'd had nightmares about this happening for years, but maybe that was it. It had happened, the thing he'd been waiting for, and the sixth sense or premonition, call it what you will, had been fulfilled. And he really wouldn't have minded so much if it hadn't been for Constance's return to Sacriston.

He breathed deeply before reminding himself he was using up precious oxygen that way.

For years he'd thought there was no chance of seeing her again. She had risen so high – why would she bother to come home now her grandma had gone? And if she did, he'd expected it to be a flying visit to see Molly and her other relatives.

But Constance *had* come back. The impossible had happened. He sat up straighter, his heart beating faster as a sick sort of panic filled him. And what had he done? Gone out of his way to hurt her and avoid her. He must have been mad. He *was* mad.

'No, not mad,' a little voice in his head stated relentlessly. There would have been some excuse if that was the case. He wasn't mad, just a coward like she'd said. He had been furious with her that day for forcing him to look at himself, but she'd been right. He *was* egotistical and bigoted and all those other things she'd accused him of. He'd known it that day on the walk home but he still hadn't had the guts to do anything about it. All his life he'd tried to act the big fellow, to be what the men around him expected him to be. You did that. It was necessary. From a bairn he'd had it mirrored in his own home. The husband and father was the man, the breadwinner, the boss. He was entitled to absolute respect. His da's position in the house had been sacrosanct.

His mouth was paining him. When he raised a probing finger he found he'd lost a couple of teeth, not that he was going to need teeth where he was going, he thought with black humour.

Did he care so much about what his pals and family thought of him that it was more important than his love for Constance? he asked himself as his hand came from his mouth. Because that was what it boiled down to. Did he? If he was honest, the answer was yes – or had been, up until he was buried alive. Now, as he looked back, it was farcical. What the hell did other people matter? All that mattered was Constance, and he would swear to it she wouldn't think any the less of him. Oh, he'd told himself she might think he was after her for her money, but that had been a get-out. He'd seen her grow up, he *knew* her and she couldn't think that way, not his Constance. Only she wasn't his Constance.

Maybe she wouldn't have wanted him anyway if he had asked her to marry him. There had been some man after her in Italy. His mam had told him that one night when he'd popped in to see how his da was. Well set up, his mam had said, with a big house and servants, and likely Constance would go back there some day soon if she wasn't happy. He had told his mam he thought that was a good idea, that she should go back, that it sounded like this man would suit the person she'd become very well, but he hadn't meant it and he hadn't slept that night. But he still hadn't gone to Appleby Cottage.

Fool. Matt nodded to the thought. Aye, he was a fool. Eighteen years ago he'd made up his mind to marry Tilly when he'd been caught in a life and death situation just like this, and it had been the wrong decision. As wrong as marrying Constance would be right. He had been given a second chance at life that day and what a mess he'd made of it. It would be too much to hope that the Almighty would give him a third chance. Why would He? If he was God he'd save the third chances for men who deserved them, men with happy marriages and wives who loved them.

But if, *if*, he got out of here, he'd go and see her. He'd crawl every inch of the way if he had to. He wouldn't expect anything, not after the way he'd treated her, but he'd go and see her nonetheless. Just so . . . she knew.

Vincent McKenzie stood quietly in the pit manager's office. There were two deputies talking to a doctor, and a priest and a vicar and several other men crammed into the small space. Outside in the yard one of the rescue teams had recently come up. Exhausted and filthy, the whites of their eyes luminous in their black faces, they'd stood aside as the next squad had gone down. They'd said little, but it was generally acknowledged that heavy casualties could be expected, although the news relayed to the gathering of friends and family outside the pit gates did not reflect this. A large portion of the crowd had been waiting for hours in the atrocious weather, some from four o'clock the previous day. It was now seven o'clock in the morning, and as some individuals left their vigil to go home for a hot meal and to see to children and other domestic matters, other folk took their place.

Vincent listened as the captain of the rescue party which had recently surfaced gave a report of what they'd found to the pit manager. A good few of the afternoon shift in question had been lucky and hadn't reached the area where the roof had fallen. When they had felt the current change they'd turned and run back towards the mothergate, and although a couple of stragglers had been burned by the ball of flames which had travelled down the roadway, they weren't seriously injured. That having been said, there were still a good number of men missing and it was these the captain spoke of. They'd heard knocking, he said, beyond the fall. A sign that someone was still alive – and with luck, a lot more than one. A fresh-air base had been established and the rescue squads were working as hard as they could, but he wouldn't like to say how long it would be before they got through to the trapped miners. He hoped it would be in the next few hours, but it was difficult to tell.

Vincent's face was deadpan but behind his closed expression his mind was racing. When the accident had happened and they'd established which miners were still underground, he'd looked down the list of names and only years of training had enabled him to remain impassive. *Matt Heath*. At last. There were a couple of other Heaths on the list but they didn't concern him, only inasmuch as he relished a certain satisfaction that the family which had interfered with his life all those years ago by saving a baby who should have died with her parents were getting their comeuppance.

He'd felt like going straight to Appleby Cottage and throwing the news in that one's face, but his duties at the pit had prevented this. The manager expected him to stay around until the rescue operation was complete; it looked bad otherwise. But once he was sure of his facts he'd take the greatest pleasure in seeing the look on her face when he told her her fancy man was no more.

It was a full twenty-four hours from when the explosion had first occurred that the rescue team reached some of the trapped men, but by five o'clock that night most of the miners who had been working the shift were accounted for. Five more were cut off from the main party in a second fall and there had been no sound from them. Three men had lost their lives but Andrew and his sons, along with George's lads, were not among them, although one of Andrew's sons had been badly hurt by a large section of the roof falling on to his back. Four other men had minor injuries. In view of the severity of the explosion and the amount of roof which had come crashing down, everyone agreed the death toll could have been much higher, but with five more men to reach there was no let-up in the rescue work. Many there feared that this last stage of the rescue was a hopeless cause, but no one would voice such negative thoughts.

At nine o'clock the pit manager told Vincent he might as well go home. The under-manager and an area surveyor were hanging on, as one of the owners was expected to arrive shortly, and normally Vincent − conscious of the fact it was good to be noted by the owners at times like this − would have stayed too. Although the manager had made the suggestion, he knew the man hadn't expected him to take it up, but for once he pretended to take the words at face value. He had more important fish to fry tonight than being seen by one of the owners.

He left, ignoring the manager's disapproving stare. Every thought, every cell in his body was concentrated on Constance.

There were only a few folk outside the pit gates now. He saw the Griffiths brothers' wives and a couple of the older children and Reg Havelock's family, along with Heath's mother and daughter, but he barely spared them a glance as he passed. They were unimportant. Village scum.

The night was clear and bitterly cold, the snowstorm of the last couple of days having blown itself out, and he breathed in the crisp icy air as he walked. He knew exactly what he was going to do. After he had changed his clothes and had a bite to eat, he was going to Appleby Cottage for the final reckoning. Matt Heath was as good as dead, which was a pity in one way; he would have enjoyed watching the man's torment as he dealt with Constance, but it would be sweet to see her face when he told her what had occurred at the pit. And he'd see to it that she never had another man.

All good things come to those who wait. And he had waited. Hell, how he'd waited for this moment. All his life had been the same.

When he reached his cottage and opened the front door, Polly shot through from the sitting room where she'd obviously been taking her ease, looking scared to death as she always did.

'I – I've kept some sheep's-head broth warm in case you came back tonight,' she stuttered, nearly falling over her own feet in her haste. 'And there's fresh bread and a jam roll I made today.'

'I'm going to change and then I'll eat.' He looked down at her head as she knelt before him and pulled off his boots. For a good while now he'd been tired of her skinny little body; even the new ways of taking his pleasure that had nearly done for her once or twice had ceased to satisfy him. It was time to be rid of her. He'd known it for a couple of years but hadn't bothered to do anything about it, but once this other had been seen to he'd deal with Polly. No one would notice if she disappeared, and there were plenty of places to bury a body where it would never be found.

It was rare she instigated any conversation, but now she said, 'The men? Are they all up safely?'

'Three dead and several injured,' he answered shortly, 'and five more still down. And I'll be going out after I've eaten.'

Polly said nothing more, but once she had taken up the hot water for his wash – he'd said he'd do without his normal bath – she stood stirring the broth in the kitchen. There were still men down and he'd come home? That was a first. And there had been a particular note in his voice when he'd said he was going out after his meal. She couldn't explain it but she recognised it from the early days when he'd first violated her – a sort of trembling excitement was the best description, but it was more chilling than that. It had been faint but it had been there. Was he going to see Constance Shelton when he left here? And if so, why tonight when he'd been up nearly forty-eight hours on the trot? He was planning something. She hadn't lived with him all these years without getting a gut feeling about how his mind worked. And whatever he was planning didn't bode well for the lass whose grandma had been so kind to her.

His meal was ready when he came downstairs. Polly made herself as unobtrusive as she could while he ate, silently placing a large helping of baked jam roll in front of him when he had finished the broth. He normally took his time over his food but tonight he practically gobbled it. Of course, that could be due to the fact he hadn't had much in the last day or so. She knew the pit manager's cook saw to it food was delivered to his office at times such as these, but Vincent had said in the past that the amount he received was meagre. But she felt it was more than hunger that had made him bolt it down. He wasn't going back to the pit, she'd stake her life on it. He was going to Appleby Cottage.

It was close to eleven o'clock when Vincent left the house. Polly watched him go and waited a full five minutes before she followed him; it would be more than her life was worth if he caught her spying on him. She slipped through the startlingly white night like a black shadow, her thick, dark-brown coat and hat and big stout boots showing up clearly against the snow. But she couldn't help that, she told herself. She'd just have to be careful. And the sedative she'd mixed in his broth would take the edge off his alertness, she hoped. There'd been about a third of the bottle of medicine left, but it was old now; the doctor had prescribed it well over a year ago after Vincent had had two teeth extracted because of an abscess in his gum, but it had been strong stuff at the time. A couple of good spoonfuls had knocked him out then.

She didn't know what she was going to do if her suspicions were right and he intended to attack the Shelton girl, she thought as she sped along. But she couldn't just sit at home and do nothing. Constance and her grandma had been the only folk in the village who'd had a kind word for her in all the time she'd worked for Vincent, the grandma years ago and Constance recently.

She had fallen over twice by the time she drew near to the cottage; the frozen snow was like glass underfoot, a thin layer of ice coating the surface and making the ground treacherous. She heard Vincent before she saw him. He was hammering on the door of the cottage so she presumed he'd only just arrived. Sidling behind one of the big trees which bordered the lane, Polly watched and listened. A light came on downstairs, Constance had obviously lit a lamp, and a few moments later the door opened.

Polly took the opportunity to move a little closer. She

was now within fifteen yards or so of the cottage and had a clear view of the doorway. Her mouth fell open as she saw the pistol in one of Constance's hands. She was holding Jake's collar with the other, and the big dog was emitting a low steady rumble from deep in his throat. Vincent had backed halfway down the garden path and although she couldn't hear what Constance said, she heard his reply.

'I'll tell you what I'm doing here. Oh aye, I'll tell you. There's been a fall at the pit and your fancy man's copped it. Didn't know, did you, stuck out here, so I thought I'd come and give you the good news in person. Him and one of his brothers and a few others were killed.'

Again she couldn't make out Constance's words, but Vincent gave a mirthless bark of a laugh. 'Whether you believe me or not it's a fact, me fine lady. Didn't know I knew about your carry-on, did you? Thought I was as dim as the rest of 'em round here, but you can't fool me. All the fine clothes in the world can't make a silk purse out of a sow's ear, and that's what you are, same as your mother. She was a whore an' all.'

Now she could hear Constance when she cried, 'You leave my mother out of this! You're not worthy to speak her name.'

'Is that so? Well, like I said, she was a whore an' all, but she didn't have your cunning, did she? She ended up marrying a pit man whereas you've aimed high and made it work for you. How many have had you over the years, eh? A good few, I'll be bound. Or perhaps you were set up by just one? Whatever, you don't get to where you are by scrubbing floors.'

He was slurring his words and as Polly watched he stumbled, righting himself immediately. The sedative had worked then, she thought, but he was still mad enough to do anything. Constance must have thought the same because her voice came shrilly: 'You take a step nearer and I'll fire, I swear it.'

'Swear it, do you? Think you've got the guts to shoot a man? I doubt it. You're all wind and water, like the rest of them.'

But he didn't move any closer.

'You get away from here with your filthy mind. You're sick, do you know that? Dirty and twisted. And my mother was a good woman, a fine woman, which is why she wouldn't look the side you were on. She loved my father and he loved her.'

'Shut your mouth! You to call me filthy with what you've been up to. You women, you're all the same. Sluts, all of you.'

'I'll shoot you if you don't go, I will.'

'I'm going, but you won't always have a pistol in your hand. Remember that, me fine lady. And I can be patient. I've had years of practice. Your mother under-estimated me, *and* that milksop she married. They thought I was nowt but I proved them wrong.'

Polly put her hand to her mouth as he swayed again with the force of the words he was spitting out and then fell backwards, sprawling on the ground where he continued to spill his venom. 'I saw to them an' your granda an' all – same as I see to anyone who crosses me. Every minute of every day you better be looking over your shoulder because your time will come. I'll make sure of it. I'll do for you the same as them.'

'My parents were killed in a fire.' Constance had taken a step towards him as she spoke, the dog still growling fit to wake the dead, and inwardly Polly shouted, '*Don't go near him, that's what he wants. Stay away!*' 'A house fire. Everyone knows that.'

'And who started it? They all thought it was a clothes horse put too close to the range, but a can of oil does a better job. Aye, that's right – you believe me now, don't you? And your granda was easy. He was still breathing when I held him under the water. All I wanted was to know where you were, but he wasn't having any of it. He asked for what he got, treating me like a fool.'

'You murdered them? My parents and my granda?'

'Ah, the penny's dropped. Not such a joke now, am I?'

'You devil, you! You evil, wicked devil! I – I'll go to the Constable and tell him what you've told me.'

'Ha! And who'd take your word against mine? I'm the weighman, remember? I've got some clout, people don't want to get on the wrong side of me. But you! You went away into service and came back flaunting your sin in front of everyone's noses. Who'd believe *you*? And what proof do you have? They'd laugh you out of the place. A woman's nerves and fancies, they'd say. And when I deal with you it'll seem like an accident, make no mistake about that. I'm good at accidents, I've had a lot of practice.'

His words were slow now and Polly noticed he was in no hurry to get up. Indeed, she wondered if he *could* get up, but then he heaved himself from where he'd been lying propped on one elbow to his feet and once again Constance retreated to her doorstep.

'With your fancy man gone you'll likely be looking around for a replacement, won't you? I hear whores get a taste for it after a time and can't do without it. So I'll make it easy for you. I'll see to it the word goes out that you're available for business, how about that? So don't be surprised if you have some callers of a night once it's dark and they can't be seen.'

'You're nothing but a filthy, stinking animal.'

'Animal, you say? You hold yourself above the animal kingdom? Well, the last time I looked there was no female in the animal kingdom who put herself out for hire for a few bob or two, or in your case, a few pounds more likely.'

'If you're not gone in thirty seconds I'll let go of this dog.'

Vincent fumbled in his pocket and Polly saw a flash of silver as he held up a vicious-looking knife. 'That'd be a pity because I wouldn't want to hurt him.' He turned as he spoke, staggering to the open gate and into the lane where he shouted over his shoulder, 'Keep your eyes and ears open, m'lady, because you never know which minute is going to be your last. But we'll have a bit of fun before you join your mam, I've promised myself that.'

The door closed on his words and as it banged he looked round and fell over again. He lay in the lane cursing and swearing and trying to get up. The sedative had clearly knocked him for six. The amount he'd had would certainly prevent him doing any harm to Constance tonight, Polly thought, but tomorrow . . . Tomorrow was another day. Another day for Constance and another day for her. And he would be back to his old self by then.

Without thinking through what she was doing, Polly stepped out from behind the tree where she'd been hiding and walked forward. He didn't see her for a moment or two, crouched as he was on all fours as he attempted to struggle up. Then he turned his head, and it was clear he was having difficulty focusing his eyes as he mumbled, 'What the hell? Is that you, Polly? What are you doin' here?'

'I followed you.' Her voice was quiet, soft. 'I was worried about you. You seemed upset tonight.'

He was upright now, shaking his head as though to clear the mugginess which was fogging his brain. 'You nosy little scut.' His words were thick and deep and he was blinking like an owl. 'But now you're here you can make yourself useful. I must be sick, I'm going down with something.'

'I'll help you.' She went over to him and then her legs nearly buckled as he put his arm round her shoulders and his body draped itself on hers. He was a dead weight.

'Get me home,' he muttered dully. 'I need me bed.'

She said nothing, but as they began to stagger along she saw his eyes were closed and he seemed to be walking in his sleep. Some hundred yards or so from the cottage she had seen a gap in the hedgerow. If she could just get him to there without him knowing . . .

Somehow she managed it. Vincent was more than twice her weight and her back was breaking when she saw the opening. She didn't pause as she led him to it. She didn't pause as they walked to the edge of the old quarry. And she didn't pause as she twisted herself free of him an infinitesimal moment before she pushed him over the edge with all her might.

It was a sheer drop and a long way down. She thought she heard a muffled scream, like someone wakening from a nightmare, but then a dull thud sounded far, far beneath her.

Polly closed her eyes and tried to steady her shaking limbs and then, terrified she'd slip herself on the icy ground, she lay down and wriggled to the edge of the rock and peered over. The moonlight was bright, reflecting off the white landscape all around but it was a moment or two before she saw him. He was lying spreadeagled in the snow at the bottom of the quarry and he wasn't moving, a black starfish against the pale background.

She was trembling so much it was a moment or two before she could sit up, and then she sat for some minutes until the quivering in her muscles subsided before she looked again. It was another ten minutes before she wriggled to a safe distance and stood up, and then she retraced her footsteps and began walking home.

She had almost reached the bottom of the lane when round a curve a dark figure appeared. Stifling a scream, her hand to her mouth, she stood stock still. The relief she felt when she saw it wasn't Vincent almost made her wet her drawers.

But of course it couldn't be him, she told herself weakly in the next moment. Vincent was at the bottom of the quarry and that's where he'd stay, and she didn't believe in ghosts. She couldn't move for a second or so, however.

Matt glanced at the thin wisp of a woman as he approached her. It was McKenzie's housekeeper. What on earth was she doing out in the dead of night and here of all places? He stopped as he reached her. She looked scared to death and he made his voice gentle and reassuring when he said, 'You all right, lass? Is there owt wrong?'

'No, no. I – I was just – just taking a walk.'

'A walk, lass?'

'I couldn't sleep. You – you're Matt Heath, aren't you? Do you know if all the men are up yet after the fall?'

'Aye, they're up.'

She nodded, turning quickly away and continuing down the lane as he stood looking after her for a moment or two.

Then Matt swung round, his footsteps quickening as he walked until he was almost running towards Appleby Cottage.

Chapter 24

Constance had got dressed immediately after she had shut the door on Vincent. Now she paced the sitting room wondering what to do. She had to find out what had happened to Matt. She didn't think Vincent had been lying, but she had to make sure. But was it a trap? Was he waiting for her out there, hoping she'd take his bait? There had been murder in his eyes, that was for sure.

Oh, Matt, Matt, don't be dead. Her face deathly white, she wrung her hands together while Jake, beside himself at her distress and the earlier confrontation, whined and pawed at her skirts.

There could have been a fall at the pit and she wouldn't have known. She'd had no need to go out for the last couple of days and had only taken Jake for a walk down the lane to Tan Hills Wood and back. She hadn't seen a soul.

Should she wait for first light before going to the village? It would be safer. And she could take Jake with her, along with the firearm. But could she endure a night of not knowing? No, she had to go now. But what if Vincent had been lying and there'd been no accident at the pit? She'd look ridiculous turning up in the middle of the night at Matt's mam's if nothing had happened. How would she explain that? But what did looking ridiculous matter if the worst *had* happened? So her thoughts continued to race as she walked up and down, her stomach churning and her mind spinning.

When the knock came at the door, Jake went berserk. Bounding into the hall, he threw himself against the wood snarling ferociously, determined that this time he wasn't going to be thwarted in dealing with the stranger who had frightened his mistress. Constance's heart was thudding as she picked up the pistol once more. She walked over to the window and peered out, and then mortally offended Jake by dashing into the hall and grabbing his thick leather collar, dragging him unceremoniously into the sitting room and shutting the door on his barking.

When she opened the front door and flung her arms round Matt's neck he was too taken aback to move for a moment, then he was holding her tight as he tried to soothe her incoherent sobbing. In the end he whisked her up in his arms and walked into the house, slamming the door shut with his foot. From the sounds coming from within the sitting room he didn't think it would be a good idea to open the door, so he continued down the hall to the kitchen, but when he attempted to put Constance down she clung the tighter to him so he sat down in one of the big armchairs either side of the range with her on his knee.

It was a full minute before her storm of weeping lessened to hiccupping sobs, and only when she was calmer did he say bemusedly, 'I never expected this welcome.'

'He – he said – he said you were dead.'

'Who said I was dead?'

'And he wanted to kill me like he did my mam and da, my – my granda too, but I had a pistol and Jake was growling . . .'

Matt had stiffened and he eased her away from him so he could look at her, his face full of concern now. 'Constance, slow down. What's happened and who are we talking about?'

'Vin-Vincent McKenzie.'

'Vincent McKenzie killed your parents?'

'He – he always wanted my mother, my grandma said so, and then he said I had to marry him and I left the village . . .'

'It was *him* – Vincent McKenzie? *He* was the man who'd been bothering you?' Matt asked in amazement. '*Vincent McKenzie?*'

Constance nodded. She was suddenly aware she had made a terrible fool of herself, throwing herself into Matt's arms and not letting him go. Her face burning, she said in a small voice, 'I'm all right now,' but when she tried to move away, his arms tightened.

'Tell me. All of it.'

'He said there'd been a fall.'

'There was a fall.' Matt paused. 'George and one of Andrew's lads are in a bad way, but what's this about McKenzie?'

Constance was mortified. His brother and nephew were injured, is that what he'd come to tell her? But why now at this time of night? And what must he think of her?

When she tried to ease herself away from him again,

Matt looked down into her swimming eyes. 'Don't look like that,' he murmured softly. 'Please, Constance, no more misunderstandings. I love you. I've always loved you, and you were right that day. I am an upstart and self-centred and bigoted and stupid, but I love you and eternity wouldn't be long enough to tell you how much.'

She stared at him, unable to believe the moment was here. Weakly, she said, 'I didn't call you stupid.'

'Well, you should have because I am. All those years ago in your grandma's kitchen, do you remember? When we looked at each other? I knew then but I was too stupid to do anything about it. You were so young and . . .'

'. . . there was Tilly,' she finished for him. It hurt her but it needed to be said. Tilly had been real and he'd loved her.

'I didn't love her, Constance. Oh, I told myself I did when we first started courting, but it was more I'd reached a stage of my life where I needed to be *in* love. Even before we got wed I knew it was a mistake but she said she loved me and I'd promised her; she would have been so humiliated if I'd broken it off. Excuses.' He shook his head. 'But it seemed the right thing to do at the time. I told you, I'm stupid.'

'No, you're not.'

'Listen.' He took hold of her face in his hands. 'I need to tell you something, something I've never told another living soul but you have to understand. I want you to understand. She was expecting a bairn when I married her and I didn't know, we'd never been together. The baby . . . It wasn't mine.'

Constance strained back a little way in order to see his face. 'Rebecca?' she asked in amazement.

'Aye, Rebecca. But she *is* mine, Constance. In every-thing that matters, she's mine, and I wouldn't be without her for anything. But I didn't see it like that for a long time. I made Tilly's life hell. Right until she got sick, we were at war and that's not too strong a word for it. And then she became ill and we talked and she told me she loved me. And I think she did. It was one hell of a mess.'

'Oh, Matt.'

'And what made it worse when she got sick was that she was so full of remorse, so sorry, and it was all too late. It should have been me that begged her forgiveness because she didn't deserve the life I forced her to live.'

'Does Rebecca know?'

'No, and she never will. She's *my* daughter. Her father — he's a nowt.' And then he smiled ruefully. 'There I go again, the egotistical side rearing its head.'

She didn't ask who Rebecca's father was, it didn't matter. Nothing mattered. She traced his eyebrows with one finger, looking into the brown eyes that contained heaven on earth. 'I love you. I always have and I always will.'

Their kiss was long and hard. It had been waiting for expression for a long, long time. And then he traced every contour of her face with his lips in small burning kisses that set her blood on fire.

It was the sound from the sitting room which brought them back to the real world. Wryly, Matt said, 'Do you think you ought to let that dog out before he eats the door?'

'He's worried for me because of Vincent.'

'Let him out and then tell me, right from the begin-ning. No, before the beginning. Start with what you know about him and your mother. I need to be very clear about all this.'

Jake, mollified and sitting on the floor at their feet now they had moved to a sofa in the sitting room, Constance began her story. When she finished, Matt's face was tense, a muscle in his jaw working. 'And he left here shortly before I arrived?'

Constance nodded. 'I would have fired the pistol if he hadn't.'

'I didn't see hide nor hair of him, only—'

'What?' she asked as he stopped abruptly.

'That skinny little mouse of a lass who works for him was at the bottom of the lane. She said she was out walking.'

Constance's brow wrinkled. 'Polly?'

'Aye, and you say she warned you about him?'

Constance nodded again. 'She was nice. Obviously scared to death of him, but nice. I dread to think what her life's been like all these years, poor thing.'

Matt wasn't overly concerned about Polly. 'You're sure he's not lurking about outside somewhere?'

'Well no, not really. I shut the door' – she wasn't about to tell him she'd collapsed against it and slid down to the floor, unable to move for a good few minutes – 'and when I looked out of the window he'd gone. Or there was no one to be seen anyway. I presumed with me threatening to shoot him he'd gone home.'

'So he could still be within the vicinity?'

'Matt, I've got Jake and I know how to use the pistol.'

'I'm staying. I'll sleep on the sofa.'

'You can't. What would Rebecca think?'

'She knows how I feel about you. So does Mam. They were waiting at the pit gates and I told them then. And once I'd got cleaned up at home I sat Rebecca down and explained why I was coming to see you. Constance' – he was struggling to get the words out, the spectre of her money rising up again despite all he'd told himself – 'I'm not half good enough for you, I know that. And you're a lady now. You know how to speak, the right grammar and all that, whereas I . . .' He shook his head. 'You've got this cottage and you're well set up. You don't need a husband, I understand that, and if you want things to remain as they are it would be perfectly understandable.'

'What are you trying to say, Matt?' It had to come from him.

'Will you marry me, Constance?' he said very softly.

'Oh, Matt, Matt, of course I'll marry you.'

Their kiss lasted a long time. Neither of them could bear to let it end and in the murmur of their whispered promises and words of love the past melted away. All that mattered was the present.

'I love you.' It seemed incredible she was free to lift up her hand and stroke his face, his dear face. 'I've loved you for so long.'

'Me too, my darling. Me too. And I promise you McKenzie won't bother you again, all right? I'll sort him.'

'No, Matt. Please, no. Promise me. You don't understand – he's not . . . normal. I believe him when he said he killed my mam and da, my granda too. If you could have seen his face you'd have believed him too. He's dangerous.'

'Dangerous or no, he needs to be dealt with.'

She clung to him, as though Vincent was in front of them and she was preventing Matt from attacking him. 'Promise me you won't do anything until we've talked it through. Please, Matt.' Vincent McKenzie had taken everyone who'd ever belonged to her – her parents, her granda, even her grandma in a way because she had never

371

been the same after her husband had died so tragically. He would try to kill Matt too, she knew it, and Matt couldn't afford to go rushing in ill-prepared. There was a devil in Vincent, a legion of them.

'Stop crying. I promise, all right? I promise. Now stop crying. You're worrying Jake and he might think I'm upsetting you. Considering my leg is quite near his jaws that's not a good idea.' Matt pulled her close, holding her so tightly she could hardly breathe as he whispered, 'I never want to let you go again, not ever. I want to remain like this, with you in my arms, for the rest of our lives.'

'Then let's.' She lifted her face for his kiss.

When Polly woke up the next morning she lay for some time staring at the window. It was snowing hard, big fat flakes in their thousands, their millions. No one would find him for days, weeks even. Of course, they might come calling when he didn't turn up for work but that wouldn't be for a day or two; they'd think he was off sick or something at first. And she could say he hadn't come back from the pit after the accident, that he'd told her it could be a long while before the men were all up and so she hadn't expected him any particular time. She could act a bit gormless, she'd used to do that in the workhouse when she hadn't wanted to get involved in any bother. And there were lots of men who wanted to do for Vincent, he'd told her that himself. Boasted about it. But no one would be able to prove it wasn't an accident anyway, he was always striding about the lanes and countryside. Everyone knew that.

Should she feel remorseful for what she'd done? Well, she didn't. He had been a monster. He'd killed that lass's parents and her granda, and he would have killed Constance too, that was for sure. And his own mother, he'd done for her. The agony that poor woman had gone through. No, she didn't feel guilty. In killing him she'd prevented him hurting anyone else, herself included. That was the way she looked at it. God Himself said an eye for an eye and a tooth for a tooth in the good book. She had done nothing wrong, and He wouldn't condemn her. Him knowing the rights and wrongs of the case.

Satisfied with this logic, Polly scrambled out of bed. She dressed quickly, since the room was icy, and as she did so she looked at the grate and promised herself a fire in there for tonight. Vincent had always had one in his bedroom but he hadn't allowed her that luxury.

Once downstairs, she stood in the kitchen, gazing around her. There was a lightness in her body, a sense of joy, and for a moment she whirled round and round before coming to rest, laughing, against the kitchen table. Bacon. She'd have bacon for breakfast and two eggs and make a pot of tea. She was her own mistress now, she could do what she wanted when she wanted. There was no one to growl at her, no one to shout and curse when she was a bit slow or something wasn't to his liking. Most of all there was no finger to beckon her.

She ate a hearty breakfast, and as she did so she thought about her situation. She didn't fool herself that she would be able to carry on living here once Vincent's body was found. It was a shame because this was a bonny cottage, but Vincent had distant relatives somewhere or other. A cousin in Newcastle she knew about, and perhaps there were more. And they'd be here like vultures once they knew he was dead, although to her knowledge they'd never come when he was alive. Had he left a Will? She contemplated this as she made herself another slice of toast.

He'd said to Constance he had plenty put by that day at the graveyard, she thought suddenly, and he'd had no time for banks – she knew that. 'Thieves and robbers', he'd called the banks. So, that being the case, he'd have a hoard hidden somewhere or other, likely a Will too. But where exactly? It had to be his bedroom.

She bit into the hot buttered toast as she considered what to do. She had cleaned every inch of the house and knew every nook and cranny, but she had never lingered in his bedroom. It was a place of torture, of unspeakable indignities, and it had made her flesh creep just to change the sheets on his bed and dust round. But ten to one that's where he would have hidden his hoard.

Her breakfast finished, she steeled herself to go upstairs to his room. When she opened the door it took a moment or two before she could force her legs across the threshold. It was spick and span, the bed neatly made. Everything was as she had left it after she'd finished her work the previous morning, except for the clothes he'd changed out of on returning home from the pit lying in a heap on the floor. She glanced round the bedroom.

It smelled of him. Her legs started to tremble. A mixture of tobacco smoke and carbolic soap. When he'd first brought her to the cottage when his mother was alive she'd thought the smell was attractive. She had been young and foolish then. Merely a child.

She had actually stepped back out on the landing before she took herself in hand. She had to do this, and do it before his relatives or other folk came sniffing about. And it wasn't stealing. If anyone had earned compensation for enduring hell on earth, she had. She'd been a slave all her life, first in the workhouse and then when she came here, and at forty-three years of age she wanted peace and quiet. And money could buy peace and quiet.

She entered the room again, telling herself if she didn't look after number one, no one else would. She could be turned out on her ear with just the clothes she stood up in and quicker than you could say Jack Robinson.

She made herself search every inch of the room, starting with the wardrobe and chest of drawers. She even went on her hands and knees and examined the floorboards to see if any were loose but they were all firmly nailed down. After going back over what she'd done in case she had missed something, she sat down on the big blanket chest at the foot of the bed. She had looked everywhere; perhaps he hadn't hidden it in here, after all. It could be anywhere. It might even be hidden in the garden somewhere in a weather-proofed box, for all she knew. She wouldn't put anything past him. He was as cunning as a cartload of monkeys.

It was while she was sitting on the chest looking out on to the landing through the open door that she thought of the hatch to the roofspace. It was a long shot, but she pulled the chest of drawers from the bedroom out on to the landing and climbed on top of it, pushing with all her strength against the hatch. It wouldn't open at first, and when it finally gave and she poked her head through the aperture she saw immediately that she was on the wrong track. No one had been up there for years, as the thick dust and cobwebs testified.

Dispirited, she closed the hatch and lugged the chest

of drawers back to its original place beside the big mahogany wardrobe in the bedroom. She then began a methodical search of every other room, which took her most of the day. At the end of it she'd had to admit defeat. She hadn't found so much as a bean.

After getting herself an evening meal as twilight set in, she filled up the coal-scuttle from the huge covered wooden container just outside the back door, which held their supply of wood and logs and kindling.

Wherever Vincent had hidden his money it was going to stay hidden, she reflected, as she lit the oil lamps downstairs and stoked up the sitting-room fire. He was cleverer than her. Of course, there was always the possibility despite what he'd said in the past that he *had* deposited his money in a bank. There was no knowing with him. How could anyone fathom how a mind like his worked? Anyone normal anyway.

Where was she going to end up, once she had to leave here? As a skivvy somewhere, that was the best she could hope for, and when she grew too old and feeble to work any more she'd likely finish up where she'd started, in the workhouse. *No, she'd take matters into her own hands before she'd allow that to happen.* She couldn't swim, and the Wear and Tyne Rivers were deep and fast-flowing in places . . .

She shook herself as though to throw off the melancholy thoughts. She'd make herself a nice cup of cocoa in a minute and have a slice of the gingerbread she'd made the day before. There was eight ounces of butter and brown sugar and treacle in it – even Vincent hadn't been able to fault her gingerbread, or any of her cooking, come to that. Maybe she could pick up a job as a cook in a small establishment, even though she didn't have any references. But first she'd go and tidy Vincent's room, which she'd left in a mess after her search. It looked as though it had been ransacked and that wouldn't bode well if anyone came to the house asking where he was and whether they could see round it. She'd been putting it off all day – going back into his room – but it wouldn't right itself, and once that was done she could shut the door and she wouldn't have to venture inside ever again.

Taking one of the lamps, she went upstairs to Vincent's room and began to put it to rights. It didn't take long. She had let his bedroom fire go out and, thinking ahead, she now cleared the ash and set a new fire as though she expected him to return any minute. It was as she sat back on her heels having finished and gave a long relieved sigh that she wouldn't have to cross the threshold of this room again, that her gaze fell on the two mahogany armchairs either side of the window. They were impressive things with padded arms and deep seats, and red hide upholstery. Vincent had had them specially made by a furniture-maker in Chester Le Street. She had always thought them too grand for a bedroom, but that had been Vincent all over – ideas above himself.

Specially made. A strange feeling came over her, shivery but nice. She had always supposed it was just Vincent showing off, but what if he'd had a different motive for wanting the armchairs made just as he specified?

Jumping to her feet, Polly sped downstairs and washed her hands clean, and then bounded up the stairs again, her heart thumping fit to burst. Excited but afraid that she was going to be frustrated yet again, she inspected the chairs minutely. They were attractive in a way but too big and cumbersome for her liking; however, the padded arms with turned spindle supports and matching legs were beautifully made. She poked and prodded the seat and back of the chair, but found nothing untoward. It took all her strength to heave one over on to its side and she brought the oil lamp close to inspect the wooden underframe. She experienced a sharp stab of disappointment, since everything looked as one would expect. But then she was looking at the screws which held the bottom of the chair secure. They were slightly rusty but in the slot in the middle of each screw there was the odd silver mark as though a screwdriver had been used recently – tiny scratches which wouldn't have been noticed unless someone was looking for it.

There had been a screwdriver on top of the wardrobe. She had assumed it had been left there at some time or other by mistake. Again she climbed on the chest of drawers, she was too small to reach otherwise, and once she was back kneeling by the chair, she found her hands were trembling so much she had to take several deep calming breaths.

She wasn't used to handling a screwdriver and it slipped and slid on each screw, but by the time she'd undone several she knew there was something in the cavity in the chair. When the last screw was out the wood fell to one side and bundle upon bundle of banknotes tumbled out on to the floor, rolling round her and scattering either side of where she knelt. She couldn't move at first; she merely stared at the money like one mesmerised. And then she stretched out a shaking hand and picked up one of the bundles, all of which were neatly tied up with string. It contained fifty one-pound notes. Shivering with a mixture of cold and excitement she undid another. It, too, contained fifty pounds. And there must be over a dozen or more.

There were twenty, and the other armchair yielded a further ten, along with a roll of various documents again tied with string. When she smoothed these out she could see they consisted of birth certificates and his parents' wedding certificate, and a lot of receipts including the stubs for his mother's funeral and even ones going back as far as when his grandfather had built the cottage. There was no Will. Vincent McKenzie clearly hadn't considered dying in the forseeable future.

One thousand and five hundred pounds. Polly plumped down on the blanket box, staring at the piles of carefully bound notes. And he had never paid her a penny, maintaining that a roof over her head and clothes on her back and food in her belly was payment enough. And if he'd been a good man who was struggling to make ends meet, it would have been enough, after her beginnings in the workhouse. But this . . .

By the time she went to bed that night the money, all but one hundred pounds which she had placed at the back of one of the wardrobe shelves so that anyone looking for it would find it easy enough, was in her carpet bag on top of the wardrobe in her room. She knew exactly what she was going to do. As soon as the weather permitted she would walk the four or five miles to Chester Le Street and deposit the money in a bank, but first she would go to a lady's outfitters and buy a grand outfit so she would look the part when she saw the bank folk. Likely when Vincent's relatives came they would sell the house and dispose of the furniture, but that wouldn't matter now. She was set up.

She hugged herself tightly, unable to sleep with excitement. She'd have to be canny but she could start looking for a place of her own. She could see it in her mind's eye. A small cottage with a picket fence and a nice bit of ground at the back where she could grow vegetables and flowers, and where her cats could lie in the sun. She could have chickens. She'd always fancied warm fresh eggs from her own chickens. Oh, it was going to be grand. *Grand*.

Chapter 25

It was a prolonged winter, even by northern standards. February and March were locked in an icy grip with the snow so thick at times it reached the top of the hedgerows and made roads impassable for weeks in the countryside. April came roaring in with bitter easterly winds and more flurries of snow until even the rugged old-timers admitted they'd rarely seen anything like it before. And then, in the last week of the month, the weather did a mercurial turn-around. Overnight, it seemed, a radiant April sun dealt with the snow. Blackthorn and hawthorn sprouted bloom in the hedges, and violets and primroses and the peeping flowers of speedwell carpeted the woods and byways.

It was another two weeks before Vincent's body was found. It could have remained where it was for much longer but for a man walking his dog on the other side of the quarry to Appleby Cottage. This side wasn't so steep, and when the dog chased a rabbit into the quarry, slipping and slithering to the very bottom where, although unhurt, he kept up a steady barking until his owner came to investigate his grisly find, the mystery of what had happened to the master weighman of Sacriston Colliery was solved.

There was only one mourner at the funeral – the man's housekeeper. Even the distant cousin who laid claim to the estate didn't bother to attend. And it was the general consensus of opinion, once the village grapevine had done its work, that the housekeeper had been treated shamefully in having no provision made for her. The cottage was going to be sold and she would lose her home and be turned out on her ear, and that after working for the man for thirty-odd years. Mind, no one was that surprised, not really. McKenzie had been a wicked devil, and whether he'd been out on a walk and slipped in the snow over the edge of the quarry as the inquest into his death surmised, or whether he had been pushed by person or persons unknown, he'd got what was coming to him. So said the village to a man.

It was a few days after the funeral that Constance went to see Polly, on a beautifully soft May afternoon filled with the scent of flowers and the snowlike pink and white blossom of apple and cherry trees. She had been awake before sunrise, listening to the soaring early-morning song of the skylarks as they heralded in the dawn chorus, and she had known as she'd listened to the birds' sweet melody that she couldn't put off visiting Vincent's housekeeper another day. Since his body had been found, Matt's sighting of the woman at the end of the lane on the very day he had apparently gone missing had bothered her more than a little.

Matt had told her to put the matter out of her mind. Whatever had happened – *if* anything had happened – it was none of their business, he'd insisted. Vincent had been alive when she had last seen him, and when he himself had arrived at the cottage there had been no sign of the weighman. Those were the facts. Anything else was supposition. And frankly, he'd continued, if the woman *had* had anything to do with McKenzie's death, he'd like to give her a medal because they could all sleep safer in their beds now he was no more. That was another fact.

Constance agreed with this. It was the reason she hadn't mentioned to anyone Vincent's visit on the night he'd gone missing when his body had been found in the quarry. Far better everyone thought he'd simply gone for a walk as apparently he'd been prone to do, and met with an unfortunate accident due to the treacherous conditions underfoot.

But he *had* come to see her. And a short time before that, Polly had warned her about him and been concerned about her. Therefore, she reasoned, it was perfectly feasible that Polly had gathered where he was coming that night by something he'd said or done and she had followed him to the cottage. And after that – who knew. But to find out if Polly knew more about Vincent's death than she'd said at the inquest was not the only reason she wanted to see her. If the stories circulating round the village were true and Polly was going to be turned out of the cottage within a few days, she wanted to make sure she was able to manage. Doubtless she had some savings, but were they enough?

The morning was so warm and fresh she decided to walk rather than take the horse and trap. The verges of the lane were a sea of bluebells, reflecting the deep blue sky. Mighty horse-chestnut trees, lush with foliage, displayed their pyramids of bloom whilst the oaks which shaded the lane were decked out in dazzling green and gold. If she was going anywhere else but to see Polly she would be filled with joy this morning, Constance thought, as she set out. Rebecca, and Matt's parents, had taken the news of their betrothal with beaming smiles and hugs and good wishes, and she and Matt were already beginning to talk about buying a smallholding nearer the coast and having part of it as a paying guesthouse in the future. She wanted him to leave the pit. He *had* to leave it.

She breathed in the sweet scent of vernal grass, watching an orange-tip butterfly as it hovered among the bluebells before fluttering off as she thought of Matt working underground.

He'd nearly lost his life twice to the pit's voracious appetite for blood. He wouldn't survive a third fall, she felt it in her bones. Neither George, nor Andrew's son, had recovered from their injuries and she knew their deaths had shaken Matt hard.

Shortly after George's funeral Matt's father had admitted his days down the pit were over, and the couple had moved in with Matt and Rebecca. Constance had offered to help out, to buy them a house, to do anything they wanted, but Matt had been adamant he wouldn't take a penny of her money and that his parents were his responsibility. When they were married, he'd said, it would be different, especially if they bought the smallholding and had a working business with the guesthouse, but he had no intention of being a kept man. She knew Ruth would come with them and Matt's mam had already talked her husband round. Rebecca was another matter. She and Larry were deeply in love and she wouldn't want to be too far away from him, but they'd cross that bridge when they came to it. Propriety dictated that a widower should wait a minimum of four or five years before marrying again. Matt had told Constance he couldn't be doing with all that rubbish and they were getting married at the end of the year. She hadn't argued.

When she reached Vincent's cottage she stood looking at it for some time before she could force herself to open the gate and walk to the front door. Ridiculous, but she felt it had a brooding quality, as though it was waiting for him to come home. In spite of the warmth of the morning, she shivered as she knocked.

It was a minute or two before the door opened and Polly was wiping floury hands on her pinny. On catching sight of Constance, she said, 'Oh, hello, lass. Come in, come in. You've caught me baking. Do you mind coming through to the kitchen? I've got a loaf that'll need to come out of the oven in a tick.'

Constance found herself at something of a loss as she followed the woman through to the kitchen. The heady aroma of bread was filling the cottage and there was a bowl of fresh flowers in the middle of the kitchen table. In a corner by the range a somewhat moth-eaten tabby cat lay in a wicker basket nursing a litter of kittens. But it wasn't just the homely nature of her surroundings that took her aback, it was the change in Polly. Vincent's house-keeper had filled out a little since she'd last seen her, and there was some colour in her cheeks; furthermore she was dressed in a deep red frock with a little lace collar, and even her pinny was a pretty one, edged with broderie anglaise.

Polly saw her glance at the cat and said, 'She was a stray. I found her outside one day, brought her in to feed her and she stayed the night. In the morning when I came down she'd had her babies. We've taken to each other.' She looked Constance full in the face. 'I think she'd been badly treated too.'

Still not really knowing what to say, Constance knelt down by the basket and began to stroke the cat, who purred loudly. 'She's lovely and the kittens are adorable.'

'She's as gentle as a lamb and I'm letting her keep her babies. The two like her are Marmalade and Honey, and the brown one's Treacle. The one with the four white paws is Biscuit and the dark brown one is Chocolate.'

'What have you named her? The mother cat?'

'Sweetheart. It might be a silly name for a cat, but that's what she is.'

'I don't think it's silly.' Constance had a lump in her throat as she looked at Polly's little face which was lit with love as she gazed at her cat.

'Sit yourself down.' Polly suddenly seemed to remember her manners. 'I'll just get the bread out and then I'll make a cup of tea. Or perhaps you'd prefer a cold drink?'

'Tea would be lovely.'

As she sat at the kitchen table watching Polly bustling about, Constance told herself that her suspicions had to be unfounded. Polly wouldn't be like this if she'd had anything to do with Vincent's death, surely?

Once they were sitting with a cup of tea and a plate of buttered teacakes each, Constance smiled into the plain little face which didn't look so plain any more. 'I had to come,' she said simply. 'I'd heard you were going to be turned out of here and I wanted to make sure you were all right.'

'That's kind of you, lass, but you needn't have worried.

I've got meself a nice little place in Lanchester. It's only three miles or so from here but the cottage is set up high and overlooks the river and it's got a bonny garden. Me and Sweetheart and her bairns'll be as snug as bugs in rugs there.'

'So this cottage *is* going to be sold?'

'Oh aye. Vincent's cousin – he's the one who inherited everything – wanted shot of it but he hasn't even been to see it. It's all been done through solicitors. He's been pleasant enough, mind. Said I could stay for a bit till I got meself sorted. I go next week, and the same day he's arranged for the furniture to be taken away. A family's moving in shortly; the man is the under-manager at Charlaw Colliery, the other side of Fulforth Wood. He's got plans to build rooms on and all sorts.'

Constance nodded. 'I'm glad you're going to be all right. I was worried you might be struggling. You know, money wise.'

Polly gave her another straight look. 'If it had been left to Vincent, I would have been – but let's just say things turned round after his death. My wages were late coming but when they did it was by way of a lump sum.'

Hastily, Constance said, 'You don't have to explain, Polly. I didn't mean to pry.'

'I know that, lass. And it was nice of you to be concerned. Your grannie was like that – I was fond of her.' Polly took a sip of her tea. 'I was sad when she passed on.'

Constance cleared her throat. It was now or never. 'Polly, I just said I didn't mean to pry and yet I'm probably doing just that. I – I don't know if you've heard but I'm walking out with Matt Heath. We've known each other years – in fact, he saved my life when I was just a baby.'

Polly stared at her but said nothing.

Highly embarrassed now, Constance went on, 'On the night that Vincent disappeared he came to see me – Vincent, that is.' She wasn't putting this very well. 'He – well, he threatened me. He said some terrible things. He told me he'd killed my parents and my granda too, and I believe he did.'

'He killed his mam an' all.'

'What?' Now it was Constance's turn to stare.

Polly nodded. 'He did. 'Course, I'd got no proof but he poisoned her, his own mam.'

'Are you sure?'

'Oh aye, I'm sure, lass.'

Constance sat back in her seat. Polly had taken the wind out of her sails and for a moment she couldn't continue. Pulling herself together, she finished her tea before she said, 'Matt came to see me that night as well, and he said . . . Well, he said . . .'

'That he saw me?'

Constance nodded.

'I wondered if he knew who I was – afterwards, I mean. Then when the body was found, I half-expected him to say something.'

'He didn't. He wouldn't. What I mean is—'

'Aye, I get your drift, lass.' Polly's voice was soft. 'He's a nice man. You're well suited. And now you're here because you want to know if you've put two and two together and made ten, or whether I pushed Vincent over the edge of the quarry.'

Hearing it put so bluntly and with such composure robbed Constance of any reply. The clock ticked on the kitchen mantelpiece over the range and in the basket the kittens mewed and wriggled as they nuzzled up to their mother's teats. Sunlight was streaming in the kitchen window and falling on the bowl of wild flowers in the middle of the table. Everything was serene and terribly normal, and yet they were discussing murder.

'The way I see it, lass, is that what happened that night is between me and God, and *only* me and God – so I can't answer your question except to say my conscience is clear and I sleep easy at nights. For the first time in thirty years I sleep easy.'

Constance blinked. It was and it wasn't an answer, but she couldn't press Polly any further. Gently, she murmured, 'I hope you'll have a wonderful life in your cottage overlooking the river, Polly. A long and happy life.'

'Oh, I will, lass. I will. Me bairns too.' Polly glanced across at the cats. 'This is where my life begins.'

Chapter 26

It was a winter wedding and very quiet, but nonetheless special to Constance and Matt because of it. Only close family were invited, the exception to this being Polly, who looked a different woman from the little mouse the villagers had been used to seeing scuttling in and out of the shops from time to time. When word had got around that the weighman must have left his housekeeper a bit, after all – for how else would she be able to set herself up in a little place of her own? – folk, in the main, had been glad for her, although there had been those who'd murmured that her inheritance had been for services of a more intimate nature than cleaning the house and cooking McKenzie's meals.

This scandal was put firmly in the shade come autumn, however, when Matt Heath announced he was marrying Constance Shelton the day before Christmas Eve.

The news caused the village to buzz with a mixture of outrage and shock, and this was further enhanced when Tilly's parents – furious that their son-in-law was slighting their daughter's memory by marrying again after only a year – put in their two penn'orth. Matt had been a poor husband and father, they announced to anyone who'd listen – and there were plenty – and their bonny lass had been a saint, an angel, and this was her reward. To be replaced before she was cold in her grave. Matt Heath was an ungrateful swine and he hadn't deserved her, and now he was spitting on her memory.

The upshot of this was that Rebecca went to see her maternal grandparents and gave them a piece of her mind, along with a few home truths, which caused them to warn her to never darken their door again. When Matt went round to try to pour oil on troubled waters, they showed him the door, and Tilly's mother continued to shout abuse after him at the top of her voice as he walked down the street, for all the world like a dockside fishwife.

This sad state of affairs had one positive outcome. Rebecca decided she didn't want to stay among folk who were speaking ill of her father and that she was going to leave with Matt and Constance when they got married and moved away. On hearing this, Larry promptly announced that he would follow her wherever she went. He'd get a job in the nearest mine and take lodgings. He further cemented his intentions by saying that once he'd got enough put by, he wanted them to get wed.

In October, Constance and Matt had found the perfect property close to the coast at Seaham, some fifteen miles from Sacriston. Bramble Farm was a little larger than a smallholding but not as big as a working farm, although the existing owners liked to call it such. Besides a very substantial five-bedroomed house, the estate boasted two small two-bedroomed cottages and five acres of land. The

cottages were in a state of disrepair, having not been occupied for some years since the owners had sold most of
their land and stock to the farm adjoining theirs, at which
time they had dismissed their farm labourers. But,
Constance and Matt agreed, the cottages were sound and
could soon be made habitable. And so they had bought
the property and once the owners had moved out at the
beginning of November, workmen had moved in.

When restoration of the first cottage had been
completed, they'd taken Rebecca and Larry across to the
property to view it one day, and Matt had put a proposal
to the young couple. He would need help with the smallholding and Constance would need assistance in running
the guesthouse. He and Constance had discussed the matter
and their suggestion was that Larry occupied one of the
cottages and received a wage for working on the smallholding with Matt, and Rebecca lived in the farmhouse
with her father and Constance but also received a wage
for her labours. Matt's parents would occupy the remaining
cottage. If, after a year, Rebecca and Larry's feelings for
each other remained as strong, they could marry on
Rebecca's eighteenth birthday. Rebecca could then join
Larry in the cottage. If, on the other hand, either one of
them had changed their mind, Larry had received experience of a life different to the one he'd been born into,
and would have been housed in comfort for a year and
paid well to boot. The pair of them were still very young,
Matt had added. Hence the condition of the year's defer-
ment. He wanted Rebecca, and Larry too, to be very, very
sure of what they were doing.

Rebecca had been ecstatic and Larry's grin had stretched
from ear to ear. Constance had no doubt that come

Rebecca's eighteenth she would be decked in white and walking down the aisle.

But this was her wedding day. She glanced at Matt sitting by the side of her and his eyes were waiting for her, their hands joined under the table. They'd decided to hold the small wedding breakfast at the Queen's Head Hotel in the village after the short service at St Bede's which Father Duffy had conducted, but once the meal and speeches were finished a coach was taking them to Hartlepool for two weeks' honeymoon. Once Christmas was over Rebecca and Larry, along with Matt's parents and Jake, were moving to the smallholding where they'd be waiting for them on their return from honeymoon. Appleby Cottage was up for sale and Constance had recently accepted an offer. It was the end of an era.

'You're breathtakingly beautiful, Mrs Heath.' Matt's voice was low and the look in his eyes brought a flush of colour to her cheeks. She was glad he thought she looked like a bride.

In view of all the controversy surrounding their marriage she had felt it prudent to forgo a big elaborate wedding dress with a train and veils. Instead she had chosen a simple but exquisitely cut white dress with a matching flared jacket trimmed with antique lace and seed pearls; her hat a sweeping affair, again in white and reflecting the trim on the jacket. In truth the slim-fitting style suited her figure to perfection and she had never looked lovelier.

'And you're very handsome, Mr Heath,' she whispered back, longing for the moment they would be alone together. She felt no apprehension about the wedding night, just an intense desire to belong to him, body, soul and spirit.

The meal was good, the champagne flowed and the company was merry, Andrew and his family and George's wife and her lads embracing her into the family as though she had always been part of it. Which they all felt she had in a way since the night Matt had caught her in his arms when he had been but a lad of nine years of age and she a little scrap of nothing.

It was just after two o'clock when one of the hotel staff came to say the coach which the hotel in Hartlepool had arranged to collect them was waiting outside.

In the midst of all the goodbyes, Matt took Polly aside and held her hands firmly between his. Constance had told him of her visit to Vincent's housekeeper and the conversation which had transpired, but he had known in his heart before then that Polly had taken matters into her own hands that winter's night. It was stretching the bounds of coincidence too far to imagine anything else. And whatever her reasons, in doing what she had she'd saved him from having to deal with the master weighman. He might not have gone as far as Polly had, but he wouldn't have been able to sleep at night until he'd used his fists on that scum, and who knows what the consequences would have been. For sure, Vincent would have been a dangerous enemy wherever they had moved to, if he had still been breathing.

He looked down into the small face that had shed its cowering, browbeaten look and had taken on a lightness that was remarkable. Softly, he murmured, 'Thank you, lass. I'm forever in your debt and our door'll always be wide open to you – I hope you know that. We won't lose touch and whatever happens in the future we'll be there for you. Remember that.'

Polly's smile was shaky. It was the first time in her life she had been touched by a man other than Vincent, and certainly the first time one had looked at her with such warmth and affection. 'I said to Constance once that you were well suited and you are,' she replied. 'I know you'll both be very happy.' She didn't allude to the hidden message behind his words. That was in the past and she was living in the present and looking forward to her future. Each day was a joy now.

'Aye, we'll be happy, lass. I'll make sure of that.' He glanced across the room to where Constance, radiant and dewy-eyed, was hugging Rebecca and Larry. 'But I want you to know that you have a friend — two friends — for life, lass. All right?'

Polly nodded. He was a nice man, a lovely man, but she still didn't like being held by him, and when he bent forward and brushed his lips to her cheek as he said, 'Goodbye, Polly,' it was all she could do not to shrink away. But soon she could get back to her cottage and her family. They'd be waiting for her, lined up on the sitting-room windowsill. Whenever she left the house, just to go shopping, she had such a welcome when she returned.

And then Constance was standing in front of her, and when she hugged her, murmuring, 'Bless you, Polly. Bless you,' she could return the embrace without fear.

When Constance and Matt emerged from the hotel in the midst of their noisy, laughing guests there was a small crowd gathered to watch their departure in the grand coach and horses, grander than anything Sacriston had seen for a long time. There were no smiles or well-wishes from the villagers, not for these two upstarts who had flouted all convention and added insult to injury by moving away. Molly hugged her niece and so did Beryl, who had made the journey from Kimblesworth with her husband; they had all partaken of a fine meal and not a little champagne, and were feeling on top of the world. It was Molly who whispered in Constance's ear: 'Your grandma would have been so proud of you the day, lass, so proud, and I'm sure she's looking down on you and smiling.'

The tears spilling over, Constance hugged her aunty hard but could voice no words, her heart was too full. And then they were in the carriage, leaning out of the window as it began to pull away. Neither of them noticed the disapproving faces of the village women. Instead it was the beaming smiles from Polly and the others they carried away with them. Rebecca, hand in hand with Larry, crying happy tears. Ruth, with her husband leaning heavily on his stick, calling out, 'Bless you, me bairns. Bless you.' Beryl and Molly with Ivy, who was now in a wheelchair, and Florence who'd made the journey from Yorkshire, waving and shouting, and the rest of their guests adding to the general bedlam.

Constance didn't know if she was laughing or crying when she sank back on to the thickly upholstered seat once they had left Durham Street behind them; maybe it was a mixture of both. She only knew she had never been so happy in the whole of her life as Matt took her in his arms and kissed her until she was trembling and aching for more. He only had to touch her hand or look at her in a certain way and her knees turned to jelly, and now he was her husband. Her *husband*. It had really happened. Until this minute she realised a part of her had been unable to believe he would actually be hers.

That Matt had felt the same was evident when he traced her lips with one finger, a note of wonder in his voice when he murmured, 'At last you're mine, my wife . . . Oh, Constance, Constance, have you any idea of how I feel about you?'

'If it's only a fraction of what I feel for you I'll be satisfied.' She snuggled up to him and he drew the thick fur rug the carriageman had wrapped round their knees up to her chin. Her wedding outfit, although exquisite, was no match for the icy December chill. It hadn't snowed for two weeks but the frosts had been thick and relentless, and the countryside was clothed in a frozen glinting sparkle which looked picturesque but which numbed noses and fingers in seconds.

Constance, warm and cosy in her husband's arms and a little light-headed with what she liked to think was excitement but which was probably more due to her first taste of champagne, looked at the winter wonderland outside the carriage window as her eyelids grew heavy. Two weeks in which they would be alone together without anyone or anything to claim their time except each other. It was heaven and she couldn't ask for more. And then they would go home to their farmhouse and start their new life with Rebecca and Larry and Matt's parents, and Jake. Dear, dear Jake. But each night it would be just the two of them again, wrapped in each other's arms. It was all she had ever wanted, all she'd ever dreamed of, a life with Matt. To be his wife down through the years, to be at his side and enfolded in his arms at night. To be the one he shared his highs and his lows with; to know when he laughed and when he cried, and to be there when he reached out for her. It would only be death that parted them and then not for long: a love like theirs had to last into eternity.

She slept, and Matt continued to hold her tightly, his chin resting on the top of her head and her hat lying on the seat opposite where she'd thrown it when it had got in the way when he had kissed her. The sky was darkening, the snow which had been threatening to fall for days was on its way, but in the shadowed interior of the coach Matt's face had lost the expression of cynicism which had cleaved deep lines between his eyes and either side of his stern mouth for many a year. The fast-falling twilight was kind to him; he no longer looked like a world-weary man of forty but someone years younger. A man just starting out in life with the woman he loved and who loved him.

Such is the power of love . . .

Epilogue

1913

It had been a truly blessed day, everyone had said so. Even the weather had done its part to make Rebecca and Larry's wedding on 2 April – which was also the bride's eighteenth birthday – very special. For once the month of March had lived up to its reputation of coming in like a lion and going out like a lamb. For a week before the big day a determined spring sun had dried up the thick glutinous mud and deep puddles left after the last snow and sleet, and new life had responded with gusto. Birds were busily nesting, buds were unfolding and the continual stir of bees declared the harsh northern winter was over.

The happy couple had been married in the little parish church close to Bramble Farm, before they and their guests had returned to the house where a wedding feast fit for a king had been laid on. Constance and Rebecca and Ruth had been cooking for weeks in preparation for the wedding day, and although the big old farmhouse had bulged at the seams with family and friends, there had been ample for everyone.

It was close on ten o'clock when the last of the carriages Constance and Matt had hired to transport the wedding guests to and from their respective homes trundled off down the winding drive, and they were free to collapse in the oak-beamed sitting room in front of the fire with Jake at their feet.

Rebecca and Larry had left in the late afternoon for their week's honeymoon in a splendid hotel in Roker a few miles up the coast, and Ruth and Edwin had long since retired to their cottage, so it was just the two of them alone in the house for the first time since they'd been married. It was Matt who remarked on this, saying, 'The fledgling has left the nest. It's just you and me, my love, and I can't say I'm sorry the day's over. I feel as though this wedding has been all anyone's talked about for weeks. The dress, the food, the arrangements . . . It's been too much for you.' His hand reached out and gently stroked the mound of her stomach wherein their first child lay.

'Nonsense, I loved it. And the dress *was* beautiful, wasn't it?' She and Rebecca had designed and made the wedding dress themselves and it had been just as Rebecca had wanted – a frothy, fairytale vision of organdie and lace.

'*You're* beautiful,' Matt said softly, gathering her up against his chest so he could stroke the silky mass of her hair. 'But with only two weeks to go until the baby's due I still think it would have been sensible to delay the wedding until the summer.'

'What has sense got to do with it when two people are in love? Anyway, you'd promised they could marry on Rebecca's eighteenth and there was no way the two of them weren't going to hold you to it.' Constance giggled.

'It's not their fault we happened to have a big production of our own about the same time.'

She had been thrilled when she'd discovered she was expecting a baby. It wasn't until she had known she was pregnant for sure that she'd admitted to herself that she had been afraid this last joy would be denied her. She had been given so much, it had seemed as if she was asking *too* much to expect more. And although the timing had been a little unfortunate as far as Rebecca's wedding was concerned, it had been perfect with regard to the guest-house plans. They'd had a separate wing built on the south side of the farmhouse consisting of ten bedrooms all with their own bathroom and indoor closet for guests, and she had recently finished fitting them out so the business was ready to get underway in the summer. The same builders had also converted one of the bedrooms in the farmhouse into a bathroom, again with an indoor closet.

The work had been extensive. It had involved creating a cesspool some distance from the house, but Constance had assured Matt that private bathrooms was the way of the future. It would give them something of an advantage over lots of other guesthouses in the area, she'd insisted, and before too long most folk would be demanding such facilities when they took a holiday.

Matt hadn't been able to see it himself, but he had gone along with the scheme simply because he couldn't deny Constance anything. Knowing this, she now reached up and kissed his chin which was stubbly with a day's growth of beard. 'Let's go to bed,' she said softly, but on the last word she stiffened as the ache in her back which had been present all day seemed to move round to her stomach and grip it in a vice.

She said nothing to Matt; she didn't want to worry him and no doubt she was simply tired. Once they were upstairs, however, she wandered into the nursery and stood looking at the crib, hung with lace curtains, and all the other furniture in the room. She had travelled into Sunderland with Rebecca in the autumn before the winter snow and storms hit the north-east, and the two of them had had a wonderful day browsing round the big shops in the town. By the time she had returned home she had bought everything she needed for the baby, and once her purchases had been delivered she'd spent hours in the nursery, arranging and rearranging everything.

Walking over to the window, she stood looking out into the quiet, moonlit night as her fingers idly stroked the thick, rich material of the curtains she had made. She didn't know why, but when she had known she was expecting a child, she'd found herself wondering about Vincent McKenzie all the more. He had been a baby once, a helpless infant relying on those around him. What had made him into the monster he'd become? Her grandma had once said he'd been a troubled little boy who had grown into a troubled youth and an even more troubled man – but why? She knew his father had been a drunkard, it had been common knowledge, and her grandma had never liked his mother, labelling her 'a cold fish', but that alone couldn't have been enough to turn a man into someone who could kill other human beings without remorse or regret, surely?

She had fought against forgiving him for what he had done to her family and what he would have done to her, given the chance. She'd felt if she forgave him it was betraying her parents and granda somehow, belittling the terrible crimes he'd committed and allowing him to get off scot-free. It had been when she'd first felt the baby kick inside her belly that she'd known she had to let the bitterness and hate go. He was dead and she was alive. Through her and her child and her grandchildren, her parents would live on, whereas Vincent McKenzie's name was already lost in the mist of time. He had lived and died without love and affection. That was his epitaph and her revenge, if it was revenge she sought. But she didn't think she did. Not any more.

It hadn't happened overnight, but gradually in the last weeks and months, his hold on her mind and emotions had lessened. It had felt as though she was recovering from an illness as the weight of bitterness had sloughed off her and the memory of that last awful night had ceased to bring a surge of hate with it.

She was free of him.

She turned and looked at the room again, prepared for the child who was going to be loved and adored unconditionally. In the next room she could hear Matt whistling as he got ready for bed and the sound made her smile. And then, as the vice gripped her stomach again, harder and longer, her mouth opened in a little O of awareness. It was two weeks early and she could be wrong, but maybe the backache which had awoken her long before dawn and which had got more uncomfortable as the day had progressed hadn't been just backache, after all.

When she was able to, she walked through to their bedroom and stood looking at Matt. He was reading one of the many books he'd bought on husbandry. He had a stack of them in the bookcase downstairs detailing various aspects in the care of animals, different feeds, which crops to sow and when, and how to make best use of limited acres. He was engrossed, but after a moment or two he became aware of her, looking up from his book and smiling as he said, 'Come on, slowcoach. This bed's not the same without you.'

She was so glad he was free of the pit. For months after they'd got married he'd woken in the middle of the night in the grip of some nightmare or other, all connected with being shut in underground. Now even his smile was different.

Quietly, she said, 'You know you thought it was going to be just you and me for a little while now the fledgling's flown the nest? Well, I think the next one has other ideas.'

It didn't register for all of two seconds. When it did, he shot out of the bed as though he'd been scalded, but as the next pain had her hanging on to the bedstead and gasping for air she didn't notice. Once he had helped her change into her nightdress and get into bed, Matt went for Ruth and it soon became clear to the older woman that there was no time to fetch the midwife.

Looking at her son, she said calmly, 'Get me plenty of hot water and towels and a sharp pair of scissors.'

'But − but it's two weeks early.'

'Two weeks early or not, it's coming, lad, and fast. Now get me that water.'

The next hour was the worst and best of Matt's life. The worst because the whole time he was terrified he was going to lose Constance, in spite of his mother telling him the pain was natural and Constance trying to reassure him between the contractions. The best because he helped deliver his son into the world. He was a fine baby boy with a shock of blond hair, and he yelled for all he was worth until he was put to his mother's breast, whereupon his cries stopped like magic. And Matt knew if he lived to be a hundred he would never forget the look on Constance's face when she held her son.

'He's ours, Matt.' The wonder in her voice reflected how he felt. 'And he's so beautiful.'

'Just like his mother.' Matt was crying unashamedly and so was Ruth, but Constance was beaming.

'Look at him,' she whispered in awe. 'He knows us.'

And it did seem as though the baby was aware of his surroundings as he looked around with huge eyes filled with curiosity. Stephen Matthew Heath. The best of blessings.

Once Ruth had cleaned Constance up and washed her and the baby, she left after more hugs and kisses. Constance had her son in her arms and Matt was sitting on the bed holding them both. 'You were incredible,' he murmured, stroking back a lock of hair from her flushed face. 'So brave.'

Bringing their son into the world wasn't brave, Constance thought. Bravery would be continuing to live and function as she had done for so many years with a void in her heart that was Matt-shaped. But she didn't have to do that any more. The struggling, the emptiness, the aching aloneness were over. She had her husband and her son. She was complete.

Now you can buy any of these other bestselling Headline books by **Rita Bradshaw** from your bookshop or *direct from her publisher.*

FREE P&P AND UK DELIVERY
(Overseas and Ireland £3.50 per book)

Alone Beneath the Heaven	£6.99
Reach for Tomorrow	£6.99
Ragamuffin Angel	£6.99
The Stony Path	£5.99
The Urchin's Song	£6.99
Candles in the Storm	£6.99
The Most Precious Thing	£6.99
Always I'll Remember	£6.99
The Rainbow Years	£5.99
Skylarks at Sunset	£5.99
Above the Harvest Moon	£6.99
Eve and her Sisters	£6.99
Gilding the Lily	£5.99
Born to Trouble	£5.99

TO ORDER SIMPLY CALL THIS NUMBER

01235 400 414

or visit our website: www.headline.co.uk

Prices and availability subject to change without notice.